The Swan Maiden

Susan King

A SIGNET BOOK

SIGNET
Published by New American Library, a division of
Penguin Putnam Inc., 375 Hudson Street,
New York, New York 10014, U.S.A.
Penguin Books Ltd, 27 Wrights Lane,
London W8 5TZ, England
Penguin Books Australia Ltd, Ringwood,
Victoria, Australia
Penguin Books Canada Ltd, 10 Alcorn Avenue,
Toronto, Ontario, Canada M4V 3B2
Penguin Books (N.Z.) Ltd, 182–190 Wairau Road,
Auckland 10, New Zealand

Penguin Books Ltd, Registered Offices:
Harmondsworth, Middlesex, England

First published by Signet, an imprint of New American Library,
a division of Penguin Putnam Inc.

First Printing, January 2001
10 9 8 7 6 5 4 3 2 1

Copyright © Susan King, 2001

PUBLISHER'S NOTE
This is a work of fiction. Names, characters, places, and incidents either are the product
of the author's imagination or are used fictitiously, and any resemblance to actual
persons, living or dead, business establishments, events, or locales is entirely
coincidental.

To Julie and Jacci, with love and thanks

Acknowledgments

To all the readers who loved Sir Gawain (the knight, not the goshawk!) in *Laird of the Wind* and asked for his story, heartfelt thanks for the inspiration.

David King, Andy Hernandez, and Mike Braid kindly gave expert archery advice, friendship, and so much more; and thanks again to Andy for finding a longbow for a short person.

I am especially grateful to Shihan Tim Gilbert, Rokudan Renshi (sixth Dan black belt in Shorin Ryu), for sharing the secret of catching arrows, and for patiently, if a little exuberantly, shooting arrows at me until I caught some myself.

Hope springs exulting on triumphant wing.
—*Robert Burns*

Prologue

I heard the sweet voice of the swan
At the parting of night and day,
And who should be guiding in front
The queen of fortune, the white swan
                    —Carmina Gadelica

Scotland, the Highlands
Winter, 1286

"In the time of the mists," the *seanachaidh* said, "when faeries danced upon the Highland hillsides, a maiden lived in a fortress of bronze and silver on an island in a loch. She granted her heart to no one, until a certain warrior wooed her and won her love."

Gabhan MacDuff, grandson of the *seanachaidh* and son of a warrior, yawned as he lay on his stomach beside the hearth fire. His parents sat nearby with kinfolk and a few servants, all quiet as they listened. He rested his head on his folded arms and watched the flames dance.

"Their love was bright as a rainbow," his grandfather went on. "And all who knew them admired them for the love they bore each other. They were to be wed—he who was dark as a raven, and she who was fair as a swan."

At the mention of their love, Gabhan wrinkled his nose. His father chuckled softly, sitting nearby, his long booted legs stretched out to the fire. He touched Gabhan's head with his big, gentle hand, reminding him to show better respect.

"But one man, a Druid, secretly wished them ill. He coveted the maiden for himself, and his heart had grown hard and dark with longing. He vowed that if he could not have her, then no one would.

"On the eve of the wedding, the Druid went out into the moonlight and spoke a spell. He took a faery bolt and shot it into the skies. Clouds gathered and a great storm arose. The waters of the loch swallowed the island, and lightning struck the fortress. The walls crumbled into the loch."

Gabhan liked the part about the destruction of the fortress. He propped his head on his hand and looked at his grandfather. The older man was handsome like Gabhan's father, with blue eyes and black hair gone gray. Gabhan's own eyes were brown, like his English mother's, though he favored his Highland kin otherwise.

"All who lived in the fortress were drowned on the eve of the wedding," Adhamnain MacDuff continued. "And the dark-haired warrior and the pale maiden were lost, too, in the deep loch."

Gabhan frowned. He did not like to imagine the warrior and the maiden sucked into the murky waters. He waited, hoping to hear that they would be saved.

Seated beside his father, his mother smiled at him, and then gazed lovingly at her husband. Gabhan knew that his mother had left her English family to come to Glenshie Castle to be with her Highland husband, also called Adhamnain, although her family thought him a savage and unsuited to her. Now she rested her hand upon his arm, her face glowing and happy, her dark eyes warm and sparkling.

Gabhan looked up at his grandfather, feeling anxious. He did not want the story to end in disaster.

"But the hearts of the lovers were pure, and the power of shared love is strong and good, and cannot be destroyed. Such love makes its own magic, and that is what saved them all . . . in a way. Every soul who drowned that night became a swan," his grandfather said, leaning forward. "The maiden and the warrior transformed into the most beautiful and most graceful of all the enchanted swans on the loch.

"The Druid saw the birds, and saw the loving pair at the center of the flock, and knew that his evil plan had failed, for he had not separated them. He fled the land. The descendants of those swans live upon that loch still, and the magic and mystery of that place will always endure. And it is said that at certain times, in certain lights, the walls of the sunken fortress may be seen—but only by those whose hearts have been opened by great love." He sat back, smiling.

"What happened to the Druid, Grandfather?" Gabhan asked.

"Some say he still lives, having found the secret of eternal life, and that someday he will return to claim the swan maiden."

Gabhan shivered at the thought. "I know that place," he said. "It is called Loch nan Eala, the loch of the swans. It is not far from here. My father took me to see the swans there. A castle is on the shore, called Dùn nan Eala, and a family lives there. And my mother told me that she and my father saw the fortress once, shining at the bottom of the loch."

His grandfather smiled. "Surely if any have seen it, those two have," he said, eyes twinkling as he glanced at his son and daughter-in-law. "It is believed that sometimes the warrior and his lady come ashore, shedding their swan skins and regaining their human forms for a few hours. They search for a way to break the spell. If they ever find it, they will be free."

"Can it be broken, Grandfather?"

"They say that a warrior who knows true love must catch a faery bolt and fling it into the heart of the loch, the opposite way that the evil man threw it," his grandfather said. "Then the spell that surrounds the loch will end at last."

"*Ach*," Gabhan said. "I could catch a faery bolt."

"Could you?" Old Adhamnain smiled. "That is hard to do."

"I could do it," Gabhan insisted confidently.

His grandfather smiled. "Faery bolts are very hard to find. And the swans on that loch are happy, after so long."

Gabhan nodded, and rested his head upon his arms once again when his grandfather turned to murmur with his parents.

Though Gabhan listened, he understood little of their discussion. They spoke of the recent death of the King of Scots, and the struggle with the English king who was sending his armies north. The English had no rights here, his father insisted. Righteous rebellion already brewed in Scotland, and he would fight in the forefront of battle if he must, to protect Scotland and his home and kinfolk.

The hour was late, and Gabhan was tired, and the warmth of the hearth and the low drone of voices put him to sleep quickly. He dreamed of a sun-sparkled loch where white swans glided. He was a swan himself, gliding beside a beautiful female. Their matched bodies were mirrored in the smooth glass of the water. A golden chain circled his neck, and hers, and bound them to-

gether. He felt the gentle tug of the links as he floated in the
cool lap of the water beside her.

Storm clouds sailed over the loch, and Gabhan lifted his
wings. Beside him, the beautiful swan did the same. They rose
from the water as one, with the chain draped between them like
a banner of sunlight. They fled from the storm, but it caught
them with a fierce, dark wind. Lightning flashed, clouds rolled
like boulders, and the wind spun them down into the water's
embrace.

Gabhan awoke with a cry, and felt his father's hand upon his
head, soothing and strong.

Not long after that night, Gabhan rode over the heathered
slopes away from Glenshie alongside his weeping mother, his
grim nurse, and an old male servant. They were leaving the purple hills and the swift streams, leaving the stone tower that was
home. His mother said they were going to England.

His father was dead. Killed. Gabhan could not think of it, for
the pain was too deep. The castle had been attacked, and his
grandfather had died as well. His mother had urged him along
on a desperate escape in the dark of the night, while he heard
shouts behind him and smelled smoke. He understood little, if
any, of what had happened.

Still, he squeezed back tears and held his head high as he
traveled. Determined to defend his mother, knowing his father
would expect that of him, he kept his wooden sword pointed
outward. His nurse told him to put it down before he hurt someone. But his mother smiled wanly, and thanked him for his
chivalry, and let him keep the sword.

At the English border, his mother traded his red plaid, which
his father had given him, to a farmwife for a brown tunic that
fit Gabhan like sackcloth. His mother told him he must speak
only English now. He must never speak Gaelic again, she said,
and he must answer to Gawain, never to Gabhan MacDuff.

He had nodded obediently, his wooden sword ready, his
back straight. He did not understand all that she asked of him,
and he missed his father so much that he ached as if he were ill.
But he loved his mother and would do whatever she asked. The

sadness in her eyes matched the hurt in his heart. He only wanted to see her smile again.

Her English kin were strangers, but kind, and the hills near his grandparents' castle were low, green, and lovely, though not as beautiful as the hills near Glenshie. He liked the long-legged horses and the dogs and cats his uncles and grandfather kept, and he often walked along a nearby river to watch the swans there. They, more than anything, reminded him of home.

Later, his mother wed Sir Henry Avenel, a handsome widowed knight who made her laugh, and who had three small sons. With his young stepbrothers, Gawain ran errands for the knights who rode in and out of Avenel Castle. Fascinated by their armor, their horses and weapons, and the endless stories of their noble deeds, Gawain yearned to become a knight.

No one ever mentioned Glenshie or the MacDuffs to him again. Gawain sometimes saw his mother gaze at him with sadness in her eyes, but she only shook her head if he asked, and turned away.

Secretly, Gawain thought of Scotland often, cherishing vivid memories. He intended to return to Scotland one day and find Glenshie Castle, to claim his rightful land and title. That must wait, he knew, until he was grown and a knight, the master of his life, the benevolent defender of others that he so wanted to be.

He grew tall, and manhood strengthened him, body and heart and soul, and he felt his boyhood dreams fade. At last he knelt before the king of England to be knighted. Promising fealty, he swore to dedicate himself to the principles of chivalry.

When he finally returned to Scotland, he rode behind his king, and beneath the dragon banner, the sign of destruction.

Chapter 1

Scotland, Perthshire
Spring 1300

Flames poured upward, fierce and beautiful, licking delicately at the door frame. Blinking in the light, Juliana stumbled back as a web of fire spread over the floor rushes. She ran to the window of her bedchamber, whirling uncertainly.

Somewhere below, she heard a crash as the blaze engulfed more of her father's castle. Struggling against panic, she reminded herself why she had come back here against her mother's wishes, just as they had been ready to escape by the postern gate. She was sixteen and a woman grown, she had told her mother; she would be safe, and would return quickly.

Now she feared that her own escape might be impossible. She fought the urge to scream. *Be calm*, she told herself. She had come back to rescue her birds, and must do so.

Fervently she prayed that her mother and the rest were already safe in the forest. Their enemies were at the gates of Elladoune like hungry wolves: English wolves with fire arrows and an appetite for rebel Scots, ready to pounce upon the castle.

Somehow she must find her own way out, but first she had to free the doves and the little kestrel she kept; she had raised the doves from hatchlings, and had nursed the wounded kestrel until its wing had healed, and she would not leave them. She ran toward their cages as dark smoke swirled throughout the room.

Carrying first one cumbersome wooden cage and then the other, she set them on the wooden chest beneath the window ledge. Unlatching the doors, she urged the birds out. One by one they hopped to the opening and glided through the window to freedom.

One dove clung to the back of its cage. Calmly, despite her rising panic, Juliana coaxed the bird toward the window and merciful release. It fluttered away, a pale blur in the night.

Heat and smoke seared her lungs, and she turned, coughing, aware that the wooden floor grew warm under her bare feet. Clad only in the linen chemise that she had pulled on when her mother woke her, she had taken no time to dress further.

Glancing at the flame-wreathed doorway, she realized that her only choice was to go through the window. Her birds had flown free, but her escape would have to be a steep, dangerous dive into the loch. Leaning her head through the window, gulping in fresh air, she looked out.

The midnight sky, never fully dark in summer, glowed eerily, and the loch was dark and deep below. The castle's back wall sheered downward to a rocky promontory at the edge of the loch. Protected by its rear location, the large window was a luxury; its tall lancet shape, divided and glassed in its upper curves, would allow her room to jump.

The glass cracked as she looked up, the pieces cascading like stars. Shielding her head, Juliana stumbled back and ran blindly into an alcove that led to a small garderobe.

The small space was cool, and fresh air swept through the tiny window that overlooked the side of the bailey yard. Juliana knelt on the oak bench seat and craned her neck to peer out. Men, horses, and glittering armor filled the courtyard.

"Come down, Lady Marjorie!" one of the men bellowed. She glimpsed him as he paced the yard on a huge black warhorse. In jet-black armor and red surcoat, he seemed wholly malevolent.

"Come down to me!" he shouted again. The English commander, leading the raid on Elladoune Castle, believed that Juliana's mother was still inside. By now, Juliana hoped, her mother had fled to safety with her little sons and the servants.

Not long ago, her mother had roused the household, and Juliana had gathered her younger brothers, one a swaddled babe, one a whimpering toddler. The English knights had come to Elladoune to arrest Juliana's father, who had left weeks earlier with his two eldest sons to join the rebels. Discovering Alexan-

der Lindsay's absence, the English had fired his castle without
a care for his family.

Always fragile in nature, Juliana's mother had been close to
panic, praying fervently while she attempted to soothe her children. Juliana had suggested that they all go to the abbey, where
the abbot, her mother's kinsman, would shelter them.

"Come down!" the commander shouted again. "Give up
your tower to King Edward's knights, or give up your lives!"

Arrows tipped in fire sailed upward, smacking into the walls
close to the window. Startled, Juliana jerked back. Fury stirred
within her. If her bow had been to hand, she would have aimed
an arrow straight into his black heart. She had skill enough for
it. But she lacked the ability to harm any creature, for which her
elder brothers had sometimes chided her. Now she felt as if she
could do it.

Coughing, she stumbled out of the alcove and ran to the
window, careful to avoid the broken glass. Climbing on the
wooden chest, she stood on the window ledge. She straightened
inside the lancet like a saint in a niche.

The wind was cool, and the loch gleamed below, but she did
not look down. She looked up, where swans winged past, feathered golden in the firelight.

Perched there, she remembered an old tale about a flock of
swans that had cradled a girl safely in a net, carrying her home.
Another legend said that long ago, a hundred people had
drowned in this very loch, and each had transformed into a
swan.

The wind batted her chemise against her body and whipped
her long hair out in a spray of gold. Closing her eyes, she
prayed for protection, and prayed that the first legend, not the
second, would hold true for her.

She bent her knees and bounded outward. As the wind took
her, she arrowed her arms toward the water.

An angel flew out of the inferno and sank into the water.
Surely it was the most beautiful and terrifying sight he had ever
witnessed. Gawain ran forward, water lapping at his boots.

He searched, but did not see the pale slip of a girl who had
leaped from the tower window. A hundred and more swans

glided on the flame-bright surface of the loch, but he saw no human form among them. Several birds launched upward to circle overhead.

Behind him, the bellow and crackle of the fire grew louder. He heard the commander, Sir Walter de Soulis, continue his demand that the lady of the castle come out and give up her home to him.

Bastard, Gawain thought succinctly. He hoped the woman and her servants, whom he had glanced earlier at some of the windows, had found an escape. But he knew they could be dead inside the blazing castle. He was not certain that the girl who had leaped free had survived, either.

"You—Avenel! Did the girl come out of the water?" a knight called as he ran toward him.

Gawain turned. "Nay. She may be gone—drowned."

Another knight came forward and peered at the loch. "Drowned or fallen on the rocks—or even killed by those birds. Swans can fight like demons."

"Sir Walter wants her captured," the first man said. "The mother and the rest have fled into the forest, they say."

"And we may find the girl's body tomorrow," the other said.

Gawain looked up at a soaring swan. "Scots claim that when someone drowns, their soul enters the body of a swan," he mused.

"How do you know that?" one of the men asked.

"I heard it as a boy. My . . . nurse was Scottish. There is a legend about enchanted swans on this very loch, if I recall. Supposedly the first swans of Elladoune, long ago, were drowned souls. Each new swan is the soul of someone deceased, they say."

One knight looked at the other. "Sir Walter will want to hear about this."

"Tell him the girl went into the water and has not come up," Gawain said. "She's gone, no doubt. A swan flew up from the spot where she fell. I have been watching."

"I saw that too," the first knight said. "Enchanted swans or none, Edward of England owns this loch now, and he wants rebels, not children or swans. Come ahead. We'll have to tell

Sir Walter the girl has drowned." He looked up at the white birds circling overhead. "How could she change into a swan?"

"The longer I serve in Scotland, the more I believe anything can happen here," his comrade drawled as they walked away.

Gawain remained to scan the water. He had deliberately told the knights that tale of enchantment so that they would hesitate to search for her. If the girl had survived, he wanted to give her a chance to escape. He dimly remembered, as a boy, having to flee in the night from unseen enemies; the girl's situation had triggered his sympathy and his interest.

The burning silhouette of the castle was reflected in the loch. As a lad, he had believed in the eternal magic of Elladoune, yet the English had destroyed a legend in mere hours.

Memories stirred through him here and everywhere he went in Scotland as part of King Edward's Scottish campaign. None of these knights knew of his Scottish origins—or the fact that his birthplace, Glenshie Castle, was somewhere close to Elladoune.

Yet he did not even know where Glenshie was located.

Glancing toward the hills, he knew one of them hid his boyhood home in its lee. Years ago, he had vowed to find Glenshie and claim his inheritance for his own. Now that he was a king's knight, that secret dream seemed remote and impossible.

He walked along the rocky base that edged the tower. The water lapped at the promontory and sparks from the blaze sizzled in the loch like fallen stars. Searching the loch's surface, he was not yet ready to give up on finding the girl.

Moments later, he saw the lift of a pale arm and glimpsed a face amid the swans. She was there, he was sure now—although he did not know if she was a drowned or a living thing.

He yanked off his red surcoat and pulled at the leather ties of his chain-mail hood and hauberk. He laid his sword and belt aside, and struggled out of the steel mesh, his quilted coat, and his boots. He piled his gear, all but his trews, in the fiery shadow of the tower.

No one watched as he slipped into the water. He did not ask for help, expecting none. His fellow knights were here to claim and conquer, not to defend and rescue.

Once he had been fiercely proud to be among them. But he

loathed what he had seen of the king's army on its northern trek through Scotland. Chivalry and heroics were replaced by cruelty, lust, and the basest qualities of mankind. Witnessing deeds even uglier than the burning of Elladoune, he had continually found ways to avoid committing direct acts of cruelty himself.

The sins on his soul bothered him, and the thought of dishonoring his vows of knighthood disturbed him just as much. Disillusioned by this campaign, he realized that not even his own king upheld the ideals or integrity that Gawain revered.

He swam toward the circle of swans with steady strokes. Treading water, he saw that pale form again, moving among the birds. She swam toward the shore, and he surged after her.

Swans lurched upward, clumsy in the transition from water to air—grace lost, grace regained. Gawain treaded water, watching.

When the commotion of swans cleared, he saw the girl again, nearing the reeds along the shore. He lunged forward to grab her. Though she struggled, he scooped an arm around her and tugged her toward shore. When she began to scream, he cupped his hand over her mouth and stilled in the water, holding her close.

"Hush," he breathed out. "Easy! I have you!"

She twisted in his arms and gasped out an angry, muffled retort. Shouts sounded on shore. He saw the glare of torches and the glint of armor. Cradling the girl in his arms, he glided into the shelter of the reeds, his feet on the soft bottom of the loch now. He held her with him, low in the water.

"Let me go!" she gasped in Gaelic, writhing. He understood her, retaining some of the language from his childhood.

"Quiet," he hissed in English. "Be still."

"Sassenach!" she spat out. He tightened his hand over her mouth. His arm banded her, encountering soft breasts.

"Let go of me!" she snapped in English, and kicked his shin. Struggling, she sank, and he tugged her up. She rose sputtering.

"I only want to help you," he muttered.

"Then dinna drown me!" she gasped. He held her more securely under the arms. When she drew breath to scream, he clapped a hand over her mouth again.

"Sweet saints, hush—be mute like a swan!"

"Not all swans are mute," she mumbled behind his hand, and squirmed like a hooked fish.

"That I see, Swan Maiden," he grunted, wrapping a leg around her thighs, tucking her against him like a lover, though passion was the last thing on his mind. "Quiet, if you value your life, or they will catch you."

She stilled then, and slipped her arms around his neck. Her face was silky and wet against his bearded cheek. He felt a fine trembling all along the length of her.

The commander and a few knights walked along the shore and pointed toward the swans, and then at the window from which the girl had escaped. A few swans flapped their wings and hissed loudly. The men backed away.

One bird, huge and gorgeous in the fierce light of the fire, rose from the water and took to the wing, flying so low overhead that Gawain felt the breeze and ducked as it passed.

The girl laughed. "He willna hurt us."

"Hush," Gawain said between his teeth, embarrassed that he had thought otherwise. "You talk too much."

Two knights waded into the reed bed and backed away hastily as the swan circled over their heads, fast and low. Gawain watched, astonished. The bird's protective action could not be deliberate, but he was grateful for it nonetheless.

The girl looked up, her hair streaming around her face. Gawain saw that her eyes were large and dark, her head and shoulders delicately shaped. Her body was lithe and lean in his arms, her breasts lush against his chest. He held her, breathing in tandem, water lapping around their necks.

"They are gone," she whispered after a moment. Her mouth was close to his. Feeling a strong, misplaced urge to kiss her, he pulled away slightly.

"The knights are there, just over the hill," he murmured.

"The swans are gone, too, farther down the loch. Look."

He turned and saw that most of the swans had disappeared. The remaining few glided elegantly over the water. The shore was empty, though shouts continued on the other side of the castle.

Gawain stood cautiously, holding the girl in his arms. The soft floor sucked at his feet as he waded to shore. Water sluiced from them as if they were kelpies rising from the depths. Slung in his arms, sopping wet, she was yet a light burden.

Glancing uneasily toward the castle, he ran along the bank away from the burning tower toward the forest. People waited there in the shadows. A woman stepped between the trees.

"Mother!" the girl said. "Set me down." He did, sweeping his arm around her to hurry her toward the trees.

The shadowed figures came closer, reaching out. A woman pulled the girl into her embrace and swathed her in a thick plaid. Someone offered a blanket to Gawain. He refused it.

The girl turned to look up at him. Her eyes were luminous; in shadows and moonlight, he could not tell their color.

"I am Juliana Lindsay," she said. "Tell me your name, so that I can ask the angels to watch over you."

He frowned. If he told her the name given him at birth— Gabhan MacDuff—she might know him for a local Highlander, and despise him for being with the English. If he told her his English name, Gawain Avenel, she would loathe him for that.

She shivered, waiting, her cheeks pale, hair hanging like strands of honey. He touched her chin with a fingertip.

"Swan Maiden," he murmured. "Call me your Swan Knight in your prayers, and the angels will find me."

She nodded, watching him. Her mother drew her back.

"They are coming this way, knight," the mother said.

"I will lead them away from here. Go! All of you—go!" He waved them back into the forest and turned to run toward the castle, where the inferno still raged, bright and ferocious. As he went, he felt keenly as if the girl and the others watched him from the cover of the trees.

For a moment, he felt the odd sensation that he left heaven behind him and ran toward hell.

Chapter 2

Scotland, Perthshire
Spring 1306

Quicksilver and pale as the moonlight, she glided out of the forest and into the clearing. Glancing over her shoulder, she heard pounding hoofbeats and the male shouts that commanded her to stop, to wait.

She turned to watch them, slowly, deliberately, though her heart beat like a war drum. Lingering would be foolhardy, but she always made sure they saw her; she had done so for years.

Nearby, she knew that a group of people ran through the forest in another direction. They conveyed a burden, large and cumbersome: a wooden war machine on creaking wheels, partially dismantled, its struts stacked on a pony cart. Once it was conveyed through the forest, the engine would be transported along the river at night, until it reached the rebel camp.

The king's men must not discover it.

She waited in a translucent beam of moonlight. The two knights spurred toward her through the trees.

"The Swan Maiden!" one of them shouted. She forced herself to be still as their horses crashed through the shadows.

Then she whirled and ran toward the loch, shedding the white feathered cloak that covered her head and shoulders and tossing it aside. She stepped into the water and crouched quickly, her pale tunic billowing around her. Her blond hair fanned out and floated as she surged.

Arrowing through the water, she neared a cluster of swans and ducks gliding on the loch and swam into their midst. The birds ignored her, accustomed to her presence. When a curious cygnet swam too close, she pushed it gently away.

Treading water, she watched the shore. The knights burst into the clearing and dismounted. Running along the bank, they scanned the loch, pointed. One of them bent, then held up a white feather fallen from the cloak.

She watched, hidden within the ring of swans. The men walked to the water's edge. One of them picked up a stone and flung it, and it sank near the birds. They scattered with fuss and noise.

Her protective circle gone, she dove under and lunged toward a rocky shelf. Pulling herself along its striated contours, she rose up and slid out of the water under the shelter of an overhanging pine.

Friends waited there, holding out a plaid. Juliana wrapped the woven length around herself, slicked back her wet hair, and smiled. Then they turned together to run into the forest.

Amber firelight danced over familiar faces. Seated on the earthen floor of the cave, Juliana scanned the group assembled there, then turned her attention to her guardian, seated beside her. Abbot Malcolm cleared his throat.

"At last, my friends," he said quietly. "What we have risked so much to gain may be in our grasp. The report I heard this day will greatly aid our effort." He spoke in rapid Gaelic. "I have a plan, but there is danger. Juliana will risk a great deal this time."

She kept her expression calm. Around the firelit circle, the people summoned by Abbot Malcolm of Inchfillan waited. Her guardian's white tonsure was pristine in the light, his round cheeks pink, his blue gaze keen as he looked at her.

"Father Abbot," she murmured. "If we can win back Elladoune Castle and gain back our lands, I will do whatever I must."

"Father Abbot," one of the men asked, "what has happened?"

Malcolm folded his hands. Juliana knew what he would say. She and her younger brothers lived in the abbot's own house, outside the precinct of the monastery, and Malcolm had discussed his thoughts with her earlier.

Anyone who did not know her kinsman and guardian well— such as the English knights garrisoned in Elladoune—assumed that he was merely a pleasant old man, concerned only about his little Celtic abbey, and the lost souls he guided along the right path.

Some of his lost souls—rebels all—watched him now.

What Malcolm hid from their English enemies, Juliana knew, was a ferocious loyalty to Scotland. He was more lion than rotund lamb. Years ago, Abbot Malcolm had taken under his wing several dispossessed Scots, transforming them into forest rebels. Juliana felt proud to be among them.

Outside the cave, trees swayed in the night breeze. Inside, Malcolm's rebels listened, and leaned forward.

"I met with the sheriff of Glen Fillan today," Malcolm said. "He asked a favor, and posed a threat."

Juliana drummed her fingers anxiously on her unstrung bow, which lay beside her. She felt a desperate urge to act, but knew she and the others must proceed cautiously.

"Walter de Soulis has never cared about our interests," Lucas, once her father's herdsman, said. "He will not help us!"

"He did not fret about the renegades and homeless in the forest and glen, as he usually does—though I try to help him with that persistent problem." Malcolm held up his hands innocently, and some of his listeners smiled.

Juliana glanced toward her two young brothers. Iain and Alec, seven and nine, slept in a corner, curled like puppies on a pile of cloaks. She knew the boys would sleep through anything if tired enough—even a meeting to plan rebellious actions.

"The sheriff said that the garrison leader of Elladoune Castle will depart soon," Malcolm said.

"Good!" one of the men said. "Farewell to him who burned our village, so that we had to live in the forest! Though we still must fend against the man who ruined Elladoune, now made sheriff over us!"

"When the commander leaves, his troops will go with him," the abbot went on. "The English king has ordered them to pursue our new King of Scots, Robert Bruce, and his men, who have gone into the Highland hills in the area north of here. Another garrison will arrive with a new leader for Elladoune."

Red Angus, burly and russet, a former farmer, shook his

head. "So one English garrison moves out, and another moves in. Now there will be new faces to learn, new habits and patrol routes. That does not help our cause."

"But this does—for a few weeks, Elladoune will be deserted," Malcolm answered. "Sir Walter wants the monks of Inchfillan to watch the castle gates and tend the sheep and gardens until the new men arrive."

"Aha, that is just what we need!" Robert, a blacksmith, crowed. "We are prepared for it too—with weapons and armor!"

"Exactly," Malcolm said. "God has answered our prayers. We can take over Elladoune."

"And claim it for Scotland!" Angus cried. Malcolm smiled.

Arms raised upward and voices rose. "For Scotland!"

Juliana smiled, and hope bloomed within her like a small flower. Soon they would live in Elladoune Castle again, and then bring the ruined village to life, farming the land and raising herds in peace.

"Juliana," Malcolm said, placing his hand on her shoulder, "will help us carry out our scheme. The soldiers shake with fear when our Swan Maiden appears and disappears as if by magic. We are deeply grateful to her for creating that illusion these past few years."

"Magic, she has—or so say the English," Angus remarked.

"The silent Swan Maiden of Elladoune, who never utters a word," Malcolm agreed. "As long as the Sassenachs believe she might be an enchanted swan, it helps us. We want them to think it, but we do not want her to face terrible risk."

"They will harm her if they capture her," Lucas growled.

"But she plays a quick and clever game," Malcolm said, "never speaking when English are near, and running away as soon as they see her. The Sassenachs are so anxious about entering the forest that we have been able to do much secret work for the cause of Scotland."

"They are fools to believe she is enchanted and not real." Beithag, the oldest woman among them, snorted her disdain. "And it cannot last."

"True." Malcolm sighed. "And that danger is the problem. Walter de Soulis has been sheriff in Glen Fillan for only a little while, but he is not convinced that Juliana is enchanted. He says she is a rebel—even a spy."

"What did you tell him, Father Abbot?" Angus asked with concern.

"I said that my ward is a simple, pious girl who does not speak because of the terrible loss of her home years ago, followed by the death of her father and the cloistering of her mother, whom she has not seen in years." He smiled sympathetically at Juliana, who nodded ruefully. She had accepted long ago that she might never see her mother again; Lady Marjorie had put herself and her deep grief in a convent in the Lowlands a year after her husband's death.

"If De Soulis thinks the girl does not speak," Beithag said, "he has never seen her in a high temper!"

"I told him," Malcolm said, "that when the Swan Maiden appears by the loch, it is a vision, and will bring good luck."

"Still," Beithag's husband, Uilleam, said, "Juliana should cease her actions and stay safe." He nodded his gray, leonine head to underscore his point, and many others nodded in agreement. Uilleam generally said little, Juliana knew, but when he did, the rebels took heed.

"Father Abbot, find your ward a husband to give her babes, and stop asking her to help the cause," Beithag said.

Juliana shook her head. "I want to continue, Mother Beithag. The Swan Maiden can help the work we do. The Sassenachs will not come near this part of the forest, and so we have stockpiled weapons and armor, and built seige engines to transport by darkness. Our work is important."

"Mother Beithag is right," Angus said. "The girl has risked much, and has lost much, and we should ask no more of her. A laird's daughter should wed a Scottish knight and raise sons for Scotland."

"I am raising sons for Scotland. My own brothers," she pointed out, indicating the two boys asleep in the corner.

"Listen," Malcolm said. "The time has come to reclaim Elladoune. We must decide how, and when. If Juliana is willing, we need her assistance."

"That devil De Soulis will destroy our plans no matter what we do," Lucas growled. "The man is invincible. They say his black armor cannot be penetrated. He cannot be defeated."

"He can only be avoided, which we have done," Angus said.

Malcolm sighed. "My brethren and I pray daily about all of these concerns. We have a hundred votive candles burning day and night to call God's attention to our plight."

"Keep those candles lit," Beithag said tartly. "We need a miracle."

"If we try to take Elladoune, De Soulis and his men will be there," Lucas said. "How can we withstand a siege or an attack?"

"Once inside, we will triumph somehow," Malcolm said. "God removed the garrison leader. He will solve this too."

"Juliana should not be exposed to this devil De Soulis," Angus said. "After all, he is the one who ruined Elladoune."

"All the more reason," Juliana said. "My father is dead, and my elder brothers are with the new king. They would help us if they could. Let me do what I can."

"Brave girl," Angus said, and nodded. "Well then. May our prayers hold sway with heaven."

"My friends, we shall pray now." Malcolm stood and joined his hands together to lead them.

Juliana lowered her head and murmured in Latin in response, although her heart quickened with fear. As the Swan Maiden, she stood at the center of the local effort, able to help—or to hinder if she should err.

More than one miracle would be needed to gain back Elladoune. Good fortune had assisted her for the last few years, and she prayed that her luck would hold.

One incident of luck in particular she could never forget. On the night Elladoune had burned, a handsome English knight had rescued her. She might have been captured and even killed if not for her Swan Knight, as she always thought of him.

He still appeared in her dreams, nameless and fascinating, dark-eyed and beautiful. Of the hundreds of Sassenach knights she had seen riding near Elladoune and Inchfillan over the last six years, she had never seen his face again.

Since that night, smaller miracles had kept her safe and out of English hands. Whether it was luck or miracles, she whispered a fervent wish that the assistance would continue.

What she wanted most of all was to bring her kinfolk and her friends—and herself—home at last to Elladoune.

Chapter 3

England, London
May 1306

The stone beneath his knees was cold and hard, yet the silence emanating from the courtiers who watched him was colder still. Sir Gawain Avenel bowed his bare head, acutely aware of King Edward's harsh gaze upon him.

"Sire," Gawain began, "I beg forgiveness of the king for my transgressions in Scotland. I offer renewed loyalty and fealty to my liege lord. I solemnly pledge my heart, mind, and sword to the service of my king." He placed his fist over his heart.

His chain-mail hauberk dragged upon his shoulders. In ten years of knighthood, his armor had never felt so heavy. The burden was one of the soul rather than the body.

He must follow this apology through or lose all. His life hung in the balance, as did the welfare of those he loved. He glanced up through the dark frame of his lashes and brows. King Edward, first of that name, frowned at him.

At least, Gawain thought, the king had not summoned the guards to haul him back to prison yet. He drew breath to continue. "I beg to be allowed into king's peace once again."

The tense silence endured. Gawain knew many believed he knelt here to save himself further trouble. He had spent the last two months in a prison cell, and he had submitted a request to retain his modest English properties earned in knight service.

In truth, he knelt here to protect his family—mother, stepfather, stepbrothers, and half sisters—from harm in the wake of what the crown, in documents signed by the king, termed his transgressions in Scotland. King Edward had a long and vengeful memory. Begging forgiveness was scant price to pay.

The recent death of his stepbrother, Geoffrey, on a Scottish field still tore at him. Gawain was certain that he had indirectly caused his brother's death by overstepping the boundaries he had danced too near for too long: he had aided Scottish rebels once again, against his orders.

Not only that, he had joined them in their quest for freedom. To him, those months had been a rare respite of true honor and integrity, yet his deed was regarded as a crime and a breach of faith. And it had brought tragedy.

He endured another irretrievable loss, kept secret from all. He had lost the respect of the Scottish rebels he had befriended. The English called them outlaws, but he knew them as righteous people with noble hearts.

And now each and every one of them—from James Lindsay, called the Border Hawk, and his wife Isobel the prophetess, to the last man among them—believed that Gawain had acted treacherously toward them. It could not be helped, he thought regretfully.

The silence continued. Someone coughed, armor chinked. The chamber glowed with tapestries, painted ceilings and floor tiles, and the jewel colors and sumptuous fabrics worn by the courtiers.

At the center of the brilliance, wearing black and chain mail, Gawain felt grim and colorless. He waited, head bowed.

"This is not the first time you have knelt before us, Sir Gawain," the king finally said.

"Sire, true." A muscle flashed in his cheek. The king had a long memory. "I was knighted here at Westminster Palace."

"I believe you knelt here another time," the king prompted.

"Six years ago, I broke my fealty . . . and asked to be admitted back into king's peace."

"Broke faith in Scotland. Yet once again you are here for the same reason, and once again beg king's peace."

"Aye, sire."

"Six years past, you aided rebels to escape near . . . Elladoune, was it not? That was the rash action of a young knight, and you were forgiven." The king flapped his hand impatiently. "But this time you deserted your English commander, Sir Ralph Leslie, and joined Scotsmen led by a known renegade. This time, you lack the excuse of youthful impetuousness."

"Sire, Leslie was a cruel man who served his own needs be-

fore those of king and crown. He brought suffering and shame
to an innocent woman. May I remind my lord king that Lady
Isobel's gift of prophecy is admired in the English court as well
as in Scotland. I chose to aid the lady."

"Defending a lady is understandable, but this one is wed to
a Scottish outlaw."

Gawain would never regret what he had done, though he had
lost his friends in Scotland, and endangered his family. At least
he could repair the risk to his loved ones. He would pay any
penance to bring them better peace.

"I upheld my oath of chivalry," he told the king simply.

"Was it honorable—or traitorous? Your father insists you
were their prisoner, not their abettor. Shall we believe him?"

"Sire, years ago I knelt here beneath your sword blade, and
swore to defend women and those weaker than myself against
cruelty and oppression. I swore to support virtue and honor
wherever I found it. Am I to be reprimanded and punished for
doing so? I pray that my liege, a paragon of knighthood himself, will trust my integrity—and forgive my faults."

"Do you sympathize with the rebels?"

"Sire," Gawain said. "I am an Avenel."

"And they are unswervingly loyal." The king grunted, a be-
grudging sound. "You have always shown integrity despite
your impulse to help those you should not. The ideals of the
courts of love do not apply on the fields of war—especially this
Scottish war."

"Sire, I pray pardon." He bowed his head. Near the dais, he
saw his stepfather and his stepbrothers. Henry looked worried,
and his son Edmund fisted a hand. Robin, soon to be knighted
himself, was pale.

"Henry!" the king called out. "Your eldest is cut of different
cloth than you and your other sons. He is dark as a raven where
you three are well-mannered brown wrens. He has a rash and
willful nature, which you thankfully lack."

"His mother and I have always been proud of him, my
liege," Henry said smoothly. "If Gawain has trangressed in res-
cuing a lady, his mother insists 'tis because he is pure of heart,
like his namesake in the Arthurian tales." Henry smiled. The
king nodded as if mildly amused.

Gawain lowered his gaze. Few, including the king, remembered that Henry was his stepfather, and Henry had not corrected the assumption. That gesture of support was humbling indeed.

"Sire," he said, "I can only aspire to be as worthy a knight as Sir Henry Avenel."

"Then aspire to behave yourself," the king barked.

"I offer my obeisance and my pledge."

The king flicked his fingers. "Very well. Your vow is acceptable to us."

"My lord." He bowed his head with relief. He hoped to be excused soon. Even this brief royal audience had required two months of prison, three petitions for leniency, and a goodly sum of money. If the king wanted to discuss the weather, Gawain would have to stay.

"We need trained knights in the north now that Robert Bruce has claimed the Scottish throne and hides in the hills like an outlaw," King Edward said. "We must send our army in pursuit. Every capable knight is needed. You are to return to Scotland with us in a few weeks. We are gathering men to journey north."

"Sire." Gawain swallowed hard. "My liege, since I am to go north again, might I make a request?" Not the best moment, Gawain knew, but he would not be granted another audience soon.

"You may try," the king murmured.

"There is a place called Glenshie in Glen Fillan, west of Perth. It was taken from the Scots many years ago, burned but never garrisoned. I wish to rebuild the property, sire."

"Why?" Edward demanded.

"I . . . If I may garrison a Highland castle, I can demonstrate my fealty. And it will be of benefit to both Scots and English."

The king beckoned to his chamberlain, who summoned an army commander Gawain recognized from among the courtiers. They murmured together.

"That location is remote and impractical," the king finally replied. "Worthless and abandoned. Still, my general suggests that you command a garrison somewhere. If your talents were

put to better use, you might be less inclined to behave . . .
chivalrously."

"Sire," Gawain said, gritting his teeth. The callous denial of
Glenshie, his childhood home, cut like a knife. Yet he could
never petition for the property as its rightful owner.

"Before you go, understand this." Edward leaned forward.
"One more transgression and your head—mayhap the heads of
your Avenel brothers too—will see the cutting block. A bad
apple may spoil a whole barrel." He sat back. "Let that guarantee your new oath."

"Sire, my word upon it." Swamped in suppressed anger,
Gawain felt loyalty rock beneath him like a boat.

"We will test the strength of your word," the king murmured.

Gawain rose to his feet and bowed, then walked away, filled
with a vague sense of dread. His stepfather and stepbrothers
came forward, their faces showing relief and pride.

No matter what he did, it seemed, their love for him sus-
tained. Such loyalty could never be fully repaid—and must
never be dishonored.

But a few months with Scottish rebels, followed by a stint in
the Tower of London, alone with his thoughts, had changed him
irrevocably. He was a different man, though the Avenels had
not yet realized it.

His promise to the king had come easily, for he loved his
family. Yet he did not know if he could honor his vow. He had
lost his beloved stepbrother Geoffrey, had lost the respect of his
Scottish friends. Now he risked even more: kinship, the firm
rock of honor and ambition, the calm horizon of the future. He
no longer knew who he was, and he could not share those
thoughts and fears with anyone.

Subdued, he accepted the congratulatory embraces of his
stepfather and stepbrothers. As he departed the hall with them,
his doubts shadowed him, relentless as a hawk.

Chapter 4

A high cry cut through sunlight and peacefulness like a blade. Kneeling on a sheltered part of the bank, Juliana paused as she tossed bits of grain to the swans and the ducks. She glanced around, knowing that her younger brothers were playing at bows and swords in the forested area between the loch and the abbey gate.

The scream sounded again, more frantic than playful. She rose to her feet, shading her eyes against the sun. Out on the water, several ducks scattered noisily, taking to the air.

Closer to the bank, six swans looked up from intent feeding. Four small, gray-brown cygnets glided behind their parents, Artan and Guinevere—a pair Juliana had named a few years ago when they had first nested on Loch nan Eala. The adults arched their wings and leaned their heads back alertly.

Something was amiss, Juliana thought; the swans sensed it too. Hearing another cry, she turned, recognizing that particular shriek.

"Iain!" she called. "Alec! Come here!"

She waited. A breeze ruffled the pale golden hair that spilled over her shoulders. Her glance took in the water meadow that spread away from the loch, its tall reeds laced with burns and pools, merging with a broad stream where the mill was located. Beyond that lay the ruined, deserted village, where hearth fires had not burned for three years.

She looked behind her. The modest grounds of Inchfillan Abbey, walled and quiet, met the banks of the loch. Past the abbey, the loch was fringed by forest that extended toward Elladoune at its other tip.

The English-held castle was not visible from here, and Ju-

liana was glad. Glimpses of her former home stirred only grief
and sadness, even after six years.

She was careful to avoid the English soldiers who rode in
and out of Elladoune Castle. They sometimes came to the
abbey to meet with her guardian Abbot Malcolm, but she and
her brothers kept out of sight whenever possible.

The screams were louder now, and she turned. Her brothers
tore out of the woods as if the demons of hell were on their
heels. Hair flying, shirts and plaids rumpled, knees bruised and
knobby, they pounded on bare feet across the meadow. They
gripped small bows in their hands, and feathered arrows—with
blunted points—flopped in leather quivers on their backs.

"Juliana!" Alec, the older boy, called. Iain shrieked repeatedly as he followed.

"*Ach*, hush!" she called. "Did you argue between you?"

"Run! Quickly!" Alec called. Iain waved his arms, still
squealing, as he rushed toward her.

Seeing genuine fright on their faces, Juliana ran to meet
them. Iain thudded into her, wrapping his arms around her
waist, burying his golden curls beneath her encircling arm.

"What is wrong?" she asked.

Iain pointed toward the forest. "The black knight!" he
yelled. "He is coming!"

"De Soulis?" She looked at Alec.

He nodded breathlessly. "The sheriff and his men are riding
through the forest! We were practicing bow shooting, and we
saw them! Iain screamed loud and they followed us. We must
hide!"

Alarmed, Juliana took their arms and began to hurry toward
the abbey. "They must not see us!"

"I will shoot them," Iain said fiercely. "I am going to win the
archery competition and best all the English bowmen!"

"You are not big enough, and hush up," Alec said. "If they
see Juliana, they will try to catch her. Hurry!"

Juliana put a hand on Iain's thin shoulder as they hastened
toward the abbey gate. Iain had been a babe in arms and Alec a
toddler when Walter de Soulis and his men had burned Elladoune. Her brothers did not remember it, but the memories

still seared her dreams, and her fear and loathing of De Soulis had not abated.

"How many knights did you see?" she asked the boys.

"A hundred!" Iain said.

"Fifteen," Alec said, glancing at his brother. "They were riding to the abbey."

Iain pointed and shrieked. "The black knight!"

Horses and riders, wearing the red surcoats of Edward's men, burst through the trees and headed across the meadow, hoofbeats heavy, armor and weapons chinking. The leader rode a black horse and wore black chain mail beneath a wine-colored surcoat. Seeing him, Juliana grabbed the boys' arms and began to run.

"There—the Swan Maiden!" someone shouted.

Three horsemen split away from the group and rode toward them, their faces grim. Juliana shoved her brothers ahead of the riders and spun to block the horsemen. One of the knights cut around her and chased after the boys while the other man rode toward her.

She swerved and went down the bank, splashing into the shallows. On the loch, a swan launched into flight, great wings beating. As the huge bird swerved toward them, the horse neighed, but the knight drew closer and reached out. Splashing through ankle-deep water, Juliana avoided his grasp.

"Stop!" he hollered, reaching again.

"Let her go," a deep voice called out. "The boys will pay for her escape!"

With a sense of dread in her gut, she slowed and turned.

De Soulis stared at her from a few yards away, his eyes small and piercing. He was graying but handsome with precise, carefully etched features, and she sensed a darkness about him that went beyond his notorious black armor.

"We have your brothers," he called. "Go into the loch if you wish." He waved a hand to encourage her. "Show us how you turn into a swan. I, for one, would like to see it."

Two knights rode behind De Soulis, Alec and Iain trapped in their arms. Alec sat quietly, but Iain shrieked and struggled as he lay over the front of the saddle, legs kicking.

"Juliana!" Alec called. "Run!"

She hesitated, standing in a cool sweep of water.

"What shall I do with them? Will you speak in their defense, Swan Maiden?" De Soulis guided his horse into the water toward her. She stepped back.

"Do not talk!" Alec shouted. "Remember the Swan Maiden!"

She glanced toward her brother. Alec bravely wanted to protect the ruse they had agreed on, while nearby, Iain still squealed and fought. She was proud of both for their spirit.

"Quiet that boy!" De Soulis ordered. Iain's captor winced loudly when he was bitten, and he smacked the child in response. Iain began to whimper.

Furious on his behalf, Juliana lunged through the water. De Soulis turned his horse to block her advance. When she stepped sideways, water swooshing, he blocked her again. Her dress was soaked, her breath and chest heaving, her hair hanging down. She stared at him, trapped, wild with a need to free her brothers.

Artan glided swiftly through the water toward them, wings raised aggressively. Nearing the horse, the cob lifted his wings and swatted outward. The bay snorted and stepped back.

Juliana moved again but De Soulis blocked her. Near her, the swan hissed. Reaching down, she touched the taut curve of Artan's neck. The bird settled low in the water and swam away.

"So, we see some of your magic after all, Swan Maiden," De Soulis drawled. In the distance, Malcolm and a few monks ran toward them, shouting. "Come to me, or the boys will be harmed."

She knew it for a genuine threat. After a moment, she lifted her arm toward him in passive surrender.

"Well and truly caught," he said. "I am disappointed. I expected more of a challenge from the Swan Maiden of Elladoune." He grasped her arm to pull her up behind him.

She grabbed his belt to steady herself, head lifted and back straight. He guided the horse to the bank and looked over his shoulder. "No plea for mercy?"

She narrowed her eyes. At close view, he was lean and taut, with sharp features and dark eyes. His chain mail, finely woven and glossy as onyx, draped over him like heavy velvet.

She stared at it curiously. De Soulis's black armor was renowned. Rumor said it was impenetrable, even enchanted. Whatever the truth, she had never seen a war garment like it.

"Juliana!" She looked around to see Malcolm and the monks rushing toward them.

"Father Abbot!" Iain yelled, struggling in his captor's arms. "Help! The black knight has us all!"

"Let my wards go, Sir Walter," Malcolm said sternly in Scots. "You have nae quarrel with them."

"True, though I confess I am curious about the girl. The rumors about her are . . . intriguing."

She twisted, and De Soulis caught her forearm in a steely grip. "You cannot fly away now," he murmured.

"Let them go," Malcolm repeated. "Leave here."

"We have business on the loch." The creamy smoothness of his voice made Juliana feel ill. "King Edward has requested a pair of Scottish swans for a royal feast. He has appointed me his new Master of Swans in Scotland. Part of my duties are to see that swans are captured to stock his rivers and grace his table. My men will take a pair of birds from those you keep."

"We dinna keep them," Malcolm answered. "The birds are wild. They choose to stay here."

"All the swans in Britain belong exclusively to the king," the sheriff said. "That includes the swans in Scotland. For now, we need but one more. We have caught one already—the Swan Maiden." De Soulis kept hold of Juliana's arm. "The king will find this pair quite amusing."

"The king?" Malcolm asked. "You canna take the lass!"

"I can and will," De Soulis answered. "With another swan." He gestured to two men, who dismounted. They took nets and long hooks from their saddles and walked to the water's edge.

Juliana gasped and twisted silently in De Soulis's relentless grip. She had known some of the birds for years, since they had been born, and she could not bear for harm to come to any of them. But she did not know how to help them now.

"Abbot, if the girl wants to protest, make her use her tongue," De Soulis said. "I am weary of this game she plays."

"Sir Sheriff, she chooses to be silent."

"'Tis said she has some magic about her."

"People say that you have magic too. That armor, I hear, is impenetrable and under some dark spell."

"Nonsense," De Soulis snapped.

"Then we understand each other."

"Mayhap. Tell me why the girl does not speak."

"She is pious and grieving. 'Tis all."

"She should be in a convent, then."

"She would be, if King Edward hadna burned most of them," Malcolm said pointedly. "The girl is kind to her brothers and to our brethren, and tends to the swans. She is an innocent. Leave her be."

"She makes a fine hostage, as do her brothers. You will hear from me soon, Abbot Malcolm." De Soulis turned his horse.

"Stop!" Malcolm shouted. "You canna keep them!"

"They provide assurance. We need the help of the monks of Inchfillan when the garrison at Elladoune departs. I suspect rebel activity in this area. But of course we can trust you, Abbot . . . can we not?"

"Certes. No hostages need ensure it."

"I will take them nevertheless. The king will want to see this Swan Maiden. As for the boys . . . what is the tradition among the Scots? Fostering? Consider them fostered by the sheriff of Glen Fillan. My wife will approve of them in her household, as she is without children of her own." He nodded brusquely. "Good day. Ride out," he snapped at the guards, and shifted forward.

Juliana gasped out, turning to look at her guardian.

"Where will you take them?" Malcolm demanded.

"Her brothers will stay at Dalbrae with my wife and my garrison," De Soulis said. "I will take an escort and convey the girl to Newcastle in safety."

"Newcastle-on-Tyne?" Malcolm asked. "Is the king there now?"

"He and his army have been making their way north toward Scotland and have reached Newcastle. 'Tis a short journey from here, a few days at most. She will be in the care of a military escort. The king will decide what is to be done with her."

Panic overtook Juliana then. She could scarcely breathe or think as she twisted against De Soulis's grip in terror. She could not go with these men, nor could she leave her brothers, or Malcolm, or this place. Desperation rose high and quick, and she shoved De Soulis. He wrenched her arm in fierce reply.

"I will come with her myself," the abbot said, "or I will send monks with her! 'Tisna right to take a female like this—the daughter of a laird—"

"Daughter of a rebel, and a rebel herself, most likely," De Soulis corrected. "A priest will be with my troops, and he can chaperone her." He spurred the horse and cantered away.

Juliana looked over her shoulder at the guards who carried her brothers. Alec's eyes were wide and frightened, and Iain emitted bold, earsplitting shrieks. Malcolm and some of the monks ran forward. The abbot ran on sturdy legs, his dark tunic flapping around his muscular calves.

Within moments, he loped alongside De Soulis's horse. "Be strong of heart!" he called to Juliana in Gaelic. "And keep your vow, Juliana—keep silent!"

Tears clouded her eyes as she watched Malcolm. He called out a reassurance to the boys, then stopped in the meadow.

"We will pray for you!" he yelled. "We will ask for a miracle!"

She looked toward the loch, where the two guards stood in the water. One hooked Artan, the large white cob, around the neck, and the other held a net, while the swan beat his wings in a fury.

Juliana turned away, stifling a sob. She too was caught, though her net was woven of secrets.

Chapter 5

A golden chain encircled her neck, yet it was a captive's chain nonetheless. Similar links bound her wrists and hands, which rested motionless in her lap. The white satin gown, embroidered with silver threads, was the finest garment she had ever worn. A close cap of white feathers covered her head, and her pale hair spilled down her back.

The precious chains and beautiful costume were meant to transform her into a human version of the swan sitting beside her in the cart. Juliana lifted her head proudly, determined to hide her fear and disgrace from her English enemies.

She swayed inside the pony-drawn cart, feeling dizzy and dull-witted. The watered wine given her by one of the guards had been bitter with added herbs, which sapped her energy and made her feel vague and slow, as if she floated through a dream.

Yet she felt as if she were caught in a nightmare.

The cart rumbled along a torchlit corridor inside the king's castle. Servants bearing large platters of food hurried past. Ahead, two men carried a huge tray displaying a castle sculpted of marzipan and adorned with sugared fruits.

Juliana glanced at the large male mute swan settled beside her in a nest of green embroidered satin. A gold chain around his long neck was attached to an upright wooden post. Artan ruffled his feathers nervously when one of the ponies whickered.

Juliana made a wordless, soothing sound. Artan lifted his orange beak, its base knobbed in black. He chirred and quieted.

Beyond a set of tall oaken doors, she heard the sounds of

music, laughter, and the clatter of dishes and knives. She knew that a banquet was in progress, attended by the king's guests.

Though her head spun from the wine, she sat aloof while a serving woman arranged the sumptuous white gown around her and adjusted the cap of feathers. Artan hissed and the woman stepped back hastily.

"That swan is a beautiful beast, but mean," the woman said. "But ah, the lady looks like a princess. Seamstresses and artists worked day and night to make this gown and the nest. 'Tis a shame, I say, that the king only means to make a fool of her and her Scottish people with all this costly finery."

"Since when are ye the king's advisor?" one of the guards scoffed. "Go tell the chamberlain that the girl is ready to be presented to king and court." The woman hurried away.

"Here, pretty bird," one guard said, chortling as he approached. He reached out and stroked Juliana's shoulder with damp fingers. She jerked away.

Artan hissed and swiped a wing at the guard, who jumped back. "That foul-tempered swan belongs on the king's table," he muttered. "And the Swan Maiden would do well in a man's bed."

"King Edward wants her brought pure and maidensome to his feast, or we will all be blamed," the first said. "Keep yer hands away. 'Tis eerielike, the way that swan defends her. Chills my bones, it do, and I'll not touch her, king or none."

Juliana fisted her hands in her lap, gold chains chinking. Several days had passed since she and Artan had been captured in Scotland. The journey south to Newcastle had been a blur of rough cart rides and chafing ropes, aching muscles and constant fear, infrequent meals of stale bread and cheese. And too often, she had been given wine mixed with bitter herbs, which induced apathy, compliance, and bouts of heavy sleep.

Walter de Soulis, who had accompanied her south, had ordered the dosings in the wine. She had tried to refuse in silence, but the drinks were forced down her throat.

White satin, golden chains, and the swan Artan beside her were an improvement, but she did not know what King Edward intended for her. She had been told that he was pleased by the capture of Juliana Lindsay, daughter of a Scots rebel and cousin of another. Would she be imprisoned, she wondered, or sealed in a convent—or put to death as a witch or a rebel?

She shivered at her own thoughts, and turned her attention to Artan beside her, smoothing his feathers.

The Swan Maiden, the English called her, claiming that she knew magical arts. Only fools, she thought bitterly, believed in such things. If she truly had magic, she would have escaped her captivity already.

And if the king discovered the truth about her, she thought, frowning, he would surely order her execution.

The doors of the banquet chamber opened wide, and the cart lurched as the ponies moved ahead. The high-vaulted chamber was filled with torchlight and shadows, voices and distant faces. Clarion trumpets blared suddenly. The swan, startled, ruffled his feathers and hissed again.

She placed a hand on his back and he busked his wings slightly. As the cart rumbled over the floor tiles, Juliana lifted her chin and straightened her shoulders.

A fanfare of trumpets accompanied the arrival of servants carrying yet another course arranged on platters. Gawain held up a hand in refusal when a servant offered a tray to him and to his stepfather and stepbrothers. Ground pork baked in colored batters in the shapes of fruits seemed highly unappealing, he thought, and turned away.

"No more appetite?" his stepfather, Henry Avenel, asked as he accepted a serving on his own bread trencher.

Gawain swirled the last of the red Gascony wine in his silver goblet. "I have little taste for wondrous foods," he said wryly. "I made my appearance here, ate something in good company, and now I am ready to be quit of this feast."

"So early? Look at the marvelous confection coming through those doors now—what . . . it looks like a girl made all of marzipan!" Robin Avenel, who had been knighted but a few weeks ago in London, craned his neck to peer through the crowds.

Gawain did not even glance at the newest wonder being offered. Edmund, Robin's older brother, slid them a mildly interested glance and turned back to the servant girl standing beside him, smiling at her and running his fingers along her arm.

He wondered how Edmund could concentrate on seduction amid the din of musical instruments and the chatter of servants and guests. Most of those attending the feast in the hall at Newcastle were knights and soldiers of the king's army, journeying north to Scotland. They needed a grand celebration, he thought, to relieve the tedium of a military existence.

"Gawain," his stepfather said, "you stayed with the barbaric Scots too long this time. If you are not enjoying the feast and the spectacle here, your tastes have turned far too simple."

"They always were simple," Gawain said. "You forget that before I was counted among your sons, and among the king's knights, I was a lad in those barbaric hills." He rarely made reference to that, he thought; the wine had loosened his tongue.

"I have not forgotten," Henry said sternly. "You had best pray the king does not remember you are not my own son."

"They say King Edward has another surprise planned for the evening." Robin leaned forward. "I wonder if this is it." He seemed frustrated when the other Avenels did not bother to look.

"Another *subtletie* sculpted from spun sugar and almond paste?" Gawain asked. The crowd blocked his view. "Another leaping acrobat? 'Twill be lost on this lot, Robin. Most of them are too drunk to care what else is brought out."

"Grand as it is, this feast hardly compares with the king's Swan Feast in London last May, when he knighted three hundred men—our Robin among them," Henry added proudly, smiling at his youngest son. "The king threw a sumptuous celebration there. This one is modest, but the food is good. The Plantagenet court, wherever it rests, does maintain quality."

"In London, the king had a pair of swans in golden chains brought to him, and he swore to destroy Robert Bruce and rule Scotland, or die in the attempt," Edmund said. "I did hear that the king will renew that vow on another pair of swans, since Newcastle is his last stop before he enters Scotland once again."

"Then I will definitely leave early," Gawain said. "Swan

meat is tough and not to my liking." The vow, rather than the meat, was his true objection.

"Aye, swans are out of season now—their flesh is most tender in the autumn," Edmund said. "But the king has talented cooks, and he brings them along when he travels. Each dish here has been more artfully crafted than the last."

"These knights are worthy men, and deserve a feast to lift their spirits," Henry agreed.

Gawain frowned. "The king's true intention is to attract new knights for his army and contributions for his Scottish war."

"'Tis wise to be generous toward the king who has recently granted you king's peace." Henry dipped his fingers in a bowl of rosewater, raising his brow at Gawain.

"I am grateful for the king's goodwill," Gawain said carefully. "I simply wish to leave the feast early. In the morning, I will journey north."

"The king has ordered you to Scotland already?" Robin asked.

"Aye. Gawain has been given a post as a commander," Edmund said, "despite his infamous transgressions."

"The king is desperate," Gawain murmured.

"See, some good came of you bowing that stubborn head of yours and begging king's peace," Henry said. "Your Scottish birth could have cost us all our heads, now that Robert Bruce has so boldly claimed Scotland for his own. Edward is furious toward any who have even remote ties to the Scots."

"Who can blame him," Gawain said, mildly and ambiguously, meaning the King of Scots.

Henry frowned. "I defended your actions in Scotland because your mother was worried about you. She still hopes the king will offer you one of his fair cousins for a bride. But you must behave yourself for that to happen," he added.

"I doubt my obeisance will earn me a bride with royal blood, if that is what you are hoping, sir."

"Whoever you marry, your lady mother will be heartsore if you are not happily wed soon, before she—" Henry stopped abruptly, and took a swift draught of wine.

"I know," Gawain said quietly. For his mother's sake, in her last days, he should marry any suitable lady quickly and find affection for his wife afterward. He had given little thought to marriage, busy campaigning in Scotland for Edward. He had wooed and trysted with high-born ladies and heath-born lasses, but had never found a love incandescent enough to light his life, and hers, until the end of their days.

Why hunger for something so rare, he thought sourly, the stuff of legends and courtly tales; most of those stories ended badly anyway. He took a swallow of wine and watched the throng around him.

He had seen true love once, seen its power and its grace. The magic between James Lindsay and Isobel Seton was the most sacred thing he had ever witnessed. He had basked in its reflected warmth, and envied it, and hoped someday to have even a glimmer of that in his own life. Now he realized that he had been a little in love with Isobel himself.

Months ago he had spent a great deal of time with them. The choice he had made had resulted in his stepbrother's death, his own imprisonment, and his humiliating plea before the king.

Even so, he would give anything to restore that lost friendship. Most likely James and Isobel never wanted to see him again.

He shoved a hand through his thick dark hair, realizing that he was a bit more drunk than he thought. Best consider marriage in the light of day, he decided, when his head was cooler and his heart was not quite so aware of its weight of sadness.

If his mother wanted him wed, so be it. He would have fetched down the moon for her if she had asked.

"Perhaps the king will grant Gawain some fair demoiselle now that our brother is back in grace," Edmund remarked. Gawain raised his wine cup in salute while the others chuckled. The wine wet his lips, but the smile did not touch his eyes.

"We cannot hope for that now," Henry said. "We can only hope the king will have no cause to doubt your fealty in the future."

"Certes," Gawain answered. "He will not."

"Will you see your mother before you go north? She will be distressed to learn that you are leaving again so soon. She . . . was not well again last week when I was there."

"I will visit her tomorrow." Gawain stood and stepped out-

side the bench. "Good night, sir. Edmund, luck to you. Sir
Robin, watch your back, lad." He clapped his youngest stepbrother on the shoulder. "New-made knights are not as invincible as they think." He smiled, just as the trumpets blared to
announce another course.

"Wait, Gawain," Robin said. "Something truly magnificent
has been brought into the hall. Do not go just yet."

"A few moments more, then," Gawain agreed, aware that his
departure might attract the king's unwanted notice.

A pony-drawn cart draped in sumptuous fabrics had crossed
the length of the great hall, wooden wheels creaking. Guards
walked in front, blocking Gawain's view of the inside of the
cart. When it finally rolled closer to where he stood, he drew in
his breath, astonished. This was what Robin had urged them to
see.

In the center of a lush green nest sat a blond young woman
and a large swan. Both were bound by golden chains. On a
wooden pole above them, a yellow banner showing the red lion
rampant of Scotland fluttered with the cart's movement.

Gowned in white satin trimmed in silver embroidery, the girl
sparkled like a diamond. A cap of white feathers framed her
face, and her smooth hair had the delicate sheen of purest gold.

"An enchanted swan for the king's feast," Edmund said. "I
swear I have never seen a sight so lovely."

The girl and the swan sat so still that for a moment Gawain
thought they were glittering statues. Then the bird fluttered its
wings, and the girl reached out to touch its snowy back.

She turned her head, and Gawain saw her face more clearly.
Perfection, he thought impulsively. Then he saw, despite the
proud tilt of her head, that her eyes were wide with fright. He
frowned.

The crowd applauded as the cart rolled nearer. Gawain stood
grim and still, watching. The girl's stiff, straight back, her apprehensive gaze, the heavy locks on the chains, and the presence of the guards made him doubt this was mere
entertainment.

She was a breathtaking sight, but Gawain suspected that the
king intended only to mock Scotland and humiliate the girl.
The cart halted near the king's table, and Edward nodded with

a smug smile. Gawain stayed where he was and studied the girl from his closer vantage point.

With a shock of certainty, he realized that he had seen her years ago. A face so exquisite was not easily forgotten.

He narrowed his eyes, studying her. Aye, she was Juliana Lindsay of Elladoune, he thought, or her double. Six years had barely changed her, though she was thinner. He recognized the oval face, the small, stubborn chin, the wide mouth, the dark-hued eyes, and the lean grace of her frame. But her hair was more pale than he remembered, with a remarkable sheen, like gold washed with silver.

How did she come to be here at the king's feast, dressed like a swan and chained like a captive? He remembered that James Lindsay had once mentioned that he was cousins with the Lindsays of Elladoune. He wondered if Jamie knew that his young cousin was being offered like plunder to a king who hated Scots.

"Is she artfully made from spun sugar and almond paste?" Robin asked, staring.

"Far too real," Gawain said grimly. "I know her."

"Who is she?" Henry demanded.

"A Scotswoman, the daughter of a rebel. I met her years ago." Gawain fisted a hand, silent and fierce, wondering if he and James Lindsay might have been able to prevent this mockery had he stayed with them in Scotland.

"'Tis madness to chain a young girl so," Henry said.

"Indeed," Gawain growled. He walked around the table toward the open area surrounding the cart. He wanted to help, but was not certain what to do, short of grabbing her and carrying her out the door. Surely there was some better solution.

The king stood. The guests rose too, in a rush of movement, dropping napkins and setting down their goblets and half-eaten portions of food.

"What have we here?" the king asked in a smooth, rehearsed tone. "A swan . . . and a Swan Maiden. Welcome to our celebration." He gestured brusquely. A servant pulled the huge carved chair aside and the king walked around the table.

Edward approached the cart, a tall, thin man, hands folded behind his back. Torchlight gleamed on his white hair, and on the jeweled collar over his magenta tunic. Age and illness bowed his shoulders.

"The sight of such a beautiful woman will surely stir our knights to thoughts of . . . victory over Scotland," Edward murmured. A ripple of low laughter followed.

Gawain frowned, watching the king pace in front of the cart. Edward peered at Juliana as if she were one of the strange beasts kept in the little zoo in the Tower of London. The girl straightened her head and back as gracefully as the swan beside her.

The bird moved then, extending its neck and hissing loudly. It batted a wing at Edward, who stepped back hastily. The guards and some of the advisors rushed forward, but the king waved them away and resumed his stroll.

"All the swans in England," Edward said, "belong to the king. No one disputes that. These two *swans*"—he emphasized the last word—"were taken in Scotland. Scottish swans also belong exclusively to the king of England. As does the land of Scotland itself." His voice rose, and he lifted his hand.

"I swore in London weeks past upon a pair of swans," he declared. "I swear again before God and this company, and upon this swan and Swan Maiden, that I will quell Scotland and the rebel Robert Bruce. All men here, swear the same with me!"

Throughout the hall, hundreds of knights repeated the king's words in an echoing, massive single voice. Gawain stood silent while Henry and his stepbrothers made the vow as well.

The king rounded upon the girl, his face flushed. She stared boldly back at him. Gawain watched her reaction with keen approval.

The swan hissed, flapping his wings. Edward raised a hand, avoiding the swan, and stroked the girl's head, cooing. She batted his hand away firmly. The smack was audible.

Gasps echoed around the room.

With a fixed smile, Edward turned to his guests. "The Swan Maiden wants taming," he said. "We shall choose an English knight for the task. She will be brought to rule by him, just as her rebellious nation will be ruled by his king." He looked around the hall. "Whoever can tame this Scottish swan shall have her. Come forward and try!"

Several knights stood, and more followed suit. The king beckoned them forward. Gawain stood not far from the girl's cart, motionless. Even when Henry urged his sons to go forward, Gawain did not move. He had no interest in this cruel game, and no taste for dominating a woman.

As the men gathered to form a line, Gawain recognized many of them by name or by sight. Some were so drunk that they swayed and stumbled. And some, Gawain knew, hated Scots as virulently as Edward Plantagenet.

He looked at Juliana Lindsay again, and saw her face grow pale. Cold fury rose in him. He could not leave now—and he could not stand here and watch this.

He stepped forward.

Chapter 6

She sat straight and wary, greeting each knight in turn with cool silence. One after another they came toward her, some bumbling and drunken, a few edgy and intense. Despite the haze of the herbal potion, she maintained dignity and quiet.

Most advances or overtures she ignored until the knights walked away to echoes of laughter. Others were bolder, rougher, pulling on her, even caressing her. Laughter rippled out like haunting music, low male voices with scarcely a female titter among them. Her sense of desperation and fear grew.

She batted hands away, turned her head to avoid drunken kisses. Beside her, the swan hissed continually, rocking his head sinuously on his neck, raising his wings to strike blows.

One of the men tried to lift her, and Artan lunged, his wing striking the man's forearm. Juliana heard the sickening crack of bone. The man howled, grabbing at his arm and stepping back.

"My wrist! The bird has snapped my wrist!" he howled. Some of those watching laughed, while some saluted the swan's prowess.

Another knight came forward and yanked on her arm. Juliana shook free of his grip, while Artan flapped his wings and snaked out his neck. The knight stepped out of the swan's reach and stroked Juliana's face, making cooing noises.

In a fury of anger and instinct, she bit his finger.

The man shrieked and jerked back his arm to strike her. In that moment, a dark-haired knight stepped out of the crowd and strode forward, his hand on the hilt of his dagger.

"Leave her be," he growled.

"Wild swan bitch," the other man muttered. "She cannot be tamed—I leave her to you, Avenel!" He stumbled away.

The knight in black stepped back into the crowd, watching Juliana steadily. She stared at him, wiping the back of her hand over her mouth, her hair wisping over her eyes. His face seemed familiar, yet she could not place the meeting or name the man.

Even without that protective gesture, she might have noticed him. He was a raven among peacocks, dressed in black amid the brightly garbed knights. Taller than average, broad-shouldered and lean, he was unsmiling, while the others grinned and chatted. His dark eyes were intense, and glossy black hair framed a face of chiseled masculine beauty. Quiet power emanated from him.

Yet he stood awaiting his own turn with her. Juliana looked away. His gesture was possessive, not protective.

Another knight came toward the cart and slurred a greeting. He reached out and grabbed her arm.

"One night in my bed will tame her! Come here, little swan!" The audience laughed and called out encouragements.

Juliana kicked and struggled, and Artan hissed, straining at his chain. The knight lifted an arm to defend against a powerful wing blow, dragging Juliana halfway out of the cart.

"Release her," the king ordered. "This grows tedious. 'Tis poor chivalry and poor spectacle. Move on. Next!"

The knight set her roughly on her feet on the floor and walked away muttering. Juliana leaned against the cart, legs shaking.

"The Swan Maiden needs taming, and requires a lesson," Edward called out. "This display has been amusing, but there are priests and ladies among us. We cannot offend them. Who here can win her obedience—and her love?"

Juliana stood straight, though her head spun and her knees were weak. She waited, proud and still, neck and shoulders tensing beneath the weight of the collar and chains.

A knight stepped forward, a young man with light brown hair and a pretty face that would mature into handsomeness. Artan stretched his neck to utter a snakelike hiss, widening his wings.

"My—my lady," the knight said. "I wish you no harm."

She leaned her head against the cart, feeling dull-witted and weary. Artan hissed. The knight glanced nervously at the bird. "Robin . . . Sir Robert Avenel is my name. My stepbrother is Sir Gawain Avenel, the man who just championed you. I would be your champion, too." He smiled awkwardly.

Her glance flickered toward Gawain Avenel, the knight in black, who watched with a grim frown.

"If you please, my lady, consent to come with me." The young knight lifted a hand toward her.

Artan lashed out and bit him. Robert leaped back, shaking his hand.

"Watch, pup, and see how 'tis done," another knight called, this one a broad man in a blue surcoat. He shoved Robert aside and grabbed Juliana's hand. He kissed her fingers, his lips hot and repulsive.

"Sweeting, let me show you the pleasures of captivity." He stroked her feathered cap. "Come with me, and discover delight."

Juliana jerked away from his touch. Artan lurched at him. Swearing, the knight stepped back.

"With that devil swan and a black knight to protect her, no man can gain the lady," he muttered. "Avenel, see if you fare any better!"

The dark knight came toward her. He reached out, as had the others. Juliana expected Artan to lash out and bite him.

Avenel opened his closed fist and sprinkled bits of bread inside the cart. Artan snatched at the food.

The knight cocked a brow and looked at Juliana. "Are you hungry?" he murmured. "I can fetch something more appealing than bread crumbs, if you wish."

Surprised, she shook her head.

"I imagine you would like to leave all this nonsense behind," he said quietly.

She nodded, looking up at him.

"Come with me, then, and all will be well."

She shook her head. His calm manner was reassuring and soothing, but his intent was no different than the others.

"Lady Juliana," he murmured, "this competition to win you will go on all night, unless you surrender to someone."

She narrowed her eyes. How had he known her name? The king had not announced it. He must be close to the king, or in league with the guards who watched over her. As for giving in to English will, she would rather live in a prison cell than surrender her body and her will to a king's man. She conveyed her refusal with a haughty angle of her chin.

Avenel reached into a pocket and took out another piece of bread, which he tore into pieces for the swan. "Not all these knights share my agreeable temper. A wring of the neck, a twist of a dagger, and your swan will not protect you for long. The only risk is the crime of harming a swan in England. Apparently 'tis no crime to mock a Scotswoman. You will have to co-operate with me if you would be safe." He spoke low and urgently.

She slitted her eyes. He leaned close, resting a hand on the cart. Artan, busy nibbling, did not even lift his head.

"The king makes a show of his chivalry, but he detests any Scot. If one of those drunken fools wins custody of you, no one will ensure your safety."

Frightened, she watched him with wide eyes. She had to put her faith in him. He had proven himself capable of decency at least, even if his intentions toward her were no doubt sinful.

"Show the king that I have tamed you. Then I can help you."

She would never submit to him just so he could gain favor with his cruel king. Anger flaring, she turned away.

"Better to be tamed by me," he murmured, "than one or more of my drunken comrades. Lady, tell me . . . did you remember the Swan Knight in your prayers, as you promised?"

Gasping, she stared at him. Only the Swan Knight himself would know of that promise.

She looked at him speculatively. Years had etched his face and made it leaner, harder, but she recognized him now. His eyes were just as she remembered, dark brown, deep and warm, framed in black lashes and serious, straight brows. This was indeed the man who had saved her at Elladoune.

He tipped his head and smiled. "I see you are still in need of a rescue, Juliana Lindsay."

Heart quickening, hope rising, she nodded in answer.

"Give me your hand." He opened his fingers, and she reached out. His grip was warm, dry, and strong. "Now do as I tell you," he murmured. "Act heartstruck for love of me." He lifted her hand and kissed it.

A thrill spun through her at the touch of his mouth. Her knees buckled, and he caught her arm under the elbow. His smile was unexpectedly boyish, tilted, and full of easy charm.

Heartstruck was not so difficult to pretend. She felt again the adoration from years ago, when he had helped her and she had asked his name. *Call me your Swan Knight*, he had said.

But she could not trust him, no matter if she wanted to do so. He was an English knight, and she was a Scottish prisoner.

She scowled at him. He kissed her fingers again. Applause fluttered amid hoots of laughter. "Smile, lady," he murmured.

The king rose from his seat and came toward them.

The warm cradle of his fingers and the brush of his lips over her knuckles stirred tears in her eyes. She had not felt comfort or gentleness for so long. Her harsh treatment had made her weak and needy, she told herself sternly. Scowling at him, she straightened her shoulders and tried to pull her hand away.

He tightened his fingers over hers. "Look at me as though your heart is mine forever," he drawled, "not as if you want to eat my heart for supper."

She closed her eyes, confused. To get out of here, she reminded herself, she had to cooperate with him. She forced herself to smile at him.

He turned toward the king, holding her hand aloft and bowing. Cheers and light applause swelled through the hall.

Artan, finished with his bread crumbs, hissed and spread his wings. Gawain glanced at the swan, whose neck swayed ominously.

" 'Twould ruin the moment if he bites me," he said dryly.

Juliana felt an urge to laugh, until Gawain lifted her hand and turned to the king.

"My liege," he said, "the Swan Maiden is mine."

Gawain glanced sidelong at the girl. Her hand trembled in his, but her lips shaped a beautiful smile that struck him like an arrow shot. He caught his breath.

The king approached the cart. Gawain had to see this through; he could not abandon the girl to the king's game. Once again he had obeyed his impulse to protect others—though that had brought him more trouble than honor in the past.

His greatest flaw, he knew, lay in his tendency to help those who needed assistance, no matter the cost to himself. It was an admitted weakness, and one he could not strengthen.

Somehow Juliana Lindsay seemed to draw that out in him. Fate had thrown them together more than once, and each time he had taken up her cause, though he did not even know her.

King Edward came closer. Gawain bowed. "Sire, I have tamed the Swan Maiden as you requested. I wish to claim her as my own." In truth, he hoped to gain custody of her and send her back to Scotland.

To his relief, Juliana lowered her head demurely. The cap of feathers and her golden hair shone like crown and veil. She swayed, and Gawain tightened his hold on her arm to steady her.

The king scrutinized them. "How did you accomplish it when no one else could? With some magical incantation?" He looked back at his audience, who laughed appreciatively.

"No mystery, my lord. I obeyed the example of my namesake, Sir Gawain, who showed courtesy and kindness to others."

"Easy to be courteous to a little beauty." The king peered at her, lifting her chin with a fingertip. Juliana turned her head aside in a clear, soundless insult.

The king frowned. "And how did you master the swan?"

"With a bit of bread, sire."

"A practical man." As the king turned, the swan lashed out and snapped at him. Edward snarled and stepped back. When he reached out to touch Juliana's arm, she jerked away from him.

"Not tame yet, either of them," the king said curtly.

" 'Twill be done, I assure you," Gawain murmured.

"Do it, or the task will go to another knight."

Gawain grasped Juliana's golden neck chain, tugging on it gently. "I assure my liege, the lady will be meek and obedient, and do all my bidding," he murmured. "So will the swan."

Juliana glared at him, while Edward nodded in approval and paced away, lanky and slow.

"Behave yourself," Gawain hissed to Juliana. "Try to act adoring. And keep that swan of yours still." He smiled, wide and showy. She smiled back, her teeth clenched.

The king swung around. "What a pretty pair of lovebirds—the pale maiden and her dark knight. With but a word from him, she turns into his loving leman. One caution, sir."

"My liege," Gawain said.

"Remember the Scots are known for the quick turning of their loyalties. You may lose her devotion without warning. Her countryman Robert Bruce has shown us the bitter side of his fealty lately, even though he renewed his obeisance three times in public audience . . . ah, much like our good Sir Gawain."

Gawain tensed at the inference. Edward paced away. "What if the Scottish Swan Maiden gave her heart to England?" He looked at Gawain, eyes glittering. "Tame the girl, and train her to your will."

Gawain frowned. "Train her, sire?"

"Surely you need no instruction for that. A woman will do all a man's will if he handles her properly." He turned to the crowd, beaming like a jester in a play, soaking in the laughter with raised hands. The king, Gawain realized, was very drunk.

His outraged silence matched Juliana's stillness.

"Take her north with an escort, and display her in golden chains," the king said. "The captive Swan Maiden led round the countryside by English knights. She will serve as an example."

"An example of what, sire?" Gawain asked carefully.

"Of the harm rebellion brings to the Scots. Teach the girl about loyalty to England. We may take her into our bosom of forgiveness if she makes a pretty oath like you did. We know that you understand the concept of loyalty by now."

Gawain flared his nostrils. "Aye, sire."

"Then demonstrate it. Teach her a pretty speech too."

"My lord," Gawain said, "the lady does not speak."

"'Tis her willful, rebellious spirit. She will surrender to your will. I want to see her in court again when 'tis done." Edward strutted now.

This was a jest to him, Gawain thought, one he would forget by morning. An urge to protest rose up in him. Then he noticed his stepfather and stepbrothers watching him, faces somber. His family would suffer if he was uncooperative now.

"As you will, sire," he said flatly.

"Good," Edward said. "She will be ruled by her English husband. Let her be a symbol of Scotland ruled by England." Edward grinned, then waved the applause into quick silence.

Gawain's hand tightened on Juliana's arm, though she pulled away like a jessed falcon. His heart pounded hard. "Husband?"

"You claimed her. Now marry her."

"Sire," Gawain said curtly. "I hoped to win her freedom."

"Your father requested our assistance in finding you a bride. This one will do for you. When she is docile, bring her to Carlisle to prove her loyalty. That will prove yours."

A bride, meted out like a punishment, and meant as a test of his loyalty. "My lord, I have renewed my oath to you."

"Your maiden swan is a rebel, hatched in a nest of rebels. This a merciful sentence for her."

"Merciful indeed," Gawain muttered.

"If she proves herself, 'twill be your success. If she rebels, 'twill be your failure."

A muscle thumped in his cheek. "Sire."

Edward's eyes glittered. "Now go and do to her tonight what we would do to Scotland." His grin grew wicked, and snickers rippled throughout the audience.

Gawain felt Juliana shudder. He held her arm, giving no indication of his own fury.

"That bird looks to be a juicy one. We will dine on it tomorrow. Tonight you will find your little swan tender and delightful, no doubt." Edward grinned again, then turned to his chamberlain. "Fetch a priest," he directed. "We will end the feast with a wedding."

"Sweet saints," Gawain muttered under his breath.

The king strode away to confer with his advisors, who gathered in a cluster, tall men with long, dark robes, gleaming chain mail, and grim faces. None of them had laughed during the spectacle, Gawain had noticed.

Juliana whimpered, the closest to a sound she had made. "I promised to set you free," he murmured to her. "But as you can see, I am not Edward's most favored knight. My apologies."

She sent him a sour glare.

The knights cleared a path as a priest hurried forward. Gawain felt as if he could hardly breathe. Juliana stood still beside him, tense in his grip. Behind him, the swan hissed.

He saw his stepfather and his stepbrothers at the edge of the crowd. Henry nodded to underscore his support, but Gawain did not feel reassured. He was about to obey the king's drunken whim and enter into a mockery of the sacred state of marriage.

At least, he thought, he could repay some of the debt of honor that he owed her cousin James Lindsay. Juliana would be under his protection now, and he could send her back to Scotland. His conscience would ease knowing he had helped a Lindsay.

Otherwise, his imminent marriage to James Lindsay's rebellious little cousin was plainly astonishing to him. He doubted the girl would ever develop English loyalties. Her kin were rebels, blood and bone, and she seemed to share that. He suspected that her insistent silence was pure stubbornness.

As the priest intoned the marriage text in Latin, Gawain repeated the phrases that bound him to her, legally and forever. He looked at Juliana. She was no loving bride, but clearly furious. Her cheeks were pink, her lips tight, her eyes dark blue flashes. In the cart, the swan hissed. Bizarre wedding music, Gawain thought.

"The lady must speak the vow," the priest said, edging away from the bird.

Juliana shook her head.

"She may nod her agreement," the priest said.

This time her head shake was more vehement.

"Is she deaf and dumb?" the priest asked.

"Not deaf," Gawain said between his teeth. She lifted her chin defiantly. He leaned down. "Nod, Juliana," he murmured.

She glared at him.

"Marry me, and I can save that bird from a roasting pan."

She glanced at him quickly, eyes intense.

"I swear it," he said. He had promised much to many of late, but he would keep this one somehow.

The priest repeated the vows. Juliana sighed and nodded.

"Well enough," the priest said, and pronounced the marriage blessing. "Give her the kiss of peace," he directed Gawain.

He bent and touched his lips to hers. Her mouth was still and soft. He felt a swirl of transient pleasure. His blood surged and his heart pounded as if he were a youth, smitten hard and floundering with it.

The king clapped his hands and came forward. "Well done," he announced. "Now take your maiden swan away, and render her a maiden no more." He walked away with a sly smile.

"Sire," Gawain said. "Might my . . . lady wife be freed from her chains now?"

Edward ignored him and beckoned to the musicians to play again, resuming his seat while servants rushed to pour wine into his goblet and offer him trays of sweetmeats.

Gawain stood beside Juliana, as silent as she was. The doors of the chamber opened wide as the next cart was brought forward, bearing a huge confection, a fruit-bedecked castle.

The entertainment he and Juliana had provided had ended.

One of the guards approached Gawain. "She's yers to take home, sir, but she is still a prisoner. An escort will go with ye tonight. Orders will be delivered by messenger in the morning. For now, we will wait in the outer courtyard."

As the man turned away, Gawain thought of something and

followed him, out of Juliana's range of hearing. She waited for him, standing, wavering slightly.

"Sir!" Gawain placed a gold coin in the man's hand. "Make certain that the swan is taken to the river and released, rather than taken to the kitchen," he said in a quiet, urgent tone.

The guard nodded thoughtfully. "For good coin, anything can be done. I will see to it. The king can eat some other swan on the morrow, eh?" He winked.

"My thanks." Gawain walked back to Juliana and took her arm to guide her out of the hall. She glanced at the swan with a whimper, stumbling, her distress obvious.

"Come, my lady. Come." He urged her toward the door.

She faltered beside him, and he realized that she must have been given some sort of potion to weaken her. He swept her up into his arms and carried her through the huge doorway.

He hurried past servants, past carts loaded with dirty platters and soggy bread trenchers. Striding through a torchlit hallway, he took some stairs that led to the courtyard.

The girl rode silently in his arms. Her golden chains chimed in rhythm with his footsteps as he descended the steps. He walked out into the cool, rainy darkness and set her down, and she leaned against him wearily.

"Not much longer," he said, looking down at her.

A guard appeared, the man with whom he had previously spoken about the swan. He led Gawain's own horses, both saddled: Gringolet, a dark bay, a sturdy destrier from his father's stables; and Galienne, a gray palfrey, a temperate mare that Gawain often rode himself to spare the warhorse.

"'Tis done, sir, what ye asked of me," the guard said. "I saw to the matter myself. 'Twill be released in the morn."

"My thanks, man." The guard drew the palfrey forward and Gawain assisted Juliana into the saddle. "She is called Galienne," he said. "Can you ride?"

She slid him a look that said the question was ridiculous, and took the reins in her manacled hands, turning the horse's head. The rain had flattened the feathers on her small cap, and turned her golden hair to sopping strands. Draped in the white satin gown, her back was straight, her hands amazingly sure.

Aye, he thought admiringly, she could ride very well.

He bounded into Gringolet's saddle and walked him forward to stand beside the palfrey. Unfastening his black cloak, Gawain swept it around Juliana's shoulders and pulled up the hood.

She looked at him, quick and wary.

"You are wet," he said simply. His stepfather and stepbrothers strode into the courtyard. Gawain waited while they mounted their horses.

All the while, his glance repeatedly strayed toward his silent, weary, mysterious bride.

Chapter 7

The patter of rain and the pounding of the horses' hooves on the cobbled stones seemed loud in the night-dark streets of Newcastle-upon-Tyne. Juliana rode at the center of a group of guards and the Avenel kinsmen. She recognized the younger of the men as Sir Robert—Robin, the others called him.

Gawain rode ahead of her through the Black Gate that led out of the castle and into the walled town, where cobbled streets, crowded with houses, looked slick in the rain. One of the guards led her horse, though she could have handled her biddable mount.

No one spoke to her, and she kept silent. She had not spoken in so long that she wondered if her voice had grown weak from disuse. She shivered in the cool rain, grateful for the cloak that Gawain had given her.

He rode ahead of her, his head bare, his shoulders broad. She glanced at him often, aware of a tenuous bond. Her husband— the word seemed strangely ominous now. Dread sat like a stone in her as she wondered what he would demand on their wedding night.

A guard carried a torch ahead of them, but it scarcely pierced the rain and shadows. The massive bulk of a church thrust into the night, and the river gleamed like a ribbon in the distance.

The riders followed a curving, steep side lane and halted before a whitewashed, timbered building whose third level canted over the street. The door opened, golden light pouring over the wet cobblestones. A woman waited as the men dismounted, and a boy came out of the house to lead the horses away.

Gawain turned to Juliana and held up his arms to lift her down. "This is the inn where my kinsmen and I have been staying. We will spend the night here." His hands braced her waist.

She slid down from the horse, and would not look at him. He led her toward the inn, and the woman stood back as they entered a dim, low-ceilinged room.

"Greetings, Dame Bette," Gawain said.

"Greetings, sir. I see ye brought a guest from the king's feast." Bette shut and latched the door and turned. She was sturdy, with gray hair haloing out from a white kerchief, and a dark gown. She appraised Juliana with a fast glance. "I do not have a free chamber for her. Who is she with? Sir Henry and the rest have gone to an upper chamber. He's called for hot wine, and says he wants to see ye right away."

Gawain lifted his cloak from Juliana's shoulders, hanging it on a wall peg by the door, and then brushed the raindrops from the sleeves of his dark tunic. Juliana turned to face Bette, hands joined in front of her by the golden chain.

"By the saints, she is chained!" Bette said. "And wearing feathers! Is she a mummer? Eek, sir—is she a harlot?"

"She is a captive of the king. We have the keeping of her."

"A prisoner! We've no dungeon here! The crown will owe us for her boarding, and it be the very devil to collect it from the royal accounting clerk at the Sand Gate. That man is a lizard."

"The crown owes you naught for her keep," Gawain replied. "I will pay. She is my bride. A gift from the king."

"Bride." Bette stared at him. Then she peered at Juliana, who stared boldly back at her. "Well, she is not ughsome, and may please a man, but Lord bless us, she is a criminal!"

"She is only a rebel Scotswoman."

Bride, Juliana thought. Scotswoman. Rebel. He had not bothered to say her name, though he knew it. She frowned.

Bette looked skeptical. "Well, she needs a bath. I'll take her to yer bedchamber, and wish ye luck of yer marriage."

"My thanks," he said. "Let her bathe in privacy, while I meet with Sir Henry. And bring her a hot meal, if you will." He took the woman's hand, and Juliana saw the flash of a coin. Bette nodded and blushed like a young girl. Gawain crossed the room and went up the stairs.

"Come dear, ye must be tired," Bette said, taking her arm. "And how are ye to bathe, in them chains? We cannot get that gown off of ye, and 'tis too fine to cut. Well, ye'll wash as ye can. Tsk," she added, scanning her critically from head to foot. "Why are ye dressed so? Ye look like a duck."

"From what the king's chamberlain told me as I was leaving the castle," Henry said, "Walter de Soulis will travel north with you and the lady, bringing an escort of men."

"Walter de Soulis?" Gawain asked sharply. He poured himself a cup of heated wine, watered and spiced, a soothing drink that his father preferred before bedtime. Given the events of the evening, he would have opted for something far stronger.

"Aye, he is the king's sheriff in the shire where the girl—your, ah, wife—comes from," Henry said. "Edmund knows something of it. Ned?"

"I inquired about the girl in the hall," Edmund said. "A shameful farce, that wedding. You saved her from a poor fate, if one of those sots had gotten her for his own."

"We know you did not mean to marry her," Robin said. He sat on a stool beside the fire. "Though that may not be so bad—she is a pretty chit."

"Lady," Gawain said irritably. "Demoiselle. Girl. Lass, if you will. She is not a chit. You are a knight now, not a boor with a sword."

Robin gaped at him, and Henry held up a hand for peace. Gawain turned away and sloshed more wine into his cup. He did not intend to drink it all, but he needed something to do.

"At any rate," Edmund said into the tense silence, "this De Soulis has been appointed the first Master of Swans in Scotland—an honorary title, I think, since a sheriff has no leisure to tend royal swans in Scotland during a war effort."

"The king seized upon the symbolic importance of swans last May, when he held his first Feast of the Swan in London," Henry said. "No doubt that is behind this appointment."

Gawain downed a long draught. "I know De Soulis. He burned Elladoune Castle the night that I was reported for aiding rebels. Juliana Lindsay lived there. 'Tis where I first saw her."

"By the saints! Did you help her that night?" Henry asked. "You never mentioned that detail before, as I recall."

Gawain shrugged. "Her, and some others—a mother and children who escaped while their home was being torched. I paid for it with a public apology. 'Tis done."

"Not quite," Henry replied quietly. Gawain glanced at his stepfather, whose hazel eyes were piercing, though his manner was calm, as usual. "Now you've met the girl again, and you have married her by king's order—and you must deal with the man who accused you years ago. Not done at all, is it?" Henry frowned.

Gawain sipped. The spiced wine burned a sweet path down his throat. "What else do we know about this girl?"

"She is yours to keep, by legal and sacred bond," Henry said. "That much we know."

"Wonderful news," Gawain snapped. He flickered a glance at his stepfather, who watched him with grim sympathy.

"Some good may come of this."

"'Tis a shock to find myself wed," Gawain admitted. "But if all that comes of it is my lady mother's contentment, then 'tis enough." He glanced around, and saw sober nods.

"True," Henry agreed quietly. "Ned, what more did you learn about Gawain's bride?"

"She lives in a place called Inchfillan Abbey, under the care of a kinsman, an Augustinian abbot."

"He's wed a nun?" Robin asked.

"Nay, the abbot is her guardian. De Soulis took her brothers into custody as well, before he brought her south with that mute swan. King Edward requested a pair of Scottish swans, and his Master of Swans obtained them."

"De Soulis has a poor sense of humor," Gawain drawled.

"One of the guards said that the girl is called the Swan Maiden in the area where she lives," Edmund said, and shrugged. "I do not know why."

Gawain swirled the wine in his cup. He knew exactly where that epithet came from. "Her brothers were taken? I heard there were two Lindsays, older than her, running with Robert Bruce."

James Lindsay had mentioned his cousins. Gawain shook his head slightly as he thought of the irony in this sure tangle.

"Now you have the responsibility of her," Robin said. "But how are you going to transform her into a loyal English lady?"

"I do not think that can be done at all, frankly." Gawain took a stool beside the fire, settling into the slung leather seat and resting his elbows on his knees. "I only meant to free her and send her back to Scotland. I never counted on the rest."

"You will return her to Scotland—and you will have custody of her for the rest of your life." Henry paced the room, rubbing his jaw. His brown hair had grown more gray, Gawain noticed. Henry was a handsome and skilled man, a paragon of knighthood in Edward's court. His advice and friendship were valued by the king, and his military expertise was respected by many. Gawain considered himself fortunate to call him stepfather and mentor.

"But to take her to Scotland, he has to show her in chains the whole way," Robin said. "Is that not what the king said?"

"Aye, so all of England can see the captive Scotswoman," Edmund said. "A devilish plan."

"I refuse to treat a woman so," Gawain said. "The king is a madman to expect it."

"He seems so, at times," Henry said. "His hatred of the Scots grows more unreasonable, I admit. But if he issues a writ saying she must be chained, and sends an escort to see it done, there is naught you can do about it."

"There might be," Gawain said firmly.

"Insubordination," Henry said, "does not honor the Avenel name."

"Gold links are soft, and impractical for a prisoner's chains," Gawain replied. "Easily broken."

"You have a damnable habit of helping others when 'twill only bring trouble for you," Henry said sternly.

"Those chains had better hold," Edmund muttered, "or all the Avenels will pay the price of it."

Gawain scowled into his wine cup, knowing the truth of that. Henry looked out the window at the rainy darkness. After a moment, he reached into his pocket and withdrew a small object. He tossed it to Gawain.

Deftly catching it, Gawain opened his hand. A tiny iron key lay in his palm. He looked at Henry.

"The king entrusted it to me," his stepfather said. "I entrust it to you. Use it wisely."

Gawain nodded and crossed to the door. "'Tis late. I bid you good night. We are leaving in the morn, my . . . bride and I. Do any of you ride north with us?"

"Robin rides for Avenel Castle tomorrow," Henry said. "Edmund and I must stay in Newcastle for now."

"Ah, then. Good night." Gawain was aware that his family wondered if he would sleep with his new bride this night. He wondered it himself. He opened the door latch.

"Gawain," Henry said. "Thank you."

He glanced over his shoulder in surprise. "Why, sir? I have run the Avenel name to near ruin with all my transgressions. Even worse, Geoffrey . . . is gone now, in part my fault," he murmured. "This evening's pageant does not improve matters."

"Geoffrey's death was hard for everyone, but no one is to blame," Henry said. "We know that you have risked much, and given up much, to protect our welfare. We are all grateful."

Gawain began to speak, but his voice clouded. He nodded stiffly, opened the door, and slipped out into the corridor.

The small bedroom was silent and dark but for the low light of a brazier and a single candle. Outside, rain gusted against the walls, making the room seem cozy. The candle's halo illuminated the bed as Gawain crossed the room and looked down.

Juliana lay in the bed against several pillows, with the fur coverlet pulled up to her shoulders. She still wore the white satin dress, although the feathered cap lay on the table. Her pale hair was like moonlight and silk, and her face was smooth and serene. Gawain reached out a hand but did not touch her.

He wanted a wife, he thought, but not like this. When war and traveling were a way of life, knights often craved the peace and contentment of a home and a family, and he was no different, he knew. Someday he had hoped to find a gentle lady to warm his heart and share his life.

Unsure what to make of this marriage, he felt numb, still stunned. He sat on the edge of the bed and watched her. She slept deeply, her breathing quiet. She was a sweet perfection, golden fair and smooth cheeked, with a soft curve to her mouth, her hands curled and slender on the pillow, wrists manacled.

Frowning, he used the little key to unlock the collar. Sliding a hand under her head, he lifted the band away, baring the sinuous curve of her throat. He stroked a finger over the pink crease the collar had made.

Next he removed the manacles, and pooled the chains on the tabletop. She moaned in her sleep, and he soothed his hand over her head.

He did not dare to touch her further, for desire coursed quick and intense through him. Giving into that was unthinkable. She had been stolen from her home, imprisoned, humiliated, forced to wed. He would not demand marriage rights of her, despite the king's crude suggestion.

He stood, blew out the candle, and walked in the darkness to the other side of the bed. Listening to the driving rain, he removed his boots and clothing, all but his braies. This wedding night was not like most. The girl might wake up and mistake him for a lecher if he kept his usual practice of sleeping nude.

All he wanted was some rest. He felt exhausted from the shock of the evening and the crazy tilt in his future. In the morning he would sort out his obligations. He would receive writs and meet the escort; he realized that he did not even know their destination in Scotland or his military duties yet.

A gust of wind and rain made the closed shutters tremble. The outer world was in upheaval, he thought, like his own world. He eased between the covers. The rope foundation of the bed creaked as he reclined and closed his eyes.

He had much to think about—too much for a weary man to sort through in one night. Listening to the rain, he felt sleep overtake him.

Chapter 8

Blessed freedom. The chains were gone. Juliana could feel the cool air on her neck and wrists. She wondered, lying in the darkness, if the Swan Feast had been only a nightmare.

More fully awake, she realized that her captivity was still real, for she lay in the bed at the inn. But someone had freed her. Relieved and grateful, she sighed and stretched.

After weeks of straw and thin blankets, the deep, soft bed felt like a cloud. She yawned and snuggled into its warmth. Just last night, she had curled in a corner of a cold dungeon cell, too afraid to sleep because of the guards outside the door.

Here she had slept undisturbed for what seemed a long while, although the sky was still dark beyond the opaque glazing in the small window, and rain still pattered unceasingly.

She rolled over, and squeaked in alarm.

Gawain slept beside her, his shadowed form motionless beneath the covers. She had not realized his presence until now; his soft snores had mingled with the sound of the rain.

She wondered if he had removed her chains—at least he had left her fully dressed. Apparently he had not attempted to ravish her as the king had suggested to him.

Yet. She sat up carefully, watching him.

In the shadows, she saw only the firm gleam of a bare shoulder, the dark mass of his hair on the pillow. He sighed, shifted his head, resumed snoring. Sure that he was completely asleep, Juliana leaned closer out of curiosity.

Warmth emanated from him, and he smelled clean and spicy and good. He smelled like comfort, she thought suddenly. She recalled the gentle kiss they had exchanged after the marriage vows had been said. She remembered how he had kept her safe, years ago, in his arms. A subtle shiver traveled through her. She wondered what it would feel like to kiss him again, deep and full, like lovers.

But he was not her lover, and their wedding night was a mockery. A husband had been forced upon her like a sentencing. He had helped her, and she was grateful, but he was an enemy to her people. King Edward had sworn to destroy Robert Bruce and Scotland, and Gawain Avenel had stood with the other knights as they repeated that vow.

She had to get away from him and this place before he awoke and tried to claim his rights as a husband. Best if she escaped Newcastle altogether, so he could not chain her again as his prisoner, albeit his wife.

She eased herself out of bed and stood. Although her satin gown rustled loudly, the knight slept undisturbed. Turning, she wondered what to wear; she could hardly flee through the night in a gown as bright as a full moon. Unlacing the neck, she slipped out of the garment and the thin, impractical slippers she had been given. She stood in her gauzy chemise.

The dark blur of the knight's tunic lay on the foot of the bed. The black serge garment was wide and large, and she tugged it over her head and slipped her arms in the sleeves. Avenel was broad-shouldered and she was slight, but her legs were long. It suited her well enough to flee in it, she thought.

Groping around, she discovered his leather belt and latched it over her hips, but it nearly thunked to the floor and she set it aside. Glancing furtively toward the bed, she snatched his boots. They were heavy and well made, and so big on her feet that she fitted them with floor rushes stuffed into each toe box.

She braided her hair out of the way, although with its fine texture it would soon loosen again, lacking a ribbon. Then she tiptoed to the door, eased it open, and slipped out.

The fire in the brazier must have gone out, Gawain thought vaguely, stirring in the bed. The sheets were cold. He rolled over and stretched out his hand in the darkness.

She was gone.

He bolted upright and grabbed groggily for his clothing. That was gone, too. Standing, swearing, he stepped in a pool of white satin. Juliana had not only fled the room, she had left him nothing to wear but his braies—or her gown and feathers.

Muttering under his breath, he went to a corner where his saddle pack lay. The previous day, expecting to ride north to fulfill his term of knight service—wifeless, he thought sourly—he had packed clothing, blankets, and other items.

He extracted a dark brown tunic and yanked it over his head. Discovering that she had taken his boots, too, he swore again and headed for the door, stubbing his bare toe on a stool.

 He made his way along the hall and down the creaking stairs quickly. The other bedchambers were occupied by king's knights, including Henry and his stepbrothers, but no one stirred.

The front door was unbarred, and his cloak was missing from the wall peg where he had left it to dry. Growling in further annoyance, he stepped out into the night.

Rain drenched him within moments. Through the darkness, he saw someone standing at the end of the street. At first, he thought it was a boy. Then he realized that Juliana turned as if uncertain where to go.

Staying in the shadow of the houses, he strode toward her and snatched at her cloak as she whirled to run. "Walking home to Scotland?" he asked.

She fought him, sputtering in the rain. He held her in a fierce grip, while the downpour slicked over his head, ran into his open collar, sluiced cold around his bare feet.

She squealed and tried to stamp on his feet with his own damned boots. He stepped neatly aside.

"You will not get far," he said. "The town is surrounded by a wall several feet thick and more than twenty feet high, with seven gates." He pulled her hard against him and pointed toward the castle that loomed over the city. "Seventeen towers, each with guards on watch, day and night. The outer wall of the town was built fifty years ago to keep the Scots out. 'Twill keep one Scots lassie inside."

He lifted her and dumped her over his shoulder. As he headed back to the inn, he struggled to hold her. She squirmed, her feet beating at his thighs. He smacked the most convenient part of her to reach, her small rounded bottom, and received a solid punch in the kidneys.

Inside the inn, he slammed the door behind them and slid Juliana to her feet. Stripping off the sodden cloak, he flung it over a hook. She stared up at him, her gaze livid, her cheeks flushed, her hair hanging in soaking strands over her face. He kept one hand tight around her upper arm.

"If eyes were daggers," he murmured.

"You would feel the prick," she snapped. Her voice was soft and hoarse, and cracked on the last word.

He raised a brow. "Ah, so you do talk. I thought so. Good. You can explain what the devil you were doing out there." He pulled her toward the stairs.

When she dug in her heels like a mule, he yanked, half dragging her up the steps. She shivered in his damp black tunic, which hung on her like a funeral pall.

When they reached the second floor, Henry peered out of an open door. Beyond him, another door opened, and Robin and Edmund looked out. At the foot of the uppermost staircase, Bette stood with a candle in her hand. All of them gaped.

"Good night," Gawain said succinctly, and pulled Juliana along the corridor. He pushed open his bedchamber door, shoved her inside, followed, and slammed the door, bolting it.

"As if that would keep me inside," she said. She folded her arms and stood staring at him.

"Determined to escape? What about that wall around the town? Do you intend to fly over it, Swan Maiden?"

"You dinna understand. I must go home." He heard a plaintive wobble in her voice, and frowned.

"I understand well enough that you must stay here."

She turned her head indignantly and did not answer.

"Back to silence, I see. What is this silence of yours all about? I remember having to hush you up, years ago. You were full of speeches when we hid in that loch with the swans."

" 'Twas long ago. I scarcely recall." Her English had the airy lilt of a Gaelic-speaking native. It tugged at him swiftly, keenly, a reminder of people and places better forgotten. "What will you do with me now?"

"I have not thought about it. I was sleeping until a few minutes ago." He pushed her toward the bed, and she sat on its edge, sending him a little glare. She was shivering markedly, he noticed. He was cold himself, and damp. "Take off those wet things and get under the covers," he said. He ran his fingers through his hair, shaking some of the moisture out of it.

"I willna." She folded her arms.

He turned to stoke the brazier in the corner of the room, adding dry sticks and coals from a bucket. Juliana stood and edged toward the door. Standing, he spun around and grasped her arm to turn her firmly toward the bed.

"I am a patient man," he said, "but no more. Sit there. And strip down. You are trembling with cold."

"Dinna think to warm me!" She sat again, glaring at him.

In answer, he snatched up a blanket from the bed and tossed it over her shoulders. She grabbed at it, rubbing at her own hair. Gawain turned and stripped off his rain-damp tunic, tossing it over the foot of the bed. Standing before her in his braies, he grabbed another blanket, pulling it without apology from beneath her. He tossed it around his own shoulders.

Her gaze skimmed his bare torso, lowered, raised again. She scooted away on the bed. "I hoped you were a courteous knight who would help me. Instead you mean to hold me against my will."

"I do not—"

"I heard the king's orders! He may be a king, but he acted like a lecherous cur! I willna be subdued for your amusement. Chain me, ravish me, if you dare! Wring my swan's neck and have him for your supper—or wring my own. But I willna be tamed!"

He stood staring at her. Pale and ethereal as a moonbeam, she housed a white flame of righteousness that would make any rebel proud and strong. She directed it at him as if he were a straw target and she a flinted point.

He held up a hand for peace. "I have no intention of taming you," he said. "Be at ease."

"At ease? In a bed with you?" She pulled the blanket closer. "The king urged you publicly to take me this night—just to show that England can rape Scotland. We Scots know that already, and I will fight to the death if you try it!"

"I do not doubt it," he drawled. "My *written* orders from the king are to take you back to Scotland and keep you for my wife. The rest of his orders I need not obey. He will forget them soon enough, drunk as he was," he muttered.

She slicked her fingers through her damp hair. "And you, are you drunk as well? Every man there tonight was sodden," she said with disgust.

"I am in command of myself, if that is what you ask."

She shot him another glare. He sent one back, then ruffled his hair to coax more wetness from it. "You will stay," he said curtly. "You are my wife now, and my obligation. And a prisoner of the crown. I will not forfeit my life for your escape."

"I am nae your wife!"

"We were wed by a priest. Or did you miss that little moment?"

She drew breath. "When ice coats the halls of hell, I will be your wife. When the faeries of Scotland serve sweetmeats to the king of England, I will be your wife!" She folded her arms tightly over her chest and lifted her chin.

He cocked a brow. "You have a talent with words . . . for a silent maiden."

"Those wedding vows meant naught. I didna speak them out."

"Naught to us, but they were legally done. Your nod was good enough, and we are joined in the eyes of God and man. To undo it, we would have to find a priest willing to request a divorce from Rome. 'Tis far easier to remain wed."

"A divorce willna be necessary," she announced. "An annulment will do, since you will never touch me."

"Will I not?" He stood staring down at her, anger rising. He was tired and frustrated, and he had been more than kind to her so far, yet she treated him as if he were a boor.

"My kinsmen will kill you if you do," she said.

"One of your kinsmen may kill me anyway, if he ever sees me again," he muttered, rubbing the blanket over his shoulders. She looked at him, puzzled, but he was not about to explain the tangle between him and her cousin James Lindsay.

"My guardian is an abbot. I live in his household."

"In a religious compound? You do not behave like a nun."

"If I were a nun, the king's guards would have left me in Scotland. Father Abbot will annull the marriage."

"We will see." He sat on the bed. She scooted away from him. "Go easy, I will not harm you," he said wearily. "And I do not want to discuss legalities, either. I just want to get some sleep." The need pulled at him like a river current.

She looked longingly at the bed. "Sleep on the floor."

"Share the bed with me," he replied. She shivered again. "Take that wet tunic off," he said abruptly.

"I willna."

"'Tis summer, but these rainy days lately have been chilly. You will be ill by morning by the way you are shivering now. Take that off and get warm." He yanked away her blanket, then drew the wet garment from her in one long pull. She twisted and squealed in protest. A quick flip draped the tunic with his other garment, near the brazier where they would dry.

She jumped away from him and stood, dressed in some thin undergarment. He saw firm, pink-centered breasts and lean, graceful curves before she grabbed up the blanket again.

"Take off my boots and get in bed," he said gruffly.

"You do mean to ravish me!"

He sighed in exasperation. "I am too tired to ravish anyone. Least of all a spitting mad little Highland lass." Tired, but not unwilling, he realized. The sight of her body had sent a fire bolt through him.

She stared at him, her breath heaving. He glanced away to ebb the desire that flowed through him. "Those boots need to dry by morn so I can wear them," he said.

She stepped out of the boots and kicked them toward the brazier. He walked over to set them to dry properly. When he turned again, she backed away.

"What guarantee do you give that you willna ravish me?"

"Do you want to be ravished?"

"Nay!"

"Then stop asking about it." He went toward the bed. She watched him warily, and shuffled away.

"Juliana," he said patiently, "you wound me. I am a knight sworn to honor, yet you give me no credence. I have proven my worth to you, yet you will not trust me."

"Trust a Sassenach?" she asked incredulously.

"If my word is . . . almost good enough for King Edward, 'tis good enough for you. Lie down."

"Go to sleep if you are tired," she said. "I am nae so weary as I was." Her eyes darted toward the door.

"Oh, ho," he said, seeing her intent. "Do not even think about it. A trick done once to me is never done twice." He stepped toward her and picked her up, dumping her on the bed. Then he sat on the edge, trapping her with his arms.

"Let me go—you gave your word—" She twisted beneath him. "I willna be a wife to you, and I willna stay here!"

"Lie still, or I will be forced to chain you here to keep you safe for the night." His blanket slipped off as he half flattened himself over her to hold her down. His bare chest pressed to the soft globes of her breasts, with only the damp, thin chemise between their bodies. He felt her nipples bead against him, and a shiver went through him.

She bucked beneath him. "Let me go!"

"That would be exceeding foolish of me." More foolish to remain in this position with her, he told himself. He snatched the golden chains from the bedside table.

"You say you are chivalrous, but you lie," she said, wriggling beneath him. "You do mean to ravish your own bride!"

"If 'twould quiet you, I might consider it," he muttered.

"Where is your courtesy?" She torqued beneath him.

"I am summoning all of it in this moment," he growled. He leaned forward, and she flattened into the pillows, staring at him. "Listen to me. You must stay here, and I need to sleep. As do you, I think. Can I trust you for the night, at least?"

"I willna stay here with you. I want to go home to Scotland. I want to be free." Her voice quavered on the last few words, and he sensed how deeply she meant it.

"I will take you home."

"Hah, in your own time, and as a prisoner!"

He sighed. "Can I trust you for the night?"

She shook her head vehemently.

"Well, you are honest at least. My apologies. You leave me no choice." He slid one of the manacles around her wrist and latched it. Then he looped the chain around the bedpost and locked the other manacle into the links. He stood and looked down at her. "Now we can get some rest."

She fumed, pulling at the manacle, while he plumped a mound of pillows to support her and then walked to the other side of the bed to lie down, pulling the covers up.

"I will have the key from you so soon as you are asleep!"

He rolled over quickly and folded her arm firmly against her, holding her wrist against her chest, which rose and fell beneath his hand. "Not unless you want to carry the rest of those chains upon you," he said. She kicked him. He turned, presenting his back.

"There must be tusks on your family crest, for you are a pig!" she snapped.

"And you," he said, "were more appealing as a mute swan." He punched his pillow.

He heard a husky snarl and felt a halfhearted shove, softened by the bedclothes between them. But she said no more, and he felt himself sliding once again toward sleep.

Chapter 9

Dawn brought a thin, clear light and a return to silence. Juliana awoke alone, and found the white gown, feathered cap, and shoes laid out on the bed. The chains, she discovered immediately, were gone. Within moments, Dame Bette knocked on the door and entered carrying a cup of ale and a slab of hot bread with cheese melted on it.

"Yer husband said ye would be hungry this morning," Bette said, grinning with delight. "It stirs the appetite sometimes, when ye've wed one what makes yer heart quicken."

Juliana blushed at Bette's obvious assumption. Just the opposite was true. She and Gawain quickened each other's hearts, but not with loving. She ate quickly, for she was hungry.

"I will lend a hand with yer finery," Bette said. She helped Juliana slip into the gown. "Yer bridegroom and his kinsmen are waiting downstairs. There is a pack of soldiers in the lane, too. Whatever ye did, my lady, they mean to keep close watch over ye. They've brought writs from the king, which yer husband has been reading this morn. He seems none too pleased."

She stood, mute and still, while Bette plaited a single braid down her back and tied it with a bit of string.

"I gather yer husband thinks ye innocent of any wrong, and so do I," Bette continued. "He has been sitting in a dark mood, shifting those chains in his hands until the clinking sound was like to drive me mad."

Sighing, Juliana thought it more likely that her husband was fuming silently over their unwanted marriage, her attempted escape, and their arguments last night. She should never have been so foolish as to break her silence with him.

She sat on the bed and slipped her feet into her flat shoes, leather painted white to go with her gown. She looked up as Bette approached with the feather cap and settled it on her head.

"There is a king's man, too, wearing the blackest armor I have ever seen," Bette said. "He is the leader of yer escort."

Juliana frowned to herself while Bette adjusted the cap; she remembered the journey south too well. De Soulis had shown no consideration for her, ordering a fast pace, tight ropes, and a regular dosing of bitter herbs in wine to keep her senses dulled. Despite Gawain's presence, she dreaded the return now.

"Sir Walter says ye must wear the feathery hat," Bette said. "He says he is the Master of Swans, and ye're the Swan Maiden, and ye're to be dressed as a swan for show, like. Oh my, and I thought ye were a mummer guised as a duck!"

Juliana smiled despite her somber mood.

"And yer husband," Bette added, "looks like he would like to strangle the Master of Swans. Hurry, now, ye've a long journey."

The cart rumbled over the old Roman road, lurching over pits and stones in the roadbed. Juliana grabbed the edge of the cart to steady herself, chains jangling. She looked out at low, rolling hills and patches of moorland. The driver, a gruff old man called John, said nothing as he guided the two sturdy horses that drew the cart, which was packed with goods and weapons.

A mounted escort of thirty men, with several squires, two servants, and the riderless palfrey she had ridden the night before, surrounded her. Gawain Avenel rode his dark bay horse just ahead of the cart, talking with a knight mounted on a brown horse even larger than the bay. Walter de Soulis, black armor gleaming beneath a wine-red surcoat, rode beside the cart.

Juliana studied her husband's head and broad-shouldered back. He wore a dark brown serge tunic over chain mail, with the heavy hood slid down over his shoulders. His hair was thick, wavy, and glossy as ink in the morning light, and his smile flashed handsomely and often as he listened to the other knight.

The two men seemed to be established friends, she noticed,

though appearing to be opposites in many ways. Gawain sat his horse with taut grace and control, while the other had a carefree lack of rhythm. Where Gawain was lean, dark, and restrained, his friend was large, sandy-haired, soft around the middle, and gestured freely with big hands.

In further contrast to her husband's sober nature, his friend laughed quickly, booming out. He even glanced back at Juliana and smiled at her, his face as pleasant as his demeanor.

Though she did not smile back, she found the big sandy-haired knight's confidence and humor appealing. But she was not ready to trust him any more than Gawain Avenel.

Riding near the cart, Sir Walter de Soulis seemed even more severe and humorless by contrast. He said little to anyone, speaking sharply when he did. And he had already forced her to drink from the wine bladder that he kept strapped to his saddle.

Though she had refused at first, he had put it to her lips and poured wine between them, so that liquid dripped over her chin. The bitter aftertaste left a grainy texture on her tongue that she wiped away on the back of her chained hands.

At the time, Gawain had been riding at the head of the escort. He turned to ride back. "Sir Sheriff," he said, "what are you doing?"

"The girl looks pale and nervous. The wine will strengthen and calm her," De Soulis answered. Gawain nodded, glancing at her with a frown before riding away.

That had been over an hour ago, and now she felt woozy from the herbs in the wine. She had swallowed only a bit, but its effect was enough to dull her thoughts and make her feel weary.

She was exhausted already from little rest the night before, and for the past several days and nights. As the cart rolled along the road, she leaned her head against a bale of hay and slid into a bleary doze that deepened into sleep.

"Laurie, I swear I am glad to see you," Gawain said with quiet relief to the man who rode beside him. " 'Tis sheer luck you were sent from York with the king's men to ride with this party into Scotland. I had not seen or heard from you for near a year, I think."

"Ha, luck," Laurence Kirkpatrick said. " 'Twould have been luckier had I been at Newcastle yesterday. I would have talked you out of staying for the king's feast. Married!" He shook his head. "How could you go to a supper and come out with a wife!"

"I only thought to help the girl. She needed a champion."

"Och, aye," Laurie answered with exaggerated wisdom. "And no one could protect the lass but you, I suppose. I heard the story from your stepbrothers this morn. Surely someone else could have stepped in."

"Robin attempted to help, but her swan bit him. I was the only one who thought to bring bread for the poor creature."

Laurence shook his head disparagingly. "Do what I do, man. Watch after yourself first. Life is more pleasant that way. I am a Scotsman born and bred, but I fight for the English king. The pay is better, and the chances of gaining land and a good life are far better."

"And the ale is good," Gawain said dryly.

"Och, well, the ale is better in Scotland, actually," Laurie answered. "But I prefer to offer sword arm and services where my skills will be appreciated and rewarded."

Gawain slid his friend a quick look. "I wonder if a certain English girl influenced your decision . . . Maude, was it?"

Laurie's cheeks burned bright. "Maude of Rosemoor. Sir Harry Gray's youngest daughter."

"Ah, Lady Maude," Gawain drawled. "Here you chide me for being a married man, yet I was sure you would be the one to wed first. Last we met, you were well smitten by that fair damsel."

"Er, uh," Laurie said. "We are wed."

Gawain laughed with delight. "When?"

"Last winter."

"So the fair Lady Maude is the reason a braw Border Scot rides for the English king," Gawain said, grinning.

"Pay and rewards were greatly on my mind." Laurie scowled.

"Oh, I am certain of it," Gawain said. "The lady is accustomed to finery, being Sir Harry's daughter."

"Ho, just wait, now that you are wed!"

"But my lady wife does not seem to care for finery and property. She cares only for freedom—and wants only to get as far away from me as she can." He frowned, thinking of the unsavory task of restraining her the night before. There was something fresh and wild about her that deserved freedom, he thought, glancing back involuntarily. She slept in the cart.

Laurie, too, looked back. "I canna blame the lass. Her English bridegroom is a somber sort."

"Aye, and sworn afresh to the king, too."

"Nae still torn between Scottish and English?" Laurie whispered loudly. "When we were lads and squires together, you used to say—"

"I said naught," Gawain hissed. "And keep quiet about it."

"Well, many are pulled between two loyalties. Change like the wind, they say of us Scots."

"I am not a Scotsman," Gawain insisted.

"Ah." Laurie nodded as if he knew better. "Then listen to one who admits that he is. This matter is much on my mind of late. Many Scotsmen have lands to protect in England—as I do, as you do. And many think Scotland is better off under English rule. The English have wealth and military might. Scotland is poor and leaderless, needing wealth and might on her side."

"Scotland has a bold leader now in Robert Bruce, it seems."

Laurie shrugged. "I will wait and watch before I decide what I think of that. Bruce was one of the finest knights in King Edward's court, and he has English lands and interests, far more than I do. Now he's gone over to the Scottish side, but following him doesna seem safe nor wise."

"Many Scotsmen care more for freedom than safety."

"I can understand it. But my wife and children, and my gear and my table, are safest kept in England."

"Children?" Gawain glanced at him.

"We'll have one by the end o' the year, Maude says." Laurie grinned, quick and fresh, his cheeks pinkening.

Gawain smiled and clapped his friend on the shoulder. "Good news! No wonder you like to keep on the safe side."

"Aye so. What of yourself? I heard you took to the hills with renegades. I thought you had joined your own at last. Yet now you have declared anew to Edward again."

"Laurie, no one knows of my birth here but you. 'Tis best you forget it if you feel inclined to speak of it aloud."

"Pray pardon, Gawain," Laurie murmured soberly. "I know you have English property to protect, though I didna think 'twas a large holding. Did Henry decide to grant you something more, though you are not his true eldest son?"

"'Tis not the land that I think to protect, but the family."

"Ah," Laurie said, nodding his understanding. "Ah."

Gawain rode in silence beside his friend. He had known Laurence Kirkpatrick since they had attended lessons together at a school taught by monks in Northumberland. They had squired together, and had been knighted in London under Edward Plantagenet's sword in the same ceremony.

Long ago, when they had been young boys, Gawain had confided the secret of his Scottish birth to Laurie, his close friend. At times, Laurie seemed full of bluster and reckless humor. Yet Gawain knew him for an honorable man, and trusted him implicitly.

"What of your new assignment in the north?" Laurie asked. "I hear you have been given command of a garrison."

"'Tis temporary only, while the current commander is out chasing Bruce in the hills," Gawain said. The writ for his assignment had been handed to him by De Soulis that morning. So far he had scanned it only briefly, but he was stunned by the conditions and restrictions placed upon him.

"Do you know the details of it yet?"

"Not all of them. King Edward wants a written report of the lay of the land. I am to ride about, scribble notes, collect them together, and deliver them to the king's army commander. As for the rest—well, this will not be an easy post, or easy tasks."

Laurie laughed skeptically. "I hear one of the tasks given to you is impossible!"

"Ah, the one where I am to tame a girl according to my whim, eke an oath of loyalty out of her, and display her as the captive Swan Maiden of Scotland?" He pinched his lips together sourly.

"Och, aye, 'twill win a lady's affection," Laurie drawled.

"And then I must bring her to court as an example of Scottish obedience, making sure she spits out that oath of fealty for the king. Just as I had to do," he added darkly.

"You didna gain the king's forgiveness this last time, my friend. He means to make an example of you."

"It seems so."

"And all this is to be done while you garrison the girl's own castle and take the lay of her lands?" Laurie shook his head. "Under the eye of that black dog, the sheriff?"

"I hope not, for I have old arguments with him."

"Easy to do," Laurie said. "You know what they say of him."

"Only that he is the king's Master of Swans in the north, and sheriff of some small Scottish shire."

"They say," Laurie began, leaning sideways and lowering his voice, "that his black armor has some spell of invincibility over it. That he practices dark arts to keep it so."

Gawain wrinkled his brow skeptically. "I have heard no such rumor, and I rode with him years ago, when he wore black armor—this suit, or some other, I do not know. But 'tis absurd."

"Look at that mail—have you ever seen the like?"

Narrowing his eyes as he turned to look at the sheriff, Gawain studied what he could of the chain mail beneath the man's surcoat—the sleeves, hood, lower hem, and leggings. The links shone like polished jet. "It looks blackened with grease and lampblack to me," he said.

"I have heard," Laurie added, "that he traded his soul for that suit, made in some foreign place."

"'Tis well made, and no doubt expensive. But not worth a man's soul. 'Tis a foolish rumor you would do well to ignore."

"They say," Laurie went on quietly, "that never a point can pierce it, or ever has. The man canna be wounded."

Gawain shook his head. "If such armor were to be had for a decent price, we would all be wearing it."

"Well," Laurie said, "he looks of a size with you. Since he has already paid for it, you should borrow it from him if you ever go into battle. I couldna get my arms into it, myself. Pity." He sighed.

Gawain grinned. "Sir Laurie, I have missed you."

"Aye, and now tell me this—is the girl's property worth all this annoyance?"

"Hardly. Elladoune once belonged to her father, but 'twas forfeited years ago. She has no hereditary claim to it, since she has older brothers in Robert Bruce's army. 'Twill never be mine, if that is what you are wondering."

"I see." Laurie glanced at him. "So you must train her to speak before the king, or lose your head? Unpleasant."

"Risky, more than unpleasant. She is a bit wild, and comes from true rebel stock. The task is unsavory . . . and the castle is too damned close to Glenshie," Gawain added in a low voice.

Laurie glanced over his shoulder at the sound of hoofbeats. "Ah, look. Here comes Sir Soul-less," he drawled.

Gawain turned to see Walter de Soulis riding toward them. He noticed, also, that Juliana slept in the jostling cart, her collar and chains glinting in the light. She leaned against one of the hay bales carried for extra fodder. All around her were piled sacks of provisions, weapons, and armor. She looked lost and vulnerable amid the trappings of war.

"Avenel," De Soulis said, guiding his horse to ride beside Gawain. "I trust you have read over the king's writ."

"Close enough to wonder why I have been given this assignment," Gawain said.

"Were I you, I would not wonder about that. I would be grateful that my head is still on my shoulders."

"There is that," Laurie commented. De Soulis glared at him.

"The king's writ does not state how long I am to be posted at Elladoune," Gawain said. "What do you know of that garrison?"

"A hundred and fifty to two hundred men have been housed there for several years," De Soulis answered. "Just now, the castle is all but deserted. The garrison commander has taken his force into the hills. The king ordered a thousand men to hunt Bruce."

"More than a thousand will be needed," Laurie said pleasantly. "Two thousand, even three. Even then Robert Bruce will not be easy to track—vanished into the mists, he will be."

"You must have some duties elsewhere, sir," De Soulis said. "Kirkpatrick, is it? Sent to us from Sir Aymer de Valence?"

"Aye. For now, according to your own orders, I am to guard the lady. As you can see, I am doing so. I will let you two near her, but no one else can come so close." He smiled.

De Soulis slitted his eyes and turned to Gawain. "No doubt you heard of the defeat of Bruce's troops at Methven a few weeks ago," he said. "Bruce fled with a handful of men."

"I heard so." Gawain had also heard that the battle had been an easy victory for the English and a devastation for the small Scottish army. "Then I am to take over Elladoune until the commander returns from his foray."

"Watch over it, aye. The commander of the king's armies, Aymer de Valence, is heading for Perth with near three thousand men. He is at Roxburgh now. We will be there by late today."

"I thought we were going higher into Scotland than that."

"First we must confer with the king's military advisors for a few days. De Valence will decide who will hold Elladoune permanently. Until it is settled, you will have to do."

Gawain flared his nostrils. He suddenly understood the value of silence as a weapon, which Juliana wielded daily. He stared at De Soulis until the other looked away.

"I am living at Dalbrae Castle in Glen Fillan," De Soulis went on. " 'Tis near enough to Elladoune to keep an eye on it."

"Sir Gawain can manage, I am sure," Laurie said. "After all, he has me for his next in command."

"You?" Gawain asked. De Soulis looked equally surprised.

"According to my renewed writ of knight service, I am to be second in command there," Laurie answered. "Aymer de Valence himself gave me the post. I have a copy of the writ with me if you wish to see it." He fumbled at his belt pouch and produced the parchment, waving it briefly at De Soulis.

"Good," Gawain said. "We need someone stalwart and loyal at Elladoune." De Soulis scowled, but nodded.

" 'Tis an honor to serve under Sir Gawain Avenel," Laurie said sternly. "Indeed, all the Avenels are known for fealty."

"So they say, but I hear there is one bad apple." De Soulis

spurred his horse to ride ahead, where he fell into pace with the knights in the lead.

"Coward," Laurie growled, glaring after him. "Stay around after you deliver an insult, and sip the brew you stirred."

Gawain looked at Laurie. "You did not say you were sent to Elladoune."

"Had nae chance yet, with that black crow around. My wife is a cousin of De Valence," Laurie answered. "When I heard yesterday that you were to take over a garrison in Scotland, I went to him and requested the post, and got my gear together quick as I could. Barely had time to write Maude a note and find a messenger."

Gawain nodded. "I am in your debt, Laurie."

"You owe me, and I am nae shy about asking for favors."

"Whatever you want, ask it." Gawain glanced behind them at Juliana. She sat slumped and asleep in the cart, the chains swaying at her throat, her feathered hat askew. Her fragility was so evident that he felt a fierce urge to protect her, and get her away from the escort if possible.

His hand drifted to rest upon his belt pouch, where the key was tucked. "I will ask a favor of you myself."

"Certes. Shall I harry a black crow for you?"

Gawain shook his head. "Just help me protect a wild swan."

"Done," Laurie answered.

Chapter 10

"Still quiet, my lady?" De Soulis murmured as he maneuvered his horse beside her cart. He spoke low so that only Juliana could hear him. Even Gawain, who usually stayed close, was out of hearing range.

She sent him a little glare. Her head felt woolly from the wine. Tempted to point that out to him, she said nothing.

"I wonder about this silence of yours," the sheriff went on. "They say that the Swan Maiden of Elladoune does not talk because of a magic spell over her. But I suspect 'tis a spoiled temperament—or a need to keep secrets. Rebellious secrets."

She turned her head away and fisted her hands in her lap. Silence was the only protection she could provide for herself. No matter what the English did to her, they could not touch her innermost self—nor could they learn what she knew about the rebels.

De Soulis leaned toward her. "Some speak of witchcraft," he said. "Such accusations are best avoided, so I urge you to speak up in your own defense."

She bowed her head and fingered the golden chain. If only she were back in Scotland, she thought. At home in the Highlands, witchcraft was a rare accusation, unlike in England.

"Very well," he murmured. "Keep your secrets for now. Someday we will talk, you and I." His tone was hard-edged. He urged his horse forward to join the knights riding in the lead.

She glanced at Gawain, who seemed deep in conversation with Sir Laurence, the knight who usually rode beside him. Her husband seemed unaware of De Soulis's threats to her—or did he know, indeed, and do nothing?

She sighed. Gawain Avenel was the stuff of dreams for

some, she thought—a perfect, courteous knight, handsome and strong, noble and skilled. He had taken risks to help her twice now, and she owed him much for that. But she could not trust him, no matter his courtesy. Their marriage was no more than a mockery.

She looked out over the low green hills of the English countryside. Her natural physical energies had flagged because of the herbed wine and the stress of these last few weeks, and her spirit had weakened too. She felt desperate to go home; only that would fully restore her.

But she wondered if she would be safe at home. Her Swan Knight had appeared twice now—years ago, and last night—to save her when she faced danger. Yet he had chained her last night again, and he had not prevented this humiliation. Somehow it suited his purpose, whatever it was, to keep her a captive.

Perhaps, like De Soulis, he too wanted to know her secrets.

One secret she kept secure with the rest: she had loved the Swan Knight for years. Formed of dreams and long in the weaving, that love would not save her now, nor could she reveal it.

Tears gathered in her eyes, and she bowed her head. Soon the soporific effect of the wine, still powerful in her body, took her into heavy sleep again.

The escort traveled along the Roman road leading north from Newcastle. As they drew near a town, farmers and harvesters stopped in the fields to stare at the king's knights. Some clustered along the roadside with infants in their arms, and older children ran beside the procession.

Gawain noticed that more people had crossed the fields to watch the military escort pass. They pointed at the strange sight of a lady chained in gold and dressed like a swan.

De Soulis cantered to the head of the train and raised his arm. "Behold the Swan Maiden of Elladoune!" he shouted. "See what befalls the Scots when they rebel against King Edward! The English can subdue even one who is said to have magic about her. Even she has submitted to English justice!"

Gawain swore, low and fierce. "What the devil—"

"Witch!" someone called, and a clod of earth struck Juliana in the back. She looked stunned and confused. Then another bit of mud caught her in the cheek, and she wiped it away with the back of her manacled hand. She lifted her head high.

"The Swan Maiden of Elladoune!" De Soulis called again. "Hooked and netted in Scotland, and taken to King Edward! We have clipped her wings, as you see! Is she magic, as the Scots say? Or is she a rebel deserving of punishment?"

"Damn him," Laurie growled. Gawain turned to see another clump of earth hit Juliana square in the chest. She gasped softly with the blow. He swore and rounded his horse to face the crowd, placing his hand on the hilt of his sword.

"Do not dare disturb the king's peace!" Gawain shouted. A few people stepped back. Two boys stopped, hiding their hands behind their backs. He glared at them and turned Gringolet.

On the other side of the road, Laurie cantered up and down as Gawain did, and other knights soon followed suit. Riding at the head of the escort, De Soulis continued to call attention to the Swan Maiden of Elladoune.

Another clod of mud sailed toward the cart. Laurie swung his horse around and rode back toward some boys who held mud balls in their hands. They scattered, shrieking, as he bore down on them.

"Enough," Gawain growled. He rode hard to the head of the escort. "What the devil is this about?" he snapped as he drew close.

"King's orders," De Soulis answered.

"You are a sheriff, sir, not a mummer with a wandering show. You shame this lady. 'Tis unbefitting to a knight."

"We are not all such exemplary knights as the Avenels," De Soulis sneered.

"That has naught to do with it. The lady is my wife."

"Then you make the announcements. My throat is parched."

Gawain sucked in a breath. "No more of it," he said.

"I am in charge of this escort so long as we are in England. If the king wants her displayed, so be it. According to this writ, you do not have charge of her until we reach Scotland."

"You do not seem to take my meaning," Gawain growled. "There will be no more announcements about her."

De Soulis glanced at him. "A threat? Are you loyal to the girl already? She must have proved a fine morsel last night."

"Have a care," Gawain warned. "You speak of my wife."

"Hot to defend her, are you?" De Soulis slid him a sidelong glance. "I remember you, Avenel. You were at Elladoune when her father's castle was taken. You helped some rebels escape. Did you help her that night too?"

"I do not recall. 'Twas long ago."

"Tell me—has she spoken to you?"

"Nay," Gawain lied.

"They say of her in Scotland that she is a creature of enchantment, and can change into a swan when she chooses."

"And they say," Gawain countered, "that you wear bewitched armor."

"Idiots. That rumor was begun long ago by some lackbrain, and haunts me to this day."

"And so for the lady," Gawain said. "She has been raised in an abbot's household. She leads a pious life, I understand."

"I know Abbot Malcolm, and you will come to know him too. He seems a mild and reverent man. I wonder sometimes if he is a fool—or a clever rebel. Either way he bears watching. You may as well be made aware of this, since you are going to Elladoune."

"An abbot acting as a rebel? Interesting," Gawain drawled.

"Some Scots clergy are more fierce than Scots warriors. The brethren at Inchfillan seem biddable enough, though. I asked the abbot and his monks to tend Elladoune in the garrison's absence, but I told my own men to watch them. If there is any suspicious activity, the trap will close on them all." He smiled. "The girl bears watching too."

"I doubt she is capable of mischief."

"Besotted already. Beware," De Soulis said. "I pity you, Avenel. Rebel or witch, you will have the full responsibility of her once we reach Scotland."

Thank God, Gawain thought.

He rounded his horse and rode back, and De Soulis followed. When Gawain positioned the bay to ride parallel with the cart once again, De Soulis rode nearby. Gawain felt as if he had picked up a pesky, biting blackfly that he could not shake. He stared ahead without speaking.

"When you reach Elladoune," De Soulis said, "and once you have a garrison there, you may be ordered to pursue rebels in that area."

"That will depend on how many men will be garrisoned there."

"Soon we will cross the Scottish border, and turn east for Roxburgh Castle. Aymer de Valence will have some word about the garrison for Elladoune."

An idea had occurred to Gawain a while back, and he acted on it quickly. "Tell me what you learn, then. I will part from your escort at the end of this road to take the east fork into Northumberland."

De Soulis stared at him. "I have seen no orders on that."

Gawain patted his tunic. "I have a safe conduct to visit my family's home at Avenel Castle." He had obtained it before the feast, the wedding, and the king's new orders. "I plan to stay at Avenel for a few days. I will cross into Scotland to meet you and the others. The lady goes with me," he added firmly.

"But she is in the care of my escort!"

"I will not leave my bride in the company of men without even a woman to care for her. Surely you realize the problems in bringing a female prisoner into a large military castle like Roxburgh."

"My orders state that the Swan Maiden is to be chained and guarded at all times. She will be put in the dungeon at Roxburgh until we finish our meetings."

"She will be well guarded at Henry Avenel's castle. King Edward himself visits there often enough, and would surely approve his friend's authority—where you seem to question it."

De Soulis groused, then relented. "One day, and no more."

"Four," Gawain replied.

"Impossible. Two days."

"Very well. On the second day hence, at midday, I will meet you at an inn on the Scottish side of the border near Kelso."

"I know the place." De Soulis nodded. "Take part of the guard with you when you depart."

"My mother will not appreciate a military guard at her home," Gawain answered. "Nor would Sir Henry Avenel."

"I do not like this. But your father, at least, can be trusted. 'Tis best not to take a female prisoner into Roxburgh, as you say. Very well. Midday on Saturday, at the inn outside of Kelso."

Gawain nodded, then urged his horse ahead to join Laurie. He looked back at Juliana. She rested again, head leaned against the hay bale, eyes closed. She drooped like a bedraggled white flower, her gown and feathered cap rumpled and soiled.

He watched the wife he scarcely knew, and wondered about the curious mix of fragility and fire in her. Last night the spark and will in her had intrigued him, and her presence in his bed had heated a passionate urge that he could barely ignore.

He wondered about her chosen silence, and the whisperings of enchantment. Had that come from the rumor he himself had started, years ago, as Elladoune burned? The legend had grown around her, and he very much wanted to know why.

"Juliana."

She awoke when a hand touched her shoulder, and opened her eyes. Gawain stood beside the cart. His face showed concern, his black brows drawn over thick-lashed brown eyes. His hand and voice were gentle.

"My lady. Wake up, now. We have reached the split in the road. Come with me." He reached into the cart, taking her arm, urging her to sit up.

She did so, head spinning. Leaving, she told herself; she was leaving the escort. That gave her strength to move, no matter how groggy she felt.

She wanted to ask him where they were going, but could not, with so many men watching them.

Gawain scooped his arms under her and lifted her out of the cart, setting her on her feet, chains chinking. The earth felt solid and good beneath her feet after so long in the cart. And his arms felt good around her.

De Soulis watched with the others, his face a harsh mask. Gawain led her toward Galienne, the gray palfrey. Then he took a small iron key from his belt pouch and inserted it first into the golden collar and then in the wrist manacles. Within moments, she was free of the burden of golden links.

She smiled up at him, but he did not look at her. Boosting her into the saddle, he turned away, golden chains glinting in his hand.

She sighed with relief, looking around, wondering if they had reached Scotland, though the landscape still looked flat and green and English to her. Something had happened while she slept. She felt mildly confused, but at least the effects of the wine had lessened.

"What are you doing?" De Soulis cantered toward them. "The king ordered her chained at all times! I agreed for you to take her, but you have no authority to free her of her bonds."

"I will not present my bride to my mother in chains." He stuffed the links into the pack behind the cantle and swung up into the bay's saddle.

She stared at him. Mother? She wished she could ask where he was taking her. She did not want to go to his English castle. How would she ever get back to Scotland?

"Take a guard with you," De Soulis snapped. "She is a valuable prisoner and cannot be let loose."

"She will go nowhere, I assure you. Look at her, man. She is so weak she can barely sit her horse. A few days of rest will not change her captivity, but might save her health."

"You should not have custody of that key! I will report this to the king and his advisors."

"Report it to whom you like," Gawain said. "Tell them I treat the woman with courtesy."

"You cannot be trusted," De Soulis sputtered.

"The dungeon cells at Avenel Castle," Gawain said, "are in good repair."

Juliana, listening avidly, gaped at him. She was to be transferred to another English dungeon—with the knowledge and consent of Gawain's own mother, apparently.

Gawain ignored her look of alarm. He took hold of her palfrey's rein and pulled as he rode ahead. Juliana swayed in the saddle, knees gripping tight. The summer air was sweet on her bare wrists and throat, but her heart beat heavily.

After a few moments Juliana heard the escort canter away in the opposite direction. Relieved to be free of the humilation of riding in the cart, she felt wary. Her Swan Knight had rescued her once again—only to draw her deeper into uncertainty.

If she could have escaped then and there, she would have done so.

Chapter 11

They left the stone road and traveled steadily over grassy hills until they followed the path of a narrow river. At last, in the distance, Juliana saw a castle on a green hillock. Gawain slowed to look at it, then started forward, leading her horse at a fast pace as if eager to get there.

The square walls and central keep shone creamy against the backdrop of a dense greenwood, and the calm river flowed past the side of the mound. Juliana gasped at the lovely picture, feeling a sense of surprise. She had always imagined English castles to be brute fortifications teeming with enemy soldiers. Avenel Castle looked like a haven out of a legend, beautiful enough to house faery royalty.

Following Gawain, she rode across the drawbridge, the horses' hooves pounding over the wooden slats, and passed beneath a raised portcullis into the cool shadow of a stone arch. Inside the enclosed courtyard, instead of armed knights, she saw two young pages run forward and wait for them to dismount.

"Gawain!" Hearing a light female voice, Juliana turned, still in the saddle. The square keep, massive and high, dominated the courtyard, and an open flight of stone steps led from its upper doorway. A young girl descended the stairs, calling out excitedly, dark braids flying out behind her.

"Eleanor!" Gawain answered. He dismounted and swept her up into his arms, spinning her around. She was slight, though tall, and giggled as she threw her arms around him. Juliana judged her to be about thirteen, and assumed she must be a sister to her husband; their dark hair and handsome features were similar.

Gawain laughed and set her down, and she beamed up at him. "Ah," he said, "'tis not Eleanor, but Catherine!"

"Aye, Catherine," she confirmed, smiling.

"Gawain! Gawain!" A second girl ran down the steps. She was a mirror of the first, from the long dark braids plaited with red ribbons to the bright blue gown banded in embroidery. Juliana blinked in amazement, and glanced from one to the other.

"Here is Eleanor!" Gawain caught the second girl as she hurtled toward him, and hugged her.

"Robin arrived yesterday!" Eleanor said.

"He said he was not certain when you would come, but that you would bring a bride when you did," Catherine said.

Both girls looked toward Juliana. "Greetings," they said together in eerie echo. "You must be Juliana," one went on. "Welcome to Avenel."

Juliana stared from one girl to the other, unsmiling despite their beaming smiles. Overwhelmed and uncertain, she felt outside the joy of the moment. She wondered if he would introduce her as his bride or his captive. She was so weary she wanted to fall from the horse, but was not sure if she would awaken in a featherbed or a dungeon cell.

"What did Robin tell you?" Gawain asked.

"That you had wed a lovely Scottish woman on the king's wishes, and that she would be exhausted when you arrived—if you arrived at all. He was not certain you would stop here."

"We hoped you would not be so cruel as that!"

He glanced at Juliana. "Lovely and tired, indeed, and very much a surprise from the king. Lady Juliana, these are my half sisters, Eleanor"—he nodded toward the one standing to his right—"and Catherine."

Juliana nodded and said nothing. The girls bowed and smiled prettily. They were dark, slender creatures with eyes of a startling gray-green. While they were old enough to display the courtesy and decorum of ladies, they seemed young enough to lapse into bubbly giggles and expressive looks and grimaces.

"Come inside and meet our mother," one of the twins said, and gave Juliana a dazzling smile.

Gawain walked toward Juliana and put his hands around her waist. "I beg you to show only sweetness at Avenel Castle, if you will," he murmured as he slid her down from the horse.

He brushed her hair from her brow in a gentle gesture that made her blink and blush. "Silence," he whispered, "might keep the soldiers away, but will only make my little sisters more curious. You may speak to anyone at Avenel without fear." He circled an arm around her shoulders and turned with her.

Both girls came forward to hug her. Juliana returned their embraces tentatively and said nothing, wholly uncertain if she should speak, or what to say.

The twins fell upon Gawain, who laughingly fended them off. "You did not send word of your marriage, you great oaf!" one chattered. "When did you wed?"

"Two days ago. The ceremony happened rather suddenly."

"We thought you would never marry," one girl said. "Mother thought 'twas hopeless. You know she has longed for this day!"

"I know," he said quietly, glancing at Juliana.

"We have, too," her sister added. "But we gave up on you—"

"After all that wooing, and all those rejections—"

"Hush, Cat, you will frighten my bride with such stories," Gawain said hastily. "How is our lady mother? Well enough to bear this surprise?"

"She already knows," Eleanor said. At least, Juliana thought it might be Eleanor, for she had noticed that her face seemed a bit rounder than her sister's, her laugh lower. "Robin told her."

"'Twas a shock, but she took it well," Catherine said.

"'A Scot,' she kept saying," Eleanor added. "'A Scot,' as if she could not quite believe you would wed a Scotswoman now, with the war on. A Scottish bride for an Avenel is not so favorable, but I think 'tis wonderful because you—"

"'Tis fine," Gawain said brusquely. "Do not fret. Come, Lady Juliana," he said, tugging on her arm, for she had stepped back at the implication that a Scottish woman might not be welcome here after all. "Come. I want you to meet my mother. Is she in her chamber, Nell?"

"Where else, these days? Robin was sitting with her earlier, but he left, and she napped for a bit," Eleanor said.

"She is awake now. I just came from there," Catherine added. "She will want to see your bride right away, of course!"

Gawain nodded and walked toward the keep, his hand firm around Juliana's elbow. She went silently, slowly, feeling as if her legs had turned to pudding from apprehension and weariness.

"What did you bring us? A book?" one of the girls asked.

"If I give you any more books, your shelf will fall from the wall," Gawain said.

"You always bring us a new book each time you come home!" the other twin said.

"Oh, aye," he said, as if he just remembered, though Juliana could tell he teased them, "there is a book in my pack. 'Tis the tale of Sir Bevis of Hampton."

"Mama told us that story. He fought a dragon and saved England, and crossed a desert to find his love." One spoke, and both sighed.

"Now you can read it to your heart's content," Gawain said.

"What did you see in Newcastle? Did you speak with the king? Did you attend a jousting tournament?" The questions came so fast, in such similar voices, that Juliana could hardly follow who said what. "Robin said you went to a great feast!"

"Aye, we did that," Gawain said, glancing at Juliana.

"Did you bring something for Mama? Or anything else for us?" One twin—possibly Catherine—smiled with such charm and candor that Gawain chuckled and Juliana smiled to herself.

"Have you been sweet and kind girls, as Mama asks of you?"

"Always." One batted her eyes, while the other giggled.

"Robin said all of you attended the king's feast, with subtleties and cakes and swans and acrobats, and met your bride there. Tell us about it!"

Gawain's fingers flexed on Juliana's arm; his touch was

oddly comforting. "There were cakes and sugar castles, and
swans and peacocks. . . . We saw the king, but not the queen,
for she is still in London. I rode in a joust and won the day,
and ate so much at the feast that night that I feared I would
burst." He grinned. "But I did not eat as much as Edmund and
Robin."

"And you won a bride," Catherine said. The girls had shifted
again fluidly, and now stood shoulder to shoulder. Juliana, despite her fatigue, tried to note who moved where to keep them
identified.

"I did. She was dressed all in white, the loveliest creature I
had ever seen." Juliana blinked at him in surprise, but he did
not look at her. "I have other news. I am being sent back to
Scotland."

"Robin told us. Mother was distraught about it."

"I feared so," Gawain said.

"You can reassure her about it. And be sure to tell her
about your wedding—and us, too," the second twin said. "Do
not spare any detail. That will please Mama. You know how
much she loved the splendid celebrations at the court, when
she and Father went there together." The girl—Eleanor, Juliana thought—pouted. "I wish you had sent word here and
invited us to your wedding. Newcastle is not so far from
Avenel."

"And miss seeing the surprise on your silly faces?" Gawain
answered. " 'Twas a wedding. They are all alike." His teasing
grin made the twins moan as they climbed the stone steps of the
keep together.

Opening the outer door, he ushered Juliana and the girls inside a shadowed foyer with three doorways and another flight
of stairs. "Stay here," Gawain told his sisters. "This must be
private." He turned them gently toward a curtained doorway,
and led Juliana up the steps with him.

She climbed, head held high, though every fiber of her body
seemed to tremble. The sound of their footsteps echoed.

"My sisters like you well," he said, "though I apologize for
their constant chatter." He glanced at her, but she did not answer as she went with him down a corridor that smelled of
stone and, oddly, camphor.

Nearing an arched doorway, Gawain paused. "Now I must ask that my courtesy to you be repaid," he said quietly.

She tilted her head, listening, waiting.

"I want you to act the happy bride when we enter that room."

Drawing her brows together, she folded her arms over her chest and looked away. Surely that was the last thing she could pretend. She could think of no reason to comply with his request.

"You can speak," he said curtly. "Answer me."

She looked at him. "Happy bride? Are you daft?"

"You act the mystery maiden well enough. Now play the loving bride. Coo and smile and cling to my arm—whatever a joyful bride might do." He held out his arm.

She pushed it away. "I am nae some happy new-made wife, loved and content," she said. "I am a prisoner. Until an hour ago, I was chained and humiliated—and will be again, I expect."

"'Twas not my choice to see you so treated."

She lifted her chin. "So in return for giving me a little freedom from my chains, you think you deserve a favor?"

He sighed impatiently. "I have done a bit more for you than that. I ask only this in return."

"I want your promise that there will be nae more chaining."

"'Tis not a bargain I can make."

"Nor can I play the happy bride." She looked away.

"Please," he whispered. That one word, ragged and plaintive, caught her sympathy and her curiosity.

"Why?" she asked softly, intrigued.

"Because I am about to introduce you to my lady mother."

"Are you so terrified of your mother that you must lie to her, and have me lie to her, about our marriage?"

"Not at all," he said, lips tightening.

"She must be a virago! Her oldest son begs favors in corridors to avoid telling her the truth!"

He stepped toward her, and she stepped back, until her heel hit the wall. "I swear," he said, "the mute swan is sweeter to the ear than the honking goose."

She glared up at him. He returned it, full bore, until she shrank back.

"Whatever your opinion," he said, "do this, and I promise courtesy—though I would far rather throttle you just now."

"I willna do it," she said firmly.

"Only pretend this in front of my mother. You can despise me all you like in private."

"Your lady mother should know how her son takes a lass across England in chains," she said. "She should hear how he binds her even as she sleeps, and willna let her go, and keeps her captive so he can gain his king's favor."

"I did what I had to do, and tried to treat you gently."

"Gentle for a guard, but rough for a husband."

"You do not want a husband," he reminded her.

"Nor a guard," she retorted. "Especially one who keeps my key, locks and looses me at his will, and wants me to play sweet bride to his courteous knight so he will look the perfect son."

He took another swift step toward her, his cheeks flushing, eyes blazing dark. Juliana pressed her shoulders against the wall as he leaned over her.

"I should never be alone with you," he said, pressing a hand against the wall. "It loosens your tongue."

"Better my tongue than my chains, some would say," she snapped. "At least you canna control my speech—or my silence."

He cast her a sour look, slanting his weight forward on his hands to trap her where she stood. "Little Swan Maiden, silent and still," he mused, looking at her. "Delicate lady in need of a champion. Wildcat and hellion, needing no help from anyone. Now a bitter-tongued Highland fishwife. Who the devil are you?"

"Just a lass who wants to go home. So much," she added in a whisper, looking away as the need to be home overwhelmed her.

"I will take you there, but first you must act glad to be my wedded wife. If you please," he added between his teeth.

She narrowed her eyes. "'Tis all you ask of me?"

"Aye."

"You dinna expect . . . wifely duties?"

His gaze slowly raked down, then up again. "None," he murmured, his expression so direct that she glanced away again. "Until you want that too, and grant yourself to me— freely."

Silence lingered. She peered at him and was caught in his dark, deep gaze. "Only this, and then you will take me back to Inchfillan Abbey?"

"If 'tis where you live. We can stop there on our way to El- ladoune. That too is home, is it not?"

"Elladoune!" She looked at him in surprise. "Why there?"

"I am to command that garrison."

" 'Twould have been a small courtesy to tell me where you were taking me. I thought I was going to another prison." Her heart beat hard and fast. She had scarcely hoped to set foot in Elladoune ever again, and now suddenly she had the chance. "We are to go there together, as husband and wife? Or as king's man and captive?"

"Husband and wife would be more peaceful, would it not?"

She frowned, thinking. Wondering. "Aye," she admitted. She glanced at him. He leaned closer, until she felt the warmth of his breath upon her lips. Without meaning to, without think- ing, as if she were spellbound, she tilted her head back and closed her eyes.

"I wonder," he whispered, "what a peaceful marriage might be like between us. Do you?"

She parted her lips, began to speak, but could only stare up at him. He closed his eyes, and hers drifted shut too, and a mo- ment later his lips touched hers, pressing gently.

As with the soft, brief kiss at their wedding, unexpected pleasure whirled through her. A flash of desire, hot and bright, followed. She almost moaned with the urge to surrender to him, but she stayed still and passive.

He drew away and gazed down at her. "Is it so much trou- ble," he murmured, "to pretend for a little time that we are con- tent, each with the other?"

She stared at him, her heart racing crazily, her breath deep and fast. She leaned toward him, breathless, then pressed back against the wall.

"Juliana," he said. "I beg you to do this for me."

She sighed. "Will you expect the same at Elladoune?"

He pushed away from the wall. "Please yourself," he growled, and turned away.

"I—I will think on it," she said cautiously.

The door at the end of the corridor opened, and a servant woman looked out at them. Gawain grabbed Juliana's hand.

"Think fast," he said, and pulled her along with him.

Chapter 12

The bedchamber was shadowed, its windows partly shuttered despite the mild weather. The woman seated in a chair beside the crackling hearth fire wore a blanket over her knees. Gawain walked into the room, releasing Juliana's hand. He looked at his mother, and his heart hurt.

She was thinner than he had ever seen her, though he had been here but a month ago. Dark-haired and brown-eyed like her son, Lady Clarice was still a beautiful woman, though she had lost strength. Her slowly progressing disease seemed to clarify her, illuminate her from within. Each time he saw her, she seemed more spirit than flesh, as if she were gradually transforming on the path toward death.

Her hair was leaden in color, her eyes were sunken and shadowed, but a light burned bright and warm in her dark eyes. The elegant shape of her skeleton was evident in her face and in the thin hands draped over the arms of the chair.

She smiled. "Gawain! Oh, Gawain!"

"Mama." He stepped forward and bent to kiss her parchment cheek. "I trust God keeps you safe in His hands."

"Safe enough for now, and better too, now that I have heard your news from Robin. My dear, you are still too thin. We must feed you well while you are here." She peered past him. "So this is your bride!"

"Juliana Lindsay," he said softly. He walked over to take Juliana's hand and lead her forward, silently praying that she would guard her tongue with his mother, if not with him. Like all the members of his family, he feared to stir the shadow of death that hovered so close to his mother.

"Lady Clarice of Avenel," he told Juliana. She nodded, her

dark blue eyes huge in her pale face as she looked from him to
his mother, and back to him again. He sensed her astonishment.
He had not told her that his mother was gravely ill. The words
were far too hard to speak.

"Robin said you had married," Lady Clarice said. " 'Tis joyful news, and such a surprise. King Edward is full of surprises
these days. Henry asked for advice in finding a match for you,
and then the king orders you wed to one of his own guests. The
Swan Knight and his Swan Maiden. How kind of Edward."

"Aye," Gawain said, understanding immediately the story
that Robin had brought his stepmother, no doubt at Henry's
urging.

"Juliana, welcome." Clarice began to stand. "Come here."

Gawain murmured in protest, reaching out. The servant girl
stepped forward to push on Lady Clarice's shoulder until she
subsided in the chair, then plumped a pillow behind her.

"Oh, go away, Philippa," Clarice said irritably. "Stop fuss-
ing. I am not a piece of glass. I want to greet my new daughter,
and you only embarrass me. The poor girl will be frightened if
she sees but an old lady in a sickroom. Help me up, Gawain."
Philippa looked at Gawain in appeal. He sighed and assisted his
mother to her feet.

She was fragile in his hands, but he sensed her stubborn
spirit. He steadied her like a worried parent. "Mama, easy—"

"Oh, hush. Welcome to Avenel, Juliana. Our home is yours."

Juliana stood before her. "Lady Clarice," she replied, and
bowed her head. "I am so honored by your gracious welcome."

Breathing a sigh of relief, Gawain took Juliana's hand and
drew her close to his side. She gave him an adoring smile,
sweet and without guile. He smiled down at her in full gratitude.

He wanted, suddenly, to kiss her again. The honey taste of it
still lingered on his lips, still warmed his blood.

"Come here, sweeting," Clarice said. "Oh, you are lovely,
though grimy from the road. Gawain, did you set a soldier's
pace? The girl looks as if she has not rested for days."

"We could have been more considerate," he admitted.
"Philippa, will you have a bath prepared in my room for my
wife?"

Philippa nodded, and at her mistress's affirmative gesture, left the room quickly. "Did you bring your things with you, Lady Juliana, or will they arrive later?" Clarice asked. "We can find something fresh for you to wear if need be. Your gown is lovely, but looks in need of repair."

Juliana hesitated. "Ah—my things—"

"Will be sent north," Gawain added hastily. "We will stay only a night or two. I have a new assignment."

"In Scotland, I know. Will you go so soon? I hoped you would remain here for a few weeks. You have been away from Avenel for years, but for a few brief visits." She squeezed his hand while he still supported her.

"I know," he said, feeling the loss of those years keenly the more he sensed his mother's waning strength. "But the king is sending three thousand men to Scotland. His commanders have ordered a soldier's pace for every group, as you have noticed. We must depart soon, but I wanted you to meet Juliana first."

"I hoped the king would allow you to stay in England this time or send you to the Welsh border. Not to Scotland again."

"I had no choice," Gawain said softly. "And I do not mind being sent back to Scotland."

Lady Clarice looked at Juliana. "My husband told me you are a Scotswoman. Lindsay . . . I know the name." She frowned as if trying to recall something.

"My father was Alexander Lindsay of Elladoune."

Clarice inhaled sharply. "Elladoune?"

" 'Tis in central Scotland," Juliana answered.

"I have heard of it." Lady Clarice looked at Gawain. "Is she a kinswoman of . . . James Lindsay, the rebel that you—"

"Aye," he said brusquely.

"Do you know my cousin?" Juliana asked Gawain, frowning.

"I have met him," he answered. "I am to be constable of Elladoune and its new garrison, Mama."

"Oh, dear," his mother said faintly. "But why would the king wed you to the cousin of the man who caused you trouble—"

"Do not concern yourself with that. I am sure the king wishes to encourage better loyalty among the Scottish rebels by matching one of their daughters with a loyal Avenel," he said.

"That must be why he recommended the marriage. But surely Juliana and her own kin are loyal."

"Surely so." He sensed Juliana watching him curiously. "Mama, please sit down." She did not protest when he helped her back into her chair. Juliana stepped forward to tuck the pillows behind her. A blanket lay folded on the floor, and she spread that over Lady Clarice's lap.

His mother smiled at Juliana in thanks. "What a lovely pair you two make, the one so pale and delicate, the other so strong and dark. Swan Maiden and Swan Knight." She sighed happily and leaned her head against the high back of the chair. "That reminds me of a legend I heard long ago . . . well, 'tis no matter. Who would want to hear an old woman's rambling thoughts."

"You are not an old woman, nor do you ramble," Gawain said.

She smiled, but her eyes sheened with tears. "I am happy for you, Gawain." She reached out for Juliana's hand and took his as well. "For you both. She is kind and lovely, and I can see that she loves you already," she whispered. "Who would not? The girls who rejected your marriage suits were dimwits."

"Mama." Gawain squeezed his mother's hand. "You must rest now. I will send for Philippa."

As he spoke, a plump ginger cat slipped out from under the bed in the center of the room and crossed toward them, tail high, followed by three kittens, white, ginger, and a mix of both. The mother cat leaped into Lady Clarice's lap, and the kittens scampered under her chair. The smallest ginger kitten reached out a tiny paw to bat at the blanket.

"What's this? They should not be disturbing you." Gawain stooped to lift the large cat from his mother's lap. "Easy," he said. "This is no seat for a great beast like you."

"But I like her company," his mother protested.

He set the mother cat down and stooped again to pick up the little ginger one, boneless and warm and tiny, and gently handed it to his mother.

"This one is less burden for you," he said. "I will send for Philippa. Juliana—" He turned to see that his bride had gone down on her hands and knees to peer at the two kittens still beneath Clarice's chair, cooing with soft delight. She straightened with the tiny white one balled in her hands. Her pale, solemn face had transformed and simply glowed with joy. Gawain blinked.

"Oh, my lady, they are so bonny!" Juliana said.

"Bonny, aye," Lady Clarice said. "I have not heard that word for years. Please, sweeting, take the kitten for your own."

" 'Tis unsuitable for our journey," Gawain said.

"Nonsense. Pippa can ride in a basket."

"Pippa?" Juliana asked.

"The twins named the white one after Philippa, even though she dislikes cats."

Gawain bent to unfasten the ginger kitten, who was scrambling around on the blanket in his mother's lap. The kitten tried to sink its tiny teeth in his finger, and he disengaged it gently, allowing it to knead its way up his arm to his shoulder.

"This one cannot stay still," he said, while Juliana and Clarice laughed. Juliana nestled her cheek against the curve of the white kitten's head. Gawain set down the tiny ginger, who ran away and came back again, nearly underfoot.

"Pippa is yours now, and you may call her what you like," his mother said. "Gawain may keep his little friend, too."

Entranced by the sound of Juliana's laughter, heard for the first time, Gawain barely noticed that the kitten was playing with the thongs on his boots. He looked down. "Ho there, Sir Bevis, do you think me a great dragon?"

Juliana laughed again, brightly, and Gawain grinned at her.

"Bevis is a perfect name for that one!" Lady Clarice said.

"And Pippa is perfect for this wee sweet thing," Juliana said as she rubbed her fingers over the kitten's head and back, her touch gentle and sure. She glanced at Gawain, her smile so dazzling that her eyes sparkled like stars in the night sky.

His heart, in that moment, melted. She had threatened to be defiant with his mother, yet she played the loving bride so well that he almost believed it himself. Each time he was with her, he saw another facet of her, like a jewel turning and changing in the light. Fascinated, thoughtful, he looked only at her.

The ginger mother came toward them again, stepping haughtily, raising a paw as if to declare that she wanted her kittens with her again. Bevis scampered away, and Juliana bent to pet the mother, keeping Pippa curled securely and happily in her hand.

"Do not touch that tabby," Gawain said. "She is a bad-tempered creature. No one but my mother can touch her."

Even as he spoke, Juliana was down on her knees, soothing the mother's long back with her free hand. The cat lifted her head and closed her eyes, purring loudly.

Lady Clarice smiled. "That tabby avoids everyone, and only tolerates me. I have never seen her take to anyone like that."

Juliana scratched the top of the cat's head gently and smiled. The third and smallest of the kittens, the ginger and white mix, with a touch of gray on the ears, crawled out from under the blanket to rub against Lady Clarice's leg. "This wee kitten loves you especially, my lady. May I name her for you?"

Lady Clarice smiled. "What name shall it be?"

"Marguerite," she said. "For she is delicate like the flower and has a soothing temperament." She bent and scooped up the kitten and placed her on Lady Clarice's lap. The kitten curled up and went to sleep immediately, quieter than her more rambunctious brother and sister.

His mother looked up at Gawain and smiled. "My dear, I think the angels have sent you one of their own for a bride."

Gawain helped Juliana to stand. He raised her hand to his lips and kissed it, filled with gratitude to her. She had done far more than he had hoped for. She had brought his mother some joy, and he was in her debt. He cleared his throat and nodded.

"Aye," he said, staring into Juliana's deep blue eyes. "She can be an angel indeed—when she wants."

Sighing loudly, Juliana sank deeper into the high-walled wooden tub, letting the steaming water soothe and envelop her. She hoped Philippa would take her time returning, for she wanted to stay here, undisturbed and peaceful. Deliciously hot and scented with roses, the water coaxed the tension and fatigue from her muscles. Rose petals floated on the surface, easing her spirit further.

She scooped more soap out of a small pot, feeling the flecks of lavender and herbs in the slippery stuff. As she lathered herself and washed and rinsed her hair, she delighted in the fragrance, the texture, the penetrating heat. The abbot's house at Inchfillan had few such luxuries, nor had there been many at Elladoune in her childhood.

The real luxury was that she was utterly alone, thoroughly clean, and beginning to relax at last, after the ordeal of the past weeks. She glanced around Gawain's bedchamber, a pleasant room, though not large, and furnished with a simple elegance. The few wooden pieces were finely carved and polished, the floors were covered with woven rush mats, the lime-washed walls were bordered in a colorful painted diamond pattern, and the window was shuttered below with genuine leaded glass above. A red-curtained bed filled one corner of the room.

That she did not want to think about at all. The sight of the bed, its pillows and thick mattress neatly covered in red brocade, stirred a curious excitement within her. Images of Gawain unclothed, his muscled torso gleaming, went through her mind. Vividly, she recalled the feel of his arms around her, and that simple but astonishing kiss in the corridor.

Groaning softly, she leaned her head back. Whatever the future held, she would face it when it came, rather than fret—or dream—pointlessly now. She closed her eyes and tried to clear her mind of the thoughts that tumbled through it.

She must have dozed, for when she opened her eyes, the water had cooled and the room was darker, but for the low fire in the hearth. Climbing out of the tub, she dried herself with a linen sheet and sat on a hearthside stool. Her fine hair dried in the heat while she combed her fingers through it. When it was damp and golden sleek, she braided it over one shoulder.

Philippa had left a gown and some other things on the bed. Juliana slipped on the garments: linen hose, tied at the knees with ribbons; a chemise of pale silk; and a mulberry gown of serge that buttoned at the neck, fit her torso and arms closely, and swelled full over her hips.

The hem, like the white satin gown, was too long—that must be fashionable in England, she thought. Her own gowns at Inchfillan were practical, leaving feet and ankles unencumbered.

She thought of home and the hills and lochside where she loved to walk. Soon she would see Scotland, but she might never have that freedom again. Her life was utterly changed now.

Picking up a white veil of sheer silk and a circlet of braided silks, she set it down again, not eager to wear a married woman's headgear just yet. Instead, she shoved her feet into a pair of leather shoes, tied with thongs, and then walked around the room, touching the dark polished wood of the furniture.

Avenel was a beautiful home, she thought. Every room was well kept, and the family seemed warm and charming. She could see how much Gawain loved them, and they him. She envied that.

Her own family had been scattered far and wide. Her father was dead now, her elder brothers were with the Scottish king's troops, and her mother had willingly consigned herself years ago to a religious life, leaving her children in the care of her cousin, Abbot Malcolm. For years, Juliana felt as if her family were Malcolm and the monks, Deirdre—the abbot's sister and housekeeper—and Iain and Alec.

At the thought of her little brothers, worry and fear rushed back. She felt anxious again, as if the restorative bath had never been. She had to return to her brothers, and to the rest of her friends and kin. The need was painful and insistent.

Every moment that she stayed in England, she felt as if another strand of her heart pulled, tore, came loose. Scotland was in her blood, was part of her soul, and she had to go back.

She fought sudden tears as a yearning ache assailed her. Deep in her heart, she longed for something else, feeling the lack but uncertain what she needed. Home, certainly; love, perhaps. She thought of Gawain then, and shook her head wearily.

Dear God, she thought, she was tired, and lonely, and frightened. Covering her face in her hands, she sobbed out. As a knock sounded on the door, she lifted her head.

"A moment, Philippa," she called. Sniffling, wiping her eyes, she crossed to the door to undo the iron latch and pin.

She opened the door to Gawain. Startled, she felt her heart bound. He smiled and tilted his head.

He looked astonishingly handsome. A trick of light and shadow, she thought, staring. He was freshly shaved, his cheeks flushed from a bath, his hair damp, the waves brushing the column of his neck. He had exchanged his dusty surcoat and chain mail for a tunic of dark green linen. A soapy fragrance wafted toward her, an herbal scent reminiscent of sage.

He tightened his eyes in concern. "Are you unwell?"

"Tired," she replied, almost undone by his tender question. She stepped back, sniffling. He entered, carrying the pack that had been strapped to his horse's saddle. He walked into the room and set it on the floor. She heard the harsh jangle of the chains tucked inside.

"Come to chain me for the night?" she snapped.

"Not yet," he said dryly. "If you are ready, my family would like you to join us for supper in the solar. My mother is not strong enough to come to the great hall for meals, so we gather in the solar with her. My sisters are hoping to read to us tonight, since I brought them a new book."

"I must finish dressing. I was expecting Philippa."

"She is with my mother. My sisters wanted to help you dress, but I thought you needed better peace than that just now. Their own little handmaid is as giggly as they are, so I told the girls that I would fetch you myself. They think I am eager to be alone with you. The thought delights them."

"But doesna delight you," she retorted. She went toward the bed to pick up the white veil.

"If you need help, I can assist. Though I know naught about weaving odds and ends into the hair, as the twins like to do."

"I am nearly done." She slid the silk through her hands. "Go on. I will join you soon."

"My dear wife," he said, folding his arms and leaning against the door, "this castle is a maze of halls and stairways. You might get lost," he said wryly.

"'Twould be a shame if I found a way out and went back to Scotland on my own," she muttered. She shook the veil, floated the rectangle over her hair, and slipped the braided silken circlet over the crown of her head.

"There would be dire consequences if that happened."

"Dire for you, bonny for me."

"Swan Maiden," he said, "do you still think to fly away?"

"They say I have that power." She reached up to adjust the veil.

He came toward her. "The thing is crooked. Let me—"

Flustered, she stepped away from him. "I can manage."

"My mother, and other married women I have seen, wear theirs just so." He tugged on the veil, cradling the crown of her head. Shivers slipped through her. Gawain picked up the silken ends and tucked them around her throat, wrapping one longer side under the headpiece. His thumb grazed the line of her jaw, just above the silk. "There."

"Thank you," she whispered. Shivers cascaded through her still, even when he lowered his hands.

He reached out to pull open the door for her, and smiled, fine lines crinkling around his warm brown eyes.

She tilted her head. "Why are you kind and charming to me at times, and so hard with me otherwise?" she asked impulsively. "What is it you want from this marriage?"

He frowned slightly. "What does any man want from a wife?"

"Since you let me be last night, it canna be lust," she said boldly. "If 'tis land, wealth, and title, you willna have those of me, for I have no inheritance worth claiming. Is king's favor enough to content you?"

He closed the door again, abruptly, and leaned his hand against it, his arm above her head. "Each time you see a chance to sting me, you try, lady. My patience grows short with it."

"My patience grows short, too," she said.

"You," he said, "have none."

"I do, when I want. Just now I want to be free. I have had enough of captivity."

"But not enough of honing your anger on me. I am not your enemy or your tormentor. I have shown you naught but kindness, and I expect it in return."

She looked away, feeling her cheeks burn, knowing he spoke the truth. She had sometimes behaved poorly toward him though he had helped her. "Likely you intend to shut me up in Elladoune and await new orders from your king."

"If you cannot rein in your damnable temper, you may just find yourself shut in a tower somewhere."

She flashed him a scathing look, and felt as if it met a brick wall. He stared at her until she glanced away. "But you may keep your kitten in your cell with you," he added when she was silent. "She is in the solar, awaiting you in a basket."

She pursed her lips. "Dinna think that will make me like you better. I have agreed to be kind to your mother, and I will, and to your sisters too. As for you—"

"Being kind to my mother is more important to me."

"I dinna wish to upset your mother. She is a good lady."

"Aye," he said gruffly. "Juliana—my mother and my sisters do not know the full truth about us, or about you. And none of us will tell them—at least not yet."

"They will cease to like me once they learn the truth."

"I doubt that, but—" He heaved a sigh. "My mother may not live long enough to learn the truth. We will not burden her—or the girls, who have enough to bear with our mother so ill—with the poor circumstances of our marriage, and the king's orders."

She nodded soberly. "For now. And later?"

"We shall see. We will go on to Scotland, and do our best to abide by the king's orders."

"Ah. Chains for me, and lessons in obedience, and land and accolades for you."

He gave a huff of frustration, and his eyes seemed to blaze. "Do you think I wanted this?" he demanded. "Do you think I like seeing you chained, and displayed?"

"You didna prevent it," she said.

He closed his eyes. A muscle moved in his jaw. "I had choices to make. There are matters you know naught about, and reasons for what I do."

"Tell me, then. Why are you part of this? You dinna seem a man to play the king's cruel games, yet you do."

"I do indeed," he said softly. "Now."

"What do you want from this marriage, and this evil scheme to keep—and train—me?"

He let out a long breath. "What I want most of all," he said, "I gave up on gaining years ago. I have new goals now."

Juliana sensed tension in him, and more—a current of sadness, even loneliness. She tilted her head in sudden sympathy. "There is something you greatly desire," she said more gently. "What is it?"

"I want whatever my king wants, of course," he said

brusquely, and opened the door. "Supper grows cold, and my family is eager to see you. Remember," he said as she sailed past him into the corridor, "for now, you adore me."

"Oh," she said flippantly, "how could I have forgotten?" She marched ahead, and heard his dry chuckle behind her.

Chapter 13

> "An elderly man, a wife he took to hand,
> The king's daughter of Scotland . . ."

Eleanor's voice skimmed over the opening passages of the story of Bevis of Hampton. Listening, Gawain stretched out a hand to scratch the ears of the old mixed breed hound that lay beside the fire.

> "This maid, I have ye told,
> Fair maid she was and bold,
> And nobly born."

He glanced at Juliana. Seated in a chair beside him, she held the white kitten in her lap while she, too, listened. Fate had certainly brought him a fair maid of Scotland, he thought. What would come next, he did not know.

A groan from Robin caught his attention. His stepbrother sat at a table, facing Catherine over a chessboard. He lamented some clever move she had just made.

Eleanor continued to read, curled at her mother's feet on the other side of the hearth, turning the parchment pages of the illuminated manuscript. Lady Clarice listened, a blanket tucked over her legs despite the warm room. She stifled a deep cough behind a cloth and took a sip of wine. Philippa looked up quickly from a seat in a corner, where she sewed.

Despite the sorrowful uncertainty of his mother's illness, Gawain felt some contentment. What surprised him was that Juliana's presence added immeasurably to that. He watched her dangle a ribbon for the kitten's amusement. He wished this peaceful, loving moment—like a little bubble containing paradise—could continue indefinitely.

His gaze flowed over her from head to foot and up again. The plum-colored gown contrasted with her pale golden coloring, and her cheeks were pinkened from the heat of the fire. The cut of the fabric enhanced her lithe body while revealing the grace of her long throat. Profoundly attracted to her, but uncertain how she felt, he glanced away. Eleanor had finished her passage, and she and her mother were staring at him.

"A fine story," he said hastily. He had read more of it on his own than he had heard from Eleanor just now. "A good adventure, though without the poetic sensibility that our lady mother prefers in a long epic tale, such as *Gawain and the Green Knight.*"

"Surely no one can surpass the Gawain poet." Lady Clarice smiled. " 'Tis one of my favorites—and mayhap why I gave my son that name." She smiled. "But this story is exciting. We shall hear more of it tomorrow evening. Juliana, have you heard the tale of Bevis before?"

Juliana shook her head, her fingers easing over the kitten. " 'Tis new to me, my lady."

"No doubt Juliana has heard many other stories," Catherine said. "Scots storytellers are said to be the finest of all. Gawain, surely you remember the tales from your earlier days?"

He shrugged. " 'Twas long ago," he murmured. "My grand—" He stopped suddenly, recalling that Juliana did not know about his origins as yet. And his mother, who did not like it mentioned, was frowning. He cleared his throat. "Er, we had no time for stories. We were . . . concerned with other matters."

"Matters of war," Juliana muttered.

He reached over to rest his hand upon hers. "Sweet lady wife." Her quick answering smile was forced.

"Lady Juliana," Robin said gallantly, "do not fret over it. Leave such matters to men who are trained to war."

She scowled at him. "Were war left to women, who are nae trained to it," she said, "there would be none." Robin blushed and lifted a hand in apology.

"Well done," Lady Clarice said, smiling.

"Juliana, tell us what you most like to do at home in Scotland," Catherine said. "Where is your own castle?"

"I once lived in a place called Elladoune," she replied. "'Twas burned by the English." Her bluntness caused Lady Clarice and the twins to gasp. Gawain frowned warily.

"My mother told my brothers and me many tales and legends about warriors and their ladies—wonderful, magical stories," she went on. Relieved, Gawain hoped she did not intend to press the other issue. "Later, we lived in the forests with outlaws and dispossessed families, where I learned to hide from English soldiers. And there, too, I heard wonderful stories, at night, by the fire, from a harper left homeless by the war."

"Oh, my," Lady Clarice said faintly. "Homeless! Dear saints. We did not realize that you were . . . a victim of the Scottish war."

"Most Scots are victims of the war in one way or another, Mama," Gawain said. He felt strangely humbled, for he had not known that Juliana had lived homeless after Elladoune. He looked down to pet the old dog, telling himself that he should have asked how she had fared.

"I lived in the forest for two years, my lady," Juliana said. "We were safe there, with other dispossessed people. We learned to fend for ourselves and to avoid the English." Aye, Gawain thought, listening. She knew how to fend for herself. And he realized why she found it so hard to trust English knights.

"Go on," Catherine said. "What then?"

"My father died fighting for freedom, and my mother entered a convent in her grief. We were taken in by her cousin, an abbot, and lived in his private house on the abbey grounds, not in the monastery itself. His sister, who is his housekeeper, lived with us there. My two older brothers had already gone to fight with the rebels, and are with them still. I have four brothers, two older and two younger than I," she added.

"How came you to be a guest in the king's court, if your family are Scottish rebels?" Eleanor asked curiously.

Gawain kept his attention on the hound by his knee, and Juliana's hands stilled on the kitten.

"She was a guest, Mama," Robin spoke up. "As I told you

when I first came here, she was invited to the king's feast to represent the king's hope for an end to the Scottish war. She was dressed as a swan, in satin and feathers, and the king himself called her his Swan Maiden. Was she not beautiful, Gawain?"

"She took my breath, I swear it," Gawain murmured. That at least was the truth. He stroked the old dog's back.

"Swan? Oh, the pretty feather cap," Clarice said, nodding.

Gawain sighed and sat back, rubbing his hand across his chin. As much as he loved his good-hearted family, he knew they found the truth often too awkward to face. If Henry and Edmund had been there, they would have supported Robin's story.

His family preferred ideals and pretty versions of the truth and avoided complex emotional matters. He had seen the habit intensify in the years of his mother's illness. Henry in particular wanted to protect her and give her happiness, even if it meant disguising the truth.

The tendency had been there earlier, as well. His Scottish origins were rarely mentioned. As a boy he had been hurt by it, but he eventually understood. His mother wanted him to become a favored knight, and wanted no taint from his Scottish name and background. He also suspected that she still grieved for his father, whom she had loved deeply.

However, she loved Henry faithfully, and he adored her. He had provided a luxurious and privileged life, and had shielded his family well at Avenel.

If they wanted to embellish the truth about Juliana, Gawain would not correct them. In his own thinking, he never embroidered or denied any matter. The early influence of his Scottish father and kin left him with a hunger for honesty.

He glanced at Juliana. She had the quick-witted frankness of a Scot, which he found vastly refreshing and reliable. That was part of the draw he felt toward her. She would not understand the unspoken rules within the Avenel family.

But she seemed to sense them, for she had gone fluidly along with what was said and done around her. Although her delicate brows were lowered over sapphire eyes, she kept her thoughts, her temper—and the truth—to herself. Once again, he blessed her for it.

"Gawain, being my son, would of course be a perfect Swan Knight," Lady Clarice went on, still talking about the king's feast. "My family are De Bohuns, Juliana. Swans have been part of our family crest for generations. 'Tis said that long ago, one of our ancestors was a legendary Swan Knight named Helias."

Juliana looked at Gawain, wide-eyed. He shrugged a little sheepishly; the idea of the Swan Knight, years ago, had not come to him out of midair.

"We have a swan on the Lindsay crest as well," Juliana said. "Swans have lived on the loch between Elladoune and Inchfillan Abbey for longer than anyone can remember. There is an old legend about how they first appeared there."

"I would love to hear that tale," Eleanor said.

"Someday I shall tell you," Juliana said. "Lady Clarice, are you unwell?"

Gawain started, for his mother had lifted a hand to cover her face. She lowered it. "'Tis naught. I am sure the swans near your home are a lovely sight." Her voice sounded hollow. "Gawain . . . would enjoy seeing them." Her gaze met his and shifted away, and he knew that she was remembering a source of grief.

"My husband will certainly see the swans of Elladoune when we go home," Juliana said, smiling.

Bless her again, he thought, for doing this for his mother's sake. He reached out to touch her cheek. For a moment, the marriage between them felt real, and good, and no pretense at all. He could easily imagine loving her.

She tilted her head away from his touch in silence.

"I am tired, and will retire to my bed now," Lady Clarice said. "My daughters must go to bed too. Juliana, welcome again to our family. I can see how much my son loves you, and you him." Tears shone in her eyes. "It makes my heart glad."

Gawain took Juliana's hand and kissed it. She curled her fingers over his, warm and gentle.

"We are glad too," Catherine said. "But unhappy that we missed their wedding celebration."

"We will have a wedding celebration of our own!" Eleanor said, and beckoned to Catherine, who came close, then nodded.

"But we had a wonderful feast at supper," Lady Clarice said.

"Without the fun of a wedding—dancing, music, guests!" Catherine said. "Juliana is the first guest we have had here in a long while, other than Father's friends, who only want to discuss military policies." Eleanor nodded agreement.

"Juliana and I have traveled far, and are too tired for dancing, and too full for more feasting," Gawain said. "'Tis best to keep the household quiet for Mama's sake. Later, when she feels stronger, we will have music and dancing, if you like."

Eleanor folded her arms petulantly. "I think you should pay a forfeit, since you kept us from enjoying a celebration."

"And kept us from the king's court," Catherine added.

"What forfeit?" Gawain asked. "Shall I dance or sing, as they do in court?"

"You will regret that if you ask him," Robin said.

The twins laughed, and Eleanor looked inspired. "We shall follow you to the bedchamber with horns and drums, and flowers and candlelight, as they do on the night of a wedding! We shall put you to bed with great ceremony and noise to bless the union, and keep the evil spirits away!"

Gawain looked sourly at his sisters. "We have already had our first night," he said sternly.

"Gawain and Juliana are too weary for revelry," Lady Clarice said. "And you two do not need to witness a bedding," she added.

"Oh, Mama, we know all about such things! Listen to what the heroine says of Bevis—" Eleanor flipped through a few pages, ran her finger down, and began to read.

> "Had I taken a young knight,
> That was not bruised in war or fight,
> As he is,
> And would me love day and night,
> Embracing and kissing with all his might,
> And make for me bliss . . ."

"Oh, for such bliss!" Catherine cried, clasping her hands. "The joy of true love!"

"Aye," Eleanor echoed. "Gawain must forfeit kisses!" Catherine squealed in agreement. She and Eleanor grinned up at their eldest half brother.

Juliana, he saw then, was laughing, her face tucked against the kitten's snowy fur. Grousing for good effect, Gawain rose from his seat and bent to kiss first one and then the other giggling sister on the cheek.

"Nay, silly, not us," Eleanor said. "Kiss your bride!"

"Each time we say, you must kiss your bride!" Catherine said, nodding to Eleanor. "That is your forfeit!"

"You owe us this! We most heartfully wanted to see you wed," Eleanor insisted. "Mama said 'twould never happen, you know, but we were hopeful someone would find you pleasing."

Gawain saw Robin smother a grin behind his hand. His mother's eyes glowed with laughter. In the corner, Philippa chuckled as she sewed a seam.

Juliana smiled, her cheeks pink. He sighed dramatically and turned toward her, bending. She tipped her cheek and he kissed it chastely. She smelled of roses and lavender from her bath. Crazily, he wanted to linger.

"On the mouth, with all your might—just as the book says!" Catherine insisted.

"Make bliss for her, you silly oaf!" Eleanor crowed.

"Girls," Lady Clarice admonished.

"Oh, let him forfeit," Robin said. "Gawain owes his bride some courtesy, for I would wager that her hasty wedding—and what followed—did not suit a lady's dreams."

Gawain sent him a scathing look. He leaned toward Juliana again, meaning only to kiss her cheek, but she turned her head and his mouth met hers. After a dizzying instant of sweetness, he withdrew.

The girls applauded. He smiled, glad to see that his mother was laughing. He felt responsible, in part, for the sadness that had come to this family lately. None of them had laughed freely or well since Geoffrey had died.

Juliana, however, did not smile, but blushed and turned her attention to the white kitten.

"There," he told the twins. "You have had your forfeiture. Now go to bed, you two."

Catherine looked at Eleanor. "We shall demand more kisses on the morrow. A proper wedding would have days of merrymaking!"

"Aye, you owe us more celebrating," Eleanor told Gawain.

"And Lady Juliana needs more bliss," Catherine whispered loudly. This sent Eleanor into a giggling fit.

"Good night, daughters," Lady Clarice said. "Philippa, take them to find their maid, if you will."

Philippa rose from her seat, while the twins kissed their mother. Eleanor picked up the volume of Bevis, and the girls left the room whispering to each other.

"Those two," Gawain said, "are heartily spoiled."

"They are young," Lady Clarice said gently. "Let them have their joy. Too soon, life may take it from them." She stood. "Can someone help me to my bed?" she asked faintly. Gawain took a long stride forward, as did Robin.

"Let me help you, my lady," Juliana said, rising. She handed the white kitten to Gawain, then turned to Lady Clarice.

"My thanks, sweeting," his mother answered in acceptance, allowing Juliana to assist her. "Philippa will come back soon. Then you and Gawain should retire too. You must be very tired after your journey." Lady Clarice moved forward with Juliana and looked at her sons. "Robin, find a page and tell him to bring mulled wine for me, and some for Juliana. Gawain, your bride has dark circles under her eyes—'tis in part her fair complexion, but she is weary. See that she rests."

"I will, Mama," he said softly, opening the connecting door that led into his mother's bedchamber. Juliana guided the fragile lady through. "God be with."

He turned back to see Robin watching him. "Your bride is not so silent after all," he said. "So that mysterious silence of hers is a ruse?"

"Aye. But we Avenels are not unfamiliar with pretense."

Robin looked sheepish. "Father told me to tell our lady mother that Juliana was a guest of the king, and chosen for you as a favor. He did not think she would react well to the truth about your bride."

"I understand," Gawain said. He looked down at the kitten squirming playfully in his hands and scratched its tiny, snowy head gently. "I wonder if any of us will ever learn the full truth about my bride," he muttered half to himself.

"I will not tell anyone else that she speaks, if 'tis a secret," Robin said.

"Good. She wants it kept among us. She has her reasons, whatever they are."

"When you get to Scotland, you will learn them quick enough," Robin said. "Good night, then. I will have the wine sent up. Blessings to you on your wedding, brother," he added with a little smile. "Mother is pleased. And that is what matters most, is it not?"

Gawain lifted the kitten and looked into its wide-eyed, innocent stare. "Aye," he said softly, and chuckled as the kitten nuzzled his cheek.

"Look at that, yet another female who wants to forfeit a kiss from you," Robin said, laughing as he left the room.

Chapter 14

"She's abed, sir. Good night and God bless ye both," Philippa whispered as she slipped out of Gawain's bedchamber. She smiled and hurried down the hall.

He nodded in acknowledgment, having waited outside the chamber while Philippa had gone inside with Juliana to prepare her properly for bed. Now he pushed the door open.

Candlelight lent a deep glow to the red-curtained bed. Juliana sat propped on pillows and covered in scarlet brocade. She apparently wore nothing at all, for her slim shoulders and arms were bare, and her combed hair flowed down like a river of gold. The coverlet was drawn tightly over her chest, and her hands fiercely clutched the fabric. Her slender legs and feet barely made a hill under the coverlet.

The kitten lay curled in the middle of the bed. Gawain remembered that Philippa had rushed out of the room to return with a bundle that must have been the cat.

He came forward. Juliana watched him in silence, her eyes the only part of her that moved. Instead of going to the bed, he bent to open the saddle pack on the floor. The jangling of the chains inside sounded clearly in the quiet.

He intended to extract a clean shirt, but first he picked up the chains and bands, wondering what to do. The king's orders were clear. He had already disobeyed them by bringing her to Avenel unbound. But her escape was a strong possibility once he went to sleep. Much as he loathed the idea, he might have to restrain her again.

"Ah," she said, watching him. "Now I must bare my neck for the golden collar. Is that the secret of our nights at Avenel?"

He glanced over his shoulder. "I cannot risk the Swan Maiden's flight."

"So you think you must chain me like a bird in your fine cage." She waved a hand at the curtains and the canopy of richly embroidered cloth above her head.

"I do not like this any more than you do."

"You could trust me," she said, "to sleep and not to flee."

He almost laughed. "This close to Scotland? I know you better than that, I think."

"And I thought I knew you. I thought you would treat me with better courtesy here. Your family has been muckle kind to me. What about you?"

"You have utterly charmed my family."

"You asked me to do so!" She sounded indignant.

"So I did. But you could not help it, I think." He stood. "You are like that kitten. 'Tis in your nature to be gentle and charming . . . yet both of you have claws."

"And I have wings, or so you think, and would pinion me."

"If I let you spread those wings, you would be gone."

"You could trust me," she said again.

He sifted the chains from one hand to the other. "I wish I could," he said thoughtfully. "I want to." He felt her gaze upon him as he watched the glitter and fall of the chains.

He hated them. The last thing he wanted was to lock them around her again. But he could not risk losing her. Too much depended on keeping her safely in his care.

As if she were a bird poised on a windowsill, he knew that she would fly if she had the chance. That was her nature, he thought, to seek freedom. He had seen the urge in her already.

"The chains are heavy," she said. "They hurt me."

He had seen the bruises, the red marks. "I know."

She sighed. "Will you fetch that for me, there?" she asked, pointing across the room to the neatly folded pile of clothing that Philippa had left on the flat top of the great wooden chest. "I canna get out of the bed," she explained, blushing modestly, and raising a hand to her chest. "Would you fetch me the silk?"

Puzzled, he nodded, and crossed the room to pick up the silk chemise and the veil and ribbons—not knowing which piece she meant—and brought them to her. The chains swung in his hands.

She motioned for him to turn away, and he did, while she slipped the heavy cream silk chemise over her head and pulled it down. That, he thought, did not bode well for a woman who claimed to be content to stay in one place for the night.

He turned to see her sliding the veil through her hands. She rolled its length and wrapped an end around her left wrist, knotting it. Then she looked up and held the other end toward him.

"If you canna believe I will stay here the night, let me prove it. You may tie this end to the bedpost. I willna go anywhere. I promise."

He watched her silently, brows drawn together, stunned by what she offered—her own fledgling trust.

"If you please," she murmured, "the chains are horrible to wear. The silk will allow me to sleep, and yet keep me here."

Still he did not speak. He frowned, hoping her opinion of him was not so low that she believed he cared nothing for her welfare.

After a moment, he flung the mass of links toward the pack, where they jangled out of sight. Then he stripped off his surcoat and tunic, and tossed them over the end of the bed. Kicking off his shoes, he strode to the bed in his braies and climbed in. The feather mattress bounded beneath his weight. He was careful not to disturb the snowy puddle of sleeping kitten as he pulled the covers up.

Snatching the end of the veil, he tied it around his right wrist, closest to her, and held up his forearm. Juliana gaped at him all the while.

"There," he said. "We will bear it together. And should you feel some urge to slip out in the middle of the night, you will have to wake me, or carry me over your shoulder."

She continued to stare at him.

He folded his hands, silk pulling slightly between her arm and his, and looked at her. "Silent again, Swan Maiden?"

"You . . . you would bind yourself, for my sake?" she asked hoarsely. Her eyes looked overlarge, as if she were about to cry. For love of God, he could not think of a reason for it.

"This solves some of our problem, does it not?" He settled

in the bed, putting his hands up behind his head. Her arm went up. "Ah. Sorry." He lowered his right arm, keeping his left up behind his head. A moment later, he leaned over and blew out the candle that flickered on a small table at his bedside. Then he lay back again.

"Good night, my lady," he said softly. "Sweet dreams."

Silence lingered for a few moments. "Gabhan," she said. He had not heard his name on her lips before. Whispered in the dark, her Gaelic accent lent it an intimate, wonderful sound. *Gav-vahn*. Unknowing, she had used his original name. No one had called him Gabhan since his boyhood in Scotland.

He pulled in a breath. "Aye?"

"I must ask a favor of you." Her voice sounded wary.

"Ask it." He expected a lecture regarding the straying of hands in the middle of the night. But he had agreed, when they had been together at Newcastle, that he would not force himself upon her. If she was to become his true wife, she would have to want lovemaking between them as much as he had begun to want it.

Judging by her behavior toward him so far—excepting the pretense they played for his mother's sake—the chances of that were scant enough, he told himself. He raised his knee and looked up at the shadowed canopy, hoping to seem nonchalant about lying in bed with her. He waited.

"I want you to take me safe to Scotland yourself," she said. "Dinna leave me in the care of De Soulis."

As at other times, he was surprised. The girl was never predictable. "When Walter de Soulis concludes his meeting with Aymer de Valence, we will resume our journey together, by king's order," he said. "In a few more days—by week's end, at least—you will be in Scotland. What does it matter how you get there?"

"I want you to take me there," she said. "He willna harm me if you are there. I—I will feel safer with you."

He glanced at her sharply. "Has he laid a hand on you?"

She shook her head. "He hasna touched me. But I fear that he will kill me one day, even so. Dinna leave me with him on the journey, or at Elladoune, when we are there."

"Kill you? Juliana, you are letting fancy and fear run with

your thoughts." He wanted to take her hand, but knew that was not wise, no matter how closely the silk joined them.

" 'Tisna fear or fancy," she said softly.

Although he made less of her feelings to reassure her, she seemed to feel real apprehension. "He is not a pleasant man, but he is a loyal king's man, a sheriff and now Master of Swans in Scotland. He will come often to Elladoune. If he disturbs you, stay out of his way."

"I dinna trust him. If you must guard me at all, I want to be guarded against him."

He frowned. "Very well."

"Thank you. And in return"—her gaze swung toward him, a sober gleam—"I will stay in your cage."

Saints and martyrs, he thought, sleeping with her proved a mighty challenge. Those luscious little sighs, the light bounce of the bed, the gentle pull of the length of silk between his wrist and hers, created sweet, prolonged torture. His awareness of her was keen and constant, though she had scarcely moved. While he had hardly slept, he knew she did, and quite deeply.

The temptation to pull her into his arms was strong. He tried to turn his back to her, but could not, without rolling her with him. He stayed on his back and stared at the curtains, which he had earlier pulled shut, enclosing him and Juliana in a warm and intimate nest. Flexing his hands, he resisted the recurrent, teasing, delicious thought of touching her.

Earlier, he had laughed with her, and had tasted her mouth more than once. The memory of that sweetness drew him to her now like a bee to a flower. He wanted her fiercely, his body aching with an astonishing need, strong and vibrant and immediate.

Perhaps he struggled only against the common exaggeration of dreams and sensations in the darkness. Perhaps it was merely the natural urge that came upon a man at night. In the morning, he told himself, he would forget this. He would scarcely remember how much he wanted her, how he throbbed for her. This would seem like a dream.

But he could not convince himself of that. He sucked in a breath and shifted his arm, feeling the tug on the silk.

Honor alone kept him from pulling her into his arms and kissing her, caressing her as he yearned. Honor kept him still, and weighed upon him as heavily as desire.

She turned on her side, facing him, and sighed long and low. He sensed, in the utter quiet, that she was awake. On his foot, through the covers, he felt the tiny pricks of the kitten's claws as it flexed its toes in sleep.

"Must we have the cat in our bed?" he asked irritably.

"Aye," she said, her voice thick with sleep.

"Why so? She will hardly protect you against me, if 'tis what you think. I fear I will smash the little beastie, all unknowing, in my sleep."

"If you canna be husband to me," she murmured, "which you canna, for 'twould be ill-done to take me in my body as England wishes to take Scotland. . . ." Her pause signaled that she expected his reply on that point.

"Aye, ill-done. We have agreed on that. Go on."

"Then I will have the kitten in the bed at night. I want some comfort. I am a prisoner, after all."

"I hope I suffer so, if I ever fall into prison again," he muttered, reshaping his pillow.

"You will, if you dinna tame me."

"Thank you for the reminder," he growled.

After a moment, she turned her head. He saw the silvery gleam of her hair and the oval curve of her face in the darkness. "In prison again? What did you mean?"

"I spent two months in the king's dungeon in the Tower of London. I was released but six weeks ago. 'Tis why my mother still thinks me too thin," he added.

"What was your crime?"

"The crown called it transgression," he answered. He did not want to offer more, not then, for there was far too much else to explain regarding that incident. But Juliana leaned closer in the dark, her curiosity clearly raised.

"Transgression? But you are the perfect courteous English knight. Surely there was something serious to warrant prison."

"There was." He lay unmoving, silent, considering. His hand was beside hers, the band of silk gentle between them.

"What was it?" she prompted.

"Betrayal," he said quietly, and turned his head away, presenting his shoulder to her.

Caught in a dream, yet riding the edge of wakefulness, she summoned back the vanishing images and thoughts, drawing them over her like a cloak woven of stars and darkness. That world seemed more real now than reality, a place of safety and love and joy. A sparkling strand of murmurings and laughter and a beloved face streamed past, and she went toward it. She did not want to rise up into the light of dawn, and another day of captivity.

Snuggling down, keeping her eyes closed, she felt lush and warm and relaxed as she sought and found her dream world again. Caresses, whispers, someone whom she adored, who loved her—

There he was—just there. She smiled and slipped into his arms when he appeared. They floated together somewhere, in a meadow, in an ocean, in a bed, in heaven—she did not know. Neither did she know his name. But she knew him nonetheless, understood him deeply, as if he were the twin half of her soul.

His slow, gentle fingers skimmed her back, her arm, her hip. She lay against him, breast to chest, her knee drawn over his firm thigh, his breath easing over her hair.

So peaceful, so warm. A wondrous feeling, unlike anything she had ever known before. She could not tell where she ended and he began. She only knew how much she loved him.

Smiling, sinking into his comfort and strength, she slid her hand over the smooth contour of his chest, feeling the circlet of his nipple harden. She explored him, sighing as he sought her as well, his hand gliding over the roundness of her breast, his thumb flicking over the nipple, creating a burst of starlight in her body, in her heart.

Breath soft in her hair, lips warm and gentle on her brow, he seemed to meld with her. She tilted toward him, and his mouth captured hers, her lips opening to him. If only she could float here forever, loved and loving, cherishing, a part of his flesh and spirit, as he seemed part of hers. Only joy existed between them, only the urge to touch, the desire to please.

His hand left her breast, making her yearn for more, stirring her heartbeat. Fingers gentle against her throat, thumb tipping her head back, finger pads tracing the arch of her neck. She tilted her head and opened her mouth, seeking within his mouth as he delved into hers.

Now his head tipped down and his hair, like midnight silk, slipped soft over her skin. His mouth was hot and exquisite on her breast, seeking, finding, and she sighed and arched into him. The dream went on, and she flowed within it.

She furrowed her hands through the heavy satin of his hair, found the rasp of his beard, played with his ear, until he sucked in a breath and came up to meet her mouth again, taking her there with such extraordinary gentleness that the rest of her melted like drizzled honey.

Moaning, she heard his deep, breathy echo. Her hand progressed along his arm, over the carved plane of his chest and abdomen, over the velvet-textured hair lower down. She wanted to know, wanted to touch, wanted to be touched. Her fingers found the waist of his garment. He was heated and solid there, rising against her hand. He took her mouth again, firmly this time, and lifted his mouth away. He whispered her name, kissed her ear.

Gasping, she lost the edge of the dream and opened her eyes.

Gawain. Not some nameless dream lover. His brown eyes stared into hers, blinked, his lashes and brows black as coal. A cool silvery light spilled over his body, over hers. She lay half on top of him, their silk-bound hands beneath them. She stilled, and he was silent. The same nurturing warmth as in the dream enveloped them. But her heart pounded through her chest, and his heart thumped against her.

His hand drifted away from her breast. Her hand was still cupped over his hardness, linen separating her skin from his, and she slid free. Her body felt lonely, cool.

Slowly, he turned his head and closed his eyes. His hand lingered on her arm, utterly tranquil.

Perhaps this was yet the dream. He was achingly beautiful in the dawn light, perfectly made, tender and strong. She felt love and passion lingering, palpable as light and fire.

A dream, she thought, closing her eyes. An extraordinary dream. She was too weary to distinguish time from timeless.

Resting her palm over his heart, she felt its rhythm, and slept before she could think, drawn back into the web of comfort that still held her.

When she awoke in the full light of morning, she was alone in the bed. The silken veil, still tied around her wrist, floated free at the other end.

Chapter 15

At midmorning he had still not seen Juliana, and neither had his sisters nor his mother. He worried that she had escaped, despite her promise. A groom in the courtyard finally told him that Robin had taken her fishing. He walked briskly through the open castle gates and over the drawbridge to see for himself.

His stepbrother and two pages sat on the bank of the moat, a favorite spot for fishing, but Juliana was not with them. They waved toward him, and pointed down the meadow toward the river.

He hurried there, crushing wildflowers underfoot, scarcely noticing the spring air or the white clouds and perfect sky overhead. Juliana was all he saw, standing in plain sight beside the calm river.

She wore the mulberry gown and the white veil. In the sun-warmed air, she had no cloak. When he approached, she glanced over her shoulder, her face lovely and innocent. Yet he saw a light that was alert and knowing, and wonderfully sensual, in her deep blue eyes. He was glad to see no flash of anger there, for he knew he deserved it.

Slowing his step, he felt himself flush as he recalled what had happened at dawn. He had awoken with Juliana deep in his arms, his lips upon hers, his hands—and hers as well—finding joy with each other's bodies.

He could hardly apologize, for he was not certain she had been awake. He knew he had been caught in the blissful throes of a dream that had merged with reality. Now, the thought of those lush moments with her threatened to arouse him again.

Forget this, he told himself sternly, though it remained agonizingly clear in his mind.

"You have swans here," she said, turning back to look at the river. "But they are nae tame."

"Aye. Wild swans have often nested on that far bend in the river. I hear that some of the Avenels who lived here long ago tamed the creatures, but none of us have that knack." He stood beside her, hands folded behind him, watching the river. Far down along a bend, a pair of swans dipped their beaks into the water. "They are wild and distant and do not come close often. My mother enjoys watching them when they are here."

"You do know how to tame a swan," she said quietly.

He glanced at her. "I doubt that."

"You brought bread to the swan cob that was with me in the king's court," she said. "You fed him, and showed him patience and gave him food. It takes little more than that."

"He was already tamed," he said.

"He was a good cob, Artan," she said faintly. She folded her arms around herself, and sighed, then sighed again.

"Juliana," he said. "Artan is free."

She glanced at him quickly. "The king ordered him prepared for the next day's supper."

"Ah, well." Gawain shrugged. "A good coin invites a favor. I would guess the king ate peacock or pheasant that next night."

She stared at him. "Artan was released?"

He was glad to surprise her, pleased by the brightening in her face. "If my gold and my suggestion had any influence, he is swimming on the Tyne even now, or searching for a new home. I bribed a guard to free the bird."

"Ah, Gabhan," she said, uttering his name in soft Gaelic. "How very kind of you."

By God, he thought, closing his eyes briefly and turning away. He loved the sound of his name in Gaelic, like some secret pleasure. " 'Twas no matter," he said casually.

"Is it just a bonny tale to ease my mind?"

"Ah." He cocked a brow. "I see you have noticed the family tradition. 'Tis the truth, I swear it." He held up his palm. "Shall we go inside? My mother would like to visit with you, and the girls asked if you would shoot arrows with them later. Robin has lately begun to teach them some archery skills."

She smiled. "I would love that."

"And tomorrow morn we leave for Scotland."

She looked up at the sky. "Mayhap Artan will be back on Loch nan Eala by the time we reach Inchfillan."

"I thought he would find a new home in England."

"He would seek his own home or burst his heart doing so, that cob. His family is there. And 'tis Scotland. He would never be content on an English river."

He watched her. "Nor would you."

"'Tis peaceful here, but I must go home. I must." She looked at him, her eyes burning blue. "It torments me to be gone so long. I feel as if I could grow ill if I dinna go back. I—I canna explain it."

"I will take you back," he said quietly. "I said I would."

She said nothing in reply, and watched the swans on the river for a few moments. "You could tame those swans, you know."

He laughed. "I cannot imagine any member of my family doing that. It needs far too much patience."

"Love and patience will tame any creature."

"Even a Swan Maiden?" He smiled.

She shrugged and walked away, and he went with her. Shielding her eyes, she peered toward the swans. "They are building a nest, see. The cob is pulling reeds and grasses out of the water and the edge of the bank. And the pen is taking them from him, and tucking them in place. She is making a circle for herself. But whether she will accept the cob when the nest is made . . . time will tell. Sometimes the cob will pull materials for three or four different nests before the pen is satisfied, and lays her eggs."

"Poor fellow! So making this nest is no guarantee?"

"None at all. She may yet fly away."

"I thought they mated for life."

"Usually," she answered, moving a few steps ahead. "But it can take a long while for them to decide upon a mate. Even then, they dinna always have cygnets every season. And," she added, "if he tires of her, or she of him, they will separate. I have seen it, rarely, among the swans on Loch nan Eala."

"You know swans well, it seems."

"I do," she said. "If you bring food—bread and grains—to

these swans every day, at the same time, they will learn to come to you and learn to expect you. They will tame a bit."

"Tell my sisters," he answered. "They would enjoy that. But the creatures are said to be ill-tempered. 'Tis partly why we leave them alone and watch them from afar."

"They only attack when their safety is threatened, or their families and territory are invaded. Treat them with respect and they are good companions for life."

"Ah, is that the secret. We Avenels do not know much about swans, I fear," he said wryly.

"Swans take care of themselves. Just make certain that this part of the river is safe from their enemies—dogs, foxes, and otters—and see that they have plenty of food available to them and good places to nest. Protect them, and they will repay you with beauty and loyalty."

"Aye." He did not mean swans. He wondered if she did.

Her glance flickered away. "They would be content here. And once they are tamed, they will march over the drawbridge and through the gate and pester everyone in the courtyard if they think to find food from familiar hands there."

He laughed. "My mother and my sisters would enjoy that."

"Ah, there they go," Juliana said, watching as the swans took a running start and lifted up out of the water into flight.

Gawain craned his head back to watch them, too.

"They willna fly much longer," Juliana said then. "Soon their feathers will molt for the summer, and for weeks they will be earthbound."

"Easily caught," he said softly, watching her.

"Aye." She glanced at him, then past his shoulder. "*Ach,* I think you should kiss me now."

He blinked. "What?"

"Here come your sisters," she answered. "Kiss me and be done with it. This morn they were determined that so soon as they saw us together, they would demand kisses between us."

"Well, then." He drew her toward him. She lifted her face and he touched his mouth to hers. She tasted sweet, warm, infinitely giving. He felt her curve into him. The powerful dream returned, pulled him under, and he was lost in the current.

His heart drummed hard as he lifted his head and looked up to see the approaching twins. Juliana turned with him.

" 'Lovelonging has caught me!'—so says Bevis's true love," Catherine said. "And true love has found our Sir Gawain. We did not even have to remind him about the forfeit he owes us!"

"Sir Gawain, whom no damsel would have," Eleanor added.

"But the Swan Maiden wants him." Catherine smiled.

"Hush," Gawain said sternly.

"Were there maidens who did not want him?" Juliana asked.

"Oh, aye, so many we lost count," Catherine said. "None of them had the lovelonging." Eleanor giggled. Gawain scowled while Catherine gestured toward the castle.

"Our lady mother looks down from her window, see there?"

"Aye." He waved, and the twins called out, waving. Lady Clarice lifted a hand and smiled, framed in the arched window.

"She is glad you wed Juliana," Catherine said. "She seems happier, even heartier, this morning than she has been in a long while. You are her first child, and your happiness is very important to her. She worries more about you than about us."

"She worried that you might never wed," Eleanor said.

"This," Juliana said, "I must hear about." She sent him a teasing smile. The twins laughed.

"Gawain offered for the hands of several heiresses and even a widow . . . and each one turned him down," Eleanor explained.

"Why?" Juliana asked. Her eyes were bright with curiosity as she looked from one girl to the next.

"My poor behavior," Gawain said hastily. " 'Twas long ago."

"I find that hard to believe—a fine knight like yourself."

"Believe it," he said. "Five refusals. I am no prize."

The twins nodded. "He could not attract a bride because of his transgressions. At least 'tis what Father said."

"I want to hear more about this transgression," Juliana said, looking at Gawain.

"The first or the second?" Catherine asked brightly.

Juliana watched him somberly. Gawain shrugged. "I overstepped my bounds in Scotland," he answered. He had not planned to tell her yet, comfortable with his habit of keeping matters to himself. And it was hardly the time with the twins here—he wondered if he would ever find a good time for it. "I begged king's peace. Twice. 'Tis done." He half turned away.

"What did you do?" Juliana narrowed her eyes curiously.

"The first time," he said, clearing his throat, "I abetted the escape of rebels in Scotland."

"At Elladoune?" Her glance was keen.

"Aye." He looked away.

"You were seen the night we met?" she asked quietly. "And punished for it?" He nodded, and she frowned. "I never knew."

"'Tis done, as I say," he answered. "I pledged anew, and was admitted into king's peace again."

"And the second time?" she asked.

"Similar to the first," he said dismissively. "I helped a Scotswoman in need, and a few months later, had to petition for king's peace again. My reputation was not the best after that, as you can imagine. Helping Scotswomen is apparently frowned upon in the English court." He glanced at her quickly.

"I am glad that you have that penchant," she murmured.

"The marriages that Henry and my mother tried to arrange were refused by the ladies' fathers or the ladies themselves. I have been left to find my own bride," he said, "and I was little interested in pursuing the matter—until now." He bowed and smiled, taking the conversation into a lighter vein.

"And so you see why Gawain is no prize," Eleanor said, turning from fervent whispering with her sister.

Juliana tilted her head to consider him. "Is he not?"

He gave her the sour look he had bestowed upon his sister a moment earlier. Eleanor, who tended to giggle and chatter more than Catherine, tittered behind her hand.

"I wish you and Juliana would stay here, Gawain," Catherine said. "Mother seems so much better today. She may not be with us long," she added in a whisper. "The physicians say—" She lowered her head.

Gawain touched her shoulder. "She is stronger than you think," he said gently. "Mayhap she will surprise us all."

Though Juliana turned away, he saw her brow fold, her eyes mist over. She was touched deeply by his mother's illness, he realized. He was grateful for her tender heart.

The girls ran back toward the castle, waving and calling to their mother. Robin and the pages walked to meet them, and they crossed the drawbridge together. Gawain strode beside Juliana to cross the meadow after them.

"I owe you my thanks," he said somberly. "You have done far more than I asked. You have brought my mother joy." He watched their feet as they walked through grasses and wildflowers.

"Do you think she will surprise everyone, and get well?"

"She is weaker than when I saw her last, even a month ago."

"Then why did you tell your sisters so?"

He sighed. "What am I to tell them?" he asked. "That she will lie in her grave by winter, as I believe will happen? That they should gather their rosaries and purchase black silks?" He swore suddenly and halted, drawing a breath against the onslaught of grief that came at him like a strong wind.

Juliana touched his arm, then lifted her face and kissed his cheek, quick and sweet.

He blinked down at her. "Are the twins coming this way?"

"That was for you," she said, her cheeks pink. "A seasoned knight who isna afraid to show love for his mother—nor is he afraid to help Scots in need. That man deserves praise and reward, for he is a rare creature indeed."

He felt himself blushing. "Ah, well. 'Tis my name, you see. I am obligated to match the perfection of Arthur's knight Gawain every day of my life. 'Tis not easy to have that name."

"You do honor to it." She smiled gently. "Tell me what ails your mother."

"A disease of the lungs, they say, that saps her strength and will kill her someday. Her physicians dose her and bleed her, and annoy all of us. They cannot help her. But she seems to have accepted it more graciously than I have." He paused. "My lady mother is one of the finest people I know, strong and kind. She and I survived . . . a tragedy together, years ago, before she wed Henry. 'Twill be hard to lose her." He could not look at her, then.

She touched his arm, a quiet comfort. "You are fortunate to have such a mother in your life for any space of time."

"Your mother," he said after a moment. "Is she gone?"

"Gone into the religious life. She will never come out of the convent she chose, and I willna see her again unless I travel there, and 'tis far. She left me to watch my brothers while she cared for her soul. 'Twas more important to her than the souls of the children who needed her," she added quietly.

"Juliana," he said, feeling a surge of sympathy. "That must have been difficult for all of you." She shrugged admittance.

"You have a wonderful mother," she said softly. "Be grateful for her company as long as you have her."

"I am," he said. He knew that his mother would love Juliana as if she were her own daughter—then he shook his head at his own fancy, for he truly did not know what would become of this marriage once they returned to Scotland.

He walked on with her. After a moment, she linked her arm firmly with his and looked up, smiling shyly.

"I must be very deserving today, to earn such affection from a lovely lady," he teased.

She grinned. "Look, I have saved you once again, I think. There are the girls—and they have a book with them. More forfeits in store for you, sirrah."

"Not more verses," he groaned. The twins waited in the courtyard, one of them holding the new volume he had given them tucked under her arm. Juliana laughed up at him.

He looked down at her and smiled. He did not think he could pay these forfeits much longer without paying a serious price in the bargain.

Avenel was paradise. She felt as if she walked through a dream world. The sun shone brightly, and love and kindness and laughter surrounded her. The Avenels and their servants, and even their dogs and cats, were attentive and friendly. She wanted to look around, now and then, to be sure they talked and smiled at her—at Juliana Lindsay, a Scottish rebel in their English nest, and not some beloved princess come to call.

A few dark notes sounded, like a heavy knell, beneath the melody: Lady Clarice's serious and undeniable illness, and the fact that the Avenels were English, and enemies to the Scots.

But the sweetest note of all was Gawain. Kissing him, laughing with him, felt heady and wonderful. Affection, kisses, and casual touches made her feel like his friend, his lover, truly his wife. When he was near, she blushed, and her heart beat hard, and she remembered the joy she had felt waking in his arms that morning. She yearned to be alone with him again.

Even if they only played at love for a little while, she felt cherished; she belonged. Surely she would melt before day's end, flow into a puddle of joy and contentment—a raindrop on the river in enchanted Avenel.

The grim world of truth waited outside the gates of Avenel, and soon they must return to it. Tomorrow Gawain would take her back to the escort, to the cart, to silence—and chains.

And to Scotland, at last, for which her heart also longed. Desperate to return, she would pay any price, play any game.

But she suspected that the game she played with Gawain would forfeit her heart and her very soul into the bargain.

Chapter 16

By late afternoon, he had kissed her so often at the twins' urging that he knew the fragrance of her, the taste, the softness of her. Each time they touched, a tide swelled within him that made his body throb, his heart pound.

He wondered how he would endure another night alone with her in his bed after a day of pretended wedded bliss. Thoughts of the ecstasy that had stirred between them, while both were half asleep and dreaming, pulled at him. He had to master his passion, and remember honor. Otherwise, he would take her up the stairs and make her his own, there, then, forever.

Awareness of their departure tomorrow cooled his ardor somewhat. As the day wore on, he dreaded leaving Avenel; he wished the surprising joy he had found here could continue.

He left his mother's chamber, having sat with her to read verses by the Gawain poet until she fell asleep. Hearing laughter through a window in a stairwell, he looked outside.

Juliana and the girls were on the practice field at the side of the castle grounds. Descending quickly, he crossed the courtyard to find them.

As Juliana's keeper, he could not let her leave the castle alone with the girls. As her husband, and as a man honest with himself, he found it difficult to stay away from her.

The large field, grazed flat by sheep, was used for jousting, weapon practices, and for exercising horses. Three large bales of hay were placed at the far end, with painted cloths pinned to them, for archery practice. The girls stood at the other end, closest to his approach. Each was armed with a short hunting bow. Robin walked back and forth among them as, one by one, they lifted their bows to shoot at the targets.

" 'Tis the bridegroom!" Catherine exclaimed, turning as Gawain walked toward them. She still held the bow and nocked arrow in her hands. Gawain turned her away, so that she aimed toward the target.

"Careful, Cat," he said. "Would you deprive the lady of her bridegroom after only a few days of marriage?"

"You will owe Juliana another kiss for making me unhappy with that remark," Catherine said saucily. She turned to release her arrow. It came down at a crazy angle in the grass barely ten feet away.

"Aha," Gawain said. "We will have no problem with field mice with this cat on the prowl."

Robin laughed outright. The twins turned mirrored scowls upon their brothers. Gawain saw Juliana grin, eyes sparkling. She stood to one side, a lady's short hunting bow in her hand, and bent to choose an arrow from a pile at her feet.

"Forfeit a kiss," Eleanor said. " 'Tis rude to mock Cat."

"Oh, come now," Gawain said. "I only teased her. I should not have to pay a kiss each time I speak to one of you."

"You made a promise," Catherine insisted. "Each time we ask, you must kiss your bride, because we missed your wedding."

"And each time you are rude or ill-tempered, you must pay a forfeit, too," Eleanor said. "And kiss Juliana."

"That was not part of our agreement," Gawain said.

"It is now," Eleanor said blithely.

"The *Fifteen Joys of Marriage* says that kisses make a kind marriage, and so a couple must grant them liberally to each other," Catherine said. "We read it just this morning, so that we could let you know the rules of a good marriage. You have never been wed before."

"I must find a book penned by a nun for you two next time," Gawain muttered.

Robin grinned. "Honor the forfeit, brother."

Looking at Juliana, Gawain lifted his brow. Cheeks pink, she gave the arrow fletching her close attention. He moved toward her, lifted her chin with a finger, and kissed her cheek.

Then, not because his sisters insisted, but because he suddenly wanted to, he kissed her on the mouth. He saw her eyes close, and his entire being seemed to whirl inside.

" 'Oh, that I loved as my own heart's blood!' " Eleanor cried, clasping her hands.

"Bevis again?" Robin asked. Catherine nodded happily.

"I will never," Gawain grumbled, "purchase another book for you if you do not desist with those quotes." The girls chuckled and walked away with Robin, who began to instruct them again.

Juliana's cheeks flamed. "You dinna have to kiss me each time they demand it," she murmured.

"I know. We are blissful newlyweds. And I like it," he added in a light tone.

"When they learn the truth, they will demand apologies, not happy kisses." She was scowling.

"They will not learn it from me or my kinsmen."

"I see that," she said wryly. She nocked the arrow and tilted the bow, aiming it, her brow furrowed. She extended her bow arm and drew the string back with her other hand. Then she relaxed her arms and adjusted her stance, readying to aim again.

"Now 'tis Juliana's turn!" Eleanor said. "Gawain, you must see what a fine archer she is!"

"Juliana's brothers taught her," Catherine added. "She has shot many times in the forests of Scotland."

"When will Father let us go bow hunting?" Eleanor pleaded.

"When you can hit an animal cleanly, so that 'twill not suffer," Gawain said.

"And when you can ride through forest or field without chattering like magpies," Robin said. "Which will never happen."

"Careful, Robin," Gawain murmured. "Next they will demand that you take a bride and kiss her in perpetual forfeit."

"I would gladly do so, if she were as comely as Juliana."

"And as comely as your sisters," Eleanor added coyly.

Robin shielded his eyes in mock horror. Gawain, despite his best effort, laughed. Catherine huffed indignantly.

"I am sure Juliana's brothers do not tease her so harshly," she retorted, tossing her head.

"My brothers," Juliana said, "are not so polite as yours. They tease me most horribly at times." The twins chuckled.

Juliana lifted the bow. The wind blew against her skirt, revealing the lean lines of her body and her confident stance. Gawain had no doubt that he watched an experienced archer: her arms were steady, her gaze intent. She looked only at the hay bale as she drew the string taut and released it.

The arrow flew true and swift, smacking into the center of the target. Gawain whistled low.

"Another stroke of luck," Robin said. "The wind seems to be with her each time she picks up the bow."

"That looked like plain skill to me," Gawain remarked.

"I will wager she cannot do it again," Robin said.

"She can!" Eleanor and Catherine cried in unison.

"Move the target back," Juliana directed. Robin ran the length of the field to drag the bale back, then returned.

Juliana nocked the arrow again. Gawain watched her raise the bow, sight, draw, and release in a fast, fluid rhythm. The arrow flew true to thunk into the painted center of the target.

Robin bowed. "If that were a deer, 'twould be dinner now."

"If 'twere a man, he would be dead," Gawain drawled. He turned. "Excellent. Is that what comes of running with rebels in Scotland?"

"My brothers taught me to defend myself."

"Ah. Ever shot an English knight?"

She looked at him squarely. "Not yet."

"The marriage treatise says a kiss is a suitable reward for a deed pleasing to the spouse," Eleanor prompted.

Gawain shrugged amiably and leaned forward. Juliana tilted her cheek for his kiss. Even so chaste a contact stirred him fiercely. Her skin was silken, her subtle scent intoxicating. He wanted to take her into his arms and carry her to some private place where he could kiss her wild and deep—and do far more.

He gave her a twist of a smile. "Little rebel," he murmured. "Best to stay in your favor. You have a lethal aim."

"I do," she agreed, and turned her head. He kissed her again, without thinking, full and quick. Her soft sigh almost undid him. He stepped back.

Eleanor and Catherine applauded. Gawain began to sense that his sisters' sport would kill him before long.

He took Juliana's wrist in his. "Come with me. We need to collect some arrows." He drew her down the field at a determined pace, walking past several arrows stuck in the grass.

"There are some—" she said. He pulled her onward.

Down the field, he reached toward a target and snatched the shafts buried in its center circle, stuffing them into his belt. Then he drew her behind a tall bale and swept her into his arms.

He kissed her deep and hard and full, as he had been wanting to do all day. She gasped out and circled her arms around his neck. Seeking hungrily, he kissed her again, and swept his hands down her back and over the curve of her hips. She pressed against him, moaned under her breath, and then pulled back.

"Oh," she whispered, "are the twins coming toward us?"

"Nay, we have time," he growled, and delved again. She tilted her head, her mouth eager. As he held her, she seemed to falter a bit, but his own legs felt strong and sure beneath him.

He knew he should stop, should restrain and deny what surged through him. But denial and restraint abounded at Avenel. He craved honesty and passion, and Juliana had both. He could not stop his thirst, once slaking had begun.

His lips lingered on hers, and she did not pull away. Another kiss filled him, rocked him, stirred his desire—and then went further, shaking the very door to his soul.

Cease, he warned himself, or take her down in the grass, here and now, to seek the greatest bliss he could imagine. Her response made it clear she was willing.

He forced himself to pull back, cupping her face in his hands. "Pray pardon," he whispered. "These forfeited kisses, a bed shared at night—'tis too tempting for a weak man such as I."

"Weak," she said breathlessly. "I doubt it." She leaned against him, her breasts soft, her body warm against his beneath layers of clothing. He stepped back reluctantly.

She turned. "Arrows," she said, sounding confused. "We had two dozen, and used them all. How . . . how many do you have there?"

He pulled out the bundle he had shoved in the back of his belt. "Four," he answered. "These must be yours, since they were dead center in that target. My sisters could not have put them there, nor could Robin. I am not sure I could have put them there myself," he added, bemused. "And I am no poor archer."

"Your sisters and Robin told me you are a fine archer with a longbow. They said you are fast and sure."

He shrugged. "I have some tricks. And I know enough to recognize genuine ability." His body, his heart, still throbbed.

She looked flustered. "The . . . rest of the arrows will be in the other targets, or in the grass." She walked around the hay bale, tucking loosened strands of pale hair back under her veil.

Gawain came with her, searching as he walked. Several arrows were planted here and there like saplings. He stepped on one or two before he saw them. A few swayed precariously at the outer edges of the hay bales. The rest were expertly sunk in the heart of another target.

"Yours?" he asked. She nodded. "You have amazing skill, lady." He fisted the collected arrows. "I have scarcely seen such accuracy from a man, let alone a woman. You would be the devil to beat in any competition—and a considerable foe in a skirmish or on a forest path."

Juliana stooped to pick up a shaft in the grass. "I started using a short bow when I was twelve. My father and my brothers Niall and Will, and my cousin James, are skilled archers. I learned much from them." She sent him a curious glance. "You have met my cousin. Your mother mentioned so."

"I have," he said neutrally.

"Robin told me, this morn as we were fishing, that you were taken prisoner by Jamie's men and escaped. You pledged your obedience to your king as soon as you got away. But I thought you transgressed and had to make a new pledge. How many times have you had to declare obeisance?"

"More than most," he answered vaguely. "I have not been the most courteous of knights in Edward's regard." He busied himself with the search for arrows. She watched him, then seemed to accept his answer, turning away to look for more hidden shafts.

The story of his capture and escape from Scottish rebels was the version his family preferred; it kept the Avenel name clean of the taint of treachery. Many men changed allegiances in the war between Scotland and England, especially those who lived near the border. The Avenels, by tradition, were fiercely loyal, and he had shattered that pattern. Yet his family loved him regardless.

He wanted to explain his secrets and his conflicts to her, but not now, not yet. He had much to resolve within himself. Glenshie, and its complications, must remain protected for now. When he could finally share all of the truth, he wanted to share it with her.

Juliana swept the grass with her foot. "We are missing two arrows."

"Not planted in some English knight somewhere, are they?"

"If I loosed them, 'twould be no accident where they hit."

"I am certain of that." Spying a flash of gray feathering, he extracted the arrow shaft from matted grass.

Juliana found the last arrow and walked back toward him. He took it from her hand, fingers grazing. "Well done, Swan Maid."

She glanced toward his sisters. He realized she expected them to demand a kiss for the collected arrows. "My apologies on behalf of my sisters, and myself," he murmured. "We need not play their silly game."

"It doesna bother me," she said.

"Their silliness—or the kisses themselves?"

She shrugged, as if to say none of it mattered. For a moment he felt hurt. He wanted it to matter to her. He wanted her blood to simmer each time he kissed her, as his did.

"My sisters' heads are full of troubadours' verses and stories of courtly love. I will talk to them."

"They are young. And I wish my brothers had been as kind and as tolerant with me as you are with them."

"Your brothers taught you to shoot as well as any man, so they certainly did not ignore you." He glanced at her. "Where are they now?"

"*Ach*, do you think to learn where the rebels are?"

"So that is why you do not speak to English soldiers. You know too much, I think." He lifted an eyebrow.

"I dinna speak to English knights because they are fools!"

"All but me," he said blithely.

She wrinkled her nose at him. "When I was the twins' age, I adored my older brothers, as your sisters do you. But Niall and Will had scant tolerance for me at that age. My father ordered them to teach me to shoot—they didna want to do it. They were demanding tutors and excellent archers. But I wouldna give in until I bested them."

"With good results. You are an uncompromising archer. Your stance, your draw and balance, your aim—all superb."

"They taught me to defend myself," she said, "and then they left me to do just that." She hurried ahead.

Thunder rumbling over incessant rain woke Juliana. She lay on her side, her wrist tied with the veil, its other end around Gawain's wrist. Snoring softly, he slept beside her. The kitten curled between them, a hillock of warmth against Juliana's knee.

Gawain had said very little to her before going to sleep. After the day's closeness and intimacies—including its startling, dreamlike advent—his coolness hurt. He seemed to be deliberately quiet toward her.

Pale light seared the room, and a loud crash startled her. She drew up her knees and winced as flashes and rumbles filled the room. Wanting some contact and reassurance, she touched Gawain's arm tentatively. He slept, but his solid warmth was comfort enough. Another crack of sound, followed by a flash of light, made her jump and squeak.

"What is it?" Gawain asked groggily, rolling toward her. "You are safe here." He propped himself on his elbow. When she flinched at a new crash of sound and light, he sat up and took her hand in his, the silk draping between them. He drew her nearer. Between them, Pippa stretched in her sleep. "Come here. Watch the kitten, now."

"You needna coddle me. Go to sleep." Keenly aware of his half-nude presence, she felt herself blush.

Thunder exploded again, and he circled an arm around her. She relented, leaning against him. He felt warm and good.

"Does the storm disturb you—or is it the thought of rejoining the escort in the morning?"

She shrugged. "I dinna like storms. And I dinna want to return to being dragged about as the Swan Maiden."

"The king put his Master of Swans in charge of you—not the Swan Knight. I would not have treated you, or any woman, so."

"Why must we go with them? We can ride to Elladoune together." She leaned against him, caught in a spell created by the curtained space, body heat, and their low, quiet voices.

"The king does not trust me well enough for that."

"Ah. You disobeyed his orders by taking off my chains."

"He does not know about that yet. And I did not ignore his orders completely." He held up their bound wrists.

"But he mistrusts you, and means to test you in Scotland."

His laugh was rueful. "As I said before, I am no prize. Get to sleep. In the morn, you will go home, as you so want."

"Gawain." She hesitated. "I like it here at Avenel, though 'tis England. I . . . I do like your family. But I must go home."

"I understand," he said quietly.

"And I understand why you decided to wed me in the king's court. 'Twas for your family. For your mother."

His hand rested on her shoulder. "In part," he said.

Beside her, Pippa stretched and made tiny noises in her sleep. Juliana stroked her, feeling safe and good beside Gawain. Although this trust and ease might not last, she savored it. But she wondered what Gawain kept secret from her—what other reason he had to marry her and go back to Scotland with her.

A tumult of thunder, like stones rolling down a slope, made her shiver. "It sounds as if the storm is cracking the world apart. All will be different tomorrow."

"This place cannot be destroyed by a storm."

"I dinna mean the castle. I mean . . . this peace between us." She drew up her knees and rested her arm there. "Avenel is like a sojourn in faery land, lovely but false. 'Twill end soon."

"When we return to the grim world," he finished. "You are safe with me. I swear it."

"But you owe your fealty to Edward. I am never truly safe with you, nor can I trust you, no matter how—" She stopped.

"Go on."

"No matter how good I feel when I am with you," she blurted.

Lost in the sounds of the storm, he uttered something low and fierce, and turned her toward him. The heat of his hands on her shoulders triggered a wave of desire that flashed through her body like an inner storm.

She tilted back her head, her heart pounding, her body throbbing with anticipation. The force that pulsed between them was strong and vibrant, and impossible to ignore any longer. She wanted him to ease its tension.

"None of this is false, I swear it," he growled, looking into her eyes. "And I swear you will be safely kept."

"But you want me to obey your king," she said breathlessly. "Mayhap that is why you are so kind to me here, why we pretend this marriage. You want to convince me to follow your will, and earn you favor at court."

"That is absurd. Obey or not. But the king wants his way, and we are caught by that."

She stared into his dark eyes. "Caught fast."

"Aye," he growled. He slipped his palm to cup her cheek then, and kissed her. She moaned, for it brought sheer relief. As she leaned back to accept the slant of his mouth over hers, he slid his hand along her jaw, his fingers weaving into her hair.

Falling into the kiss as if she dropped through air or plunged underwater, she protested on a whisper when he pulled away. On a silent plea, she tipped her face toward him.

He kissed her again, his fingers cradling her head. Resting her hand on his chest, she felt smooth, heated skin, a pounding heart. Pulled close to him, she slipped her hand over his shoulders, seeking his strength, seeking something she could not name or define, but yearned to discover.

Bound by silk, his hand entwined with hers, while his other hand soothed over her back and hip. Lush and hungry, his mouth met hers again. When he tipped her back and stretched out beside her, she turned toward the hard pressure of his body.

The silence and the enclosed bed created a haven of privacy, erasing outside boundaries and creating new ones. She felt an honest, fervent desire between them, obvious within this sanctum. Here, she trusted him. He would give her pleasure and comfort, and she would offer the same, wordlessly, eagerly. In that, at least, she felt safe with him.

His hand gentled over her breasts, and his fingers lingered, coaxing. When he settled his mouth on her nipple, hardening her there, shivers cascaded through her. She writhed, gasped out. The silk twisted between them as she gripped his hand and wrapped her fingers tightly in his.

The day had started with a dream of exquisite loving, and now had come full circle. She sighed and rolled to allow him greater freedom with her body, and she traced her fingers along the hard, sleek contours of his back, sliding lower. Her body craved his fiercely; desire flowered in her, powerful and new.

When a tiny moan escaped her lips, his mouth captured it from her. The kiss deepened, and she melted further as his hand soothed over her breasts again. She moaned again, turning.

He paused and drew back. Cool air filled the space between them. Suddenly he rolled away, moving so quickly that she turned with him, dragged by the tug of the silken bond. She stared at his back, her heart slamming, her body keen and lonely.

The center of her being, somehow, ached. "What," she said breathlessly, "was that?"

"Male weakness," he replied hoarsely.

"It didna seem weak to me."

"Go to sleep."

"I canna sleep. The storm." That, and her wildly beating heart that would not calm.

"I can. And must, or ravish you here and now in this bed. Or is that what you want?"

"I dinna want . . . ravishing, exactly," she said plaintively. A moment ago she would have pursued it boldly, but now she could not. He had closed himself off from her, and the outside world had somehow come galloping into the gap.

"So be it. No ravishment," he said, his voice low. "You swore you would be mine on the day that hell turns icy, and faeries serve the king of England—or whatever the devil you said. I will not dishonor you, or my own word."

"What if I changed my mind?" she asked faintly.

He punched his pillow. "I crossed a border with you just now, and I did not mean to do it. I would not want you to think poorly of English knighthood," he added sourly.

Regret rushed through her like icy water. But he was wise to end this now, she told herself. The surprising haven of their shared bed, for all its potential and wonder, could not alter what separated them outside of it.

"Gabhan—" She said his name in Gaelic without thinking.

"Good night to you," he snapped.

She sighed, angry, hurt, and confused. Her body told her to do one thing, her mind told her another. Her heart was ensnared in the middle. He struggled, apparently, with something similar.

The Church had taught her that lust was a trap, and now she knew how sweet a trap it was. Clarity of insight told her that passion, within a truly loving union, was a bridge to something beautiful. She wanted to cross the bridge with Gawain, but he did not want that.

Thunder crashed again. She inched closer to him and tucked her fist against his back. He did not turn to take her into his arms as she wished, but he did not move away. She drifted to sleep again behind the battlement of his back, while the storm raged outside.

Chapter 17

The morning clouds were leaden gray through the open window of Lady Clarice's chamber, and the air was cool. Gawain turned to latch the window shutters, and stopped. There was gloom enough here already, he thought.

He watched his mother murmur to Juliana, who wore the white satin gown beneath a blue cloak, a gift from Lady Clarice. Juliana leaned down to kiss his mother's cheek, holding the white kitten tucked in her arm.

"Aye, I promise," she responded to Lady Clarice's quiet question. "We will return to Avenel as soon as we can." She embraced his mother.

Watching, Gawain felt a tug on his heart and blinked in astonishment at the sheer strength of his feelings. He loved his mother and family deeply, and knew it. Now, as he looked at Juliana, something similar stirred within him.

But the feeling had more layers, more texture: affection wrapped with passion and bright hope.

Last night he had wanted her intensely. He had turned away to quell his desire, aware that the boundary he had inadvertently crossed was more than physical desire. The depth of his feelings for her had amazed him, even frightened him.

Love, an inner voice whispered. He answered it—*Nay, it cannot be*. How could he have come to love her so quickly? Yet it was strong and undeniable. And he did not know what to do.

Juliana held out the snowy kitten to Eleanor and Catherine. "Please keep Pippa for me," she told them. "She is too young for a long journey. Mayhap I can claim her when she is older and we . . . are settled in our home." She glanced at Gawain, her eyes filled with doubts that only he understood.

He wished he could reassure her. "Juliana, we must go."

She kissed the kitten's head and handed her to Eleanor. "Keep her safe for me," she said, her voice breaking. She embraced the twins and walked to the door, dashing her hand over her eyes.

Gawain folded Lady Clarice into his arms, careful of her frailty. The tears in her eyes disturbed him, but he smiled and said he would see her soon, though he wondered if this might be the last time. He hugged his sisters and turned away.

Juliana led the way out of the chamber and toward the stairs. They descended the stairs in silence, the hem of her blue cloak sweeping each stone step. He watched its brightness in the shadows, and fought grief and regret.

He was leaving Avenel too soon, but he had no choice. Riding beside Juliana beneath the portcullis and over the drawbridge, he turned and waved farewell to Robin, who stood in the courtyard, framed by the stone arch.

Juliana rode silently, fair and perfect beside him. As sad as he felt to leave Avenel, he was aware of the comfort of her gentle strength. And he felt a burgeoning hope: soon he would find Glenshie at last, and claim it.

He urged Gringolet ahead. The palfrey, Galienne, hastened to keep up as they took the road that stretched over the moors.

Just as Juliana had said, their days at Avenel did indeed seem like time spent in faeryland—beautiful and unreal, and flown with the light.

He led her along the road toward the Scottish border not far away, where De Soulis and the escort would be waiting. After an hour, the horses cantered through a stand of trees. Recognizing the area near Kelso, he slowed his horse, and Juliana guided hers to a halt.

He dismounted and reached up, and she skimmed to the ground in his arms, watching him warily. He turned to take the golden chains and bands from the pack behind his saddle.

He did not speak, nor did she, for he did not know what to say. Should he apologize or beg forgiveness? Should he explain that their marriage, and his assignment to Elladoune, might gain him a long-cherished dream? Should he tell her he loved her?

Husky and quiet, he asked her to remove the veil so he could put the chains on her once again. He felt like a coward.

Juliana unwrapped the veil. Her hair was coiled over her ears, and she pulled the ivory pins free so that the golden sheen spilled over her shoulders. The white silk veil drifted down like a wisp of cloud.

He caught the veil and stuffed it in his pocket, never taking his gaze from hers. He did not want to do this. But the escort had ridden into sight over the rim of the hill. He heard the horses' hooves and saw the men from the corner of his vision.

Juliana lifted her chin, gazing past him. Her eyes were dull, their blue spark turned to smoke. He slipped the collar around her throat and closed it, then lifted the wrist manacles.

She held up her hands passively while he closed the bracelets and attached the chains. She was as cool and delicate and as still as marble under his touch.

Anger at himself, at his king, made his fingers tremble. If he was ever to defy his orders again, he ought to do it now.

Yet he was manacled even more securely than she was. If he broke faith with the king again, his family would suffer. And he would never find Glenshie.

His fingers brushed her slim throat as he checked the collar. "Does it pinch?" he asked.

She did not answer. Chains chiming, she reached inside her sleeve. Drawing out the white feathered cap, she set it upon her head. She acted as if he were not there.

Once again, she was the silent, beautiful Swan Maiden.

She turned and waited. Gawain boosted her into the saddle, then mounted the bay. He took Galienne's lead and rode on. In the distance, he saw the escort heading for the inn tucked at the base of a hill, just over the border of Scotland.

When he reached the yard, the party waited there. Gawain tethered Juliana's horse to a tree and turned to see De Soulis and Laurence Kirkpatrick coming toward them.

All the while, he avoided her glance. He felt too ashamed of himself, and the whole of English knighthood, to look in those beautiful eyes.

*   *   *

"She is tired," Gawain said to himself, watching Juliana, who sat her horse out in the yard. He studied the drooping lines of her shoulders and her bowed head, and saw fatigue there, and something sad and poignant. He felt as if he had caused it.

"Some of the goodwife's fresh ale and that excellent cheese will revive her," Laurie said, standing beside him. "You speak of her more like a husband than a guard. Is it so?"

Gawain glanced at him. "If so, 'tis my own business."

"I've kept a good hold on your secrets in the past," Laurie muttered, as if bothered by Gawain's reticence. "And my guess now is that you are lovestruck." Gawain scowled to dispel the impression, but Laurie only rolled his eyes.

"Dame," Gawain told the innkeeper's wife, who walked near them, "if you will, bring some ale and food for the lady in our party." He handed her a coin.

"The lady, sir?" she asked, pocketing the silver.

"The king's prisoner," De Soulis said, approaching them.

"The *lady*," Gawain said. The woman nodded and hurried away.

"According to the king's writ, I am to decide what is best for the prisoner," De Soulis said.

"Food and ale are necessities."

"True, but you spoil her. I allowed her to be taken to Avenel so that we could avoid bringing her into a garrison town. But do not fancy yourself her keeper yet. We are not at Elladoune."

"But we are in Scotland," Gawain said. "And according to the orders, she is now in my charge. And she is my wife."

"Eager to take over her care? You wax lovesick. That marriage was no love match, but a jest of the king, I thought."

"Aye, a poor joke indeed," Laurie remarked, "to fasten two people in marriage just to make a dull feast more entertaining."

De Soulis glanced at him. "Go tell the men to mount up. We will be leaving soon."

"Fine. I will tell them we will depart once the lady has eaten. Surely they can organize themselves in the time it takes her to swallow a few morsels." Laurie went to the door.

"I am glad he is going to Elladoune with you, and not to Dalbrae with me," De Soulis grumbled. "He annoys me."

"He does not bother me," Gawain murmured. "Tell me— how many men did Sir Aymer decide to send to Elladoune?"

"A few of the men out there will go with you, and later a full garrison will be sent, though that is still being debated," De Soulis said. "You know what you are to do once you are there. Ride the land, take note of its features, and write them plainly—Latin or French will do—for the commander of the king's armies. He is most interested in learning where his armies can set up tents or stage battles, how far the villages and abbeys are, and so on. Deliver the notes to me."

Gawain nodded. He disliked the task, but saw the advantage for himself: he intended to search out Glenshie.

"Since you seem inclined to pamper the girl," the sheriff added, "I must remind you that she is to enjoy no privileges until she declares her loyalty to King Edward."

"Of course not," Gawain repeated flatly, his sarcasm lost on De Soulis. He frankly loathed the man, he decided.

"I took liberty with the king's orders for you once, but I will not do it again. Was she treated as a prisoner at Avenel or cod-dled there?"

"She received courtesy from my family," Gawain snapped.

"Although she committed treason against England."

"From what the guards told me in Newcastle, she tried to prevent a few swans from being stolen. How is that treason?"

"All the swans in Britain belong to the king," De Soulis re-torted. "And I suspect her of rebel activities, which may be proven when we return to her territory. Watch her closely."

The innkeeper's wife approached, and De Soulis took the wooden cup from her hand. Gawain accepted the bread and cheese she carried, then turned to tell the sheriff that the cup was intended for Juliana.

"One thing more before we go outside," De Soulis said. "At Roxburgh, I saw the list of Scots fallen and taken prisoner at Methven. Your wife's brothers were captured, and will be ran-somed. The Lindsays of Elladoune were listed in the notice sent to the guardians of the realm of Scotland. The other two are in my custody at Dalbrae. We took them when we took the girl."

"Other two?" Gawain frowned, realizing that her mention of her brothers had omitted the full truth about them—another sign of her distrust. Now he would have to tell her that two of them had been taken, a task he did not relish. He assumed that the two held at Dalbrae were rebels as well. "Where are the brothers who were taken at Methven?"

"I do not know." De Soulis slid Gawain a quick look. "Let me give you some advice. Do you hope to hold Elladoune and eventually claim it as the lady's husband?"

"I admit it has occurred to me," Gawain said cautiously.

"Refuse to pay the ransom. Her brothers will be executed."

"Jesu," Gawain burst out. "You are a cold man!"

"I am practical. They are proven rebels, and may never be released or even ransomed. Their kin cannot pay. You are their brother by law, so you can refuse to pay the ransom. Once their sister pledges to Edward, Elladoune can be reinstated to her family. And with her elder brothers gone, she could be named heiress. Therefore, the property would be yours."

"That scheme stinks of dishonor," Gawain snapped. "What of the younger Lindsay brothers?"

"Young scoundrels," De Soulis said. "Rebels in the making."

Gawain frowned, wondering what those two had done. He was about to ask when he saw De Soulis take a small parchment packet from his pocket and empty it into the foaming ale.

"What the devil is that?" Gawain asked, distracted.

"A potion. She will sleep on the journey. We will of course have to carry her in the supply cart, as before."

"A sleeping draught?" Gawain demanded. "Have you given her that before?"

"I dosed her with this a few times since we first took her out of Scotland. The herbal mixture quiets her, without harming her. She has been far more docile with it than without it. Surely you have noticed the difference in her mood."

Gawain narrowed his eyes. "I thought she was drugged at the king's feast, but I did not realize she had anything after that."

"On the way out of Newcastle, I gave her some in wine." De Soulis shrugged as if it was unimportant. "'Tis poppy and a few herbs. Give this to her now, and she will sleep or sit nicely until it wears off. You will be glad of it, I assure you. She can

be wild without it, as you may have discovered. Mayhap you
will want to continue the remedy once you have her at Elladoune."

"You have no reason to give that to her," Gawain ground
out. He suddenly remembered Juliana's plea to him at Avenel,
that she feared De Soulis would kill her someday. Surely this
was why. His breath increased with fury as he glared at the
sheriff.

"You are too soft with her. She is a rebel. If you want to present a loyal, obedient wife to the king, you must take a stern
hand with her now, or she will overtake you entirely."

"Kindness fares better than harshness with wild creatures."

"Such creatures take advantage of kindness, which they
sense as weakness. She has a volatile female temperament and
must learn her limits. Had you seen her in Scotland the day she
was taken, you would understand my actions."

"She fought you." Gawain did not need to be told. He
watched the man through a flat glare.

"Tooth and nail. She struggled so that I had to stop along the
way and ask a wisewoman's advice—she was the one who
gave me this mixture. That girl is like a bird, impulsive and
simpleminded. She would fly away in an instant."

"You found the chains and potions necessary, then."

"Aye. We tied her securely and gave her the medicines. The
king ordered the golden chains made up for her in Newcastle—
he liked that tiresome conceit about the Swan Maiden. Those
chains are more valuable than the girl. Why do you think we
have a full military guard for one Scotswoman?"

"Ah. She wears an earl's fortune around her neck," Gawain
drawled. "How foolish of me to overlook that."

"If she escapes, we lose part of the treasury for the Scottish
campaign." As he spoke, the sheriff stirred the ale with his finger and offered it to Gawain. "Take this to her. You will be
pleased by the result."

Gawain lost his hold over his anger then. Snatching De
Soulis's surcoat, he yanked him forward. The ale sloshed over
both of them. He could smell its bitterness.

"Are you ten fools in one?" he ground out. "A coward en-
cased in black armor? Are you are so frightened of a girl that

you must poison her to control her?" He let go without warning, so that De Soulis stumbled and spilled the rest of the ale.

"You exaggerate this—I mean her no harm."

"If that potion had harmed her," Gawain growled, "your life would have been mine."

Turning, he stalked toward the door and yanked it open, striding across the yard. He heard De Soulis follow. Laurie hastened toward him.

"We are leaving now—on our own," Gawain said. Laurie cast a grim look at De Soulis and turned to mount his horse.

Reaching Juliana, Gawain handed the bundled bread and cheese up to her. "My apologies, lady," he said. "There is no ale. We will stop for water from a clean stream."

He took the key out of his pouch and quickly unlocked her collar, sliding it off and unlatching the manacles, piling the whole glittering mass in his hands. Juliana widened her eyes.

"Avenel!" De Soulis yelled, coming up behind him.

Gawain spun. "You had better keep these. They are worth a king's ransom." He dumped them in de Soulis's hands. "I am sore tempted to wrap them around your neck. The lady is in my safekeeping as of this moment."

"If you take her, I will report it—and you will be wearing these chains! No doubt you are aware that nobles enjoy the privilege of hanging on golden chains!"

"I simply obey my own orders, as you did yours. We are in Scotland now, so she is in my keeping. I will ride out with her now. Sir Laurence will accompany us. You can send the men to Elladoune later." He turned to Juliana. "We must keep to a tough pace," he told her. "Are you up to it?"

She nodded and took up the reins. He stepped aside and mounted his own horse, turning to see that Laurie was waiting.

"You will not survive your treacherous action this time, Avenel," De Soulis said. "The king will not show you lenience again—no matter who your family is."

Gawain almost laughed as he imagined De Soulis learning his true Highland origins. "If King Edward, the Flower of Chivalry, condemns a man for defending his wife, he is not the worthy knight and leader he once was."

"I will send a report to him by messenger before I leave this inn," De Soulis growled.

Gawain inclined his head to acknowledge the threat. He picked up his reins and glanced at Juliana. She sat alert and ready, back straight. He blessed her for it.

He urged the bay to a canter and left the yard, Juliana and Laurie following. They thundered along the road and left the inn far behind without being pursued, and Gawain relaxed slightly.

Soon enough, he recognized the air as distinctly Scottish—brisk, clean, scented with peat and heather. Riding past hills and streams, he felt the magic of Scotland more keenly than ever. His anger began to clear like fog in sunlight.

He wondered what the devil had possessed him, once again, to risk so much to defend Juliana. The girl did not even seem to like him, marriage or none. But he knew the answer.

He loved her. It must have begun years ago, on the night he had saved her, the night he had bound himself to her with a secret—the Swan Maiden and Swan Knight. Now the bond had looped out into time and caught him fast in its net.

Tucking the revelation away with the rest of his secrets, he rode onward.

Chapter 18

The air held the soft promise of rain. Juliana felt the damp breeze caress her bare throat and wrists. She closed her eyes briefly, reveling in freedom. Hungrily, she pulled in deep breaths of Scottish air.

Although they had left De Soulis's escort, she still maintained her silence. Only Gawain had heard her speak, and she felt certain that he would keep that secret. Not knowing his friend well enough to trust him, she stayed quiet.

She drew silence around herself like a cloak, a passive defense. Constant silence, she found, was meditative and protective in the midst of uncertainty. She took peace from it like water from a stream.

She glanced often at Gawain as they rode at a steady pace. As if she had spoken aloud, he seemed to understand her silences, and responded whenever she wanted to go slower, or needed to rest or to refresh herself.

The warmth he had shown her at Avenel had cooled. She missed that easy affection—but Avenel had been a dream, and they were all awake now.

She found his subtle expressions and moods readable, as if she knew him well. Sometimes his dark handsomeness had a hard, compelling edge, when sharpened by anger and impatience. At other moments he seemed more angelic, even boyish, laughing with Laurie or glancing around quickly for her reaction.

Always, though, she saw in him an awareness and concern for others, like a golden thread in all he did. She marveled at it. If his king had been half as decent as this one knight, she thought, Scotland would have no war and no tyrant.

As she rode on, she succumbed further to the charm of brown eyes framed in thick black lashes, to his tilted smile, to the low timbre of his voice, as if—

Her breath caught. As if she were in love. *This is not the way,* she told herself sternly, *that a captive regards a captor, that one enemy studies another.*

Yet it is the way, a gentle voice in her head answered, *that a woman looks at the man she desires. It is the way a wife regards her beloved husband: admiring, fascinated, loving.*

Sighing, wondering if it was so, she rode on.

The three horses spread out, spacing one behind another, to follow a narrow drover's track up a long, steep hill. The wind blew harder as they rose higher. Gawain slowed the bay to ride beside Juliana, while Laurie rode ahead, out of hearing.

"I must speak to you," Gawain said. "De Soulis told me news of your brothers."

"Alec and Iain?" She spoke quickly.

"The two with Robert Bruce."

"Niall and Will. Are they—?" Her eyes showed true alarm.

"They live," he assured her, and heard her sigh in relief. "They were taken at Methven, and may be ransomed for return."

"Where are they kept?"

"I only know that they were listed as prisoners on the roll sent to the guardians of the realm of Scotland."

She nodded. When she lifted her head to gaze at the purple mountains that rose above the moorland, he saw the gleam of tears in her eyes. One tear slipped down, and another, and his heart turned with the sight. He could not bear it.

"My kin and I canna pay a ransom," she said.

"Juliana, I will make no guarantee," he said carefully. "But I will inquire about them, and see what can be done."

A fat tear slid down her cheek as she nodded mute thanks.

"What of the other two?" he asked. "You did not tell me of them, nor that they are in De Soulis's custody—he told me himself."

"I assumed you wouldna help them. They would be rebels too, if they had the chance. And if my elder brothers are released, they will fight the English again. 'Twould be unwise for you to help the Lindsay brothers. Your king would be much displeased. You shouldna risk his wrath for the sake of some young lads."

"I have a heart," he snapped. "Though you think I do not."

"I think you do," she said quietly. " 'Tis what frightens me most." Clucking to the palfrey, she passed him.

He watched her go, and blew out a long breath in frustration. Spurring Gringolet, he surged up the hill past the palfrey and struck out over the drover's track to catch up to Laurie. At least, he thought, he need wrestle no challenges from that quarter.

"What do you think your wee Scots swan wants of you?" Laurie asked Gawain almost as soon as he caught up to him.

He shrugged. "To be free," he answered. "To go home. She wants naught more from me, I can tell you that." He scowled.

"Nay? I notice that while she may be cool as ice, there is a true fire in her eyes for you. And a fire in your own, for her. It just makes me curious. I have seen you besotted, but never like this." Laurie gave him a quick, appraising glance.

"I am not besotted," Gawain ground out. "Nor is she." He was tempted to ride far ahead for a while, where no one would speak to him. He needed silence, as did Juliana again—she now lagged far behind, he saw, as he glanced quickly at her.

"Are you sure she doesna want wee English babes with you? Sweet dark-eyed Avenel bairnies, who will grow up privileged at court, marry well, and own land on both sides of the border?"

Gawain slid him a long look. "I assure you, she does not want that," he said firmly.

"So what do you want? I am just curious," Laurie said, smiling mildly. "I am a wondering sort of man."

To find Glenshie, Gawain wanted to say; to find my home, and learn the truth—about many things. But he would not tell even Laurie, not yet. He frowned as he guided his horse along the ridge of the hill, its slopes thick with early heather blooms.

Overhead, a flock of ducks arrowed through the sky. He glanced up. "I want to be free as well," he answered. "Free of this infernal questioning."

Laurie grinned fleetingly. "What else to do on a long journey but talk, eh?"

"And free of this ridiculous task that the king has set for me.

The real question is what the king wants. We may pay dearly for leaving De Soulis's company."

"Why should we? No one stole the king's golden chains. Well, if you must prepare another apology, I will help you pen it. I have a knack for words."

"I am done begging for king's peace."

" 'Tis obvious to everyone—except the Master of Swans—that you acted within your rights as a husband in taking her away from De Soulis. He was mistreating her. She will still be in English custody at Elladoune, so there is no harm done."

"If I am lucky," Gawain muttered.

Laurie drew a breath and looked around. "My God, Scotland is a beautiful land. I seem to forget that when I am away."

And I have never forgotten, Gawain thought, *not for a moment*. But he kept it to himself.

Patting her horse's neck, Juliana let Galienne stay back. Ahead, Gawain and Laurence Kirkpatrick traveled side by side: one dark, lean, and quiet, the other broad, his laughter rippling, his gestures wide and free.

Rain clouds hovered above as they moved north. Juliana looked around with rapture, as if she saw Scotland for the first time—beautiful, wild, exuberant, and vivid. As they left the rolling Lowlands and moved into the rumpled, heathered skirt of the Highland hills, she regretted her silence, for she could not share her joy in her surroundings so easily.

The horses slowed as they climbed hills thick with heather and yellow gorse and green ferns, past walls of dark rock where bright flowers danced in crevices. Hawks called in high flight, sheep moved like tiny clouds over distant slopes, and red deer skimmed the crests of the hills.

She lifted her face to the cool, clean wind and breathed Scotland into her lungs and her soul.

When the sun sank and the sky turned lavender, Juliana recognized the shape of the hills and knew that she was near home at last. She sat straighter, felt brighter despite fatigue. The wind touched her like a friend.

They rode past Highland herders in belted plaids and shirts, urging their sheep along the slopes as the enemy rode past;

elsewhere, they saw women in plaid shawls, with bare feet beneath simple gowns, watching them with wary eyes. Several bare-legged, pink-cheeked, curious children made her think of her younger brothers. She had not seen Alec and Iain in so long that her heart ached with need, as if she were their own mother separated from them.

Soon, she told herself. *Soon, soon.*

She urged her horse forward and soon caught up to Gawain and Laurence. Gawain glanced back at her and smiled briefly.

"Now that an English escort has been seen riding north, word will spread that we are here," Laurence remarked to Gawain.

Juliana listened with interest whenever the Lowland Scot spoke, for she liked his mellow voice and easy manner. He intrigued and puzzled her. She had already learned that he was a boyhood friend of Gawain's, and was a Scotsman who sided openly with the English.

"Aye, they will spread the word," Gawain agreed, "and since we have a Scotswoman in our company, hopefully we will have no trouble from the locals."

"Unless they think to rescue her from the enemy," Laurence remarked, glancing at Juliana.

"'Tis possible. We are close enough to Elladoune now that some of these people may recognize her." Gawain and Laurence glanced up as two children ran like young deer and disappeared over a hill. Juliana watched them go, too.

"No doubt they carry word that the Swan Maiden of Elladoune is on her way home." Gawain turned to glance at her.

"You know the area well to know where we are," Laurie said.

"I rode through these hills long ago," Gawain answered. "I have never forgotten the way." He sounded thoughtful.

Juliana frowned. Although he was an English knight, he sounded almost like he was a man glad to be in Scotland again.

"Well, at least we are close to Elladoune," Laurence said. "God gave me a lazy nature. Journeying is not for me. A seat by the hearth, a cup of ale, a soft bed—give me those night after night and I am content. That is, if a decent bed and decent ale can be had at this castle," he added wryly.

"We shall find out," Gawain said. "We will cross a narrow pass between those two hills"—he pointed—"and enter a forest, if I remember properly. The woodlands are considerable in this part of the Highlands, but there have been king's troops in this area for years. The paths should be well marked. Is it so, my lady?" His dark gaze swept hers briefly.

She did not answer. Perhaps, she told herself sourly, like Laurence, he thought only of cup and hearth and bed as well—and knew immediately that would not be true of him.

Bed, she thought next, and frowned. What would happen when they reached Elladoune? Would Gawain expect her to behave as his wife, once there? She shivered inwardly, deliciously, at the thought of deep kisses at Avenel—and then admonished herself to stop. Too much was unknown and uncertain in this situation.

"We will ride northwest for a while," Gawain told Laurence. "Then the forest will open into a glen with a lake called Loch nan Eala. In the Gaelic, that means—"

"Loch o' the Swans," Laurence translated. "I have Gaelic from childhood, man, as you do—my nurse was a Highlander like yours, if you recall."

Juliana listened, fascinated. Gawain's nurse had been Highland, and he knew some Gaelic? He had never mentioned it to her. She wondered why that had been allowed for an Avenel son.

"The abbey of Inchfillan, I am told, is at one end of the loch, and Elladoune Castle lies at the other. Lady Juliana?" He looked at her again. "Is it so?"

She nodded.

"If we go astray, mayhap the lass will speak to us long enough to set us on the right path," Laurence said. He turned to smile at her, his eyes sparkling blue. "I hoped she would speak to me at least, since I am a Scotsman born and bred."

Juliana lifted her chin haughtily to show him what she thought of Scotsmen who rode with English.

Once inside the forest on the muffled path, she recognized the track and urged her horse ahead. Gawain and Laurence caught up, each beside her. She peered into the green-shadowed trees, and at the high canopy overhead.

The greenwood held far more than an abundance of flora and fauna, she knew. Men, women, and children lived in the forest and in caves in the glen, forced out of their homes by the English. Most of them were friends and rebels, some officially outlawed by the English. All of them were honest men and women, renegades by necessity, dispossessed by King Edward's army.

Riding beside Gawain now, she fervently hoped that the forest rebels would let them pass without incident. Any party of king's men would be noted, she knew, and one with her in it would definitely be followed. If the foresters tried to rescue her, a deadly skirmish might be the result.

Gawain placed a hand on the hilt of his sword as if he sensed the watchers. The horses filed along the forest track, while birds called repeatedly in the trees.

Some of those calls were human-made. Juliana's heart pounded as the horses slowed over a narrow stretch of the path where the trees arched overhead. She glimpsed movement, limber and quick, high up in the trees, and she saw a steely flash through the leafy cover. An owl sounded somewhere.

They were here for certain, with weapons to hand. Red Angus's owl call often preceded an attack. She had to prevent a confrontation. Desperately she looked around.

She thought of a quick way to signal that she was safe. When she heard further rustling, and more bird calls, she reached out to grasp Gawain's arm. He looked at her, startled. She leaned toward him, smiling.

"Lady?" Gawain slowed his horse with hers. "What is it?"

He looked at her, clearly puzzled, riding so close that his thigh grazed hers.

She stretched toward him and kissed him on the mouth. He responded fast and sure, his lips moving on hers, though she knew he was surprised. When she drew back, he cocked a brow.

"My sisters," he drawled, "are nowhere near, I assure you."

Behind them, Laurence laughed softly, for he had been told about the twins' antics at Avenel.

A blush heated her cheeks. However ill-done or hasty, that kiss was the quickest way to show that she was safe, though she rode with an English escort. Gawain had saved her often enough, she thought. She owed him at least one rescue.

He lifted her hand to his lips, startling Juliana in turn. "Are you so glad to be home, lady, that you kiss your new husband for joy?" He spoke loudly enough to be heard within the trees.

Angling a glance at him, she wanted to answer tartly that she had just saved his life.

"I suspect," he went on quietly, "that strange birds and some rather large squirrels are watching us. If they see a happy bride, they may leave us in peace." He let go of her hand.

With one hand easy on the reins and the other wary on his sword hilt, he pulled ahead, his eyes scanning the trees. The party advanced along the forest track, and the rustling in the trees grew quieter.

The forest opened onto a meadow in a golden wash of sun. Juliana urged the palfrey toward a stream that flowed to join Loch nan Eala. Juliana could see the sparkling surface of the loch not far away.

The silhouette of Inchfillan Abbey was visible above the treetops. She urged her horse across the shallows, sparing no glance for her two escorts behind her.

She was nearly home.

"At the pace she is flying along that bank, your wee swan will disappear," Laurie said. "If we lose her, the king will definitely be in a temper."

"Let her fly," Gawain answered. He watched Juliana as she galloped, her blue cloak flying out, her white dress rucking up over her slim legs. "We will not lose her. Let her go home," he added to himself.

He could still taste that sweet, surprising kiss. She was as unpredictable as the wind, and he savored her spontaneity. And he very much suspected that she had saved him and Laurie from an attack by rebels. She must know them well to know what was imminent; that realization made him frown thoughtfully.

"Hopefully that place ahead is not her home." Laurie pointed toward a cluster of stone-walled houses as they rode past. Juliana had galloped past the place with scarcely a glance, but the escort party slowed.

Gawain frowned as he and Laurie drew closer. Several buildings of thatch and stone, and a few of wattle and daub, were arranged along a long earthen lane. The village was deserted, its shared field beyond the last house unplanted and bare, its street overgrown with grasses and weeds.

The houses were fire-damaged and skeletal, thatched roofs missing, walls crumbling. The field had been plowed into distinct rows, but had gone bleak and wild, with a broken plow leaning at its heart. Not a soul, human or animal, stirred among the ruined houses or field. Ghosts might walk here, he thought, but no one else.

"What happened here? I wonder," Laurie mused, walking his horse slowly beside Gawain. "This place has seen some disaster."

"I would wager that whatever befell these people was brought on by the English, and quite a while ago."

"Where are the cottars? Those houses look empty. There has been no attempt to rebuild, either."

"Walter de Soulis did not mention this place when he told me about Elladoune," Gawain said. "If the garrison was the cause of this, I should have been told of it."

"If Elladoune's knights attacked this place, 'twould explain why we were watched so closely along the forest path back there."

Gawain glanced sharply at Laurie. "You sensed it too?"

"Aye. I was sure we would be attacked any moment. But your lady broke the tension with that charming kiss. Lucky man." Laurie grinned briefly.

"There must be a host of dispossessed families in the forest, judging by the size of that deserted clachan," Gawain said. "'Tis a problem in Scotland. The last garrison I was with encountered a stubborn faction of homeless renegades."

"Ah," Laurence said. "The very ones you joined." He gave Gawain a curious glance. "'Tis a tale I want to hear in full from you, since I have heard bits of it only. There are many rumors about what you did."

"I am sure there are. And I want to know why you are still in the king's army when you swore you would sail to France."

"Land and title are temptations, my friend, available in France as well as England," Laurie said. "But the ale, ah, Scottish ale. I would miss that too much."

Laurie grinned, but Gawain narrowed his eyes. He sensed another layer to Laurie, one that went deeper than a taste for comforts. He wondered if his Lowland friend was as conflicted in this war as he was himself, yet had not admitted it.

"Ho, look there! She's riding to that place—a monastery?"

"The abbey of Inchfillan," Gawain answered. "Augustinian."

"Ah," Laurie said, nodding approval. "Brethren with a practical bent. Nae recluses, but likely nae overblessed with coin, either, in this part of Scotland. Though that church and cloister are quite fine."

Gawain watched Juliana ride toward the foregate of the small stone-walled compound. Beyond the high wall, he saw the roofs of several buildings. The stone church that faced the meadow had a high west entrance tower; its smaller bell tower, above the nave, looked partly ruined by fire.

Juliana tugged on a bell rope, and the iron gate swung open. She entered, dismounting quickly, handing the palfrey's reins to a black-cassocked monk.

As Gawain rode with Laurie across the meadow, he watched Juliana embrace an older man and turn to greet other monks with hand clasps or quick hugs, as if she were indeed home instead of visiting a religious house. Their joy in her return, and her own, was obvious even from a distance. They were her family, he realized.

As he neared the gate and noticed the other inhabitants of the yard, he reined in. Laurie followed suit.

Swans filled the abbey yard, more than a dozen in various sizes. They meandered and waddled between the gate and the group of monks that surrounded Juliana. The largest of the swans—and there were several impressive creatures—turned. With great wings outstretched and necks extended, hissing loudly, they rushed toward the two horsemen entering the gate.

Gawain controlled Gringolet, who snorted and bucked. The

yard seemed filled with a veritable sea of white-feathered, irritated birds. He calmed his mount and looked over at Juliana. Standing in her white gown amid the dark-robed monks, head high on her long, slim neck, she looked like an enchanted swan herself. He stared at her in astonishment.

"Strange watchdogs," Laurie remarked. "I think I will stay right here. Those beasties bite, did you know?"

Chapter 19

"The wee lads are well," Abbot Malcolm answered as he wrapped Juliana in a hug. As soon as she had seen Malcolm hurrying across the yard, she asked about her brothers, and blurted out that she was married to a Sassenach. Despite his shocked expression, she insisted on hearing about Alec and Iain first. "They are still at Dalbrae. I saw them there last week."

"Pray God they are treated fairly and not imprisoned," she said in Gaelic. She glanced through the gate at the two knights, who had not yet ridden into the enclosure.

"The lads have some freedom there," Malcolm assured her. "I saw them recently. They are fine, though anxious to come home. Juliana, there is news of Niall and Will."

"I heard," she said. "Taken."

He nodded sadly. "And we cannot buy their release. Our abbey is poor. Even if we had the coin, the Church would not allow us to pay a war ransom with it."

"There may be another way. My husband"—the word felt odd, yet surprisingly right somehow—"may be able to help them."

"No more delays. Tell me about this marriage."

"*Ach*, Father Abbot," she said, sighing. "It happened so fast." While she spoke, Malcolm walked with her toward the foregate, his tunic and her white gown sweeping the grasses.

The swans circled around them, clapping their beaks and extending their necks, looking for food and attention. The birds frequented the abbey yard almost daily, waddling up from the lochside and through the open foregate. Juliana noticed that one of the monks in the yard produced a cloth sack and began to toss out bits of grain, attracting the swans toward him.

Succinctly and selectively, Juliana recounted her weeks as a prisoner. Malcolm listened, brow knitted with concern. She spoke of the king's feast and the impromptu wedding, then touched upon the return journey, where she had been displayed and chained as the Swan Maiden. Finally she mentioned her warm welcome at Avenel. She kept the nights, and the kisses, to herself, but her cheeks burned as she remembered.

"Father Abbot," she finished, "Gawain was with the men who ruined Elladoune. He is the one who saved me that night."

"Your Swan Knight himself? *Ach,* God loves irony." He shook his head. "The marriage need not stand if you do not want it. We can annul it, though we must first petition the bishop's replacement in Glasgow and wait for an answer from Rome."

Her heart seemed to twist in protest. "My husband did not want this marriage or this assignment in Scotland, but he has no choice. He must obey the king's orders. If the marriage is annulled, he will face dire consequences."

Malcolm peered at her. "You care about him."

She made a vague, noncommittal sound and shrugged.

"Juliana, are you . . . the man's wife truly now? Is it even possible to annul it? Certainly you can preserve the marriage if you want to do so," he said gently.

"I—I do not yet know what I want," she mumbled, and blushed hotly. Turning away, she looked around the abbey yard. Earlier she had noticed some damage to the bell tower of the church, and she looked there again.

"Father Abbot, what happened to the tower?" The upper stones of the tall projection were blackened and collapsed.

"There was a fire," Malcolm said. "No one was hurt, but the inside is gutted, and we will need to rebuild. Thank heaven no lives were lost. The tall entrance tower and the rest of the church is unharmed. And our old bronze bell, which Saint Fillan himself once rang out, is fine. But we must repair the tower before the market fair in a few weeks, since so many come to Inchfillan during that time."

She murmured agreement, and turned around as several swans surrounded them, followed by three of the brethren.

"Father Abbot." Juliana recognized Eonan, a young lay

monk. Lanky and dark-haired, he was a quiet, intelligent youth who had come to Inchfillan as a boy; his father, like Juliana's, had been killed by the English. Two elderly monks stood with him, their faces somber. "Father Abbot, if I may speak."

"You may, Brother Eonan," Malcolm said.

"We heard that Juliana Lindsay is married now," Eonan began, nodding respectfully to her. "Is it possible that her marriage will prove fortunate for . . . those people who wish to . . . to come to Elladoune?" Eonan spoke cautiously, glancing toward the gate.

"Ah, true," Malcolm said. "Juliana, you can help the cause, for you will already be inside Elladoune."

"I—" She paused, confused and uncertain.

"We will bring the news to those in the forest," Eonan said. "They will be glad that Juliana is safe, and they will want to start preparations again. Efforts ceased when you were taken, mistress," he added. "The sheriff's men have been searching the forest with a vengeance—even destroying parts of it."

"Juliana's marriage is a boon that could ensure our success." Malcolm spoke hurriedly in Gaelic, glancing toward the two knights who entered the yard. "De Soulis and his men suspect that there are rebels in the forests near here. They seem determined to find them. You can help them, Juliana."

"I—" She hesitated again, unable to refuse, yet unable to betray Gawain as they clearly expected her to do.

"For now, go with him to Elladoune," Malcolm said. "He is your husband, and that is not easily altered. We will talk, and plan, and proceed carefully, whatever we do. Did you keep your silence, my girl, while you were held?"

"I did, except with Gawain."

"Just as well. Which one is he? Introduce us."

The knights—or their horses—seemed reluctant to enter the compound. Juliana stood surrounded by a ring of swans and backed by a crescent of monks, and looked toward the knights.

Turning like a white wave, the swans hastened toward the newcomers. Laurie's horse backed away, while the bay danced and bucked. The swans hissed, wings lifted, and waddled aggressively forward. Gawain steadied his mount, and Laurie struggled with his sidestepping horse.

Then Gawain dismounted and walked forward, moving without hesitation through the feathery surf. Heads wavered on taut necks, but no swan attacked as he strode through their midst. They turned fluidly, weaving back and forth in his path as he approached Juliana and the monks.

A large female reached out to tap her beak on the leather pouch suspended from his belt. Gawain ignored the bird.

"Abbot Malcolm of Inchfillan?" he asked. "God give you good day. I am Sir Gawain Avenel, the new constable of El-ladoune—"

"Aye, and husband to Lady Juliana," Malcolm finished in English. He stood placidly in the center of a gaggle of swans, and Gawain seemed unbothered as well. "She has told me of your marriage. Welcome, Sir Gawain. We expected a new garrison leader, and we hoped that Juliana would be returned, but we didna reckon upon a wedding."

"Nor did we," Gawain said. He glanced at Juliana.

"We prayed daily, and entrusted Juliana's fate to heaven," Malcolm said. "God watched over her and kept her safe, but you are an unusual angel, I admit."

" 'Tis the way of heaven to be unpredictable," Gawain answered, still looking steadily at Juliana.

Malcolm tipped his head. "Do I know you, sir? Your face seems familiar to me."

Something quick and keen flickered in Gawain's eyes, and Juliana wondered at it. "We have never met, Father Abbot."

Malcolm shrugged, then clasped Gawain's hand briefly. "Let me welcome you and wish you good fortune in your marriage. May there be goodwill between us for all concerned."

"Indeed." Gawain sounded vaguely surprised. "My thanks."

Juliana stared at the abbot, amazed by his acceptance of Gawain. She assumed that his hearty welcome must be part of some new plan that the abbot no doubt was devising.

The swans fluttered and circled around them as they spoke. One of them pecked at Gawain's leather pouch again. Gawain did not flinch as he looked down.

"She means no threat," Malcolm assured him. "She is a greedy pen, and thinks your pouch holds food. The swans are fed in this yard every day, so that they are as tame as wild swans can be. They are accustomed to Juliana in particular."

"I see." Gawain stood calmly amid the birds. Juliana noticed that Laurie remained on his horse, looking distinctly anxious as he eyed the swans.

Gawain looked up. "You have had a fire."

"We have," Malcolm said. "We must rebuild."

"Have you applied to the sheriff for timbers? King Edward maintains a policy of support for the local churches."

"We will send word of our need to the sheriff. I hear he hasna yet returned from his southern journey."

Gawain turned again, as they all did, at a sudden commotion. The largest cob had spread his wings and was charging the two horses, causing them to whicker and buck again.

"Cùchulainn! Stop, you!" Malcolm called. "Brother Eonan, stop that cob!" Eonan ran to wave the swan away from the horses.

Malcolm turned back to Gawain. "Sir," he said, "do you know that the sheriff holds my wards, Juliana's younger brothers, hostage at Dalbrae?"

"I recently learned of that."

"We want them released. Will you see to it? They are good lads and shouldna be held. Her older brothers have recently been taken as well, kept elsewhere by the English."

"I will look into both matters. But I can promise naught."

Malcolm studied him soberly. "Three years ago, after the burning of our local village, the brethren of Inchfillan came to an understanding with the garrison at Elladoune. We do God's work here and tend to our flock of souls, and they in turn leave us in peace. 'Tis a truce without signatures."

"I will respect that agreement," Gawain said. "I do not yet know all my duties at Elladoune, but I do not war on monks and innocents. Inchfillan will stand safe so long as I am there."

Malcolm bowed his head in gratitude. "You seem an honorable man, though a Sassenach. We will talk soon. Juliana, my dear, God keep you safe." He pressed her hands in his. "Come back when you are rested. Go with him," he added, whispering. "I think you should."

"My lady," Gawain murmured. "We must travel on to the castle. The horses—and Laurie—seem eager to be gone."

She bit her lip. The moment to depart Inchfillan, and all that was familiar to her, had come too soon. She had always longed to return to Elladoune, but now she felt as if it was not her home after all. She hesitated.

Gawain tipped his head and held out his hand. "Juliana?"

She glanced at Malcolm, then at Gawain. She hardly knew her husband. A few nights together, some days on the road—despite his courtesies and the dilemmas weathered between them, she did not yet fully trust him.

Yet she remembered precious hours wrapped in the wondrous privacy of a bed, where trust and affection—and more—had existed between them. She wanted that concordance with him again. Going with him to Elladoune was the greatest risk she had ever faced.

Gawain was her path to Elladoune, to home. Unbidden, she wondered if he was the pathway to even more—to a home for her heart.

"Juliana," Gawain murmured.

She glided silently past him through the froth of swans and walked toward the gate.

Chapter 20

The slope leading to the castle gate was familiar, although she had not traveled its worn track for years. The steep hill that supported Elladoune was a promontory of slate that jutted into the water. High on its flat summit overlooking the loch, the castle, built from honey-colored stone, soared upward.

Juliana smiled to herself, excited as a child, despite her exhaustion. She looked up as they approached.

The gate stood open, its iron portcullis drawn up into the overhead arch, for Malcolm had sent Brother Eonan running ahead to bring word of their arrival. The rounded corner towers were massive sentinels pierced by arrow slits.

Gawain slowed his horse beside hers as they wended their way up the hill. "I was not certain you would come with me, once we were at Inchfillan," he said.

"I had to come home to Elladoune," she answered.

He nodded, and looked up. " 'Tis not a large castle, by the breadth of those walls, but looks to be a strong one, and built well—two generations ago, I would guess by its design."

"My great-grandfather rebuilt an older fortress. There have been keeps here for generations. We call it *Dùn nan Eala* in the Gaelic, though in my father's time it became known as Elladoune—easier for the English to say," she added, frowning.

"Fortress of the swans," he murmured.

She glanced at him. "You know what it means?"

"I have a little Gaelic," he said, and then rode ahead on the sloping track.

She was the last to ride beneath the portcullis, following

slowly to absorb the sight. The last time she had been here, Elladoune had been in flames, and she had taken a terrifying leap
into the loch—where she had first met Gawain.

The shape of the castle was a square pulled askew, with
round towers at each corner and a fifth one over the gate. The
tower in the farthest corner, pulled out beyond the others, overlooked the loch. Its outermost wall sheered down to meet the
promontory just above the water. As the largest and best protected of the towers, it served as the laird's keep.

Inside the courtyard, she saw Brother Eonan and a few lay
brothers and monks whom she recognized from Inchfillan.
Two carried buckets and sacks, and another shooed a few
goats and chickens out of the way of the incoming horses. A
monk pushed a wheelbarrow toward the large, lush kitchen
garden.

The garden was larger than she remembered, and the kitchen
building had been enlarged by an addition. More food would
have been required to feed a full garrison of a hundred or more
men, she realized.

Other changes, too, were evident. New buildings clustered
inside the high curtain wall, structures of wattle and thatch.
Those, she saw at a glance, were used for stables and livestock,
for blacksmithing and armory, and for cooking, washing, storage, and garrison quarters. They were quiet and empty.

Elladoune was different, yet the same. Memories from her
childhood assailed her even before she dismounted. The castle
was deeply familiar, yet was no longer her home. War was con-
ducted here; enemy soldiers had lived here.

The signs of that were everywhere. Weapons and harnesses dangled in the enlarged blacksmith's building; the stables had more stalls, with room for dozens of horses; rocks
for use in catapults were stacked against the wall, and a huge
grinding stone for sharpening weaponry stood inside an open
shed.

She slid from her horse and stood looking around. A monk
led her palfrey away, and Gawain dismounted to speak with
Laurence. Then he came back and took her arm.

"Come inside," he said, and led her toward the corner keep.
Her legs trembled as she climbed the wooden steps to the

main entrance of the keep tower. He opened the door, but she paused on the upper platform, turning to survey the bailey yard.

"Is it much changed?" he asked after a moment.

"Aye," she said. "And nay." She sighed. "Some things I dinna recognize—and some seem so familiar."

"What is the same?"

She was surprised that he would want to know. "There," she said, pointing toward the east battlement. "On those stone steps, there is a long crack where I tripped when I was seven and broke my arm. My father had the step repaired, but it kept opening again. I see it still."

"Then the stone should be replaced," he said.

"There, in that tower"—she pointed again—"my older brothers and I played hide-and-seek, and took turns watching the loch for water monsters."

He smiled. "A serious task. What else?"

She was grateful that he let her share her memories, which were precious testaments to her childhood and her past. "Down there," she continued, "on the south side of the bailey, we ran races and played ball, and set up targets for archery. There, in that corner shed, where hay was stored, my brother Niall shot an arrow into my leg as I was climbing the loft. He said the shaft was warped, and that he was aiming for the apple in Will's hand."

Gawain whistled low, shaking his head.

"Over there, my father kept a mews for his falcons and hawks, and I was allowed to raise a small kestrel myself. The mews must be empty now—the door hangs from the hinges. In that corner beside the stable, we buried our favorite pets after they died—do you see the wee stones? I still remember the names carved upon them."

He nodded soberly. "I see them."

"Here in the tower"—she turned to indicate the doorway behind them—"was where we lived. My brothers and I were born here, and my father, and grandfather, and kin for many generations before that."

He glanced up. "What is that above the door? A stone plaque

with a design cut in it—a swan with lifted wings, and an arrow in its beak? 'Tis worn some."

"Aye," she said. " 'Tis the crest of Lindsay of Elladoune."

"This was indeed a home," he said to himself.

"And now 'tis a place for warmongers," she said bitterly. "You didna ask what is different, only what is the same."

"What has changed, then?" he asked quietly.

"More buildings," she said. "More dirt than should be tolerated—the bailey has no grass left, worn to earth by horses and carts. That midden pile behind the kitchen shed is huge and needs tending. There are harnesses hanging outside the sheds, and weaponry, and . . ." She stopped and sighed dismally as she looked at the curtain wall.

"And traces of the fire?" he murmured.

"Aye. The blackened stone along the curtain walls has never been cleaned fully. And a section of stone, high up in this tower, is of a different color. That part has been replaced."

He glanced up. "The tower was nearly gutted afterward. Much rebuilding was done, I heard."

"Were you here then, after . . . after you helped me?"

"Not here. I was sent elsewhere in Scotland."

"Ah, you had to make your apology." She tilted her head to study him. "Your first apology. I want to know more about you," she murmured thoughtfully. "And about your transgressions. Why would a fine English knight risk his own welfare for Scots?"

He glanced at her. "Tell me your secrets, and you may learn some of mine."

Her heart pounded. She looked away quickly, regretting her impulsive tongue. If she pursued her keen curiosity about his secrets and his past, she would put hers to equal scrutiny—and that would endanger her friends. She could not ask any more about Gawain until he was ready to offer his story to her.

"You are fortunate I speak to you at all, Sassenach." She said it lightly, and he chuckled a little.

"Well," he said, "true. My lady, will you come inside?"

She turned and stepped past him through the doorway.

*   *   *

He followed Juliana across the narrow foyer and looked with her into the great hall, a large, plain chamber with whitewashed walls, a timber ceiling, and planked floor. Tables, benches, and a few chairs furnished it, but no colorful hangings or cushions warmed its starkness.

She said nothing, and turned away to go up the turning stairs. Gawain paused with her at each level to glance into the rooms that opened off the landings. They walked together through rooms that were sparsely furnished and obviously used as military quarters. Juliana made no comment, and climbed the stairs again.

The uppermost level was divided into a bedchamber, solar, and garderobe. Juliana stepped into the main room and turned, the bedraggled hem of her white gown pooling on the wooden floor.

" 'Tis all so different," she murmured. "I recognize little of it—the rooms or the furniture." She walked to the window. "Even the shape of this window has changed. The view is the same, over the loch to the mountains," she added softly.

Gawain surveyed the austere chamber. A bed filled one corner, enclosed by a green canopy and long curtain suspended from iron rods attached to the ceiling. The few pieces of furniture—a wooden chest, a table, stools, and a heavy chair beside the stone fireplace—were solid and unadorned. The floor still bore traces of swept-out rushes.

"Did you think 'twould be the same?" he asked. "Naught could have survived that fire, Juliana." He walked toward her.

"There were mural paintings on the walls in the rooms below this, where my parents slept," she said, staring out of the window. "They are whitewashed over. In the great hall, there were embroidered French tapestries on the walls that my mother was proud to own—gone, too. Likely burned," she added.

"Aye," he agreed. "It must have been a lovely home, but 'tis a garrison now—not cozy, but practical."

"This floor had four chambers—two for my brothers, one for me, one for servants. I . . . jumped from this window on the night of the fire. 'Twas a tall lancet then."

"I remember," he murmured. He saw a moist gleam in her

eyes as she looked out. A fierce need to touch her, hold her, welled in him. He doubted she wanted that from him, an English knight.

"I wanted to come back," she said. "I hoped one day my family would be reunited here. Foolish of me." She shrugged. "But I am home now, and I thank you for it. What next?"

"You need some rest. I need to find out about food and sleeping arrangements. We will have a garrison here soon, I think, from what De Soulis said. I suspect Laurie has already seen to himself."

"And what of you?" she asked.

"I am not overly tired. There is much to be done here."

"I mean—where will you sleep?" she half whispered.

He glanced at the bed curtained in green, and looked through the side door into the solar, which contained a bench in a wide window niche. A man could sleep there if he had to, he thought.

He sighed and leaned against the window frame, and thought of their nights together. Sweet secrets and unspoken truces. He wanted more of that with her. He hoped she did, too.

"Where do you want me to sleep?" he asked quietly.

She blushed. "Do we pretend the happy marriage here too?"

"Do you object?"

She shook her head. "Nay. But . . . 'twas necessary at Avenel. Here—here 'tis different. You are to tame me and make me loyal to your king, and show the Scots the proper direction for their own loyalties."

"Ah. Shall we begin, then?"

"The proper direction for the English," she said, as if reciting, "is to go south."

He laughed. "Ah, there is the Swan Maiden I know. 'Twas apprehension that subdued you today—not surrender."

She scowled. "I willna surrender, nor will I tame."

"I do not expect it of you," he murmured.

"Am I to be treated as a prisoner, or as a wife?"

"How would you be treated?"

"Courteously," she answered. "Without chaining."

"May I remind you that I no longer have the golden chains."

"De Soulis has those chains. If he insists that I am to be kept that way again, what will you do?"

"You are my wife, and in my safekeeping now. Do you think I will chain you?" He tilted his head. "Do you think that disobeying De Soulis would disturb my conscience?"

Her cheeks tinted rose as she shook her head. "But if I must act the constable's happy wife, then I want the privileges his lady would have—freedom to do what I like, and go where I choose. I am at home now, with no reason to run."

"You will have freedom, but you must cooperate. You may go anywhere between here and the abbey, and anywhere else within sight of Laurie."

"Cooperate with what?" she asked carefully.

"There is an oath of obedience and fealty to learn, so that you can say it nicely for the king."

"That," she said, folding her arms, "I canna do."

He inclined his head to acknowledge her stubbornness, but he would not give in to it. "The oath will be taken, sooner or later. Also, I must have your promise that you will always return to me at the end of the day."

Her eyes seemed to search his. "Aye," she whispered.

"One thing more—do not involve yourself with rebels."

"There are no rebels at Elladoune." Her eyes grew wide and ingenuous, startling blue in the light from the window.

She was good at ruses, he thought. "Do I have your promise in these matters?"

"What will you promise me in return?"

"To trust you."

She studied him. "I need a guarantee."

"So do I." He drew closer. "Shall we seal it?"

She nodded slowly. He rested his lips upon hers, soft as a butterfly alighting. When her body curved toward him, his heart knocked like a drum. "There," he said, " 'tis sealed."

She bit her lip and then slowly shook her head.

"What?" He almost laughed. "Not enough?"

She shook her head again, staring up at him.

He growled low and took her by the shoulders. As her head tipped back and her eyes closed, he kissed her profoundly, deeply, as he had wanted to do ever since he had woken beside her that morning in the heavenly quiet of Avenel.

Her hands rested on his waist. Desire poured through him. His mouth moving over hers satisfied only the edge of his hunger. He wanted to sweep her up and carry her to the curtained bed.

Heart pounding, he drew away. Her head stayed back, eyes still closed, simple ecstasy on her face. Her breasts were soft and firm against him. The sensation drove him closer to madness.

"Is that binding enough for you?" he asked hoarsely.

She nodded. "Better than chains." She sounded breathless.

"Some manacles," he said, cupping the side of her face, "are not made of gold or steel. Some chains are invisible, yet bind the heart firm."

"And what chains are those?" she whispered.

"If you do not know," he said, " 'tis no use to tell you."

She stared up at him and did not answer.

"My dear wife," he murmured, taking his hands from her face, "you are tired. And I have duties as a constable that I cannot neglect longer."

Striding from the room, he closed the door behind him. The coolness of the stairwell and his forceful step subdued the heated throbbing in his body. But nothing diminished the tug he felt as he walked across the yard, as if a golden cord spun out, linking him with the girl in the tower room.

Late that night, Gawain stood in the small solar and looked through the window. Entranced by the view—a sweep of lavender sky above dark mountains and the sparkling indigo loch—he stood unmoving and thoughtful, his foot resting on the stone bench.

In the room behind him, Juliana slept deeply, as she had for hours. Earlier he had brought her some fresh ale the monks had supplied, and something to eat—a burned oatcake proudly produced by Laurie. She scarcely roused enough to swallow a little watered ale before sliding back into sleep. He had not disturbed her since, although he had looked in on her a few times, touching her head gently before closing the curtain again.

Though the hour was late, he could not sleep. Laurie had claimed the largest chamber on the floor below, declaring it his privilege as the second in command at Elladoune. The monks had returned to Inchfillan Abbey, after explaining to Gawain and Laurie the features of the castle, and showing them its stores and livestock. Laurie had prepared supper from garden vegetables and salted venison, found in the storeroom.

Gawain wrinkled his nose at the thought of that thin and unsavory pottage. A cook would have to be found, he told himself; Laurie was willing, but not up to the task. He wondered if the abbot could lend some of his monks to work in the kitchen, or if Juliana could find a local goodwife to come to the castle.

In the advancing darkness, the swans floated on the loch, tiny, pale blurs. He remembered that they had been out there on the water the night Elladoune had burned. But of course they would still swim and nest here. Swans were creatures of habit. The fire and the garrison had not frightened them away.

He thought of the legend of another disaster, long ago: a terrible storm, brought on by magic, had destroyed an island fortress in this very loch. Hundreds of people had died here. According to the tale, they had transformed into swans.

He frowned, musing about the legend and remembering the first time he had heard the tale from his grandfather. The ruins of Glenshie were not far from Elladoune, he knew—but where?

Across the loch, mountain slopes thrust upward. He studied each shape, searching for a certain contour, an image that he remembered from childhood: an old woman's face in a mountainside.

As a boy, he had called it *Beinn an Aodann*—mountain of the face—imagining that a giantess lived there. He could not recall the local name. He stood for a long while, searching the profiles of the hills.

He was not trying to avoid going to his wife's bed. Sooner or later, he knew that he would go there. An implicit agreement had occurred between them, although he was not sure when or how. But he felt it with conviction in his heart. He suspected that she did too. Time—and gentleness—would tell.

The lure of the enclosed bed, with Juliana inside its sanctuary, was strong. She slept, and needed sleep, but he hoped that she would at least turn to welcome his arms. He wanted no more than that just now. Being here, so close to Glenshie and yet so far from it, he desperately craved solace for his soul.

The only place he could find that was alone with Juliana. Yet he lingered, searching the skyline for the giantess's face.

Wherever that was, he would find Glenshie.

Chapter 21

They came as they always had, gliding in toward the shore when she appeared, their graceful white bodies reflected in the rippling mirror of the water. Leisurely they swam toward her, without greeting or flurry, as if no time had passed.

As if she had not changed to the core of her soul since the last time she had stood here.

She tossed grain from a small sack and watched the swans feed. Their heads dipped, their bodies spun as they sought the offerings. Life was simple and direct for them, peace amid wildness. They accepted the food, just as they accepted her presence or her absence.

Only a few weeks had passed since she had last been here, but she had changed. She felt wiser, deeper, more aware of her need for peace, and home—and love. The doors of her life had opened, and Gawain had walked in, like a torch in the darkness. And nothing would ever be the same again.

She frowned to herself, remembering with an exquisite shiver how she had awakened in the middle of the night to find him asleep beside her. She lay beside him, savoring his warmth and the reassuring cadence of his breathing before she slept again.

She stepped toward the water, careful not to wet the hem of the mulberry gown that Gawain's mother had given her. Until she sent for her things at Inchfillan, she had only this or the white gown. Though the white satin held unpleasant memories, the mulberry serge was a comforting reminder of Avenel and the brief happiness she had felt there.

She looked over her shoulder at her chaperones. Laurie Kirkpatrick sat beneath a tree, while Brother Eonan sat nearby, pulling blades of grass as the two men talked. Each, now and then, glanced toward her. As usual, she kept a careful silence.

After awakening late that morning, she had breakfasted on some unappetizing oatcakes, which Laurie proudly claimed were of his own making. He then told her that Gawain had ridden out to Dalbrae to see the sheriff.

Exploring the castle more thoroughly after breakfast, she had noted further changes, and recalled more memories. Then she had gone to the loch with Laurie and Brother Eonan, who had come to the castle with some monks to tend the garden and the livestock.

The swans moved slowly in the water, and she walked along the bank, tossing grain to them, deep in her thoughts. Past a curve in the bank, she entered a little cove that was protected by a thick fringe of birches, out of sight of Laurie and Eonan.

Beyond the cove's outermost point, the loch narrowed like a waist, hardly wider than a river. Pine trees edged the opposite shore, fronting the dense forest where her rebel friends and kinsmen hid.

She felt a sudden urge to ignore her imposed boundaries and cross the loch to visit the forest rebels. Eonan might realize where she had gone, for he knew the rebels' hiding places as well as any of the monks. But he would not tell Laurie, she was sure.

Stripping out of her gown, she folded it and stuffed it under a fallen tree limb. Clad only in her linen chemise, she slipped into the water. Its coolness surrounded her as she sank down to her shoulders with a quiet sigh. She had always loved the sheer freedom of water.

The swans circled her, and she drew a breath and dove beneath them, surging far out in the water before surfacing for another breath. As she turned, arms treading, she saw that a few of the swans had glided out with her, forming a perfect shield.

On the shore, Laurie and Eonan sat with their backs to her. She took a breath and shot under the surface like an arrow, coming up for breath only twice more before reaching the shore.

Finding the familiar rock shelf below the water level, she grabbed it and pulled upward. Hidden by the low-hanging eaves of a huge pine, she climbed out, water sluicing from her.

This spot had long been a rendezvous. Sheltered beneath the swooping arms of the pine, she reached inside a fallen tree trunk and pulled out a canvas sack that she knew would be there.

As she expected, she found spare clothing: a bleached linen chemise, two tunics, a shirt, and soft boots. She pulled off her wet chemise and tucked it out of sight to dry, then dressed in the shirt, the serge tunic, and boots, which she had appropriated years ago from her brothers' belongings and kept here for her use. In the little cove, she kept a similar cache of belongings, including a white, feathered cape.

Within moments, she ran along a half-hidden track, her feet silent on a thick carpet of pine needles and bracken.

Struck to her soul, she stood in the entrance of the cave where the rebel families hid and looked out over the forest. She blinked against tears. A large portion had been laid waste by fire. Charred stumps of trees thrust upward, separated from the dense greenwood by a wide stream.

"What happened?" She turned to look at Red Angus and Lucas, who sat by the fire with some of the others. "While I was gone, what happened? Father Abbot mentioned nothing of this!"

"The sheriff's men rode here," Lucas answered curtly. He came forward, a short, dark, powerful man with anger etched in the folds of his face. "They suspect rebel activity in the forest, although Father Abbot has told them that only homeless innocents live here."

"The sheriff intends to eliminate any rebel threat in this area, so they are destroying the forest bit by bit," Red Angus said. He came forward from the fireside, too, so tall that he had to duck head and shoulders to stand with Juliana and Lucas. "Soon there will be nowhere to live. We have too many already living in these caves." He gestured toward the rocky hillside, split with a few narrow cave entrances.

"We will be forced to leave Glen Fillan entirely," Lucas growled. "De Soulis will persist until he destroys us all!"

"We have weapons and armor put by, and enough men to wield them," Juliana said. "We can fight back."

"Fight back, says you? The girl who will only lift her bow to stick a target?" Lucas asked.

"We cannot defeat De Soulis," Angus said. "That black armor of his is impenetrable. You know what they say of it. Not one of us will rise up against a man who practices the black arts!"

"He is just a king's man. Remember the stories said of me— there is no truth to them. I practice no magical arts. Why do you believe such rumors about him?"

"We have shot arrows at De Soulis from the treetops," Lucas said. "Every bolt bounces off his armor. He cannot be stopped. He bought it from the devil, they say."

She frowned. "Surely there is some way to stop him."

"He and his men will search the forests until every one of us is taken or killed. We have children and elderly to protect. Our only choice is to go elsewhere," Lucas replied.

"Juliana," an old woman said. She turned to see Beithag shuffle forward, her head and shoulders bowed beneath the plaid pulled over the crown of her head. "You can help us now."

"Mother Beithag, I doubt it, now. De Soulis does not believe in the ploy of the Swan Maiden," Juliana reminded her.

"But now you are wed to the garrison commander at El-ladoune," Beithag said. "Let our men into the fortress at night, so they can take it over, as we have planned so long."

"You can do that," Angus urged, nodding.

Juliana frowned, feeling pressured, resisting a scheme that weeks ago she had supported. But she could not see it through if it would compromise Gawain's well-being. Sighing heavily, she looked from one hopeful, dearly familiar face to the next.

"My husband would suffer for it," she said. "I . . . I cannot betray him."

"*Ach,*" Lucas muttered with disgust, turning away.

"Only let us in," Angus said. "We will do the rest. We have weapons and armor stored away—"

"Please do not ask this of me!"

Lucas scowled. "Before, you would have helped us!"

"Look at her face—leave her be," Beithag said. "She has feelings for her Sassenach husband. A wife should never betray her husband. Find some other way of taking the castle."

"Gawain Avenel has shown kindness to me, and so I cannot play him false," Juliana explained defensively. "That is all."

"*Ach,*" Lucas ground out again. "Now what? We have been kind to you too. Some of us are your kin. We have children here, a woman with child, others who need help and shelter. Will you turn your back on us?"

Anguish yanked at her. Angus's glance was sympathetic, but Lucas glowered; he would never let her be about this, she knew.

"Juliana," Angus said. "We men can fend for ourselves. Some of us want to join the rebel army, but we cannot leave our families like this. You can ask your husband to help us."

Lucas snorted. "Not him! He has already begun his campaign against us!"

Juliana frowned. "What do you mean?"

"My sons saw him this morning," Lucas said. "He was riding the paths and the hills. He stopped on his horse, and watched the forest and the hillsides, then rode on, and stopped elsewhere to do the same. My sons tracked him for a while."

"He is curious about the area," Juliana said, wanting to defend him, though she found herself wondering at his actions.

"No doubt he looks over the land to send word back to the sheriff. More of our forest home will be destroyed. More land will be trampled by Sassenachs."

"He might help us, if I asked him," she ventured. Lucas shook his head and growled his doubt.

"Listen to Juliana," another man said. Juliana turned to see Uilleam, Beithag's husband. Bent and grayed, he maintained a quiet but strong presence among the rebels. "If he cares for her as she seems to do for him, she could ask a favor of him, and he would grant it."

"What favor, husband?" Beithag asked.

"Ask him to go to the sheriff and demand that he stop the raids here, so that we can live in peace. This part of the forest is on Elladoune's property. He has a right to ask."

An idea blossomed in her mind. Juliana looked around at them. "All of you could live at Elladoune," she said. "There is no garrison there, and plenty of space."

They stared at her. Lucas lowered his brows. "Live under the same roof with Sassenachs?"

"Lucas, we could keep your family there, so you would be free to join Robert Bruce's army," Juliana said. "Angus, you could go with him. I will ask my husband to shelter those made homeless by the Sassenachs. But for now, I must get back, or my long absence will appear suspicious."

"Hah," Lucas muttered, "she has to slip away to come see us, but she is sure we will all be welcome at the castle! Girl, just let us into the castle by night. We will see to the rest."

"I cannot do that," she said. "But the women and children and old ones can find shelter at Elladoune." Surely Gawain, who had an innate kindness, would allow that. "He is an honorable man, my husband, for a Sassenach."

"Bah," Lucas said.

"Smitten," Beithag said, nodding to Uilleam.

"It is better than staying here," Angus said slowly.

"I will be back," Juliana said. "I must go, and hope that my chaperones will believe that I have been playing in the loch with the swans and sunning myself like an otter."

She bid them farewell, and jumped lightly down from the cave mouth to run back through the forest.

Emerging from the water inside the cove on the other side of the loch, she sluiced back her wet hair. Then she hurried to the fallen tree and reached under it.

Her gown was gone. She knelt to grope beneath the trunk, finding only old leaves. Rising to her feet, leaves and dirt clinging to her sopping chemise, she turned, confused, thinking she must have made a mistake.

"Looking for this?" a man asked.

Gasping, startled, she flung her arms over her breasts in the wet linen, and turned. Laurie stood amid the birches, her mulberry gown draped over one broad shoulder. Brother Eonan stood well behind him, a hand over his eyes.

Laurie turned. "Brother, if you think it a sin to see her thus, stay back. I mean to have a few words with the lass. My lady," Laurie went on as he strode toward her, "just where the devil have you been?" he finished impatiently.

Silently, she lashed out an arm for her clothing, and then covered herself hastily when he did not relinquish it.

Laurie put his hand on the gown. "This? You want this?"

She nodded, shivering, dripping, fuming.

"You willna have it until you and I talk some," he said. "Och, stay, dinna flee from me. I have sisters and a wife. The sight of a wee wet lassie doesna fret me as it does poor Brother Eonan, there."

She backed away, eyeing him warily, arms crossed. He took a couple of steps toward her.

"It wounds me to my soul that you dinna trust me," he said. "First you willna speak to me, then you steal away from my company, and now you think me a lecher."

She gulped and watched him, wishing she had not tried to fool him earlier. He was a strong man in a fierce temper, and suddenly she was not sure of him at all.

"Listen to me," he said sternly. "I see that look upon your face. I would never lust after my friend's own wife. Fine as you are, lassie, you are like a saint to me. Understand?"

Nodding with relief, she inched forward, then lunged to grab the hem of the gown.

He caught her arm firmly in his big hand. "Nae yet. Now tell me. Went for a swim, did you?" She nodded vigorously. "I saw you cross the loch and run into the trees on the other side. Where did you go?"

She shivered, growing colder in the shade of the trees despite the summer heat, and shrugged. Laurie let go of her hand.

"Questions require answers. You can speak, lass."

Juliana only scowled at him.

"You trust Gawain enough to talk to him," he said. "I have seen it. If you have secrets, I dinna care to know them. But I am tender in my heart, and I hoped you would like me well enough to trust me too. Hey," he murmured, "remember I am a Scotsman. Doesna that count for something?"

A Scotsman who rode with English, she wanted to reply. But he was Gawain's friend, and she appreciated his gentleness with her now, and she was strongly tempted to trust him.

Silence rolled out. Birds twittered, the breeze rustled the leaves. Brother Eonan turned his back, clearly tired of holding his hands to his eyes.

"Tcha," Laurie said in exasperation, whipping the gown from his shoulder. "Take it before you catch an ague. Gawain would have my hide for that."

She snatched the gown. "Thank you, Sir Laurie," she said.

His sudden smile was bright, and he bowed. "Lady Juliana," he said gallantly, "You willna regret the faith you put in me." He turned to give her privacy.

She stepped behind the shelter of some trees, stripped out of her wet chemise, and pulled on the dry gown. She draped the linen over a tree limb to dry and walked back toward Laurie. He turned when she murmured his name.

"The Swan Maiden likes to swim, does she?" he asked as they walked companionably toward Eonan.

She nodded. "I love it."

"And what then, in the trees? Did you seek out the rebels to betray your husband and his duties here? I must ask that, you know." He frowned.

"I wouldna betray my husband," she answered carefully. "I have friends in the forest, but they are homeless people in need, good people. Not warriors or enemies."

"Ah. Harmless, are they."

"Oh, aye," she said.

"And all you did was play a bit with your wee swans?"

She drew a breath. "Swimming is something I have always done here. It feels like flying to me . . . it feels like freedom."

"Ah well," he said. "You do need more of that, I think. Mayhap you can go swimming—if your husband approves."

She tilted a brow. "And if he doesna?"

He pursed his lips, thinking. "I am a lazy man," he said. "I dinna care to chase you about the hills like a nursemaid when I can rest on the shore while you go splashing. Shall we have a pact between us? Trust me, and I will trust you."

She smiled. "I would like that."

"Good. But dinna get me into straits with the constable of Elladoune. He isna so mellow a man as I." He winked at her.

Chapter 22

Evening spilled amethyst color into the loch as Gawain rode back to Elladoune. Once again he scanned the dark shapes of the mountains reflected in the water. He had traveled the hills for hours, but had not yet seen the stark and craggy face he sought.

He had ridden to Dalbrae, too, having learned its location from the monks. The gatehouse guard had told him that Walter de Soulis had not returned from his journey; the Lindsay brothers were inside, but Gawain lacked official permission to see them.

With the rest of the day free, he had ridden over rough tracks, past greenwood, moors, lochans, and hillsides, moving toward the high mountains north of Elladoune. Beinn an Aodann was there somewhere, he was sure.

By the end of the day, he mistrusted the memory. He thought Glenshie lay north of Loch nan Eala, but he had been a boy when he had left. Perhaps he was wrong about the location.

Yet he could ask no one. No English knight would answer his inquiry without questioning it or reporting his interest. He could raise no suspicions, nor could he ask locally and risk revealing who he was.

His mother surely knew where it was, but he could not bring himself to mention Glenshie when he had been at Avenel. He had not confessed to her his lifelong dream of claiming his inheritance. Unable to remind her of something so painful, he had kept it close.

Regardless of today's disappointment, he had to find the castle. The need sat in his belly like a great stone. Shoulders slumping, he felt weary in spirit and body as Gringolet took him toward Elladoune's gate.

He thought of Juliana waiting inside, and his discouragement lessened. Being with her—alone with her—would be heaven enough to ease his private hell.

Supper, shared with Laurie, consisted of old ale and some sort of burned meat. Gawain ate sparingly and thanked Laurie for preparing it, then asked where Juliana was, since he had not yet seen her since his return an hour or so earlier.

"Claimed she wasna hungry and retired to her tower chamber before you came in," Laurie answered.

"I was just there, writing down my notations on the landscape I saw today," Gawain said. "She was not there."

"She is elsewhere in the castle, then," Laurie said. "I am sure of it." He cleared his throat.

"You do not sound so certain," Gawain observed. "Laurie, did you lose sight of her today?" he asked, suddenly suspicious.

Laurie shrugged. "She, ah, slipped away when we were down by the loch. But she only went for a swim with her wee swans. She said she likes to do that," he added.

Gawain lifted a brow. "She spoke to you?"

"Aye," Laurie said proudly. "The lass trusts me now."

"She cannot be allowed to stray too far and get herself—and us—into mischief," Gawain warned.

Laurie nodded with brusque conviction. After bidding him good night, Gawain walked out to search for Juliana, wondering if she was in the kitchen or the stables, or walking in the bailey.

He saw her standing on the wallwalk overlooking the loch, watching the night sky darken over the mountains. She seemed to hold her own light, pale as a moonbeam. He climbed the steps and walked toward her. She did not turn as he approached, as if she knew he was there and calmly accepted his presence.

A long plaid woolen shawl was wrapped around her shoulders. Under it she wore a simple linen chemise. Her hair poured over her shoulders, brushed to a silvery sheen in the darkness.

"The sky is beautiful," she said, looking across the loch.

"Aye," he answered. "I was admiring it myself while I rode back here. I saw the swans out on the loch, though 'tis dark. A lovely and peaceful sight."

She nodded agreement. "The swans will swim all through the night, resting briefly here and there. In the course of a day and night they travel the loch and the water meadow and streams near the abbey and the mill." She pointed out their path with a sweep of her hand from one end of the loch to the other. "Early in the morning, they are here, and at midday, they are at the abbey, for they know the monks will feed them. Each evening they come back to Elladoune. They always find their way back here."

"As did you." He glanced at her.

"My path was hardly the peaceful circuit that the swans make. Gawain, Father Abbot sent word this morn to invite you to the abbey, but you had already left to ride out to Dalbrae."

"I plan to go to Inchfillan soon."

"So you saw the sheriff and my brothers?"

"I went there, but De Soulis has not yet arrived. I was not permitted to see your brothers, though the guards assured they are well. After that, I rode the hills."

"Looking for rebels?" she asked tartly.

"Exploring," he answered. "Learning the land."

"Ah. Every garrison commander must know his territory."

"I suppose. And what did you do today? Swim for freedom?"

She shot him a quick look. "The day was warm, and the water is lovely this time of year. I often swim in the loch."

"I remember. I pulled you out of there once."

"As if I needed it. I would have made it to shore all on my own that night," she said, folding her arms.

"But you would not have made it past the Sassenachs."

"I did today," she said crisply.

"Promise me you will not disappear like that again. Laurie was concerned, and embarrassed to have lost you. Though he is pleased you decided to speak with him," he added.

"I like him well," she said. "But you can hardly expect me to disrobe in the open if I want to swim a bit."

"Do not go swimming at all. 'Tis dangerous."

"I am a strong swimmer. And the loch is calm."

"De Soulis and his men are the danger," he pointed out.

"So am I a prisoner, then?"

"We agreed you would stay between the castle and the abbey for the time being. Would you rather De Soulis set the rules?"

"You may set them." Her meek response surprised him. He expected more argument. "Gabhan—I must ask a favor."

As before, she softened his name to Gaelic. She could not know the effect that had on him, but she used it unerringly to her advantage. He was ready to grant her anything. "Aye?"

She hugged her arms over her chest. He wondered what she guarded so close. "There are people living in the forest near here. Some are my kin, and the rest are friends. They are homeless since the English destroyed their village."

"I saw the ruin of it."

"Now the sheriff's men have burned part of their forest home. Father Abbot mentioned it, and then I saw the damage myself today, when I . . . went for a swim. They need shelter and safety. Gabhan, I want to bring them here to live at Elladoune," she went on quickly.

He glanced at her in surprise. "You expect me to allow Scots rebels to quarter in an English-held castle?"

"I hoped you would act the charitable knight, not the king's man," she said curtly. "They are good folk in need of help, not warriors. There is plenty of room here with the garrison gone. This was once my family's home." She sighed, shook her head. "You dinna understand."

"I do. You are loyal to your friends. But there may be troops here soon. What then?"

"I heard De Soulis say that Elladoune might be closed down by the English king."

"So you think to give the castle over to the Scots before the English have even left it?"

She looked away. He saw her brow fold, saw her mouth work in anger—or distress. "They are in need. There are children among them, and women, and elderly folk. A woman great with child, her four bairns, a man who is a dimwit, a blind man, old ones gone feeble but keeping their pride—"

"Stop." He held up a hand. "Do not weaken me so." He said it sincerely. "I have obligations to consider."

She bowed her head. "Please," she whispered.

He blew out a breath, unable to refuse her even if he had wanted. "We can shelter the neediest of them here. No more. Certainly no rebels."

Her smile glowed for an instant. "My thanks. I will go to-morrow to fetch them. You willna regret it, I promise."

"I will, if I lose my head for it," he murmured.

"We willna say who they are, if the sheriff comes by," she said. "They will have ready hands for the chores and can tend the livestock. They can be pages and grooms and serving maids. And there will be women to bake and brew and cook—"

"Now that," he drawled, "you should have said first. I was wondering how long we could survive on Laurie's concoctions."

She smiled. "And I could have a few ladies' maids, too."

"A few? How many do you have in mind to bring here?"

She tilted her head. "How fine a lady do you want me to be?"

He laughed, and she smiled again. Pale and beautiful in the moonlight, she seemed ethereal and magical. For a moment, he found it easy to believe that she was an enchanted swan.

"I am grateful," she said. "I hoped I could trust you to be the Swan Knight I remember—chivalrous and willing to help those in need. Just think how often you have saved me."

Her words touched him deeply, but he would not show it. "Ah, well. You seem to need saving, now and again."

She tilted another glance toward him. The pull between them felt strong and clear. Suddenly he wanted to take her into his arms and kiss her—yet he would never force that on her.

He looked away, his gaze scanning the magnificent view over the loch. "Those mountains—what are they called?"

"Those are only hills. The true mountains are in the upper Highlands."

"They look like mountains to me."

"*Ach,* well, the Sassenachs have only low, plain hills in Eng-land." A little smile played around her mouth.

"Aha. And what is that tall peak called, over there?"

"That high one we do call a mountain—Beinn Beira."

"Mountain of Beira, the old Celtic goddess of winter," he said. She turned with him, and they strolled on the wallwalk. "You do have a little Gaelic." She sounded impressed.

"Aye. Is there one near here called . . . Beinn an Aodann?"

She shook her head. "I have never heard that name. Why? Are you ordered to claim some new property for your king?"

He shot her a quick look. "I was just curious. It means . . . mountain of the face."

"It does. But I havena heard of it." She paused. "Tell me how a privileged English knight knows Gaelic."

"A Highland nurse watched over me from birth. She remained with us until I was old enough to become a page. I never forgot the Gaelic. 'Tis a beautiful language. What of you? Your English is very good." He wanted to deflect her questions away from his upbringing.

"Me? I was born at Elladoune. We were happy here," she whispered. She looked out over the battlement. "And the monks taught us to read some, and taught us English and Latin." She paused. "Gawain, please help me free my brothers—all of them."

The wallwalk ended where it met the largest corner keep at the part of the castle that overlooked the loch. He stopped in the shadows. "I will ask after them. The two in De Soulis's keeping—what were their misdeeds? You have not said."

"Alec and Iain are scarce more than babes. The sheriff took them to keep a tight fist on Inchfillan and the abbot."

Puzzled, he looked askance at her. "Babes?"

"Seven and nine."

"God save us," he murmured. "Children. I did not know."

"You see why I must have them back safely, and soon."

"I will do what I can." He reached out to brush a windblown lock of hair from her brow.

She lifted her head. Her eyes gleamed like the night sky, indigo sparkled with stars.

"You remind me of a swan at times," he murmured. He skimmed his palm along her sleek hair to her shoulder. "Slender, pale, gracefully made." His heart beat fast in his chest. "Faithful. Passionate. Loyal."

"If I am like them at all, it is in my need for my freedom. And in my need for an established home as well . . . *Ach*," she said. "You canna know—you have never lost a home."

"I understand," he said firmly, "far more than you think." Like her, he craved liberty and sought his true home. But he stifled one need and pursued the other secretly. Her own passions were clear and candid. He admired that. He loved it.

Reaching out, he traced his fingers along her jaw. She lifted her chin, lengthening her throat. Heart drumming, he leaned toward her.

She shifted her head closer, and he felt her breath upon his lips. He touched her arm slowly. Wanting to pull her close, he knew it must come from her first. He would stand in shadows and moonlight forever if he must, and wait.

A tilt of her head, and the tip of her nose nudged his, seeking. Then her lips touched his in a faerylike caress.

He leaned forward to kiss her full upon the mouth. The taste and feel of her was blissfully familiar to him now. She opened her mouth easily, with a breathy little moan. The sound made him throb, fill, harden. He kissed her again, heart and blood surging.

Passion laced with tenderness streamed through him, followed by a sense of love so pure that it rocked him. His private sadness over his futile search for his home began to lessen. He realized that she was a haven for his spirit and heart.

The evening wind blew through his hair and hers, weaving the dark and light strands together. She pulled back from his kiss.

"Come away," she said breathlessly. "We will be seen."

"We are wed," he murmured, and sought her lips again.

"Come away," she whispered. She turned toward the door of the tower.

He opened the door, then drew her inside and up the spiral steps, where moonlight poured over the stone.

Preceding him as they climbed the stairs, she was aware of her thundering heart, and she was aware, too, of a tumult of anticipation. Beneath it, she felt utter calm and certainty. Their kisses had sparked the hunger that had begun at Avenel.

She wanted to be with him inside the sanctuary of their curtained bed, where passion could burn clean between them. The knots and tangles that surrounded them in the outer world would blissfuly dissolve for a while there.

Gawain reached the upper landing and opened the door, waiting for her. His stillness told her that he offered her the chance to stop now, to turn away or change her mind.

She walked past him and drew upon his arm as she went by. He came behind her, closing the door. She turned into his embrace and sought his mouth again, more boldly than before.

Cradling her face, he kissed her again, this time so slowly and thoroughly that she felt herself melt like honey in sunlight. She wanted to sink into his arms, into his skill and surety, into the allure of what was to come.

Her knees felt uncertain, and the floor seemed to drop away beneath her feet. She stepped back toward the bed. Unfastening the silver brooch that closed her plaid, she let the woolen cloth slip to the floor.

The room was dim, with pools of bright and dark created by flickering candlelight. She walked to the bed and sat. The divided curtain parted around her, iron rings chinking.

He stood watching her, utterly still and silent. She realized that he waited because he wanted this decision to be hers: she could end this, or continue it.

The gap between them felt too wide, a tug of the heart. She yearned for his strength, his warmth, his vibrancy. Shifting inside the shelter of the bed, her invitation was clear.

He turned away to remove his belt, kick off his boots, strip off his tunic, slow and deliberate. She knew he still meant to give her time, but she did not need it.

His body gleamed golden in the candle's glow. She had never seen him fully nude, and she drew in a breath, stunned by the elegance and strength of his body. He bent to blow out the flame, and turned in the shadows to face her.

Desire took sure form in a man, she knew, and she studied him, curious, intrigued, wondering. He stepped forward through the divided curtains, placing a knee upon the thick, fragrant heather-stuffed mattress, so that it sank a little.

She rose, kneeling, and drew off her chemise slowly, letting him see her in shadows as she saw him, though her heart pounded at the boldness of it. He drew the curtain shut and moved toward her. Scant light seeped through the fine weave of the cloth.

Inside the private sanctum of the bed's interior, he wrapped his fingers around her arms and pulled her toward him. His body pressed against hers, his skin firm and fiery, touching her all at once. Kneeling with him, she looped her arms around his shoulders and leaned into him, breath quickening.

His kiss was rich and potent, and she opened her mouth to his exploration of her. He slid his hands down the sinuous curve of her spine, his palms hot as they rested upon the lowest slope. Her body curved against his warmth and hardness, and she shifted her hips to deepen the cradle. He groaned low.

When his hand swept her breasts, she felt herself pearl and grow firm beneath his fingers, then between his lips. She arched back, shivering, and he supported her with a hand at the small of her back, kissing, suckling, until she cried out. His touch felt new and alive and astonishing, but her body had an urge, a questing insistence. She wanted—needed—far more from him.

He lowered her to the bed and she stretched out, wrapped in his embrace, closing her eyes at the simple ecstasy of the moment. As he kissed her again, she slid her hands over his shoulders, his back and torso, skin layered smooth over muscle.

The beat of his heart was fast and strong under her palm, and she sank her fingers into the thick silk of his hair. Glossy as midnight, it was the only softness she found in him. The rest was hard strength tempered with tenderness, the quiet hallmark of his character.

He explored her, lips and fingers cajoling and stroking. In turn, she sighed and sought his body with her own hands and lips. She savored its planes, its fluid, shifting grace and power. The sensations of touching and being touched had a potency like dark wine, warming her. Longing for more, she ached inside.

When his fingertips traced lower, she opened to him. Wild yet gentle, rapture stirred and flashed in her, and took her like a storm. Cresting, crying out, she subsided in his arms.

She pulled at his waist, urging him toward her, and he bent to kiss her again. He slid closer and she moaned, impatient with need: the throbbing inside of her could only be soothed by him.

Carefully, he covered her, sought her, parted her, and slipped inside. A breath, a moment's pause—she felt him there, steady and rigid. The small pain passed, and he eased deep, surging. Another storm, sweet and wild, arose, and she entered its current with him. Love filled her, overflowed in her.

When he kissed her soft on mouth and separated, he reached out for the curtain. Murmuring a protest, she drew him toward her. She did not want their sanctum breached, even by a thread of moonlight. Not yet.

Chapter 23

Late the next day, Gawain stood in the bailey yard of Elladoune. The portcullis had been raised high by two monks,
who stood in the yard watching with him as a group of people
walked up the hill toward the entrance arch.

Juliana strode in the lead, her hand in the elbow crook of an
elderly woman. On her other side was a young man, large and
soft-bellied, carrying a basket filled with ducks.

Behind them, Laurie led his horse, on which a woman
perched, pretty, dark-haired, and in late pregnancy. Four children walked behind them leading an elderly man by the hand.
Behind them came another group of women and children,
along with Brother Eonan.

Most of them carried bundles, while the children and the
women herded several animals up the hill. He saw two shaggy
ponies with netted panniers containing a host of clucking
chickens, and behind them, a few goats, several sheep, a small,
shaggy, black-haired cow, and two long-legged dogs.

As they straggled through the gate, Juliana walked toward
Gawain with the old woman. "Husband," she said, "this is Beithag. She says she would like to be our cook, if you will have
her." She murmured to Beithag in Gaelic, so low and rapid he
caught only some of it. *Dàimheach,* he heard: friend.

"Welcome," he said in Gaelic, smiling.

Beithag peered up at him warily, her eyes dark and keen, her
face wizened over strong bones. A plaid *arisaid* covered her
from the silvery crown of her head to her feet, a rich weaving
of red and brown and dark purple. He frowned slightly, looking
at the pattern. A thought flitted in and out of his mind too

quickly to grasp. Juliana beckoned to a tall old man who came forward, surrounded by children and panting dogs.

"Here is Beithag's husband, Uilleam MacDuff," Juliana said. "And these are their great-grandchildren . . ."

Dumbstruck by the old man's name, he hardly took in those of the children. Gawain noticed that Uilleam wore a wrapped and belted plaid, similar in pattern to the cloth worn by Beithag.

MacDuff. Likely one of his own kinsmen, Gawain realized.

Smiling, although his heart pounded, he bid the old man welcome. Uilleam grunted and peered at him intently, then hesitated as if he would speak. Gawain waited, wondering if the old man recognized his face; he knew that he resembled his father greatly. If Uilleam saw anything familiar in the Sassenach, he said nothing. Gawain let out a breath.

Uilleam turned away to join his wife. Gawain watched the old man shuffle away, scarcely able to think clearly. The dogs circled him, sniffed him. He petted them, one by one, distracted but outwardly calm.

"And there is the children's mother, Mairead, on Laurie's horse," Juliana went on. "She is the wife of Adhamnain Mac-Duff, Uilleam and Beithag's son."

Adhamnain. His own grandfather and father had been called that; it was a common baptismal name among MacDuffs, he knew.

"Her husband is away," Juliana was saying. "And the young man is called Teig." She pointed to the stocky, smiling youth who carried the basket of ducks. He waved to Gawain and grinned at the children, who ran back toward him.

"Is he a MacDuff, too?" Gawain asked.

"He is a nephew to Uilleam. Beithag is a cousin of mine and my mother's. Teig MacDuff is a simple lad, but he is kind, and the children love him. He is strong too, and will work hard in the stables and pens with Uilleam, who knows all there is to know about horses and livestock. The children will help them. Mairead and Beithag and some other women will work in the kitchens with the cooking and brewing. Do you approve?"

"Whatever you think best," he said vaguely. He still felt

stunned. More people came through the gate, a few women, some children, another old woman. The chatter in the yard rose to a crescendo around him. Laurie grinned and gestured as he attempted, through Brother Eonan, to communicate to Beithag his request for a hearty supper.

"The women just arriving wish to help with the keeping of the chambers, the linens, the laundry, the sweeping and scrubbing," Juliana said. "Most of them are widows who have been living in the forests on the charity of others. They are glad that we need help at Elladoune. None of these people would accept charity—especially from a Sassenach."

Gawain nodded, scanning the little crowd in the bailey. "Tell them they are welcome here, and we are grateful for their help. The other women who came in—are they, ah, MacDuffs?"

"One or two are MacDuff widows. Their husbands were killed by Sassenachs, and their homes burned."

He had to know. "And Uilleam? Was he . . . a laird near here?"

She shook her head. "He and Beithag had a stone house in the hills, where they raised sheep and cattle and garron ponies. The commander of Elladoune burned their house and took most of the animals. Years ago, Uilleam had an older brother, Adhamnain, who was laird of a castle near that tallest mountain."

"Aye?" Gawain asked casually, though his breath caught.

"I have heard him mention those kinsmen. They were killed, I think, in a battle with the English, after King Alexander died falling from a cliff—the start of our troubles in Scotland. The laird's wee grandson was taken away by his son's wife, who was Lowland or English. 'Twas long ago. The property was ruined by the Sassenachs, shorn to the ground. Made useless."

His heart pounded, his fists clenched as he held them behind his back. Silent, yet in turmoil within, he stared over the wall toward the mountaintop beyond the loch.

Juliana walked away when one of the women called to her. Soon she gathered the newcomers and led them toward the tower keep to settle their belongings and begin their chosen tasks. The monks led the animals into the pens and stables, and Laurie walked the horse toward the stable with them.

Gawain remained alone in the bailey, rooted to where he stood. Unknowingly, Juliana had filled Elladoune to the brim with his own kin, who needed his help. The world seemed to turn on irony at times, but this coincidence utterly astounded him.

And he had to keep silent. He could not tell them that he was not just a Sassenach commander whom they would never trust or respect. He was, in fact, Gabhan MacDuff, born among them, the grandson of the laird who had once held Glenshie.

He watched Beithag and Uilleam, his great-aunt and great-uncle, climb the steps to the tower. He knew, then, where he had seen that red, brown, and purple pattern before.

He had worn it himself, on the day he had left Glenshie. His mother had traded his plaid to a Lowland farmwife for a dull brown tunic for him. That day, she had crossed with him into England, and had changed his name from Gabhan to Gawain, altering his life and future forever.

Inside an ivory box at Avenel Castle, tucked away in a storage chest, he still owned a piece of that plaid, a small, tattered scrap. He had clutched it in his sleep every night for years as a child, and later had kept it to remind him of the home and the father and the life he had lost, so long ago.

He stood awhile longer, then walked toward the tower. Strangely, he had never felt so alone as he did in that moment.

On the following day, Gawain waited with Laurie in the bailey, while Juliana and Eonan led another group inside.

"The eldest one, there," Laurie said, "was once a blacksmith and will shoe horses and repair our tools." Like the day before, Laurie and Eonan had accompanied Juliana into the forest to fetch her friends. "With Juliana is a farmer who was blinded when his house was burned and his family killed. The man with the withered leg and crutch is a harper, I understand, and will play his tunes to entertain us in the evenings. The two women are wives to the blacksmith and the harper."

Gawain nodded as he observed the newest arrivals. He

greeted them with Gaelic phrases, receiving shy or gruff replies.

"What does Brother Eonan have in that basket?" he asked, as the young lay monk came into the bailey behind Juliana, who held the hand of the blind man.

"Three baby squirrels," Laurie said. "They had fallen from a tree. I told your lady wife that they were tender for the pot, but she insists that she and the children can raise them for a bit, and put them back in the forest when they are old enough."

Gawain nodded and sighed, beginning to realize his wife's penchant for strays of all sorts. "And how many of these folk," he said, "are named MacDuff?"

"The blind farmer and the blacksmith," Laurie said. "Why?"

By the end of the week, Juliana had ushered six more people through the gate, including two orphaned boys named Mac-Duff, an old man whose name Gawain did not learn, but suspected was MacDuff, and a straggling line of young greylag geese.

"They have lost their mother," she told Gawain. "The blacksmith's wife will tend to them with the chickens and ducks."

"Beithag could take one of those for the cooking pot," Laurie said, walking toward them.

"*Ach,* she willna," Juliana said, and herded the birds past them hastily. "Nor will you eat the baby squirrels or a swan. This isna a barbaric royal court, you know."

"'Tis more like a Lammastide market, this place," Laurie answered. "I was teasing about the roast swan, but she didna think it amusing," he muttered to Gawain.

"No doubt." Gawain suppressed a smile. He enjoyed the fact that his wife and Laurie had become friends.

"Tell me this, lassie," Laurie called after her, "when will you learn that oath o' yours, so you can go to the royal court yourself? And we may live in peace here?"

"When hell turns icy, and the English king eats sweetmeats served by wee Scots faeries," she answered over her shoulder.

"What the devil does that mean?" Laurie mused.

Gawain groaned in wordless exasperation and turned to look

around the bailey. "It means that I cannot get her attention long enough for her to learn even the simplest oath for the king," he said. "She is too busy, she claims, and will attend to it later. If she does not find time soon, I will face some unpleasant explanations when we are summoned to court."

"I know, man. I have tried myself to bring the subject up with her as we walk through the forests each day. She would rather whistle the homeless out of their trees, and doesna want to hear about the king. A stubborn lass, your wife."

"She has no intention of becoming a loyal English subject," Gawain said grimly. "That has been clear to me from the first."

Laurie nodded, turning, hands on his hips, to survey the yard and the castle walls. "And what is her intention with this castle? The place has changed in the space of a few days. Stables swept out, outbuildings repaired, the animals penned in . . . the gardens trimmed back and harvested . . . the smells of savory cooking and sweet baking from the kitchen . . . and brewing, thank heaven, brewing begun as well. We will have good Scots ale before long."

"The very reason you returned to Scotland," Gawain said, and chuckled. He pointed toward a corner of the curtain wall, where two men worked with brushes and buckets. "Look there—her newest project. She has them whitewashing the traces of the old fire."

"And so I ask again, what is her intention here?"

Gawain frowned. He appreciated the changes at Elladoune. Fresh linen for the beds, fragrant heather and myrtle in the mattresses and pillows, clean rushes on the floors, good food on the table. His clothing was clean, and a steaming bath had been readied in a tub in the bedchamber the other night.

The horses were exercised and groomed each day, and armor and weapons had been cleaned with sand and repaired. After supper in the evenings, the old harper had played poignant tunes that had made Gawain's throat constrict to hear them. The music was achingly reminiscent of his childhood.

He had ridden out nearly every day to search the hills, and made observations about the terrain in his head. Each evening, back in Elladoune, he recorded his notations on parchment.

As yet he had found no trace of Glenshie. Although he had been tempted to ask some of the MacDuffs if they knew where the place was located, he had spoken little to Uilleam MacDuff or his wife Beithag. Uilleam seemed to pause now and then to study him, but never expressed his thoughts.

Every day, Gawain took time to thank them for the fine work they were doing, and complimented Beithag on the excellent food she prepared with Mairead and the others. And he made sure to mention the care that all of them took to improve the castle.

Though he wanted to ask about Glenshie and mention his childhood, his Gaelic was no longer good enough for a long conversation. He could not reveal who he was—even to Juliana. At times, the urge was overpowering, especially when they lay in their bed, enclosed and sated, loving and trusting of each other. Even so, he could not speak of it.

He was happy, God forgive him. He was content and falling more in love with her. He did not want to disturb that joy. Knowing that she would be ecstatic to learn who he was, he looked forward to telling her. Although it might be a point of pride, he had to find Glenshie first.

Once she knew of his origins, Juliana might expect him to change allegiance and become a rebel and a traitor. He could not risk that happening again. He loved his family at Avenel and owed them much. And for now, he was grateful that Juliana cared for him even though she thought him a Sassenach born and bred.

"Aye," Laurie said, still assessing the castle with his gaze. "Your lady wife has clear goals here. She has transformed this place, filling it with comforts and children and willing hands to work. She has made it into a home, man. And how you are going to explain that to the commander of the king's army when he sends a garrison here, I canna imagine."

"Let alone how I am going to explain how it has become filled with Scots," Gawain remarked. *And my own Scottish kin as well,* he thought; one more reason to keep his own goal secret.

"A quandary indeed. What will you do?"

"I had best think of something," Gawain answered as they walked toward the tower keep. "De Soulis will have arrived by now, and I must ride to Dalbrae to talk to him. Juliana pleads with me often to free her brothers."

"I will go with you if you like. Well, my friend—a week has passed. Do you suppose, since tomorrow is the seventh day," Laurie said, "your lady will rest from making miracles?"

Gawain snorted his disdain for the pun and ran up the steps, eager, as always, to see his wife.

Juliana lay enveloped in silence, warmth, and darkness inside the curtained bed. The only sound was the easy flow of Gawain's breathing. She cuddled next to him, and felt his arm encircle her, even in his sleep. His whiskered chin lay against her cheek, and she turned to kiss him. He slept on.

Gray light filtered through the curtains, and she sighed to see it. Dawn was coming, and she should rise, for there was much to be done. Today the floors in the tower rooms were to be scrubbed clean and sanded to remove the black marks of boots and spurs. Teig and some of the older children would whitewash another part of the inner curtain wall. And Beithag had promised to send someone back to the caves to collect lengths of plaid stored there, which Juliana wanted to hang upon the walls in the great hall and bedchamber.

She looked forward to the warmth of color on those plain walls at last. Elladoune was no longer the home she remembered, and she knew it would never be the same. But this week she had begun to hope that a home could be made here after all.

A home, with Gawain. She snuggled against him. Her hopes were perhaps unrealistic, but in the quiet of their enclosed bed, dreams seemed possible. Elladoune could be a haven again, a loving place, where she could live with her husband, her friends, and her brothers back from captivity. And someday, she thought, children of her own.

A fragile dream, she knew, easily shattered if the king's commanders decided to send a new garrison here. She prayed that they would not. English soldiers were needed elsewhere just now.

If her dreams were fully realized, the English would never garrison Elladoune. And Gawain would never leave it.

She wrapped her arms around him in the dark, and pressed against his warmth and firmness. A wave of love and desire poured through her—desire edged with poignancy, for although she had fallen in love with the Swan Knight of her early dreams, he was still a Sassenach.

Yet in their bed, she could keep hold of her hopes and joys. Here, she was home . . . and he was home for her heart. She kissed his cheek, and settled her lips upon his, and woke him slowly with gentle hands.

Chapter 24

Dalbrae, high on a grassy hill ringed by a ditch and earthworks, was a fortress even at first glance, its gate sealed, its battlements guarded by soldiers. Gawain had inquired at the gate often enough to be admitted this time without question. He and Laurie, who had ridden out with him, entered and dismounted.

Unlike his previous visits, this time they were told that the sheriff was there and would see them. Grooms led their horses away, and Gawain and Laurie followed a young page to the great hall inside the massive central keep.

As they stepped into the large chamber, Gawain was startled to hear a high scream. It emanated from somewhere in the gallery, a walled area protruding above and extending the width of the entrance wall. Gawain glanced upward, but saw no one through the windows that pierced the wooden wall. Another scream sounded, followed by thunks and shrieks.

"God save us, they are tormenting the wee laddies," Laurie muttered, looking around. "We should have come sooner."

Gawain frowned, but said nothing. Walter de Soulis rose to his feet from a chair beside a huge stone hearth and waited. He greeted them somberly and indicated seats on a bench beside a stout oaken table. Dressed in black serge and silver trim, rather than the distinctive black armor he usually wore, the sheriff sat in his carved chair. The shrewdness of his narrowed eyes was evident in the well-lit chamber.

Alarming noises continued in the gallery. The sheriff beckoned to the page hovering near the door. "Wine," he snapped.

When three wooden goblets were filled with claret, De

Soulis drank of his own, then wiped a hand across his mouth. Gawain cast a look at Laurie and cleared his throat.

"Sir Sheriff," he said. "We are here to discuss several matters, but first I must ask after my wife's brothers . . . what the devil is that noise?" he finished abruptly as a horrifying scream rang out into the room.

"That," Walter said, "will drive me mad."

"And us with it, but what is that infernal commotion?" Laurie demanded. "Are you dragging them on a rack up there?"

"It is the sound of my wife's indulgence," Walter muttered, and downed more wine. A clacking sound echoed through the hall.

"Apparently you have some reason to hold these boys hostage from their family," Gawain said. "But now that I am wed to their sister, and commander at Elladoune, I expect you to release them into my custody."

"I cannot do that, much as I might like to."

"They are babes, not criminals. Give them over to me."

"Babes? You do not know them, I think."

A shuttered window in the upper gallery, meant to allow musicians to be heard playing, smacked open. Gawain looked up.

A small, blue-covered behind emerged from the opening, and a back, shoulders, and legs thrust outward after it. A wiry boy in a blue tunic, legs bared, clung to a rope securely knotted to a rafter in the hall, its length pulled inside the gallery.

The boy pushed out of the window opening, swung outward into the great hall, and dangled for a moment waving a wooden sword at the three men gaping at him from below. On the return swing of the rope, he smacked the soles of his bare feet into the gallery wall, landed deftly, and looked up.

"Three of them," he called, "armed and ready!"

Gawain was pushing to his feet until he saw that the boy was not only safe, but already scrambling up the knotted rope to clamber back into the gallery. Beside him, Laurie jumped up.

"Saints in heaven!" Laurie cried, crossing the room quickly. By the time he stood under the gallery, the boy had disappeared through the window. Another pair of arms appeared, belonging to a smaller boy than the first. A little bow and a blunted arrow pointed downward.

"Get back," Walter said dryly. "They will shoot."

"English dogs! Surrender!" the small bowman cried.

"Come and get me, Highland pig!" Laurie boomed.

A stunned silence followed. The bow pulled back and the shutters smacked shut.

Gawain rubbed his hand over his jaw to hide a grin while Laurie took his seat again. "A good game," the Lowlander said gruffly. "Played it with my own brothers, as bairns."

"I take it," Gawain said to De Soulis, "that my young brothers-by-law are allowed some freedom at Dalbrae."

"So I discovered when I returned yesterday," De Soulis replied. "You, boy," he told the page, "find my lady wife and tell her to bring the Lindsays here." The boy nodded and hastened away.

Gawain slid Laurie a quick look. Laurie lifted a brow.

"How goes it at Elladoune?" De Soulis asked. "Have you prepared those notes on the territory for Sir Aymer de Valence?"

"I am working on that."

"Bring them soon." De Soulis poured himself more wine. "I hear you have allowed a bunch of ruffians and rebels to enter Elladoune. Why?" he asked brusquely.

"I invited some of the locals into the castle," Gawain said. "They provide willing hands for the daily tasks. I arrived there with but one man and my wife, and no one to tend to the cooking, the chores, or the livestock."

"The monks of Inchfillan can do that for you," De Soulis answered. "And the fact that you arrived with one man is but your own damned fault. I will report that to the king. Do not think I have forgotten. I have had no time to pen the report. Your behavior was out of bounds."

"I took my wife away from your escort for her safety. I intend to cooperate with the garrisoning of Elladoune and fulfill my duties as constable there."

"Then why do you allow rebels inside there?"

"Homeless women, children, and a few old men," Laurie said, "are hardly dangerous malcontents."

"They undoubtedly have connections with the rebels who hide in the forests," De Soulis answered. "My men have spent weeks searching them out and burning their nests—and you take them under your wing!"

"Where did you expect them to go?" Gawain asked, bitter and low. He stared at De Soulis.

"They should flee indeed, but not into one of our own castles. You will have to turn them out again."

"They are servants at Elladoune. There is naught wrong with that. Any garrison commander I have ever known has taken advantage of the local populace to maintain the castle household. Surely you have a host of Scottish servants here."

De Soulis grunted. "None of them are rebels."

"What proof do you have that my servants are?"

"Those are the same people who have been running about the forests and hills at night. We chased them down and found a site where they were constructing a war machine. Your servants are not simple, I warn you."

"Interesting," Gawain remarked. In truth, he did not find it hard to imagine at all. He slid a glance at Laurie, who was listening intently.

"Some of my men were recently patrolling in my absence," De Soulis went on. "They saw the people entering Elladoune's gates and recognized some of them. My sergeant at arms rode to Inchfillan to speak with the abbot on some minor matter— they had a fire in the bell tower and asked for assistance in rebuilding it. The Scottish Church never seems to have the means to help their own parishes and abbeys."

"I noticed the damage," Gawain said. "I told Abbot Malcolm that the sheriff, as a king's man, would probably be willing to support the needs of the Church."

"The king encourages our goodwill with the Church here, though some of them are rascals. My seneschal approved a gift of lumber," Walter said, waving a hand as if it mattered little. "The abbot admitted to my sergeant at arms that these people you call your servants have been living homeless and indigent near Loch nan Eala. Whether or not the abbot knows it, they are rebels. Allowing them inside Elladoune is foolhardy."

"Better they are where I can keep an eye on them," Gawain said, "than building war machines in the forest."

De Soulis frowned. "You cannot keep them under control without a force of men."

"Courtesy is enough. These are good folk, glad for food and shelter, and eager to help. I sense no spirit of trouble among them. Sir Sheriff—the other reason we came here is to receive our orders regarding the garrison for Elladoune. I trust you have that information now."

"I met with the king's commanders in Perth, but that decision has not been made yet. Word will arrive shortly, I am sure. Ah, my dear," De Soulis said suddenly, rising to his feet.

Gawain looked around to see a woman enter the hall, ushering two boys with her. His gaze was drawn immediately to the boys. They were dressed in matching blue tunics and yellow surcoats, their hair shorn short, their feet bare and dirty. Both were clearly Juliana's kin by similarity of features and coloring.

The smaller one was fine-boned and fair, with golden curls and wide, pale blue eyes, while his elder brother—who had swung out on the rope—had light brown hair and the same deep sapphire eyes as his sister. Both wore wooden swords in their belts, and both scowled furiously.

The woman, Gawain noted, was plump, curvaceous, and brilliantly colored in a fitted red gown that emphasized her big breasts and swaying hips. Her face was pretty, full, and rosy, with large brown eyes and full lips. The hair barely tamed beneath a sheer white veil was brown and curly.

With a boy's hand in each of hers, she lowered in a curtsy that belonged in a royal court. "My lord," she said, her voice light as a girl's. "You summoned us."

"Lady Matilda," De Soulis said. He introduced Gawain and Laurie. "My dear, Sir Gawain is wed to the boys' sister and has come to see them."

"My lady, greetings." Gawain stood. "What are your names?" he asked the boys.

"Alec Lindsay, and this is Iain," the oldest said, eyeing Gawain suspiciously. He put a slender hand on the hilt of his wooden sword, the gesture of a wary knight more than a child.

"I am Gawain." He half sat on the edge of the table so that he was close to their level. "I am your sister's husband now."

"Our sister doesna have a husband," Alec replied. While he spoke, Iain half hid behind Lady Matilda's ample hips and eyed the sheriff nervously.

"She does now," Gawain said. "Are you well, lads?"

"We are," Alec said, chin high.

"She makes us wear Sassenach gowns," Iain complained, looking at Lady Matilda. "She took our plaidies, and cut our hair, and said we were savages and must learn manners."

"But she gives us sweetmeats when we are courteous," Alec added. "How fares our sister, sir? Is she well?"

"Very well. She would like you to come home to Elladoune."

"We dinna live at Elladoune," the little one ventured. "The Sassenachs live there." He kept glancing at De Soulis.

"You, both of you," De Soulis said, beckoning, "come here."

Alec stepped forward boldly. Iain shuffled a step or two, peering nervously at the sheriff.

"Frightened of me, are you?" De Soulis barked at him.

"Aye." Iain's voice quavered. "You have invisible armor."

"Invincible," Alec hissed.

De Soulis glared at Alec. "Swing in my hall like that again, and I will have you caught and skinned."

"Walter!" Matilda exclaimed. She surged forward and wrapped her arms around the boys. "How can you scold my dear little puppies!" She kissed their heads. Iain gazed sweetly at her, and Alec beamed too.

"They need scolding," De Soulis told her. "When I returned to Dalbrae, I found these Scots brats doing whatsoever they pleased. The cook complained the cabbages were shot up with arrows. The stablemen said the harnesses were knotted together. The butler said our good wooden spoons were floating in the pond—"

Matilda cuddled Alec and Iain. "My dearlings are high-spirited! They will try better to behave, will you not, my sweetings?" The boys nodded vigorously, and she kissed each one again. Alec wiped the kiss away when she turned.

"They had better behave," De Soulis growled.

"Walter, I have written a message to my lord father, who sent word asking after my welfare. I told him of your kindness in bringing two little ones here for me. He will tell the king how courteous you are—and what a fine sheriff, too."

"My dear," De Soulis said smoothly. "Of course you must let your father know how contented you are here."

"I told him that you let me have whatsoever I want."

Gawain watched, arms folded, intrigued. He recalled the sheriff's remarks to him about keeping Juliana under his control and authority; apparently that advice was hard to implement at home. Beside him, Laurie listened avidly, nearly grinning.

Gawain saw Iain reach inside the neck of his tunic and pull out a tiny wriggling mouse, which he slipped to the floor. When it ran in front of the woman, she shrieked.

Alec drew his sword. "Lady Matilda, I will defend you!"

"I will! Me, I will!" Iain said, pulling out his own sword and rushing after Alec. The mouse scurried into the shadows, and the boys pounded toward the door, bare feet slapping the floor.

The sheriff glowered at his wife. "Those boys should be punished," he said sternly. "I will see to it if you do not."

"Walter," she said, tears pooling in her eyes. "Do remember how dear they are to me. I have so longed for a child . . . I am grateful you decided to foster Alec and Iain. They are like our own children now!" She clasped her hands, smiling tremulously.

He waved her away. "Go now, and try not to cry again, madame. And keep those boys out of my sight."

She gathered her skirts and ran sniffling from the room.

Gawain returned to his seat in the silence and picked up his wine goblet. The three men quaffed their wine all at once.

"Fostered?" Gawain asked. "Not hostaged?"

"She lacks temperament for the truth," De Soulis said.

"Ah," Gawain said, nodding. He fully understood that. "She would not do well with the truth, so you altered it."

"Nor would her father do well with it," Laurie muttered.

"I may make pages of those boys," De Soulis said. "They can foster here and become knights for the king, if the wildness can be tamed out of them."

"I will take them back with me," Gawain snapped. "Your

wife treasures them overmuch. And you clearly do not enjoy their presence."

"I will keep them, nonetheless," the sheriff said, waving his hand in the dismissive gesture common to him. "My wife wants them. She will return to England soon, for she is unsuited to long stays in Scotland. They can travel south with her if she desires it."

"You have no right to send them anywhere!" Gawain burst out.

"Their sister is an official prisoner of the king, though you need reminding of that," the sheriff said bluntly. "She cannot retain custody of them, nor can you, for your tenure here is still undetermined. For now, I will keep the boys. But if they continue thusly, I will not guarantee their safety."

"Guarantee it," Gawain said flatly. "Or give them up now."

De Soulis slid him a dark look. "They will not be harmed."

"I will be back to ensure it," Gawain said. Barely keeping hold over his temper, he stared steadily at the sheriff.

"Do you doubt the abbot's loyalty?" Laurie asked. "Is that why you keep the boys? Abbot Malcolm seems a capable guardian for them. He seems a passive man, neutral, as he should be."

"Seems so," the sheriff answered. "And I want him to stay so. I do not trust him."

"Do you trust anyone?" Laurie asked mildly, though he, too, stared hard at De Soulis.

"Certainly not you two," De Soulis barked.

"The other matter to discuss," Gawain said abruptly, "has to do with the elder Lindsay brothers taken by the crown's army. Is there further word of a ransom list?"

"Aye, what of it?"

"My wife wishes her brothers' freedom paid."

"And you intend to pay it, to free two Scots rebels? Are you truly so besotted by that creature you wed?"

"If the Lindsays' kin produce the ransom, there is naught I can do about it," Gawain drawled.

"Nay? Remember that I am watching you closely," De Soulis said sharply. "I hope your oath of fealty was a sincere one."

Ignoring that, Gawain rose to his feet. "Since you have no further information for me, and you refuse to release the young Lindsays, our business is concluded for now. Good day." He stalked out of the room. Laurie followed.

Outside, Gawain strode quickly through the busy yard, heading for the stables in angry silence. He simmered over the frustrating results of the visit. His future at Elladoune seemed extremely uncertain, and he had not gained back Juliana's brothers, any of them, as he had hoped. At least he could report that her young brothers were holding their own under the circumstances.

"Ho," Laurie said, "look there. De Soulis's warning didna last long for those wee rascals."

Gawain glanced where Laurie pointed. Alec and Iain stood in the midst of the garden, bows and arrows busy while they shot at vegetables lined up along a low stone wall. From the kitchen, a young servant boy was running, arms waving.

Wheeling, Gawain headed toward the garden at a stiff pace. He stomped inside, greens fluttering around his booted ankles, with Laurie following.

Iain pointed his weapon at a head of lettuce and pulled back the bowstring as Gawain angled through the planted rows. Striding toward the garden wall, Gawain took note of the boy's aim and his target.

Just as he heard the arrow leave the bow, he lashed out his hand and snatched the arrow in midair. He brandished the shaft.

"Come here, Iain Lindsay," he growled.

The boy gaped at him. Behind him, Alec stared too, then gave his brother a shove forward. Laurie waited, hands on hips. A small crowd gathered to watch the scene in the garden.

"Is this how you behave at home?" Gawain asked.

Iain gulped and looked up at him. "N-nay, sir."

"And you," Gawain said as Alec walked timorously forward. "Do you set a good example for your brother?"

Alec lifted his head. Gawain had seen that gesture often in the sister: pride and courage. "I do, sir."

He lifted his brows in surprise, still clutching the arrow, from which Iain could not seem to take his astonished gaze.

"Swinging on ropes when men are in meetings, shooting vegetables, letting go of mice to scare ladies—this is good?"

"We wouldna do so at home, for Father Abbot and Juliana
wouldna allow it. But these are Sassenachs here," he added
ominously.

"And we are rebels. Sir," Iain said, gazing at him anxiously.
"If you please."

"Ah." Gawain kept his countenance as grim as he could
manage, though it proved a challenge. A few feet away, Laurie
shook his head, shoulders shifting.

"We canna waste in prison," Alec added. "We must fight!"

"I see." Gawain weighed the arrow shaft in his hand. "Well,
consider this. As hostages, you are kept as guests rather than
prisoners. Play at swords if you will, and shoot at targets if you
are given permission. But harm no property and frighten no
one. Especially not the sheriff's wife—she is good to you."

"*Ach,* we let the wee mousie go only to show her how we
could protect her," Alec said. Iain nodded in vigorous agreement.

"Show a lady gentleness," Gawain said, "and you will be all
the stronger for it." The boys frowned as if that puzzled them.
Gawain handed Iain his arrow. "Next time, ask first."

Iain stared at the arrow. "Sir, how did you catch it?"

"A great deal of practice. If you both behave very well here,
I will show you someday. But do not try it on your own. There
is a secret to it. Promise me."

The boys nodded and spit on the ground to fix it. Gawain
smiled and touched Iain's head, the curls soft and baby-fine. "I
will tell your sister you do well and show much courage, shall
I? Farewell, then. I will see you again, soon."

"Promise?" Iain asked.

Gawain spit on the ground.

He could not stop searching the skyline. As he and Laurie
returned from Dalbrae, even with the conversation lively between them, his gaze continually strayed to the hills.

"I had forgotten about that trick of catching arrows that you
used to practice years back, when we squired together," Laurie
said. "You always did that with such ease. And gave those wee

bits a startling! They will never cross you!" He laughed with
delight.

Gawain grinned. "I was not sure I could still do it after so
long. But 'tis simple enough with practice, and if one has a
keen eye and a fast hand—and a sharp ear to listen for the
twang of the bow, for that is the real secret to it."

Laurie nodded. "A fine, unique skill, though I never could
manage it. You were determined to teach yourself to do that
when we were squires—always after me to shoot at you, making me swear it all secret. What gave you the urge to learn such
a strange thing? Something about catching a faery bolt?"

"Aye, a legend I heard as a boy," Gawain said. "Foolishness,
I suppose, though I did master the trick."

"You kept at it until you could snatch it with ease. Nae such
a practical thing, for what can you do with it? Frighten wee
boys?" Laurie grinned. "Now you will have to show those lads
how to do it."

"When they are much older, I will." The promise gave him
an odd thrill of surety; he would have to be with their sister in
the future for those lessons to take place. He almost smiled.

"They are good lads. They will be fine rebels one day,
too . . . unfortunately," Laurie said.

Gawain murmured agreement, his gaze scanning the distant
slopes. He had not yet seen the only landmark he knew, a
craggy face in a steep rockface. He sighed, aware that his
search for Glenshie depended on a child's memory. He had
been but Iain's or Alec's age when he left Scotland with his
mother.

They rode over a meadow beside the loch. Buttercups and
bluebells scattered over the grass, and the water sparkled blue.
Far out, swans flowed elegantly over the surface.

Lately his memories came more frequently, but were still
elusive. He remembered seeing this very loch and its swans as
a boy. His father had knelt with him on a high hillside where
the wind blew fresh and cold. He remembered his father's mellow voice as he pointed toward the loch below, and told the legend of the swans of Loch nan Eala, and of the fortress sunk
deep in its waters. He remembered a small waterfall where they
had stopped to drink.

But which direction was that? He twisted in the saddle, glancing at another hill, and frowned as a new memory emerged.

Six years old he had been on the day of his first plaiding.

His father wrapped a plaid around his only son—a rich pattern of red, brown, and purple—and handed him a wooden sword. *Gabhan,* his father called him. With other kinsmen, they marched together over heather-deep hills. He remembered his father's blue eyes, his black hair, his laugh.

He had felt so proud. The feeling came back, intense, pure.

He remembered the *ceilidh* his kinfolk held, with singing, dancing, and storytelling to celebrate the plaiding of Adhamnain MacDuff's fine young son. Uilleam must have been there, he thought, and Beithag, and some of the others who now stayed at Elladoune under the guardianship of Gawain Avenel.

He sighed and guided Gringolet carefully over a hillock and tough, bright heather plants.

"What's caught you so deep in your thoughts?" Laurie asked. "A few memories," Gawain answered.

"Your Scottish childhood?"

"Aye," he answered. "Thoughts of home." Through the fringe of trees, he suddenly saw the golden stone walls of Elladoune, and rode ahead quickly.

That night, silently, gently, he took Juliana into his arms again. Each kiss, every touch, was deep and sincere, fluent with feeling, profoundly comforting.

He cherished their secluded chamber and the privacy of their bed. The freedom there with her, without words, without explanations or questions, was bliss in itself. As before when he loved her, he was aware of natural concordance and deep mutual passion. He followed its compelling course like a swan on a stream.

Exploring her, he let her discover him, body, heart, soul. He burned for her until the brightness of it took him into itself. From the simplicity of a perfect kiss to a sensuous, incandescent ending, he savored it all, and gave all he could, and held her close afterward.

He wondered how he could ever have bound her against her

will, and he knew that he would never be able to let her go if he was ordered to leave Elladoune. Uncertainty whispered to him constantly from the shadows. He did not know what was to come. He only knew, now, how much he loved her.

Resting in her arms in the quiet and the darkness, he thought about her silences and his own reticence. They had discovered the honesty of their bodies, but a host of secrets still lay between them. Yet inside the refuge they had found with each other, none of that seemed to matter.

Chapter 25

The first rays of the sun lifted over the slopes beyond the loch. Standing on the bank, Gawain saw mist rippling over the water, and through it came the swans, gliding toward the shore.

Juliana walked past him. Rosy light glowed over her fine, sleek hair. Although she was a married woman in every sense now, he knew she preferred not to wear a wife's veil yet. He was glad; he liked to see the soft gold of her hair.

Several swans arrowed through the water, creating wavelets. Most of the birds were white, though the few cygnets among them were feathered in brown and gray. Juliana waited for them to approach, tossing barley grains into the water.

The birds dipped, found the grain, dipped again. She threw another handful and edged backward, stepping onto the grassy turf on which Gawain stood. The swans came forward, finding every morsel as they glided nearer the water's edge. Two large birds waddled onto the beach as Juliana walked backward.

A few more birds left the water to pursue the trail of grain. Their short legs and webbed feet, set well back beneath their heavy bodies, gave them an awkward gait, and they toddled forward comically. Gawain watched, smiling, for Juliana was soon surrounded by a wave of white swans.

The swans enveloped him now, bumping against his legs, beaks snapping. She handed him the sack of grain. Filtering barley through his fingers, he watched the swans feed.

"If we do this every day at the same time," she murmured, "they will come here to meet us."

He let more of the food pour out of his palm. "A bit later in the day would be better. Must we leave our bed so early?"

"Have I married a lazy man?" she murmured, smiling.

"Not at all. Just a man who likes his bed well when his wife is in it." He glanced at her, lips twitching in a smile.

A blush colored her cheeks, and her eyes sparkled a dark, rich blue in the early light. "We can come out here a bit later, but always at the same time, and always together."

Together. He caressed her cheek. "That would be fine."

"The swans will come to us," she went on. "If you make the same call when you come here to feed them, they will expect you. They will swim to this spot and wait for you." She scooped barley from his hand and dribbled it downward, cooing and talking softly to the swans.

"What sound should I call?" he asked.

"Anything you like."

He nodded, thinking. "Your cousin James sings a phrase to his goshawk—*kyrie eleison*—and the bird flies straight to him each time."

She looked at him curiously. "I didna know that. I havena seen him for a year or more. How do you know that about him?"

"Most anyone who has seen him lately has seen the goshawk he has trained," he said. He turned, thumbs tucked in his low-slung leather belt, to look out over the calm, rippling water. "Swans cannot be trained like hawks, of course—and I cannot sing at all. You do not use a call," he ventured, glancing at her.

"The swans know me by sight, and mayhap by my silence, for that in itself is distinctive, too."

"Juliana," he said, "when will you explain to me the reason for the silence?" He watched her carefully.

She shrugged. "I canna explain that so easily to a Sassenach who looks for rebels and holds a Scottish castle."

"Ah," he said. Intent on her, he did not notice one of the swans come closer. The bird nipped his hand, and he winced. Juliana turned.

"Feed them, if you will hold the grain sack. They are annoyed with you. They willna come to you if you irritate them."

He sprinkled more food, amazed at how much they could

take of the dry grain, working it sinuously down their throats. "You do know your swans," he said.

"They come here every spring, and stay till late in the year. I have seen the same ones season after season. I have watched them and fed them; I have helped protect them against otters and foxes and dogs. I even swim with them. They are as familiar as kin to me. That cob, there, is the largest and the oldest of this group. I call him Cùchulainn, after the great hero of the ancient tales." She indicated the great white bird who pecked at the grain more aggressively than the others. "His mate is over there—Eimhir àlainn."

"Eimhir the beautiful," Gawain said quietly. "The faithful, strong-willed wife of Cùchulainn."

She glanced at him. "You know the old tale? Your nurse, I suppose? She must have been quite a storyteller."

He shrugged casual admittance. "Do they all have names?"

"Aye. That one pulling at your tunic is Fionn, after the great Fionn MacCumhail, and his mate is Gràinne—but unlike the Gràinne of the legends, she has been utterly loyal to her mate. The two at the water's edge are Naoise and Deirdre, and those two far out on the water are Aenghus and Caer."

"Caer, who turned into a swan, and Aenghus who searched for her for years," he murmured as he let barley fall from his hand.

She studied him. "You *do* know the old tales."

"Some. Those names are all great Celtic lovers."

"True. The four little cygnets there, near their mother, I call Fionnghuala, Aedh, Fiachra, and Conn—after the children of Lir. The tale is beautiful but tragic, and very old."

"The three sons and the daughter of King Lir were turned into swans by their stepmother, and forced to spend eternity in that form," he said. The story came easily into his memory, for it had been one of his favorites at his grandfather's knee. "Finally the pure note of a bronze bell rang out and broke the magic spell. But they were so old, by that time, that they died as soon as they regained their human form."

Juliana stared at him. "How does a Sassenach know that?"

He smiled, shrugged. "I have a good mind for stories. I never forget them once I hear them."

She nodded thoughtfully. Gawain watched the golden-pink sun move upward behind the highest mountain and squinted at the brightness. He felt a strong temptation to tell Juliana the truth about where he had learned those stories.

If only he could tell her everything—his father's name, his own true name, his search for his childhood home. He wanted her to know that she had filled his home, and his heart, with the kinfolk of his childhood. He longed to tell her how much that meant to him, and how much more he loved her for it.

But he kept silent, intent on his private quest. He had to find and claim his home. Only then could he speak of it aloud, even to Juliana. He had his own reasons for silence.

The swans wandered back to the water, lowered, and swam out. The mother pen stayed near the shore, nosing her beak at one of her four cygnets. While Gawain watched, she sank a little in one spot and seemed to float there. One by one, her little cygnets clambered onto her back. When they were securely folded into gray-brown balls of fluff, she swam out. He noticed that she always kept herself distant from the other birds.

"Poor Guinevere," Juliana said. "She is lonely now. Artan was her mate. He has not returned, though I hoped he might."

"Perhaps he found another mate in Newcastle," Gawain said.

She shook her head. "Not he. Total loyalty, that one, for his Guinevere. Something must have happened to him." She sighed and glanced at Gawain. "I thought when you heard the swan's names, you would only recognize the names Arthur and Guinevere. You surprise me with your knowledge of Celtic tales, Sassenach."

He smiled. "You surprise me," he murmured, taking her arm, "almost daily. Come back to Elladoune now. I intend to ride out to see the sheriff this morning, but I will meet you later at Inchfillan Abbey. I want to meet with Abbot Malcolm again." He walked with her across the meadow.

"He will be glad to hear more news of my brothers' pranks."

Gawain chuckled. His tale of the boys' courage and spirit while in the sheriff's keeping had cheered Juliana and Abbot Malcolm greatly. The abbot missed his little wards keenly, and Juliana desperately wanted them back with her at Elladoune.

But when he returned to the sheriff's castle later, he might have orders to leave Elladoune. He sighed. This enchanted place and its swan maiden had woven a spell around him; like a man caught in faeryland, he never wanted to leave.

As the sun rose higher, he glanced over his shoulder once again. He stopped suddenly. Juliana rounded with him.

Mist sat in fragile rings around the bases of the mountains, and golden light poured over the tallest slope. An elusive face appeared near the summit, as if carved in the black rock. Light and shadow created deep-set eyes, cheekbones, a mouth, a straggle of hair: an old woman.

"Look there," he said hoarsely. "On the side of Beinn Beira. Do you see that face?"

"That?" She shaded her eyes against the brilliance of the sun. "'Tis old Beira, the queen of winter, trapped in the mountain. She escapes once a year, they say, and brings winter, and must be sent back again to her imprisonment. Sometimes her face can be seen in certain light."

Gawain took Juliana's hand, watching while the sun shone more brightly on the face in the mountainside. Gradually, the light washed away the image in the rock, and it disappeared.

"They say," Juliana went on, "that good fortune comes to those who see Beira's face. 'Tis a good omen to catch a glimpse of her still in the mountain, for it means that summer will continue." She smiled up at him. Her eyes were blue and deep as the loch, her head and throat as pale and graceful as a swan's.

He leaned forward and kissed her. "My thanks," he whispered, tipping his brow to hers.

"For what?" she asked as she turned to walk with him. "For telling you a new story? I am surprised you didna know that one, Gabhan." His heart turned with joy every time he heard her say his Gaelic name, though she did not know the effect she had.

"That one," he said, grasping her hand, "I did not know."

The world was bright with summer color, and with hope, as Gawain rode northward. He kept the eastern face of Beinn Beira in sight. Bluebells formed a purple-blue carpet beneath the oaks and larches, and ferns grew lush and green in places.

Sweeping over the slopes, heather blooms grew thick and tufted, and the air was warm and fragrant.

He left the forest track and headed up into the foothills, then made his way carefully among the steeper slants. Rock became more prevalent than turf, and wildflowers bloomed yellow, blue, and violet in crevices. Sunlight highlighted the old woman's countenance as he made his way slowly upward.

No castles or ruins appeared, and few homes were set along the steep hillsides, but for an occasional shieling hut or a thatched homestead—each one deserted. This area had been overrun by the English years before, he knew. King Edward's commanders had burned out, killed, or chased away virtually everyone who inhabited the area surrounding Loch nan Eala.

He knew, for he had been among those men six years before.

After a while, he dismounted the bay, for Gringolet had faltered more than once; Gawain did not want to risk a hoof injury or a broken leg for the animal. He secured the reins to a hazel bush and left the horse grazing near a narrow burn.

The water ran into a narrow gorge, with walls of twisting vines and bracken and rock that rose upward to meet another slope that footed the mountain itself. Gawain headed beyond the burn, toward a long, steep, straightforward hillside. Once he moved higher, he thought, he could better survey the view.

Climbing with a long, sure stride, he was glad that he had worn only his tunic rather than the weighty chain-mail hauberk and gambeson. Sweating freely in the summer heat, he stopped to scoop a drink from a stream of water that danced over some rocks.

Moving upward, arduous but steady, he wondered if once again he had gone wrong in his search. Nothing lay ahead but the dark, towering bulk of the mountaintop and scree-covered sides.

He paused, a booted foot on a rock ledge that jutted out over the glen below the mountainside. He saw the horse grazing by the burn, and far beyond, the smooth blue sheet of Loch nan Eala, with the white dots of its swans on the surface. On the opposite shore, in the distance, the honey-colored walls of Elladoune rose on its promontory. All was perfect in miniature.

He rounded, and looked up the slope. A jumble of bushes

and heathery patches fringed the bulk of the mountain. A narrow waterfall, the source of the trickle below, sluiced among some dark rocks, well above and behind the scrub.

He narrowed his eyes. He remembered that waterfall, a white frothing tail over the rockface. This slope, too, seemed familiar. Long ago he had stood here with his father to look down at Loch nan Eala.

Turning, he hurried upward, scrambling in some places. Finally he attained another ledge and looked toward the mountain.

Just above and beyond the fringe of growth, he saw a square thrust of stone. Gray and broken, a remnant corner of a tumbled tower, its shape struck deep chords in his memory.

His heart lurched, and he strode upward. Climbing with new fervor, he pushed his way through the dense skirt of bracken and scrub until he burst through and saw Glenshie Castle at last.

Chapter 26

Later that morning, Juliana walked along the bank of the loch again while Laurie waited nearby. She had returned to check on a nest that had been plundered by otters more than once in the last few weeks. The pen and the cob had recently produced another cluster, even though it was late in the season.

To her relief, she found the nest unharmed; the pen perched calmly on her four eggs, and the cob, who paused to stare at Juliana, pulled at the reeds nearby. She turned to walk back toward Laurie.

Out on the water, she saw Guinevere nudging her little cygnets onto her back. Juliana felt a wash of sadness for the graceful pen, who still mourned her missing mate and kept on the outskirts of the flock, staying attentive to her young.

"Juliana!" She looked up to see Brother Eonan hurrying toward her. "Father Abbot says he must see you!" he said breathlessly as he approached. Laurie came with him.

"Is something wrong? Are Alec and Iain—"

"They are fine, Abbot says. He went to see the sheriff this morning." Eonan stopped. "I do not know what has happened there, but he seems very agitated."

"I will go there now," she said. "Laurie, when Gawain returns from his morning patrol, tell him I went with Eonan."

"Well enough," Laurie answered. "Gawain plans to meet you at the abbey later, after he and I go to the sheriff's castle ourselves, but now he will be more than anxious to get to the abbey after hearing this. I will see you—what the devil!" He stopped as he turned, glancing across the meadow.

A man melted out of the edge of the forest and walked toward them. Laurie put his hand to the sword sheathed at his belt and stepped forward. Juliana gasped and hurried past him.

"Ach Dhia," she breathed, recognizing the man as a friend, and a cousin—James Lindsay walked toward her.

Dressed like a pilgrim in a somber brown cloak with a scallop shell pinned to the shoulder, he was tall and strong, and moved with a natural agility. Sunlight glinted off the dark gold of his wavy hair. He lifted a hand in greeting.

"Jamie!" she called out.

"Pilgrim," Laurie said. Juliana turned to see him coming near, with Eonan behind him. "If you seek the abbey of Inchfillan, 'tis that way. They will admit a pilgrim who wishes to pray and rest. Otherwise, move on."

Juliana hastened toward Jamie and took his outstretched hand. He bent to kiss her cheek. "Cousin," he said.

"Cousin!" Laurie echoed.

"Aye, sir," James answered. "I am glad to see that my cousin Juliana is well protected." He pushed back his hood, his keen glance the same dark blue as Juliana's, a legacy from a shared grandfather.

"I thought you were some rebel come to challenge us," Laurie said gruffly, sliding his sword into its belt sheath.

"Oh, never that," Juliana said earnestly.

"I travel in peace, on pilgrimage," James said. "I intend to visit Inchfillan Abbey. 'Tis a pleasant surprise to see my cousin here, on my way to the abbey."

"Just a pious man anxious to be at prayer," Juliana added.

"Och, nae doubt," Laurie said wryly.

"Allow me to speak with my cousin and tell her news of our kin," James said. "I assure you she is safe with me."

"Walk with her if you like, but only in our sight," Laurie said as James moved away with Juliana. "And dinna go far."

"Did you really come here to see Father Abbot?" she asked.

He nodded. "He sent word to me." James glanced back at Laurie and Brother Eonan, who watched them. "He wrote that you were taken by the English, and the wee lads taken too, and that he needed help to free all of you. I came as soon as I could. I have another mission as well here, on King Robert's behalf. But I am glad to see the abbot found a way to gain you back."

"The lads are still held, though the Sassenachs brought me back. King Edward wed me to one of his knights—the new commander at Elladoune. Now I must pledge fealty to the king."

"Wed?" James looked astonished.

"Aye, to Sir Gawain Avenel—you may know his name. He is now constable at Elladoune, although there is no garrison there as yet. The king's orders—Jamie, what is it?" She paused.

"Jesu," he murmured. "Gawain. I know him well."

"Aye, he mentioned that he met you."

"Met me? He ran with us for a few months."

"He fought with Scots rebels?" Juliana gaped at him. "When? How? He is King Edward's loyal man!"

"I heard that he pledged his oath anew." James frowned. "He was a good comrade, but loyalties change often in this war. Men must choose between their heads and their hearts. Some side with the Scots for the love of liberty, and stay the course. Others declare for the English to protect their inheritances."

"But Gawain is English . . . he never—" Juliana felt stunned.

"He sided with the Scots for a bit, lass. Or so I thought."

Juliana stared, her head spinning in confusion. "But—"

"He is a solitary man. Courteous and of a noble spirit, but he keeps his secrets close. He had some good reasons to side with us and change back. Inheritance, most like. My wife liked him well, and she has a fine eye for character."

In spite of the distracting revelation about Gawain, Juliana gasped. "Wife? You do have news! The Border Hawk is wed?"

His smile was quick and charming. "Aye, caught fast. My wife is Isobel Seton of Aberlady."

"The prophetess? I have heard of her! So the rebel softened enough to take a wife." She smiled widely. "I never thought 'twould happen. You nearly became a monk!"

"Aye, true." He laughed ruefully. "You must meet Isobel."

"I want to, and soon. But for now, tell me more of you and Gawain. He never said he ran with rebels!"

"I doubt he wants it known, especially if he has resworn his fealty. He helped Isobel and me in a bad situation, and stayed with us for a while. He fought at my back and I trusted him well." He frowned. "One day the English camped nearby, and there was a skirmish. The next morn he was gone. We saw him riding with the Southrons, while we hid in the forest."

"*Ach Dhia.* Did he . . . betray you?" she nearly whispered.

"I never knew for sure, but it appeared so. He went back to England, I heard, and knelt before the king to beg forgiveness. And got it, I see, if he is now constable at Elladoune, complete with a bride given him by the king—and the bride my own cousin!"

"I didna know," she murmured.

"He was a good friend—or so I thought." James shrugged. "What he did for Isobel and me canna be repaid. But he broke our trust later. I never suspected him for a traitor, so it surprised me. Mayhap Isobel and I liked him too well and somehow missed the truth." He looked at the loch and watched the swans.

She bit at her lip, remembering that Gawain had told her he had spent two months in prison—for betrayal. He had explained little, but she wondered anew what he had meant by it.

"Juliana, I have news of the lads."

She looked up quickly. "We heard too. I dinna know what we will do, for we canna pay any ransom. And Alec and Iain are in the sheriff's keeping now. He refuses to give them up."

"We had best go see the abbot. There is much to discuss."

She frowned. "Jamie, you should know this—Gawain will be coming to the abbey later today to see Abbot Malcolm."

James cocked a brow. "That will prove interesting."

Glenshie burned bright as a lantern in his mind, even as he sat in De Soulis's hall with Laurie. While the page poured out cups of golden, cool ale, he remembered the sunlit stones of Glenshie. When De Soulis complained about a delayed delivery of several tuns of wine and barrels of salted fish from Perth to Dalbrae, Gawain thought of the view of Loch nan Eala from the hill below his grandfather's castle; his castle by right, now.

The place had been a ruin, a stone shell, some of its higher level tumbled. The foundation walls were still sound, but choked with ivy. An abundance of green ferns filled the inner bailey, and the steps leading to the tower keep had collapsed.

But he had recognized it, and relived childhood moments

that nearly brought him to the brink of tears. Exploring the castle's remnants and perimeters much of the morning, he thought about rebuilding. He envisioned Glenshie clearly in his mind: a strong stone tower once again.

After leaving the mountain and meeting Laurie for the ride to Dalbrae, he kept silent about his discovery. Though he burst to tell his friend, he hoped to reveal his news—and the blessed relief of the full truth—to Juliana first.

He fixed his attention on the conversation. He had come here to check on the boys and to learn his orders, and to discern the possible lay of his future.

"Has the king's commander decided what to do with Elladoune?" he asked De Soulis.

"Aye, but there are some matters for us to address first. I have writs from Aymer de Valence, and one from the king himself, to convey to you."

The sheriff reached over to the end of the table and drew toward him a flat wooden chest. Opening its silver latches, he removed a few folded parchments with broken seals. He sifted through them, his fingers sly, somehow, along those edges.

"I believe that you have a document to deliver to me, as well," De Soulis said. "Is your report complete?"

Gawain thought about the folded parchments tucked inside his tunic. He had brought them, intending to deliver them, but some inner caution made him hesitate. "Almost," he said. "A week."

The sheriff scowled. "De Valence wants that information." He reviewed the page in his hand. "This first matter does not concern you directly, but you should know. As the king's Master of Swans, I am to capture swans for the king's rivers in England," he went on. "The mute swans of Elladoune are among the best known in Scotland, and so some of those will be taken up in the next few days. You will see us at the task."

"The swans' feathers are molting just now, I believe," Gawain said. "They are unable to fly."

"And that makes them even more suited for upping, when they are hooked and netted, and transported. The younger ones are easier to catch that way than the aggressive adults. We will snare a few cygnets and young swans and send them south."

Gawain narrowed his eyes, thinking of Juliana's unchivalrous capture several weeks earlier for the same reason. He thought, too, of Guinevere's four young cygnets, who were exactly what De Soulis wanted. He felt a sudden, strong compassion; the proud and beautiful female swan had already endured the loss of her mate. Her offspring should not be taken from her, too.

"King Edward has more than enough swans on his rivers as it is," he said. "Why does he take the time to send out writs for Scottish swans when he has a war to concern him?"

"The king has a special fondness for the birds. They are good omens. And he particularly wants Scottish ones."

"Nae content with owning all the swans in England, is he," Laurie muttered. "Sir Sheriff, where are the wee lads? We didna see them as we came in today. We want to make sure they are well. Their sister is concerned about them."

"Her kinsman the abbot was here this morning and saw them. I invited him here to discuss the orders for Elladoune and Loch nan Eala, some of which will affect him and his monks."

"Oh? How do my orders affect the abbey?" Gawain asked, frowning in surprise.

"You will know shortly. The boys are with the priest at their prayers and lessons just now. They have been more courteous of late. My wife has promised them a trip to the market fair next week, and I have given my permission. And I have decided to send them with her into England when she leaves in a few days. You will see them at the fair—"

Gawain leaned forward. "You do not have the authority to take those children out of Scotland," he growled.

"We shall see. Now you will want to hear of your orders." De Soulis opened two parchments and pressed them flat in front of him. "This writ is from the king himself," he said, showing them the red seal and trailing ribbons. " 'Greetings,' etcetera." He waved his hand impatiently. "He requires that a written statement by Lady Juliana Lindsay be sent to him at Lanercost Abbey."

"Lanercost?" Gawain asked. "He was to go to Carlisle."

"The king has been weakened by illness—'tis temporary, his physicians say—and rests at Lanercost before going on to

Carlisle. The journey from London has been very draining. His health this year has not been good."

"A written statment from the lady?" Gawain asked then. "What does he expect in that? And who is to deliver it?"

De Soulis perused the page. "He wants her sworn fealty in writing, and wants an affidavit signed by witnesses that she made a pledge of . . . 'her loyalty and that of her kin and acquaintances, and all those attached to the lands of Elladoune, to the king of England.' " He passed the parchment to Gawain.

He took it and read it. " 'If the lady cannot write a fair hand, she is to make her mark upon a written oath, and two witnesses, civic and religious, must swear that she has said the oath aloud and with good intention.' " He glanced at Laurie.

This was unexpected luck. Still, he doubted that Juliana would be any more willing to swear fealty this way than she would have before the king himself. She simply would not do it, and had avoided all of his efforts to rehearse her pledge. He suspected, by Laurie's skeptical frown, that his friend had the same thought.

"Well, at least he doesna demand that she come to court," Laurie said. "That is good—if the lady agrees."

"Indeed." Gawain looked at the sheriff. "Is Edward so ill?"

"He wisely attends to more important matters," De Soulis answered. "Once the oath has been accepted, I believe the king will release her from her formal captivity. I will witness the oath-saying myself, of course, as sheriff of this glen. Her kinsman the abbot will do for the religious representative. I will have my own priest present, too, for I trust him better."

"My lady wife can handle a pen for her name, I think, though she was not schooled for writing out words. When will the signing take place?"

"At the market fair," De Soulis said. "Will she say the oath aloud? If she refuses, she will not fulfill the king's order."

"I will explain that to her," Gawain said carefully.

"I suspect that she speaks to you, even if she insists upon her foolish silence with the rest of the king's knights."

"My wife has found ways to communicate with me," Gawain said, staring evenly at him.

"No doubt," De Soulis drawled. "Tell her that she must comply, or she will be at the mercy of the crown. Bring her to the market fair next week. She can say her oath in full public view. Plenty of witnesses." He smiled flatly.

Gawain narrowed his eyes, but kept outwardly passive. He still doubted Juliana would say an oath under any circumstances. "We shall see what happens," he said. "As for her brothers, if you try to take them away, be sure that I will get them back from you."

"We shall see, as you say. As for the rest of these orders, a messenger came yesterday from Perth. He brought a writ from the king himself, and a writ from the commander of the king's forces. De Valence has decided to close down Elladoune."

"Close it down," Gawain repeated. He clenched his jaw.

"You knew it might happen," De Soulis said smoothly. "You understood you were there temporarily."

"I expected a garrison to be sent there, since you are so concerned about rebels in that area."

"I argued to close the castle. I can deal with the rebels myself, through my own authority."

The decision came as a shock. A host of consequences battered his mind. Not only would he have to turn out his own kinfolk, but he would have to turn Juliana out of her home again. And he would lose the only home he had known with her. No doubt he would be sent elsewhere—England, somewhere in Scotland, even Wales or France. His heart slammed hard in his chest.

"Why withdraw forces from there now?" Laurie asked.

"De Valence has decided that it is not necessary to place a garrison there. Extra men will be sent here to Dalbrae, rather than to Elladoune. We will extend our patrols along the length of the loch and into the hills. This can be managed with fifty extra men at Dalbrae."

"Ah," Gawain said bitterly. "Send fifty to Dalbrae rather than a hundred and fifty to Elladoune. A savings of men, time, supplies, and coin."

"Exactly," De Soulis said.

Flexing his jaw to restrain his anger, Gawain merely nodded. He played with the stem of his cup, his mind whirling.

"What, then, for the rest of us?" Laurie asked.

"You both may be useful here. Or anywhere that Sir Aymer decides to post you. I will inquire on your behalf, of course."

"Of course," Laurie snarled.

"And Elladoune?" Gawain said. "Closed for how long?"

De Soulis took a sip of wine, pursed his lips, and slid the other parchment page across the table toward Gawain. "This is the king's latest writ with a new list of orders. It states what is to be done with Elladoune."

Gawain scanned the neat French script until he came to the lines that contained the orders he sought. He stared at it, then read it again.

Until no stone remains standing.

"What is it?" Laurie asked.

"Elladoune," Gawain replied softly, "is to be burned, and every stone torn down."

Chapter 27

"Friend or foe, he is wed to your cousin, so he is your kinsman now," Malcolm said, speaking Scots for James Lindsay's benefit. "Tell me this, Jamie—can Gawain Avenel be trusted?"

Catching her breath, Juliana looked at James. Seated beside her, he sipped his ale calmly. They both faced the abbot across the table in the small, whitewashed solar of the abbot's house.

"He is a man of integrity," James replied. "But I wonder where his fealty lies. The man I knew would help any man, woman, or child who needed it. But I dinna know the man who left us as he did and renewed his oath to King Edward. My instincts tell me I could trust him with my life, but his actions contradict that."

"He ran with your men, then rejoined the English. You told us that incredible story," Malcolm said. "Difficult to believe 'tis the same man you knew."

Juliana listened, feeling stunned. James had recounted events in Gawain's recent past that she had never suspected. Last year, Gawain had joined James's rebels for a while, giving them crucial help; then he had left suddenly after a skirmish, without explanation. Gawain had told her nothing of it himself.

Aware of his previous transgressions, including when he had helped her at Elladoune years ago, she could easily believe that Gawain would risk his own life to help Isobel and James. And she could even imagine him declaring for the rebel cause. Why he had left them was another matter.

Whatever had happened, she believed in his core of integrity. Yet if he had stayed with the Scots, there would be no obstacles between them now, she thought sadly.

"Did he betray you?" Malcolm asked. "Is he a spy for them?"

"It could be," James admitted.

Juliana gasped softly. *Betrayal,* Gawain had said himself of his crime. "But you said he sided with the Scots!"

"His inheritance is in England. He chose the safe course," James said. "As for betrayal—it may be. I dinna know."

"Gawain has been helpful to our friends," she said in his defense. "He may be English, but he is not like most of them."

"There is something you both must know," Malcolm said, his tone grim. "I met with the sheriff this morning, who reported some disturbing news indeed. First of all, Juliana must declare her loyalty to King Edward before the sheriff and witnesses."

"If it keeps me away from the king's court, that is welcome news," she said. "And mayhap we can find a way around the oath."

"That may be, but listen—there is more. De Soulis intends to send Alec and Iain to England with his wife soon."

"Ach Dhia!" Juliana felt the news like a blow. "He doesna have the right!"

"'Twillna stop him. He told me something else. Elladoune is to be closed," Malcolm said bluntly. "The king's commanders have decided it doesna serve them to garrison it."

Juliana stared at him, stunned. She had never expected that. "Its gates shut? Will Gawain—be sent elsewhere?"

"Very likely. He is a king's man." He frowned. "We didna suspect how much a king's man he is."

"What do you mean?" James asked sharply.

"De Soulis said that Gawain is preparing a report for Edward's commanders on the lay of the land here. He is to describe the terrain and detail where troops can camp, where water sources are, the distances between landmarks, the best routes for cavalry, and so forth. Did you know that, Juliana?"

She shook her head mutely, feeling as if her heart sank like a stone. She was aware of Gawain's daily patrolling and the writing he did sometimes at night, on parchments that he locked into a little box with the few valuables he had brought with him. When he had told her the pages were only some thoughts he wanted to record in ink, she had assumed that he had scholarly habits because of his upbringing and education.

What a fool she had been. She cupped a hand over her eyes for a moment, then looked up. James was watching her steadily.

"We have all seen him riding out in the forests and hills each day," Malcolm said. "He has been collecting the information for the king's commanders to use in fighting Scots."

"He wouldna—" She wanted to defend him, but doubts flooded her. Apparently there was much she did not know about Gawain.

"The English hold Elladoune," James told Malcolm. "If 'tis to be closed, Gawain will be the one to shut its gates. And his report to the king will gain him some much-needed favor."

"This canna be," Juliana gasped. A sense of betrayal swamped her, followed by a rush of fear. Now she could lose Elladoune again—and with it would go her hopes and dreams.

"Cousin," James said, reaching out to touch her arm. "We will find some way through this," he said in a soothing tone.

"But, Jamie, he wouldna be so traitorous as to close Elladoune, and toss us all out, and leave us—all to gain the king's favor! 'Tis betrayal—I canna believe this of him—"

"It may be duty rather than betrayal," James said.

"What can we do?" She bit at her lower lip fretfully, thinking of the people who had found shelter and welcome at Elladoune. "Where will our friends go now?"

"We will gather everyone to leave the castle," the abbot said. "As for Gawain, there is naught we can do about him. Only he knows what he does, and why he does it."

Tears welled, and Juliana put a hand over her eyes as she tried to regain her composure with a quavering breath.

"My dear girl, this is hard, I know. But we have matters to decide," Malcolm said gently. "Now we must gain Alec and Iain back ourselves, and Niall and Will as well."

Jamie leaned forward to discuss that quietly with Malcolm, and while they spoke, Juliana looked away. She would lose Gawain—perhaps she had already lost him out of her life, but he was not gone from her heart. No matter what he did, she did not think she could ever stop loving him. Her cheeks heated as she recalled deep kisses, and so much more, in the privacy of their bed. She had been so content, so foolishly in love.

If he had done what they said, and planned this betrayal of all of them, he was not the man she had thought him. Had she been so misled by her dreams and her heart? A tear slid down her cheek, and another. She dashed them away.

"We will pay the ransom ourselves," Malcolm was saying.

Juliana looked up. "How?" she asked. "We have no coin!"

"I have a scheme," Malcolm said. "And a scheme to fetch the wee ones back as well." He smiled, and she saw the effort and the sadness in it. He, too, was affected by the devastating news about Elladoune—and about Gawain, she thought.

"We do have a source of gold," Malcolm continued. "The archery competition."

"A bow-shooting contest?" James asked.

" 'Tis held each summer at the time of the midsummer market," Malcolm explained to him. "The final prize is an arrow—the Golden Arrow of Elladoune, 'tis called. 'Tis solid, good gold. The competition has been held for generations. Lindsays of Elladoune have always won the arrow—until the last few years."

"Ah, I have heard of it," James said. "Juliana's father won it many years in a row, and his father before him."

Juliana nodded. "For six years, English bowmen from the garrisons have taken the prize." She looked at Malcolm. "Even if we could win that arrow, 'tisna enough gold to pay two ransoms. And we would have to melt it down."

"I am thinking the sheriff will pay good coin to keep the Golden Arrow in his garrison's possession," Malcolm said.

"Ransom the arrow to pay the fee?" James asked.

Malcolm nodded. "De Soulis has boasted all year that his men have the arrow now and will win it again. He says 'twill always be kept at Dalbrae. That pride will cost him."

"An intriguing idea," James said. "Win the arrow, and charge him well for it—enough for two ransoms."

Juliana sat straighter as an idea occurred to her. "My father always won that prize . . . I think I could take it."

"You?" James tipped his head, considering her. "You do have the skill for it."

"Of course she does." Malcolm smiled broadly at her.

"I have the bow skill," she said, "but I am a woman, and under the custody of the crown. De Soulis would never allow me to compete."

James shrugged. "He doesna need to know. You could pass for a youth—though you had best hide that shining hair and . . . your shape." He lifted a brow expressively. Malcolm cleared his throat.

Juliana nodded. "I can do that. But the Golden Arrow of Elladoune is an unusual contest. The shot is difficult, nearly impossible for some. I have never mastered it myself, and have hardly attempted. The fair is but a week from now. Even if I enter the competition, I dinna know if I can take the prize."

"You can," James said, and Malcolm nodded agreement.

"Jamie, I know you must leave soon, but can you stay long enough to help me practice?"

"I wish I could, lass. I came here only to see that you were safe, and to conduct a matter for King Robert. I willna even stay the day, for I must go west again to meet our king, and then south to Wildshaw. My wife's child will be born in a few weeks, and I intend to be there."

"A child!" Malcolm congratulated him, and Juliana smiled at Jamie's news. Inwardly, her heart thundered.

She wondered if she had the courage to pull off this ruse, yet she had no choice. The Golden Arrow had to come back to the Lindsays—not only for the sake of tradition, but so they could bribe De Soulis with it and free her brothers.

"Well, cousin?" James asked. "Are you decided?"

She nodded. "I will do it."

"Good," Malcolm said. "Now, let me tell you my scheme to gain back the wee lads. The sheriff said his wife will bring Alec and Iain to the fair to watch the archery." He looked at each of them. "And then we will snatch them back."

"But stealing them away would be dangerous and might cause a skirmish in the town," Juliana said. "What about the Golden Arrow? We can use that to get the lads back from him."

"We will take advantage of that for the older lads. First, 'tis most essential to steal the bairns. 'Twill be easy enough if they attend the Golden Arrow competition, since that is held just outside Inchfillan's gates. We will inform our rebels, and make a plan."

"But the rebels willna go against De Soulis, especially in public like that," Juliana said. "They fear him and his black armor! They willna risk his wrath directly."

"Black armor? Ah, then I have heard of this man," James said. "I doubt 'tis as frightful a garment as rumor says."

"I agree. Sometimes I wish the man would take a wound wearing that armor," Malcolm said. "Then everyone would lose their fear of him and his armor quickly. Just a wee wound."

"Father Abbot!" Juliana said, pretending shock at his confession. James lifted a brow.

Malcolm shrugged. "Somehow we must convince the rebels that they needna fear De Soulis, so they will agree to steal the lads away. I will talk to them. For now, we agree—Juliana will take the Golden Arrow."

"There is one other matter to discuss," James said. "King Robert will be disappointed to learn that my mission here wasna successful."

"Not successful?" Juliana asked, puzzled.

"I came here in answer to the abbot's summons about you," James told her. "But King Robert also sent me to inquire about another war machine. The last one your forest rebels sent to him, secretly and in pieces, was assembled elsewhere and greatly aided the rebellion. But Abbot Malcolm told me that the sheriff's men burned the site where the rebels were building another engine."

"True, but I have been waiting to tell you some good news," Malcolm said. "We have another one. 'Tis hidden where the sheriff's men will never find it." He gestured toward the window, where a summer breeze entered.

Juliana looked out to see the top of the scaffolding for the new bell tower. "Where?" she asked. "And will the bell tower be completed in time for the archery competition? We hold it on the steps of the abbey church each year," she told James.

"My girl," Malcolm said. "Look again."

She stood and looked out the window. A wooden scaffold had been erected beside the broken bell tower. Two monks had climbed up to hammer upon another framework of timbers constructed on the roof, surrounding the broken tower. She narrowed her eyes, and then gasped. "The scaffolding!"

James got up to look out the window. "By the saints . . . 'tis a siege engine! I hadna looked closely at it! Father Abbot, you are a bold fellow." He turned to grin at him.

"If Bishop Wishart can build one and take it against the English, surely I can do the same," Malcolm answered. He beamed. "It only needs wheels and the catapult arm, which are hidden in the dormitory. Tell the King o' Scots he will have his engine. Bring him word that we will transport it in pieces, by night, as soon as 'tis completed."

"He will be pleased. This is brilliant," James said.

"Foolhardy." Juliana scowled. "What if De Soulis sees it?"

"He has seen it," Malcolm said. "So have his men. No one seems to have noticed what we have done with the timber that the sheriff's men brought us for our new bell tower and scaffold."

James shook his head. "Brilliant, but Juliana is right. All of you at Inchfillan take a great risk with this."

"We are rebels," Malcolm replied soberly. "We take risks for Scotland."

"This secret must be protected until the machine can be moved," James said. "The English must be kept away from here."

"They dinna come here often," Malcolm said. "We can move it this week, during the fair, when there are fewer sheriff's men patrolling at night—they will stay close to the market town."

James nodded. "Juliana, what of Gawain? You said he was coming to Inchfillan this afternoon."

"He said he would do so after he saw the sheriff," she said.

"We must learn how the wind blows with him."

She sighed. "If what you and Father Abbot say is so, he willna help us. And I canna bear to see him just now—nor can I ask him for help again. Not yet, if ever."

James nodded. "Then I will speak with him myself," he said grimly. "'Tis time, I think."

* * *

"Wait here, Sir Gawain," a woman said. Deirdre, the abbot's rotund elder sister, who kept his house and helped look after his wards, showed him into a room that held a table and benches. "The abbot will be with you shortly. There is ale on the table."

"My thanks, Dame Deirdre," Gawain murmured. He stepped inside the room alone, where he noted three cups on the table beside a jug of foamy ale; one cup was unused, upside down on the table. He poured out some ale, swallowing quickly. It was cool and light, watered stuff well suited to a warm summer day.

The ride from Dalbrae had been torturous, not because of the day's heat, but because his head was full of troubled thoughts—and his heart was full of torment.

He looked out the window at the new wood going up next to the shattered bell tower. Something seemed odd about it. Frowning, he did not notice the door opening behind him.

"Gawain."

He turned, expecting to greet the abbot, and saw James Lindsay. He stared, heart slamming. A moment later, recovering himself, he set his cup down.

"Jamie," he said simply.

James shut the door and sat on the bench. Gawain sat opposite him. His hands trembled, his heart raced. Casually, he picked up the jug of ale and offered it.

James shook his head. "I had my fill earlier."

"Ah." Three cups, he thought; there had been a meeting, presumably between the abbot, James, and Juliana. Gawain knew that his wife was here, since Laurie had brought him her message when they had ridden to Dalbrae. Laurie had also mentioned a visiting pilgrim at Inchfillan, but Gawain had been so distracted by his thoughts of Glenshie that he had hardly listened. "I see that I was left alone in here for a reason."

"Aye, at my request. I thought we should talk."

Gawain sipped his ale, but it tasted dull now, and no longer quenching. He set it aside. "I do owe you an explanation."

"I heard that you recently made an obeisance to King Edward." James's tone was cold and flat. Gawain sensed the tension and anger beneath the surface.

He remained still and cool himself. "Your spies are always about, even so far as London."

"They are," James agreed. "I didna come here to confront you. Every man must make his own choices in this war. I made mine. You obviously made yours."

"I did." He frowned slightly. "How is it you are here?"

"The abbot sent word that my cousins needed help. I came as soon as I could. Thankfully, Juliana is safe, though the lads are still in custody. Juliana told me much of what has gone on." He watched Gawain steadily.

Gawain realized that James's eyes were the same dark, rich blue as Juliana's. He had not noticed their color before—but now, with his mind so constantly upon Juliana, he saw the strong familial resemblance between the cousins in their eyes, in their fair golden coloring, and in their fine-boned, handsome features.

"Then you know about the marriage, and my post at Elladoune." Gawain replied.

"I do. Felicitations on your marriage," James murmured. "I willna congratulate you on your post. It might please a Southron, but it poses some difficulties for me and mine."

"I will be released from my obligations at Elladoune soon enough. No doubt you heard that, too, since the abbot spoke with the sheriff earlier today."

James nodded, and studied him in the quiet, serious manner that Gawain remembered well. "What of your obligation to my cousin, your wife?"

"I intend to honor that, though I cannot say what she will want. I doubt she will consent to return to England with me, or even elsewhere in Scotland, once I am reassigned."

"Ask her," James said. "If she will speak to you. She seems greatly upset about what she has learned of you today."

Gawain played with the rim of his ale cup. "I am not surprised, though I am sorry for it. I wanted to tell her myself. I wanted to tell her . . . many things."

"Seems to me that you should have done so already. She didna even know the extent of your involvement with us."

"I never found a good moment to explain that. If I had told

her that I ran with you, she would assume that I am loyal to the Scottish cause, and expect me to change allegiance."

"Oh, well, canna have her thinking that," James drawled.

"The marriage came quickly for both Juliana and me," Gawain snapped. "There is still much to explain. And much to guard, between us. She keeps her secrets too."

James scowled. "She hasna guarded much from you."

"What do you mean?"

"She loves you. I see it plainly in her. Juliana has given you all of her heart, all of herself. This revelation about you has devastated her. I warn you, if you hurt her further—"

"No need to warn me," Gawain said brusquely.

"Ah, I see," James said slowly. "'Tis mutual, this feeling between the two of you. A tangle indeed, then."

"Well knotted," Gawain admitted. He stared out the window, where the scaffold of the bell tower topped the abbey wall.

"Juliana said that you met years ago, when Elladoune was burned, and she and her kin were cast out by De Soulis and the king's troops. She said you saved her then—and were the first one to call her the Swan Maiden."

"An odd coincidence, but true."

"I dinna believe in coincidence," James said. "I believe in an ordered world directed by God and his angels. I believe therein lies fate, through those means. I have been its victim—and its beneficiary—often enough."

"Then I am a victim of fate."

"Or its beneficiary."

"That remains to be seen," Gawain said. "Sometimes I think I am caught in a purgatory of ironies, where there is no escape." He shoved a hand through his hair and exhaled in exasperation. "I have new orders that your fair cousin will not like at all. 'Twill shatter the marriage, I think. 'Twill shatter . . . her. I do not know how to tell her."

"Just be honest," James said quietly, watching him. "She knows what the abbot told us both—that you have orders to close down Elladoune," he said. "If there is more, tell her."

Gawain tightened his mouth and turned his cup in his hand. "The truth about my orders is not pleasant."

"The truth can seal where we think 'twill sever."

"Not this."

"Did you know," James said, "that I fired my own wife's castle, on the very night I met her? I suspect your orders are something similar."

Gawain raised a brow at James's astuteness. "Did Isobel forgive you for it?"

"Once she understood why I did it, and once she understood me . . . aye," he said quietly.

"There is much I must explain to Juliana before she would understand."

"Such as your betrayal of her cousin?"

"I thought you did not care to confront me about that."

"Still, I think I must." James fisted his hand on the table, knuckles white, wrist bones strong.

"Then do so," Gawain said. "Say what you will."

"The morning you left," James answered, low and fierce, "the Southrons hunted us mercilessly in the greenwood. But you know that—you were with them." His gaze was sharp and cold.

Gawain remembered that day. His stomach clenched inwardly. He swung the cup like a small bell, listening.

"Patrick was wounded, and Quentin nearly captured," James went on. "We had lost one of our own that morning, when you disappeared," he added. "We didna care to lose more."

"I am glad no one among you was killed," Gawain said. James said nothing. Drawing a deep breath, Gawain went on. "You knew that my fealty was originally to King Edward."

"You helped Isobel and me, and you defended her—and for that I will always owe you, no matter the rest," James said. "But you deserted us abruptly."

Gawain studied the flecks of foam in the ale as if it contained a map of life's mysteries. The air in the room seemed oppressive. He could relieve it with the simple truth.

His stepfather and stepbrothers would have already mollified James. They would have apologized, soothed him with logic, while screening what they wanted to hide to protect James—and themselves—from further distress.

But he was not like them, he knew that now. He wanted to

deal only in clear, refreshing honesty. The truth had to be known. It might seal, as James had said, what was severed.

"We had skirmished with the English the day before," Gawain said. "Do you recall?"

"I do. You fought well. And left before dawn."

"We saw the faces of some of the men we killed, from the trees where we hid."

"Those deaths couldna be helped."

"My stepbrother Geoffrey was among them," Gawain said bluntly. "I saw him fall. I went to their camp to find him." He drew a long breath. "One of our bow shots killed him. I do not know who loosed it. Mayhap even myself."

"Jesu," James breathed out. "Why did you not say?"

"Geoffrey came into Scotland to search for me," Gawain said. "My stepfather sent him. I was seen by the English knights and welcomed as if I had escaped from the enemy. I couldna get back to you without leading them to you. And my brother was dead, Jamie," he murmured. "I took his body home."

James rubbed his fingers over his brow. "And then you had to stay and make amends."

"Aye," Gawain said curtly.

"Isobel swore you had good reason for what you did. With her gift of the Sight, she was sure that leaving our band of rogues had been a difficult decision for you. I assumed it was some dilemma of loyalty versus inheritance. A question of convenience."

"'Twas a question of guilt, and obligation." *And grief.*

"I see. You didna betray us."

"Never that. I gave naught away."

"Were you suspected, or lauded for escaping rebels?"

"Both, actually. I stayed two months in the Tower of London for trangressing and aiding the enemy—specifically for helping you free Isobel from her captor. It ended with my formal apology. My stepfather circulated the rumor that your men had taken me captive. He wanted to spare the family more disgrace."

"So you decided to stay with the English."

"I had no choice. King Edward has a formidable temper. My

family suffered because I helped Isobel, let alone what I did on behalf of your rebels. They will suffer, even now, if any of this becomes known. I must act cautiously. My mother is ill—I doubt she has the strength to bear any more strain from my quarter, after Geoffrey's death," he murmured.

"How much does Juliana know of this?"

"Very little," Gawain said. He sighed, aware that the damage to his marriage might be irrevocable. "I know I should have told her sooner. There are other matters that I have not confessed to her as well. She will not be pleased by any of it. But she must learn the truth sooner or later."

"Truth and sweet oil," James said, "rise to the top. She has a few confessions to make to you, too, I think."

"I am sure of that," Gawain said wryly.

"Talk to her. She is still here in the abbey."

Gawain looked away. Relief and shame mingled in him; the urge to tell Juliana the truth was strong, but he knew that his secrecy had hurt and angered her. And he did not know how he could save his marriage if he must ruin Elladoune.

"I must leave now," James said, "since King Robert awaits my report, and he will be moving on soon. Though you, Sassenach, dinna need to know that." He cocked a brow.

"I never heard it," Gawain said quietly. "I never saw you."

James nodded. "Isobel will be glad to know of our meeting," he said then. "She never doubted you."

"Even when you did."

"I did," James said. "And I was wrong, and glad of it."

Gawain stared into his cup. His throat tightened.

"We will meet again soon, I hope," James said. "I would stay if I could, but Isobel is expecting a child soon—I promised her I would be there."

Gawain smiled. "Tell her—give her my congratulations, and my apologies," he said. "For not being a finer friend."

"She holds no grudges where you are concerned. I only hope you can convince Juliana to do the same."

"She will have to come to that for herself, I think."

James huffed in rueful agreement. "I must ask a favor of you." He leaned forward. "In a way 'tis a question of loyalty again. You may have made a pledge to your king, but you also took a binding oath with Juliana."

"So I did." Gawain frowned, waiting.

"That makes us kinsmen by marriage, and makes you kin to her brothers as well. They need protection, especially the wee lads. I canna stay here to make sure of it, but they must be taken out of the sheriff's keeping."

"I will do what I can," Gawain said. "Children should not have to suffer because men create war."

"True. So if some attempt is made to snatch them," James said, "look the other way."

Gawain nodded slowly. "Well enough."

James stood. "Farewell, then," he said. He went to the door and opened the latch, then looked back at Gawain. "Had you stayed for the Scots," he said musingly, "*Ach Dhia,* what a warrior for our side." He closed the door behind him.

When Gawain walked through the abbey yard, no one spoke to him. Monks who previously had been friendly now turned away. Laurie waited at the abbey gate, mounted on his brown stallion, with the dark bay, Gringolet, saddled beside him. The Lowlander's face was grim and watchful.

James was gone already. Gawain was not surprised, knowing his friend's habit of vanishing quickly. He was glad that James had pushed the matter to a conclusion. The truth had lifted an oppressive weight from his shoulders. The very air felt clearer to him.

But other shadows remained. He had to talk to Juliana, but he must approach it cautiously. Although he was certain of his heart regarding her, he was unsure how to resolve the conflict in his loyalties. Another day or two, he thought, would give him time to sort it through, and perhaps talk to De Soulis again. He would not hurt Juliana unduly—nor would he give her undue hope that might later be shattered.

A few swans wandered in the yard, as they often did, and Gawain walked without hesitation through their midst. A couple of the birds hissed, extending their necks and busking their wings, but he sensed no real threat. He knew they looked for food from a man they were now accustomed to seeing.

"I have naught to give you, Eimhir," he murmured as he bumped his knee against the large pen. She undulated her long neck and head and nipped at his leather pouch.

The swans waddled away from him, turning like a wave. Gawain glanced after them, and suddenly stopped in his progress.

Juliana walked into the yard, soon surrounded by a writhing, begging ring of white swans. She held out a palm full of grain and tipped it down, scattering seed.

She looked steadily at Gawain. He watched her without moving, though his heart slammed as if he had been running.

Like a pale golden flower in a garden of white blossoms, she stood for a long moment, her hair shining in the sun, her body long and slender in a flax-colored gown. He knew those graceful, lithe curves so well that his own body reacted at the mere sight. His heart thundered harder.

He took a step toward her. A tilt of her chin lengthened her fragile neck. Then she spun away from him deliberately, hair swinging, sleek gold. Aloof and silent, she walked away.

He wanted to go after her and ask the question that burned in his mind—*Will you love me, trust me, in spite of what you have heard of me?*—but he already had his answer.

Pride made it impossible for him to go after her now. He would wait until he had cooled, until she had cooled. He would find her here tomorrow.

A moment later, he leaped into the saddle and turned his horse's head. With Laurie following, he rode hard through the abbey gate.

Chapter 28

Sighting the centermost circle of the target—a painted cloth nailed to a tree—Juliana raised her bow with the arrow nocked. She adjusted her stance, squared her shoulders and hips, and grew still to sense the wind and the quiet. Drawing back the bowstring, she opened her fingers.

The arrow whistled away to thwack into the center of the target, leaves spitting downward as the force jarred the tree.

Applause sounded from above. Angus, Lucas, and Lucas's three adolescent sons peered from the dense leafy canopy overhead. Seated on a log nearby, Mairead's two daughters and two sons giggled and clapped. Juliana smiled, then chose another arrow from the quiver on the ground.

"By Saint Fillan, the girl never misses!" Angus said from his perch on the branch of a huge oak. "Try the wands next, with that other target. Split them if you can."

"And step back farther," Lucas advised. "You are too close. That last shot was no challenge for you!"

"None of it challenges her," one of Lucas's sons said. "Someday we will learn her secret, and then we will have to win the Golden Arrow from her—for she will surely take it from the Sassenachs at the fair!" Laughter echoed among the trees.

"Hush, you," she said, looking up, "or the Sassenachs will take you instead."

Walking toward another target, she stepped back farther to please her critics. She adjusted her leather wrist guard, then turned her toes inward for better balance. Narrowing her eyes, she studied the new target the men had set up for her.

Four stripped saplings were stuck upright in the ground in

front of a tall mound of raw earth. The difficult challenge, she knew, was to nick a wand as the arrow went past into the target.

For a moment, she considered the shot. When she felt ready, she chose a steel-tipped, pointed war arrow, a type she rarely used. Neither the wedged hunting arrows nor the blunted practice arrows that she preferred, with their pear-shaped ends and short points, would do for this.

Nocking the arrow, she lifted the bow and tilted it, drawing back the string in one fluid movement. The arrow balanced lightly between the bow shelf and her drawing fingers. She sensed the tension, the spring, her own readiness.

Each step came so easily to her, after years of practice, that she gave little thought to the individual elements. Like swimming—or like making love, she thought with a sigh—archery was a physical pleasure that felt natural and exhilarating. She was fortunate to be able to bring innate grace and strength to it, and she preferred to let instinct and intuition guide her.

That was the only secret she knew. When a shot hit the center mark, she had given herself over to instinct; when a shot missed, she had applied too much logic and disrupted the essence of the act. No one had taught her that aspect, and it was not something she knew how to teach in turn.

Although she did not bow hunt, and had never fought in a skirmish, she shot often at targets, and rarely missed. Most of the men she knew, kinsmen and friends, admitted that she was the most accurate shot they had ever seen. She had simply been born to the ability, and accepted that, and was grateful for the gift.

Gazing at one wand, she lifted the bow, tilted it, and pulled the string to her jaw. She sighted along the arrow to its deadly point, and beyond to the sapling. When she felt the tension peak, she let go. The arrow struck the wand in passing, biting into it, and embedded in the turf mound.

Loading another war arrow, she shot again, splitting the next wand in half. Whistles filtered through the treetops. She missed the third, heard her audience's dismay, and began again.

She gave the sequence of movements a dancelike flow and

rhythm. Stretch, balance, tense, release: she poured body, heart, and mind into each shot.

"Well done," Lucas called, high praise from him. "Now practice those overhead shots again, straight up into the trees."

"Not while I am up here," one of his sons said. Mairead's children laughed. One of Lucas's sons dropped down, and another followed, while the others stayed up in the branches, well away from where she stood.

She walked to the edge of the clearing and loaded her bow again, leaning back to make the difficult upward shot. As she pulled the string, she heard an owl's call, a hiss of warning, a rustling. She straightened and glanced around.

Lucas's sons were gone. The trees, above, were silent. Mairead's children sat on their log, looking at her with wide, uncertain gazes. They were not alone.

Gawain stepped out of the green light of the forest and into the sunny clearing. She stared, propping the bow upright.

Days had passed since she had watched Gawain and Laurie ride away from the abbey. She had not gone to Elladoune since then. Although Gawain returned to the abbey asking for her, she had refused to see him. She was angry, afraid, and devastated, even though James, before he left, urged her to talk to her husband. Not yet, she answered, not feeling ready.

Now she sucked in a quick breath. He was breathtakingly handsome, all her dreams realized. Her first sense was joy and sweet relief. But she tried to look aloof as he came closer.

The lush summer light glossed his raven-dark hair, and added a golden warmth to his brown eyes. A tunic of moss green draped over his broad shoulders and lean body, with a belt and dagger slung low on his hips. He moved toward her with masculine assurance and restrained power. She simply stared at him.

"My lady," he said. "I have been looking for you."

Gathering her wits, she turned away to nock a blunted arrow. Love rushed in to drown reason, and she fought that power.

"Silent again, Swan Maiden?" he murmured. He leaned a shoulder against a tree and tipped his head, watching her.

All she truly wanted was to drop the bow and run into his

arms. She wanted to kiss his face, where dark whiskers met a pink rinse in his cheek; she wanted to kiss those firm, bow-curved lips; most of all, she wanted to forgive, and be happy again with him.

Even though she loved him, she could not trust him. She had spent the last few days feeling furious and hurt, yet missing him dreadfully. Each night, she had cried in her narrow bed in the abbot's house, a bed she had not occupied for months.

Silently, she raised the bow and spread her feet wide. Pointing the arrow straight up, she paused.

"An unusual shot," he said, stepping forward deliberately, so that he was a handspan away, and she could not release. "What are you after? Birds? Squirrels?" He peered upward. "Rebels?"

She glared at him and aimed again.

"If you truly want to hit something up there," he said, "I suggest you get down on one knee. You will be more stable that way, and less likely to waver in your aim."

Juliana frowned and turned away, deciding not to shoot. He went with her, so close that she stepped on his booted toe. She whirled. "What is it you want?" she demanded.

"She speaks," he said, showing a flash of temper. "Eonan said you might be here." His tone softened. "We must talk."

"Have you time for that? You have a castle to empty, and Scots to harry," she snapped. "And land to explore for the Sassenachs, so they can use it against us, and take it away from us. Be sure to tell them about the mountain, since you were so curious about that."

"God save us," he growled, "you have a sharp way about you."

She jammed her arrow into the quiver in answer. Setting the tip of the bow on the ground, she stepped through the arc and pushed on the bow to remove the string. With the stave upright in her hand, she lifted the quiver and walked away.

"Children," she said to Mairead's brood, "come ahead."

The tense quiet that had descended in the forest when Gawain had appeared lingered. She did not glance at the trees, where the others still hid, but motioned the children to follow her along the forest path.

Gawain went with them. "You left your arrows behind," he soon observed.

"Oh," she said, flustered. "Gilchrist," she looked at Mairead's oldest son, who was Iain's age, "will you fetch the arrows? We will wait down the path." She spoke in Gaelic. The boy ran off, and she led the children toward another clearing.

Birch trees edged a wide overhang, and the loch spread below, sparkling in the sun. She set bow and quiver against a boulder and sat, inviting the two girls and the smallest, a boy, to sit with her. When the little one scrambled up, Gawain lifted him to her lap. Then he perched a booted foot on another rock.

"You can go," she told him. "I dinna need a guard. Ah, pray pardon, I am still a prisoner of your king. Have you been ordered to find me?" She slid him a glare. "Chain me?"

"Juliana—" he began, and shook his head, looking away.

She drew a breath, and fought tears. Circling her arms around the children, she sat silent, trying to calm herself.

Far below, swans looped in lazy paths on the water, or slipped through reed beds to enter a stream that fed into the loch, or explored the water meadow near the abbey and the mill.

"They cannot fly," she said after a moment. "Their wing feathers have molted now. They are helpless. Earthbound."

"And you feel like one of them," Gawain murmured, his back turned to her, the wind lifting the raven silk of his hair.

"I do," she said, "sometimes."

Gilchrist came running back then, and Gawain took the arrows from him, sliding them into the quiver while Gilchrist climbed up on the rock with his siblings.

Juliana watched Gawain as he looked out over the loch. Her heartstrings felt taut, for she wanted to be in his arms. The sadness and loneliness she sensed in him hurt her in turn.

Somehow, part of her had become part of him, caught in a constant weaving. Her anger lessened with that realization. If only they could be together and shut out the world, she thought. Perhaps then they could both be happy again.

"Look at the swans, Juliana!" Gilchrist said. She smiled. He reminded her of Alec and Iain, whom she missed fiercely.

"Tell us again how the swans came to Loch nan Eala," Ailis, the oldest girl, said. Seona, her little sister, nodded.

Juliana resettled the little boy in her lap. "Long ago in the misty time," she began, "a beautiful maiden, lovely as a white swan, lived in a fortress on an island in the loch. She loved a warrior who was as dark as a raven, handsome, and strong . . ."

In simple Gaelic, she told them of the lovers, and the plans for their wedding; of the Druid who summoned magic to destroy them; of the faery bolt he shot into the clouds to raise a storm. She described the shattering and sinking of the island fortress, and how everyone inside had drowned in the deep waters.

The four children listened intently, the little one staring at her in fascination, his blue eyes wide.

Gawain listened too, his back to her, his hands folded, the wind pushing against him as he stood overlooking the loch.

"The Druid discovered that his magic had failed," she went on. "He had not destroyed the two lovers, for they were transformed into swans. The warrior and his maiden would be together always, in that form."

"Sometimes the maiden swan comes out of the water, and leaves her swan skin on the shore," Ailis added. "She meets her warrior, who leaves his swan skin there as well."

"Sometimes," Juliana agreed. "Most of the time she stays with him on the loch. There, they are protected. There, they are happy, in a world of their own—"

She caught her breath, thinking of the similar haven that she and Gawain had found in their bed, behind a curtain of protection.

"Can the swan spell over the loch ever be broken?" Ailis asked. "Will they ever be free?"

"There is a way," Juliana said. "But I have forgotten. It has been a long while since I told this story—"

"Only a warrior whose heart is true, and who feels a love like theirs, can free them," Gawain said softly, in English.

She stared at him. He glanced at her over his shoulder.

"Tell them," he said. "A warrior who knows true love can free them. He must catch a faery bolt and fling it into the loch. 'Tis the only way to break the spell that holds the fortress, the warrior, the lady, and the swans."

"How—how do you know that?" she murmured.

He turned away. "I have heard the tale before. Tell them."

She told the children, her thoughts tumbling. Ailis sighed, loving the ending, but Gilchrist rolled his eyes.

"No one can catch a faery bolt," he insisted.

"Some have tried, their whole lives, to do it." Gawain looked at her, his eyes penetrating. "Just to prove it can be done. Just in case the spell could be broken someday."

Juliana repeated what he said, though it astonished her. She lifted the smallest child into Gilchrist's arms and ushered them toward the forest path, instructing them to wait for her. Then she walked toward Gawain.

"Tell me how you knew that," she said. "'Tis a local legend. Few people outside this glen know of it."

"Someone told me the tale, long ago."

"'Twasna your nurse," she said.

"Nay," he said. "Someone else."

She watched his profile, elegant and spare against the sky. "You have some secrets—and I want to know what they are."

"What of your secrets?" He slid her a glance. "I came here to ask if you will listen to me—and talk to me."

"I will tell you all," she said. "But first I must know what you have been keeping from me. If we are ever to be together again, we must have total honesty between us."

He hesitated, wind whipping at both of them. Then he turned and took her face in his hands. His eyes were deep and steady and warm. And yet she was sure something troubled him deeply.

He lowered his black-lashed lids, still hiding his secrets. He kissed her, soft and slow, then pulled back.

"My God," he whispered, "do you know how much I love you? How much I love your honest nature?"

Her tears welled then, and her lip quivered. He kissed it, his mouth gentle. Her defenses crumbled, and she whimpered a little in relief. Tears slid freely down her cheeks, and he kissed them away before finding her mouth again.

Like water for deep thirst, after so long without him. She circled her arms around him and accepted his strong, hungry kiss, pressing her body against him.

"Juliana! Juliana!" The children's voices sliced anxiously through the trees. She broke away from Gawain, and he stepped away quickly, grabbing her bow and quiver and following.

"What is it?" she called, alarmed.

"The swans! The swans!" Seona and Ailis cried out.

"They are hurting the swans!" Gilchrist said, pointing.

Juliana ran along the path to another vantage point, where the loch, and Elladoune, could be seen clearly.

Soldiers were on the bank near the castle, with nets and long hooks. Some of them were knee-deep in the water. All around them was a froth of white as the swans struggled. On the shore, a man in black armor watched.

"What is it?" Gawain said, coming up behind her.

"The sheriff's men," she said, turning. "They are upping the swans." She whirled and began to run down the path.

Hurrying with the children in their wake, Gawain followed Juliana toward the loch, carrying the smallest boy. He set the child down once they reached the meadow that edged the loch near Elladoune.

Several knights, the sheriff among them, thundered across the meadow just as Gawain and the others emerged from the forest. They headed in the direction of Dalbrae. Secured in baskets on three packhorses, several white swans struggled, netted and tied.

Juliana ran toward the loch and stopped. The summer wind dragged her pale tunic against her legs, whipped out her hair. Gawain strode quickly to stand beside her.

From Elladoune's entrance, he heard shouts. The MacDuffs came through the gate, waving and running. The children crossed the meadow to meet their kinfolk.

Juliana bent to retrieve a few white feathers that lay on the pebbles at her feet, close to the waterline. She cupped them in one hand and stood again to look at the loch.

Out on the water, several swans circled, still agitated, their necks extended, their wings busked in white arcs. A pair of females curved their heads to nudge at their offspring, while Fionn, one of the larger males, patrolled the outer cluster, gliding in a wide circle.

Cùchulainn was in a fury, driving across the water, wings out, broad chest lifted. He charged a group of hapless geese, who swam out of his way, then turned and approached a flock of mallards, who skimmed away as well. Then he streamed in an orbit around the other swans, neck curved, head erect, wings slightly lifted, a proud, angry guardian.

"They took Eimhir *àlainn*," Juliana said. "She is gone. Cùchulainn is in a rage. And his territory has been invaded."

"Who else is gone, can you tell?" Gawain asked.

She shaded her eyes, her fingers trembling. He wanted to put an arm around her, but hesitated. She stood strong and firm beside him, her voice calm, head lifted, back straight. She would not welcome sympathy now.

"Some of the older cygnets are missing," she said. "Three with feathers that are mostly white, with a little of the infant gray left. One is a female with no mate—a maiden swan," she said, glancing at him. "I called her Etain, after—"

"After the princess who was wooed and lost by the king of the faeries, and transformed by magic into many creatures, including a butterfly," Gawain said. "Yet her lover found her, finally, and took her home." The story had bubbled up in his memory without effort.

Her shading hand hid her expression. "You know that one, too," she said softly. "Who are you, Gawain Avenel?"

"Later," he murmured. "Four or five swans have been taken?"

"More," she said. "Where are Guinevere and her babies?"

He frowned, scanning the loch, unable to find the elegant pen and her small cygnets. At the sound of voices, Gawain turned to see the Highlanders from Elladoune—mostly Mac-Duffs—hurrying toward them. Laurie and Eonan were in their midst.

Uilleam was shouting and pointing, and Teig lumbered past him, waving his arms anxiously. Juliana ran to meet them, listened, then returned to Gawain.

"Guinevere!" she said. "They saw her from the wallwalk—she is in the cove! Something is wrong!" She ran with the others.

Passing them all with a long running stride, Gawain was soon joined by Laurie and Juliana. They crossed through the trees to emerge on the narrow shore of the cove.

Guinevere swam in anxious circles, wings busked, neck stiffened. Cùchulainn joined her, rushing back and forth in the water as if pacing. When Gawain and the others appeared on the shore, the birds swam toward them, hissing in clear distress.

"Where are her babies?" Juliana asked. She stepped into the water, her gown floating around her as she surged toward the swan. Breast-high in the water, she turned.

"There!" she called, pointing toward the end of the cove. "One of them is caught—there!" She swam with fast strokes, the swan floating alongside of her.

Gawain ran on land, followed by Laurie and the rest, to the end of the cove's arm. Inside a bed of tall reeds, green tipped in gold, he saw some debris and recognized it as netting.

Caught in the tangle of rope, a small gray-brown cygnet splashed, flapping its wings, opening its beak. The infant's gurgle of distress seized him in the region of his stomach.

The cygnet strained, rising and sinking, water sloshing deeper over its back, struggles that could drown it. Nearby, Guinevere circled in obvious distress. At the edge of the reeds, her other cygnets swam safely.

Juliana pushed through the reeds, gown swirling, until she stood breast-high beside the little bird. Gawain saw her reach out to examine the agitated cygnet.

She drew a breath and sank under the water, then rose up, water streaming from her hair. "His legs are caught!" she called. "There is a trap here—a net!"

While she pulled frantically at the net, Gawain paced on the shore. After a few moments he could stand it no longer. He kicked off his boots and dropped his belt, then stepped into the loch himself, surging through cool water to reach the reed bed.

She stood shoulder-deep in the water. "Gawain!" she gasped. "'Tis such a tangle—help me!"

He stood with her, feet in the mucky bottom, and began to work at the knots. The rope was wadded around the cygnet's legs and webbed feet. He and Juliana struggled together with the tangle. Once he drew breath and went under to budge a stubborn snarl. Surging up again, he stood beside her.

The water seemed to be getting deeper. The level had at first been at his waist, and now was at his chest. He realized that he was sinking in the soft silt at the bottom of the reed bed. Juliana's shoulders were submerged. She looked at him, her eyes wide with alarm.

"We will get the little one free," Gawain reassured her. "And we will get out of here—quickly." She held the cygnet securely while he pulled at the wet, interlaced rope until finally a loop slipped free and the knot loosened considerably.

Juliana released the little bird, and it scrambled away, swimming toward its mother. Guinevere swept her long, elegant neck down and pushed at him with her beak. Then she sank her tail until he clambered onto her back along with his three siblings. She glided out of the reeds toward Cùchulainn.

Juliana smiled up at Gawain. He laughed and pulled her into a wet, mucky embrace, recalling another time when he had hidden among the reeds with her, on the night Elladoune had burned.

"Come, my love," he murmured. "Out of the water." He drew her along with him.

But the silt sucked at his feet, drawing him deeper. Juliana gasped and grabbed his waist, sputtering, her shoulders well covered, the water lapping at her throat.

"Gawain!" someone called. He looked toward the shore. Laurie stepped into the water, followed by Eonan, and came toward him, reaching out. Moments later, Uilleam, Beithag, Teig, and the MacDuffs, who had watched the rescue from the shore, lined up behind them.

Laurie stretched out his big hands to grasp Gawain's arm. Behind him, Eonan grabbed Laurie's belt, and Beithag took

Eonan's, and Uilleam took his wife by the waist. Each grasped another until the last person—Teig, with his solid strength and great heart—pulled on Uilleam's belt and stepped backward.

Embracing Juliana, Gawain felt himself move slowly out of the muck and toward the shore. He looked back in wonder at the living chain that connected them to the shore of Elladoune.

Wet and joyful, Juliana wrapped her arm around Gawain as they walked with the others toward Elladoune. She laughed at some remark Laurie made, delighting in the feel of her husband's arm around her shoulders. Although her wet tunic slapped cold against her legs, the grass beneath her bare feet felt warm and smelled fresh in the sunlight. She felt healed and renewed.

Whatever Gawain's secrets, and hers, she hoped now that peace would prevail. He had come for her, and they had worked together to save the cygnet. Surely he would stay with her and they would resolve their differences.

She smiled up at him, but he slowed beside her, looking up, and stopped. His arm tensed and dropped away. She glanced toward the castle.

De Soulis and some of his knights waited on horseback at the top of the hill outside the gate. Dressed in his black armor, the sheriff watched them. He beckoned to Gawain. With a wave of his hand, he sent one of his guards riding toward them.

Gawain looked down at her. "Go to the abbey," he growled low. "Take the others and go."

Heart pounding, she turned her back so that De Soulis would not see her speaking to Gawain. "What does he want? Are we to be expelled from the castle now?"

"I will wager he is displeased to see me consorting with the locals, and means to speak to me about it," he said. "Let me deal with this alone. The . . . closing of the castle is to be done later. I have been instructed to send you all away. 'Tis part of what I wanted to explain to you—"

"Gawain, how can you allow this to happen—"

"Go to the abbey. Now. Let me speak with him. Hurry."

"Why?" she hissed, furious. "So you can give him more of our secrets? Another piece of our life to take away?"

"Go," he said sternly, "before he decides to take you again. I will come for you at the abbey."

"If you mean to follow your king's orders," she said angrily, "dinna ever come for me!" Sobbing out, she whirled and ran across the meadow, past the people who already walked toward the abbey.

Chapter 29

Feet planted firmly, Juliana raised the bow and drew the string taut. Balancing the arrow shaft, she grew still, intent on the upright wand over a hundred paces away. She ignored the noise of the crowd behind her. Wisecracking and impatient, they urged her—or rather, the hooded, cloaked youth she pretended to be—to take the shot, since others waited their turn.

After a moment, she released the bowstring. Her arrow chipped the wand and sank into the straw target behind it.

She ignored the applause and turned to face a merchant and a contest judge, who offered her the prize: a tiny silver bell, identical to the four she had already won that day. With a nod, she accepted it and walked away. Bow fisted in her hand, she shouldered her way through the crowd in the market square.

Brother Eonan and Teig, instructed by the abbot to act as bodyguards, hustled beside her. A crowd of children and youths followed; some were part of the rebel forest band—Mairead's oldest children, Lucas's sons, a few others—and the rest were from the surroundings of the town, located in the triangle of territory between Dalbrae, Inchfillan, and the loch.

The market area, dominated by an ancient stone cross, was dusty and busy, jammed with people and bright with cloth-draped booths. A variety of goods were offered there—leather, silk, spices, tin, iron, savory foods, cool ale. She looked at none of it as she walked past. The day was ending and the booths would be closing soon; almost everyone would travel to Inchfillan Abbey to watch the final archery competition.

Earlier in the day, she had won the other contests easily, gaining top placement in each successive round. This last win, with its prize of a little bell, entered her in the final contest. That one would award the Golden Arrow of Elladoune.

Several archers had advanced with her, most of them English bowmen from the garrison at Dalbrae. Only Juliana, so far, had won silver bells for all her shots, awarded for special skill. That had singled her out, although few knew her identity.

She had bells enough—she had come here for another prize altogether—and she handed this one to Teig. He slid it onto a ribbon around his neck, along with the other silver bells she had collected. He laughed, delighted with their tinkling sound. She smiled at him.

"Now we can go to Inchfillan," she said to Eonan.

He extended his arm protectively as several horsemen thundered down the street toward the road that led to Inchfillan Abbey. She saw De Soulis in the lead, with several knights. In their midst, on a creamy palfrey, rode a woman in a red gown. On either side of her were two more guards, each with a boy mounted pillion behind him.

Alec and Iain. Juliana gasped and stared at the first sight of her brothers in weeks. Disguised and hiding in the crowd, she could say and do nothing to catch their attention.

The last two riders passed by her: a tall, sandy-haired man on a brown horse, and a lean, dark-haired knight in deep brown surcoat and chain mail. He sat his dark bay horse with agile grace, staring ahead of him.

As Gawain passed, riding Gringolet, her heart leaped again. She pulled the hood of her dark cloak to shield her face more completely, but he did not seem to glance at her.

"Come," she told Eonan and Teig. "It is over a league to the abbey. We had best get some ale before we set out on the walk. Do you think they will take one of these little bells in payment for ale?" she asked. Teig protested, and she sighed.

"I will ask for ale in the name of holy charity," Eonan said, "and we will share whatever they give us. And for love of heaven, let us hurry—you cannot be late. We have much to accomplish today!"

*   *   *

Throughout the day, he thought he saw her in the crowd: a sunlit sheen of hair, a laugh like a trickle of water, a face like an angel. Each time, when he looked, it was not her.

No reason, he told himself, to expect to see her at the market. He felt her presence nonetheless; she tugged upon his heart, upon his thoughts. He constantly looked for her.

As he rode through the town, he saw Eonan and Teig standing with a youth in a short dark brown cloak and hood that obscured his face. Odd clothing to wear on such a warm day, he thought. Then he realized that the lad was likely one of the forest rebels whose existence Juliana continually denied.

The knights arrived to find the meadow outside the abbey church filled with spectators. The crowd kept back from the church to form a wide clearing. Tables for the sale of pies and ale extended along one side of the field, and a platform had been erected for the sheriff and his party. The abbot waited on the church steps for De Soulis, who came toward him.

Gawain dismounted and assisted De Soulis's wife and the boys to the ground. Alec and Iain chatted with him, protesting when Lady Matilda whisked them away, but she soon seated them on the dais. De Soulis and the abbot joined them there, along with the merchants who were to judge the shooting competition.

Laurie came toward him, carrying two wooden cups. "This is excellent Scots ale!" he crowed, handing Gawain a cup, then slurping and sighing.

Gawain sipped. "The archery contestants are here," he said as the knights entered the field. He recognized the archers as knights from Dalbrae. They walked into the clearing, set down their quivers, strung their bows, and chatted with one another. "I hear this is not the usual competition," he remarked.

"And I hear that Sir Soul-less is intent upon his men taking the prize again," Laurie said. "'Tis a gold arrow. Garrison knights from either Elladoune or Dalbrae have won this contest for years, and he is determined to keep it among his own."

"The shot, they say, is toward the bell tower," Gawain said.

"But the tower is collapsed, and still being rebuilt. The scaffold would be in the way."

" 'Tisna toward the bell tower itself," an old man standing nearby said. "To that bell up there." He pointed toward the high entrance tower of the church. A sturdy pole had been fixed at the top. From its outwardly projecting end swung a small bronze hand bell.

"Why is that wee bell hanging there?" Laurie asked.

"Tradition," the old man answered. "The archers must shoot straight up and ring the bell. Whoever does will win the prize—the Golden Arrow of Elladoune."

"A curious tradition," Laurie said.

"Long ago, they say, an evil man shot a faery bolt upward into the skies and raised a storm that brought down the first fortress of Elladoune," the man said. " 'Tis in remembrance of that old legend that archers try every year to shoot the bell."

Gawain stared upward. "My God," he murmured half to himself. "The faery bolt."

"Aye, in honor of those who drowned and became swans," the old man said. "Though suchlike magic doesna exist, eh?"

Gawain frowned in silence. He noticed several men placing shields, brought in a cart from Dalbrae, at the inner edge of the crowd, like a bright border along the grass.

"What are the shields for?" Laurie asked.

"To protect those closest to the archers," the man said. "The arrows go straight up—and then must come down again! They use blunted tips, but still, those can do damage. Och, look, the last shooter is here. The contest will soon begin."

The final archer walked across the field. Gawain recognized the youth he had seen with Eonan and Teig in the town.

" 'Tis the lad who won the silver bells today," the old man said. "None ken who he is—some say he comes from Perth."

"I watched him earlier," Laurie said. "I have never seen such a precise archer in all my life, and consistent with it."

Hearing that, Gawain narrowed his eyes.

The youth loaded his short hunting bow, different from the longbows that the English archers all used. He adjusted his stance and stretched his arms wide in a practice shot. Then, like his fellow contestants, he bent back and tilted the bow toward the sky.

"God save us," Gawain muttered, recognizing the graceful curve of that slender back.

The moment was nearly upon her. Purpose and vengeance should have kept her cool and deliberate, but her hands shook. Juliana stood to one side with the other competitors and watched another archer take his turn. Like those who had already shot, the man spread his legs wide, leaned back, and aimed upward.

The arrow sailed cleanly past the bell and soared over the top of the abbey tower. The shields went up at the edge of the crowd, but the arrow clattered on the church roof. Applause rose for the archer, who shook his head and walked away.

A tall, blond Dalbrae knight, who had nearly bested her in every contest that day, and had taken time to compliment her politely on her skill, walked toward the church step next.

"De Lisle," the man beside her, another archer, murmured. "He's taken the prize two years now. Ye're talented, lad, but look to the best, just now." He nodded toward the archer.

De Lisle, a tall and powerful-looking man, assessed the shot, then loaded his longbow. He placed one knee on the porch step, angled his leg, and reared back with his bow. His blunted arrow went straight up and chinked against the bell's rim.

Loud gasps rippled out and the shields went up. The archer himself scuttled out of the way. His arrow came down to embed in the grass, just missing the edge of the crowd. He bowed and left the field, nodding again to Juliana, as if to wish her luck.

"Close," a man said beside Juliana. "A shame. The bell must ring clear, or the shot is no good. Your turn, lad."

She walked forward, holding her quiver and bow. Her knees shook and her hands trembled as she withdrew a blunted arrow from her quiver. In a moment of cold fear, she wanted to run, unsure she could do this after all.

What she feared was not the shooting contest, but its aftermath. When she had seen her brothers, and De Soulis, she knew she had to take a stand, no matter the risks.

Her friends were willing to snatch the boys, but the guards were thick here. The rebels would be caught and hung for their crimes. Something else had to be done.

She could not appeal to Gawain, who was obviously following his orders. Soon he would close Elladoune, and leave—perhaps even leave Scotland. She would not go with him. Although she knew she must accept it, she felt empty inside.

Steeling herself against the turmoil and heartache within, she looked up at the little bell suspended from the tower. For now, the bow shot was paramount.

Her hood obscured her view, and she pushed it down, revealing the close-fitting leather cap with long earpieces that covered her hair. She hoped her face was plain enough to stir no interest. If anyone recognized her, no one mentioned it.

The crowd stayed hushed and still, and she ignored them. Nor did she look at her brothers, seated near De Soulis—or at Gawain, standing near the platform. She could not risk giving herself away. Not yet.

Choosing a blunt-tipped arrow, she nocked the bow and spread her feet. Leaning back, swinging the bow upward, she sighted along the arrow shaft.

The little hand bell, over eighty feet above her head, moved slightly in the wind, making the shot enormously difficult. Shooting upward into the trees scarcely ensured her prowess on this one, and she doubted that she had practiced enough.

Widening her stance farther, leaning back, her left arm parallel with the arrow, she began to draw back the string, but hesitated as the bell swayed gently. She felt her body waver slightly. That alone could throw off her aim. The arrow must hit the center hammer to ring it, or the shot would fail.

She remembered what Gawain had told her in the forest: getting down on one knee would give her better stability. The archer ahead of her had nearly taken the prize that way. She knelt on her right knee, extended her left foot, and aimed again.

Hesitating, she sighed out. Too much thinking, she warned herself. Send the arrow upward, straight and true; let it be an extension of sight, will, and instinct. Only then would it succeed.

She lowered the bow, curling forward. Then, on a deep breath, she swung upward until the arrow tip aimed toward the clouds. With a smooth unity of motion, she sighted, tilted, and drew the bowstring, fastening her sight wholly upon the bell.

Heart and soul seemed to move within her, and she released.

Holding his breath as he watched her, Gawain had never loved her so much as he did in that moment. Grace, she was, and beauty, and perfect skill. The dull male clothing she wore might disguise her—but in his eyes, she shone like an angel.

He knew why she did this. Somehow she thought to gain her brothers back through this means, though he could not guess how.

She stretched her left leg out, her weight on her right knee, forming a triangle of grace and strength. She curled into herself, pausing. The crowd was hushed and expectant.

Ah, love, you can do this, he thought fervently. He stood without moving, but inside his heart pounded for her, and for what she faced.

She moved then, rising like a wave in a fluid arc, and released the arrow. The shaft soared, and struck the bell. The peal began, clear and true.

Even as the shields went up in the crowd, cheers swelled around her, mingling with the mellow sound of the bell. Juliana rose to her feet and ran backward as the arrow hit, turned, and hurtled downward. It slammed into the earth only inches from where she had been standing.

More cheers and loud applause rose around her. Juliana smiled, tears starting in her eyes as she listened to the wild peal of the little bronze bell. She walked back into the clearing to stand beside her quiver, propping her bow upright in her hand. Turning, she smiled at the audience, searching for the faces she wanted—needed—most to see.

Alec and Iain were hopping up and down on their bench, cheering and smacking their hands together, their heads bright in the sunlight. They must have recognized her by now, she thought, giving them a private little bow.

Gawain smiled, applauding, while Laurie whistled and cheered loudly beside him. Her gaze met Gawain's, and he smiled wider—so dear to her, despite all the hurt. Tears pooled in her eyes.

She looked away, searching the crowd for others—Angus, Lucas, and the rest who waited near the boys, ready to reach out for them as soon as she gave the signal. But if she did that, all would be lost. She had another plan in mind now.

De Soulis rose to his feet, glaring. She did not know if he had recognized her; soon enough, he would. Abbot Malcolm accepted the prize in its leather casing from the frowning sheriff and walked toward her. The abbot of Inchfillan traditionally awarded the Golden Arrow to the winner.

"My dear," Malcolm said, smiling as he held out the leather sheath. "A beautiful shot. And here is our arrow, back again."

She nodded, and took the casing, drawing the arrow free. Of solid gold, it was shaped like a war arrow with a narrow tip, its metal fletching etched to resemble feathers. The gold was cool in her palm and gleamed clean and brilliant in the sunlight as she held it aloft to more cheering.

Then she drew off her cap and shook her braided hair free in a flaxen spill. The cheering was replaced by gasps.

De Soulis, seated on the platform, shouted out something. Laurie took a long step out of the crowd and raised his hands to clap them loudly. Gawain did the same. Eonan and the monks followed suit, along with all the residents of Elladoune and the forest, scattered throughout the crowd. The cheers and shouts arose, even more delighted and joyous than before.

"Oh, dear," Malcolm said, standing beside her. He watched De Soulis, who had turned to one of his knights, pointing toward her and giving an order. "What now? You had best run, my girl."

"Father Abbot." Juliana shoved the Golden Arrow into his hand. The crowd shifted and scattered as the sheriff's men walked toward her. "Go into the church and the safety of the abbey precinct. When the lads are released, hide them in the sanctuary of the church. Please—go!"

He nodded, aware of part of the scheme, although no one knew what she had planned. Turning, he hurried up the church steps.

Juliana reached down to her quiver and snatched a war arrow from it. She nocked the shaft quickly and raised the bow. Angling, she turned her back to the church steps. Only the abbot stood behind her, with a look of pure amazement on his face.

"Walter de Soulis!" she called out. Murmurings erupted in the audience. Some of those who had recognized her still believed she did not speak.

He froze in his chair on the platform. "Ah, the Swan Maiden has a voice after all! What is it you want?" he asked smoothly. "Ready to give us your oath of fealty?"

She narrowed her eyes and trained the arrow tip toward him. "Release my brothers to the abbot's custody," she called out.

De Soulis looked around. "Take her! And guard those boys—do not let them go!" Two knights advanced toward her, and another pair stepped forward to grab her brothers. Alec and Iain cried out and struggled.

"Stop! I will shoot him if I must!" she called out. The knights walking toward her halted uncertainly. She flexed her fingers on the bow wood. "You know I willna miss!"

Silence descended. She felt a hundred and more gazes upon her. Then Gawain stepped out of the crowd and walked toward her.

"Stop," she told him, without taking her gaze from the sheriff. "Please," she begged, when he kept coming.

"Juliana," he said, standing within an arm's length of her. He spoke quietly, so that only she could hear. "You have never shot a man."

"I have never shot a bell before either," she snapped. She changed her tone as he had, private and low. "But I struck it, and I can strike him. And he knows it. That armor he wears willna stop my aim. There are seams and laces, tiny openings—you know I can hit whatsoever I sight." She kept the arrow pointed at De Soulis, who stiffened in his chair and glared at her. Her arms trembled but she did not let them waver.

"What will this prove?" Gawain asked.

"That he can be stopped," she said. "That he canna be a tyrant here. I will only nick his skin. But I must show that his armor can be penetrated. I think—I hope—it can."

"Jesu," he said. "I thought you had gone mad, and meant to kill the man in revenge." He sounded relieved.

"Then you dinna know me," she said flatly.

"God knows I am trying," he muttered. "But you have never been predictable."

"'Tis time the people of this glen resisted him. He holds my brothers unfairly, and willna give them up. He will close Elladoune and cast the people back into the forest. And he burned Elladoune years ago—you know that, you were there!"

"Avenel!" De Soulis yelled. "Take her down! She is your wife, man—this is foolish!" He laughed, though no one else did.

"My wife is in earnest, Sir Sheriff," Gawain said. His calm voice projected over the crowd. "And she has a deadly aim."

"Go away," she told Gawain firmly, though she felt grateful for his steady presence beside her. "Leave me to this. You are one of them. You canna help me."

"Juliana, please—"

"Gabhan," she murmured plaintively, her gaze entirely on De Soulis. "You canna save me this time. I must do this. Alec and Iain are my brothers. My responsibility, nae yours. Mine."

"I will do what I can for them. You risk your life here."

"Go," she said bluntly.

He stayed where he stood, a long step away. She felt his gaze penetrate her to her soul, but she could not look at him.

"Sir Sheriff," she called out. "These people fear you, and that accursed armor you wear! No one will fight you, despite your cruelties. But if my father were alive, or my older brothers here, they wouldna fear you. And neither do I!"

De Soulis pointed at her. "You do not fear me, Swan Maiden," he said, "because you understand magic."

"Magic?" she asked. Insight came to her. "I understand the power of illusion—whether or not the illusion is true."

She wondered if he would admit it. Suddenly she knew that his black armor had no mystical invincibility. Rumor invested it with power, and he used that advantage. She understood that, for she had relied upon the mysterious aura of the Swan Maiden to protect the forest rebels.

De Soulis smiled flatly, inclined his head. "Just so."

Admittance enough, she thought. He watched her, his eyes piercing black, his countenance filled with anger at being publicly challenged. She faced him, arrow unswerving.

Her arms ached fiercely. The ache spread into her back and to her shaking legs. The compelling tension in the weapon demanded release soon. She breathed hard, as if she were running, but she would not give up.

"What do you want?" De Soulis growled. She knew then, by the lowering of his hand, that she had won.

"Let my brothers go," she answered. "Here and now, into the sanctuary of Inchfillan. And dinna try to claim them again."

He flicked his hand in a wave. A guard guided Alec and Iain away from the platform, even though De Soulis's wife cried out and reached for them.

Keeping the arrow aimed, Juliana watched from the corner of her eye as her brothers walked through the crowd toward the church. The abbot ushered them into the shadowed foyer, then stood protectively in the doorway once they were inside.

Tears welled up in her eyes. She blinked them away. Her limbs trembled violently, but she kept the arrow directed.

"What now, love?" Gawain asked quietly.

Hearing that, she wanted only to turn to him, and could not. Would not. She was not certain herself what came next. Judging by De Soulis's furious glare, as soon as she lowered the bow he would order his men after her. She had not thought this through entirely, she realized. Her plan had been born of desperation.

She slid her gaze around the crescent of people. To the right, she saw a cluster of familiar faces. Angus, Lucas, Eonan, other Highlanders from Elladoune, and the monks of Inchfillan had gathered together in the crowd. They began to draw apart slowly, forming a narrow aisle of escape.

Beyond them lay the sparkling surface of the loch.

Between her and that corridor to freedom stood Gawain.

She pulled the bowstring taut, aimed, and let go. The arrow slammed into the wood of the platform, just at De Soulis's feet. He stood, shouting for his guards to capture her.

Juliana dropped the bow, whirled, and launched into a run, streaming past Gawain, bow clenched in her hand. He turned and winged out his arms to stop the guards who rushed toward her.

Running fast, she cleared the opening her friends made. The gap closed behind her as she headed toward the loch.

Her heels pounded the grass, quick and sure. Behind her, she could hear De Soulis screaming orders, heard chaos and shouting. Moments later, the distinct thudding of horses' hooves sounded behind her.

To her left lay the blue expanse of the loch, but the shoreline was open here. She would be an easy target for bow shots. Ahead, trees spread away from the loch to join the forest. Beyond the copse was the cove, and past that, another meadow, and Elladoune. She ran toward the trees and safe cover.

Shouts sounded behind her, and an arrow thunked into the ground in front of her. She zigzagged between the tree trunks, surging onward.

Another arrow split the ground behind her. She stumbled through a green skirt of ferns as high as her knees, her booted feet crushing and cracking through the undergrowth.

Cool shadows enveloped her as she swung toward deeper forest, a dense thicket of greenish light. More arrows zinged by her, smacking into the undergrowth, whizzing past her ears.

She glanced back. Guards followed, some on horseback, others on foot, crashing through the quiet with heavy feet, burdened by armor and weaponry, bellowing after her to stop.

She never slowed, even when she felt the punch and sting of an arrow that tore through her side, ripping her tunic. The blow took her breath, and she staggered, but kept her feet, and ran on. Putting a hand to her waist, she saw blood on her fingers, but felt only a small, painful cut that she hoped was not deep.

Thrashing and shouting sounded everywhere now. She skittered sideways and headed down a steep slope. Her footing slipped, and she slid on her bottom into a bed of ferns.

Rising to her knees, she braced a hand at her side, for her wound wrenched painfully when she moved. Guards had reached the top of the hill, but they had not seen her. She stepped forward, ready to bolt.

A steel-clad arm snatched her from behind, clamping around her. She was slammed backward into a hard, armored body. Gasping with pain, she kicked fiercely, finding his shin. He grunted and dragged her into dense tree cover, falling with her into shadows.

Chapter 30

"If you kick me again," Gawain muttered, "I may just leave you here." He pulled her deeper into the thicket.

She twisted, staring up at him. "Gawain—oh, Gawain!"

"Hush," he urged. He glanced at the slope, but saw no knights. Holding her, he ducked down into a nest of ferns at the base of an oak, hiding behind the breadth of the wide, ivy-covered trunk. "Be still."

She wrapped her arms around him, resting her head on his shoulder. Her breathing was fast and ragged. He stroked his hand over the tangled silk of her hair, immensely relieved to have her safe in his arms, at least for now.

He leaned his back against the oak, shrouded with her in shadow. Tense as a cat, motionless, he listened, and glanced over his shoulder.

Saplings quivered as the guards descended the wooded slope. They shouted, their voices echoing slightly. Gawain held her close and waited, his hand quiet on her hair.

Although the sheriff's men searched perilously close to their hiding place, the knights soon departed, climbing back up the hill, rustling and calling as they left.

Gawain let out a long breath. "There, Swan Maid—it seems you needed one more rescue."

She tightened her arms around his neck, and her little sob tore at his heart. Then she pulled away. "Go," she said, skittering back. "I can get away."

"Ho, come back here," he said, and yanked her toward him into the shadow of the oak, gripping her around the waist.

Juliana cried out, clearly in pain. He took his hand away and swore, low and keen, at the blood darkening his palm.

"You are bow shot," he ground out.

" 'Tis naught," she said quickly. "A nick only. Let me go."

"Stay here. We must be certain they are gone." He circled an arm around her, and with his other hand put pressure on the wound, located in the slim curve of her waist.

She winced and tried to shift away, but he held her tightly. "Leave me here," she said in a fierce whisper. "If you dinna join them soon, they will hunt you as well!"

"Will I leave you in danger to save my own hide?" he growled. "Do you think so little of me?"

She shook her head. "But you must go," she murmured.

"Hush." He tucked her head against his chest. "Just hush."

She quieted, and he sat warily, listening for the return of the sheriff's knights. He kept a hand over Juliana's wound. The bleeding had stopped, but it would need attention.

After a while, certain of the quiet surrounding them, he exhaled. "They have gone elsewhere to look for you."

"If they find me," she said, "what then?"

He cocked an eyebrow. "What did you think would happen when you cooked up your scheme?"

"I hoped De Soulis would let my brothers go, and allow us to live in peace, if I could show that he was naught to fear."

He wanted to laugh. He leaned his head back against the trunk and huffed out in disbelief. "There is more to defeating the man than proving his armor . . . invisible, as Iain says."

"I know that. I couldna think what else to do."

"You could have waited for me to do something about it."

"I . . . we couldna trust you to help us."

Gawain blew out a breath, wordless and remorseful. He slid his fingers through her hair. "You can," he said hoarsely.

She closed her eyes. " 'Tis hard to trust a Sassenach. Even you," she added in a whisper.

He said nothing in reply, and pressed his brow to hers, realizing how much ground he had lost with her, how much he must tell her. He felt the pain of it like a wrench in his own gut.

"What would you have done," she asked after a moment, "if I had shot De Soulis? Would you have captured me, as a prisoner and a criminal, or would you have let me go?"

He drew back. "He would not have been shot."

"He would. I never miss my aim."

"I would have snatched the arrow before it hit its mark."

She stared up at him. "You couldna do that."

"I could. And I would not have missed my aim, either." He shifted to his feet and helped her up. "Come. Can you run?"

She nodded. He led her along a fast course, where the trees were dense and high. As they ran he watched for the guards. The loch was to the left, and he angled toward its long tip.

"Elladoune?" she asked. "We canna hide there."

"Not there. Around to the other side of the loch. A long walk, I know, but there is a place we can go for the night. I want you to rest and be safe." Near the edge of the greenwood, he stopped in the shade of an elm, his gaze scanning the loch. At the nearest end, Elladoune rose high on its promontory, silhouetted against the tinted sky that waned toward twilight.

"There is a shorter way. Come with me." She grabbed his hand and turned toward the little cove between Elladoune and the abbey. Gawain ran with her into the shelter of the trees. She stopped in the green shade of a stand of birches.

"Quick," she said, "take off your mail!" She fumbled at the leather thongs that tied his chain mail hood to the hauberk.

"Do you mean to swim across the loch? Are you mad?"

"'Tisna far from this point," she said. She yanked at his belt. He sighed, realizing she would not listen to arguments. He removed the sword belt and sheath while she tugged at his surcoat and the lacing of the hauberk.

He slid free of the hauberk, taking it from her to drop it on the ground. Juliana untied the laces of his quilted gambeson.

"But your wound—" he began as he pulled the garment off.

"'Twill be cleansed in the water," she said. "I will be fine. Hurry," she urged as he slid out of the padded tunic.

"Juliana, this is madness," he said.

She pulled on his shirt. "Can you swim?" she asked bluntly.

"Aye, but you should not swim so far, with your side—"

"If you dinna want to go, I will go myself," she said. Pulling on his leggings, she stopped. "*Ach*, you should stay. The sheriff will hunt you and arrest you for escaping with me. The king will have your head. 'Tis safer if you stay here, and protect

your good reputation in England. Your orders are to leave Elladoune." She looked up at him. "Leave Scotland."

He took her face in his hands. "Show me the way across this
loch," he said fiercely. "And then I will show you something."

Gaze searching his, she nodded. She bent again to divest
him of his armor. When he was down to his braies, he knelt to
shove his sword, boots, clothing, and the mound of chain mail
under a fallen tree trunk.

He turned to see that she had stripped off her cloak and
boots and stood in a long shirt, her bare legs lean and well
shaped. She ran along the bank to the cove's outer edge, where
tall reeds verged, and slipped into the loch. Gawain followed.

The cool shock of the water soon faded, and felt refreshing
in the lingering warmth of the day. He treaded water quickly
past the reeds, keeping his feet free of the silty bottom. With a
deep breath, he plunged after Juliana, surging with long strokes
and deep kicks to where a group of swans circled.

He glanced over his shoulder and saw men and horses on the
shore. Beyond Juliana, a flock of white swans glided nearer.
Gawain hesitated, knowing how territorial and tempestuous the
birds could be.

Juliana dove under, coming up in the middle of the circle of
swans. She waved toward him.

He skimmed under the water too, and came up beside her.
She cast him a quick smile and stroked ahead, staying inside
the ring of white swans. Astonished, Gawain went with her.

Sooner than he expected, they reached the other side. Juliana dove under again, and he followed her along the layered
stone of an underwater cliff. They came up under the shelter of
huge pines that hung out over the water.

She climbed onto the bank and he followed. The swans had
accepted their presence, staying with them all the way across
the loch. Now they skimmed away. Juliana ducked low under
the protecting branches of the pines.

From a shaded hiding place, she produced a cloth sack.
Gawain, sopping as he knelt behind her, watched in amazement
as she pulled out dry clothing. She shoved something at him,
and he grabbed it—a woolen blanket.

Yanking off her wet clothing, she knelt, nude and dripping,

under the eaves. She turned to him, tugging at his tunic. A moment later, stripped and wet, he took her into his arms.

The breathless kiss he gave her was somehow the finest, the most pure, he had ever shared with her. His hands skimmed the graceful curve of her back, and her breasts, nubbed and firm, rubbed against his chest. He nestled against her, rising hungry, and kissed her again. Her arms encircled his waist.

He wanted her fiercely, yet he inhaled sharply and forced himself to turn away, to cool his passion. This was not the time. Snatching up the blanket, he wrapped it around her.

"Your wound," he said raggedly. "Let me see it."

She turned to show him a small, ugly tear in the perfection of her skin, below the lowest rib on her left side. Though it was clean and scarcely bled, he saw a flash of pink muscle beneath the gap of skin. He frowned, and turned to rip a wide bandage from a shirt in the sack of clothing.

Wrapping her slender form securely, he picked up a dry gown of bleached linen that lay folded on the ground. He drew it over her head and arms, tugging it down.

He kissed her chastely, quickly. "Later," he said, "when your wound is healed, and we have time, this secret place of yours could serve a fine purpose."

She nodded, teeth chattering. "Dress now, and hurry. They may have seen us cross the loch!"

"I think your swans hid us well," he said, but he grabbed the blanket, a tartaned length, and pulled it around himself. Then he stopped and looked at it.

The plaid was the red, purple, and brown pattern of the Mac-Duffs. He held its bright thickness in his hands. Slowly, deliberately, he spread it out on the ground. He had seen a leather belt in the pile of clothes, and he grabbed it, sliding it under the cloth.

He pleated the plaid carefully, leaving a length free, as his father had showed him so long ago. He had not forgotten, although he had not been aware of it until that moment.

Juliana knelt and watched him in silence. He lay on his back, wrapped the gathered plaid around his waist, and stood, head and shoulders ducked under the tallest part of the pine overhang. He fastened the belt quickly and flipped the extra cloth over his bare left shoulder. Then he looked at her.

She looked puzzled. "Where did you learn—"

He watched her, heart slamming. "My father taught me."

"Your father?" She gaped at him. "Henry Avenel?"

"My own father," he murmured. "Adhamnain MacDuff."

"MacDuff . . . Gawain," she said, and gasped. "There was a wee lad who left long ago . . . Gabhan MacDuff. He was taken south by his Lowland mother—oh! His English mother!" She raised shaking fingers to cover her mouth.

"Aye," he said quietly. "I am he." He held out his hand, while she gazed wide-eyed at him. "Come with me. There is something I want to show you. *Mo cridhe,*" he added.

My heart. The phrase came to him so easily.

She stared at him. Somehow, in the space of a few breathless, wondering heartbeats, she had watched him transform from a king's knight into a Highland warrior.

"Gabhan MacDuff?" she said again. Blinking, she wondered suddenly if he had gone mad, surrounded by Highlanders and stories and legends for so many weeks at Elladoune.

"I am he," he repeated. "The one who left here, so long ago." He took her hand to draw her with him out of the pine eaves and into the forest. Turning, he strode so fast, barefoot and plaided, that she could not ask the host of questions that rioted through her mind.

She followed him through the trees and up a hill. He slowed and took her hand to help her over some rocks. Wildflowers tumbled in crevices and heather swayed, bright and beautiful in the dimming light.

They passed a rushing burn, and she paused, breath heaving, her hand to her aching side. Gawain—*Gabhan,* she corrected herself, as she had always called him without knowing—stopped, looking back at her.

Somehow, he belonged on that hillside, with the heather cushioning his feet. Behind him, the mountain was dark and cragged, the setting sun bright on its upper face. For a moment, she saw the countenance of winter, old Beira, on a high slope.

"The face," she said. "'Tis there again."

"I know," he said quietly. "Come." He held out his hand and led her upward carefully, slowing for her, placing his hand, warm and strong, at her back.

They passed a trickling waterfall, where Gawain stopped to drink with her. He took her up a long, grassy slope, a wide pathway deliberately cleared of rocks by the hand of mankind.

At the top, he drew her with him through a wild, feathery edging of bushes and bracken. On the other side, she saw a high and broken wall of gray stone.

"Oh!" she said. "What is this place?"

"Glenshie," he said. "I was born here."

Again she gaped at him. Mad, certainly, she thought—yet in her heart she knew that he was in deep earnest.

He pulled her with him inside the perimeter of the square keep. She sat on a fallen stone, while the gloaming descended, soft and purple, around them.

Propping a foot on another stone, staring out over a slope that overlooked the loch far below, he began to speak.

And she listened, and at last began to understand his secrets.

"I betrayed them all," he said, after telling her much of his story—his childhood, his secret dreams, his gradual disillusionment as a young knight. He had even explained his mother's reticence. He finished by telling her about his sojourn with James Lindsay and his rebels.

Through it all, she had listened quietly, and he was grateful for her patience and acceptance. The night darkened and deepened toward dawn, yet he still sat with her among the stones of Glenshie and talked. With each new revelation, he felt a burden lift from him, heart and soul.

"I betrayed everyone, Juliana," he continued. "They had faith in me. But I went over to the Scottish side with your cousin and his rebel band. I betrayed my family, and the English heritage my stepfather had granted me. I broke the word I had given King Edward—more than once. My stepbrother died because of the choice I made." He had explained the forest skirmish and its aftermath. "And I abandoned the friends who needed me."

"You betrayed no one," she said. "You acted for honor,

which many of your comrades didna do—and so it seems wrong, when 'tis right. Now that you have found Glenshie, and found the part of you that you thought was lost, you will have peace of mind."

He sat on a fallen stone and stared at his hands in the darkness. "Peace? I cannot redeem what happened to Geoffrey."

She sat forward, placed a hand on his arm. "But death is a risk of war, and every knight knows it. You didna kill him. Be true to your own heart, Gabhan. You think much about others, but forget to tend to yourself."

He smiled a little. "I do tend to what I need. I looked for Glenshie. And I allowed myself to fall in love with you."

She rubbed her hand along his arm. "And I am glad you did. But now you need to tend to the rest."

"My allegiance," he said softly.

She nodded. "You love Scotland."

He looked at the mountains. "I always have," he murmured.

"Then you must choose as best suits your heart."

"I know what you want to hear from me. But 'tis not so easy to cast off all that I am, and take up the plaid, and the cause of Scotland with it."

"I understand you better now," she said thoughtfully. "You are one of those who are caught in this war. One side and the other pull you fast between them. You care for both sides."

He folded his fingers together. "If I declare for the Scots, my family in England will bear the brunt of it."

"The Avenels love you. They would tell you the same. Go the way of your heart, and let the rest tend to itself."

In the darkness, she glowed like moonlight. He slid his hand over the satiny crown of her head. "You sound like Laurie," he said, smiling wearily. "Please myself first."

"Laurie is another with a foot in both lands. He decided for England, and willna waver."

"Oh, I do not know about Laurie," he said. "He wavers more in his heart than he lets on. His wife is English, and Laurie likes life to be easy. He says he only comes here for the ale." He smiled a little. "But he respects the Scots and he does not like this fight. 'Twould not take much to sway Laurie to the Scottish side someday."

"Would he follow you if you came over?"

"He is not a follower. He goes his own path—as I do mine."

"When you were looking for me in the forest, the day we rescued the cygnet," she said. "What were you going to tell me?"

"Who I am," he said. "What I had found here at Glenshie. I wanted you to know all of it. Including what I have been ordered to do at Elladoune."

"Close it," she said.

"Raze it," he said. "That is the full truth."

She gasped, and gasped again, and sat up, turning away from him. "Nay," she whispered.

"Juliana, it torments me," he murmured. "With you there at Elladoune—with MacDuffs there—how could I do this? But my orders will not change. Naught will change just because I wear a plaid in this moment. My chain mail is hidden away, but it still exists. 'Twill not go away."

She was silent for a long while. "I think," she said, "you made your decision long ago. For England."

He let out a regretful sigh, as if he could release some of his sadness. "I am a knight of King Edward. I have a chance to gain the right to Glenshie by that means."

"Ruin my family's castle," she said, "to save your own."

He puckered his brow. "I never intended to destroy Elladoune. As soon as I can, I will ride out to see the king's commanders myself and argue for it. But I will clear it and close it down before I leave. That will satisfy De Soulis until I can appeal to the king's generals—if anything can satisfy him. He will do whatever he can to ruin me now, I suspect."

She kept her face turned away, and said nothing.

He reached out and touched her hair, a silken sweep of light in the darkness. "You thought I would choose for the Scots."

"I hoped you would. I still hope so. I think your heart lies there."

"Juliana, regardless of which way I lean in my heart and soul, I need to do what will serve all those whom I love—my family in England, my kin in Scotland. My honor as a knight. You," he whispered fervently. "I can ensure your safety if I remain with the English. Do you not see that?"

"Safe," she said, "without you?" She glanced over her shoulder. "What serves you in this?"

"That I can help others, and protect them," he said. "It means much to me, that, though some think it my greatest flaw. If I sacrifice something of my life, I gain in other ways. Mayhap you would still love me," he said softly, wonderingly. "If so, 'twould be more than enough."

"You I love," she murmured. "But a Sassenach who rides through Scotland, ruining it for his king—'tis hard, that."

He stood abruptly and stepped away, placing his foot on the rubbled wall. "So that is your answer. You cannot love a Sassenach."

She stood and came toward him. "You I love. You. 'Tis my own flaw. My own weakness. Or my strength," she whispered. She touched his arm.

He turned with a low groan, overwhelmed by what he felt, what she offered. Gathering her into his arms, he tucked his chin over her head and stood silently with her.

"There is another way to claim this place," she said, looking up at him. "Claim it through your king—your own king, the King of Scots. You were born a MacDuff, not an Avenel."

He looked over her head at the night landscape and did not reply. There was irrefutable truth in what she said, and undeniable risk.

"Robert Bruce will take this land back from the Sassenachs one day. Scotland will be free, I know it in my heart. Glenshie is yours by right. Your own king wouldna dispute such a claim."

"Unless the claimant fought for the English." He sighed. "I have been tempted to put my faith in Robert Bruce and his campaign, I confess it. He is a true king, noble with it."

"Would you give your fealty to a man who has himself transgressed against King Edward, and made his obeisance three times? Would you pledge to follow that man, now that he has followed his heart and become King of Scots?"

He huffed a flat laugh at the irony she pointed out. "You are asking me to change my allegiance."

"You did so once."

"I need to ensure the safety of my English and my Scottish

families," he said gruffly. "The best way to do that is to serve my knight's obligation, and earn what privileges I can—for your sake and for the Avenels both."

"You choose obligation, not love. Loving us, you could still follow your own heart. We would understand that."

"Understand this. I obeyed my heart once, and went over to the Scots. It ended in disaster."

"Then try it again."

He stared out at the mountains and the loch. "'Tis a beautiful place, this," he murmured. "I remember it well. I always wanted to come back. But I love the Avenels, too."

"You have family here—your own MacDuff kin."

"I know. I must speak to them."

"And someday," she said, taking his hand and placing it on her abdomen, "there may be others who are kin to you."

He kissed her temple. "Would you want that, with a Sassenach knight?"

"I want that with you," she murmured decisively.

He framed her face. "Would you go with me to England, if I asked that of you?"

"To visit your family, but I canna live there. My soul is here."

He nodded his understanding. "You bargain hard, my love."

"'Tis worth the price," she said. "I willna give up."

"Give up for now," he murmured. "Here, in this place, we need have no loyalties but the one between us." He bent close, so that his brow touched hers.

She smiled sadly. "Just while we are here, then," she whispered. "Hidden away."

The night wind was soft around them, and stars glittered in the indigo sky. He slipped his hands into the silk of her hair and tipped her face upward. He kissed her tenderly, and drew her down to the cool grass. While the cool wind caressed his skin, he bared hers gently, and surrounded her with his plaid.

With slow, deliberate, gentle caresses at first, he skimmed his hands over her body, cherishing her, feeling her warmth surround him, succor him. Kissing her deeply, luxuriantly, he groaned low when her knowing touch stoked the fire within him.

Unable to hold himself back any longer, he felt urgent with an intense need that was more than physical. The sun would rise soon, and the obligations of the outer world would return with it. When she arched in sweet and silent ecstasy, he filled her, and loved her, and lost himself within the boundary of her soul.

The water was dark and calm, swathed in mist, and the sky paled as dawn approached. Gawain walked away from Glenshie to stand on the long slope that overlooked the loch. Long ago, he had stood here with his father, and had first heard the legend of the swans of Elladoune.

He turned to see Juliana coming toward him, folding her arms around herself, her hair and tunic pale in the darkness. She had slept only a little, he knew, as he had, until the cool, damp air had awoken him.

He took her hand and looked back at the loch. A sense of peace surrounded him. No matter what he did, she would love him. And he would always love her, to the depth of his soul, and beyond. Nothing would alter that.

Soon they would have to cross the water and face what had been wrought around them, and between them. For a while, he just wanted to be here with her, immersed in tranquility.

Dawn emerged, soft and cloudy, a pale, opalescent pink, the hills soft blue-gray, the loch silver. Swans floated, white crescents upon the breast of the water. The mist slipped away on gentle winds.

At the heart of the loch, he saw a shimmering veil of gold. The dawn light was growing faster than he wanted it to come.

"Look," she whispered. "Do you see it?"

Frowning a little, he looked again. Juliana shifted closer to him, and he put his arm around her.

A wash of golden color hovered below the water. It wavered, and took the shape of walls—windowed walls.

"Dùn nan Eala," she whispered. "'Tis the fortress of the swans. The sunken castle. Do you see it?"

He saw it. Though he could hardly believe his own sight, there it was. If he blinked, the vision might disappear. He drew her closer in the circle of his arm.

" 'Tis a gift," he murmured, and kissed her hair. She slipped her arm around his waist and nodded.

Time suspended, misted and still. A moment later—a blink, a breath—and the legendary place vanished.

Juliana turned full into his arms, and he heard her sob. He felt stirred enough to weep himself. He cradled her close.

Lifting his head, he looked again. No trace existed of the magical fortress. Above the loch, the sky brightened, its upper region heavy with clouds. He glanced at the opposite shore.

Something moved among the trees in the forest. He narrowed his eyes, watching more carefully. Shapes emerged—figures in long, dark robes, hauling a structure of some kind.

"What," he said, "is that?" Whatever it was moved away from the abbey into the deeper part of the forest.

"Ach," she said softly. "You dinna see that."

"I do see it," he insisted. "It looks like they are moving the bell tower. God save us," he muttered, watching as the tall timbers swayed, as if on a base of wheels. "It looks like a siege engine."

" 'Tis naught. Come away." She pulled at his arm.

"Naught? A siege engine in the forest, propelled by a bunch of monks, naught?"

She turned to him, her face earnest. "Gabhan MacDuff—I will call you that so long as you wear that plaid—you needna think upon it. You wear a Highlander's garment, and stand on your own Highland property, and speak to your Highland wife. And so you dinna see that, over there."

"Juliana," he said crisply, "why are the monks moving a siege engine?"

She sighed. "They are taking it to the King of Scots."

"Ah," he said. "I see. The scaffolding. Malcolm and his brethren built this under De Soulis's nose. Under mine as well."

"They did," she said. "De Soulis burned the other one the rebels had made, which was already promised to the king."

"Juliana," he said, "what rebels?"

"The ones in the forest," she admitted. "The ones in your own, ah, castle."

He rubbed a hand over his face. "Let me guess," he said. "James Lindsay came here to claim that machine for the king."

"To check on its progress," she said. "In part."

"So I have been harboring rebels under my roof, and consorting with them daily."

"You have."

"And I am married to one of them."

"You are." She glanced up at him anxiously.

He stood quietly, taking all of it in. Then he shook his head and laughed. Putting his hand over his eyes, he laughed yet again, a rueful sound that ended in a groan.

She smiled up at him. "Heaven willna stop playing its games with you until you give in, I think."

"Give in to what?" He looked down at her in surprise.

"Being the Scot you were born to be," she answered.

He shook his head, still smiling. He had no immediate answer for her, but the truth of his feelings was abundantly clear. Yet he had followed heart and instinct before, when he had gone over to the Scots. And he had held himself back from doing so ever again, no matter his leanings.

What would happen if he followed his heart again? He had much more to lose than before. He rested his arm on Juliana's shoulders.

The sky was a soft blush color, its upper layer filled with heavy gray clouds. Rain would come later in the morning, he thought, feeling the cool dampness in the wind.

He looked across the loch, and drew his brows together.

The image of the castle was there again, tipping the waves with golden veins of color. This time, the image was brilliant orange-gold, floating on the surface of the water.

"Juliana," he said warily.

"What?" she asked, and lifted her head, and cried out.

"Elladoune is burning," he said.

He took her hand and began to run down the hill.

Chapter 31

"Is there no boat?" Gawain asked when they reached the pine tree at the edge of the loch. "We would cross faster."

Juliana nodded, breathless with running. She realized he was right, though she used the boat only in cold weather. Turning, she skimmed along the forest path with Gawain until they reached a narrow pebbled beach below the level of the trees.

Hidden in the shallow water in a reed bed was a small round boat made of hide, with one cross seat and a triangular paddle inside. Gawain helped her into the boat, which spun a little. He leaped inside and took up the paddle.

"I have never rowed a curragh," he said. "Though I remember riding in them as a lad."

"Rhythm," she said as he began to move them out of the reed bed. "Rhythm and stroke will balance it."

He nodded. Despite some crazy wavering, he dipped a curving stroke to each side and mastered the skill quickly. The little boat struck out over the loch, creating quiet waves.

The swans glided out of the mist and surrounded them, floating alongside, some of them taller than the low-slung hide boat. Their escort and the pockets of fog on the loch concealed them from sight as the boat skimmed toward the other shore.

Juliana watched Elladoune. Bright flames licked the inner side of the castle walls, and smoke billowed from one corner of the bailey. "Only the kitchens are on fire, I think," she said. "'Tisna the great keep. And the stables are on the opposite side. Surely whoever is in there will get the horses out!"

"We will be there soon enough," he said as he rowed. "And

Laurie and the MacDuffs will be fighting the fire, no doubt. If 'tis the kitchens, the blaze can be put out and the place saved."

"Look," she said, pointing. "The sheriff's men are outside, on the hill leading to the gate. They must have shot fire arrows into the bailey. 'Twasna an accidental fire."

"I want you to know this was done without my knowledge." He glanced at her. "De Soulis must have ordered the firing of Elladoune."

"I know. If the sheriff's men are at Elladoune, they will be patrolling the forest too. They will see the brethren and the rebels with the war machine!"

"Then I hope your friends have sense enough to abandon their engine and seek the safety of the abbey precinct."

"Hurry!" she said, leaning forward as if that could make the curragh fly faster over the water. "Hurry! There is something to be done to help them!"

He glanced at her as he dipped the oar along one side, then the other. "What is that?"

"You showed me your secret," she said, heart pounding. "Now I will show you mine. But you must never tell, Sassenach."

"I am a keeper of secrets, my lady," he said. "Trust me."

She waited while Gawain slid them effortlessly into the shelter of the cove. He leaped out into the shallows and beached the boat on the pebbled shore, then handed her out of the boat.

She ran toward the cache of belongings that they had left beneath the fallen tree. With shaking hands, she pulled out his chain mail and gear, and her own clothing.

Gawain picked up his quilted linen gambeson, pulling it on over the belted plaid. He strapped his sword belt over the war garment and pulled on his long boots. Juliana handed him the chain-mail hood and bent for the hauberk.

"Not that," he said. "There is no time. This will do." He took his sword and slid its length into the sheath at his belt.

"Highland men," she said, "often wear only the quilted coat and helmet over their plaids. Most canna afford a full suit of chain mail. Now you look even more like a Highland warrior."

He slid her a wry glance. "You will not stop, will you, now that you have this possibility at hand."

She smiled brightly. "Never, *mo cridhe.*"

He looked toward the castle, where a rim of flame edged one wall. "We must go. Hurry." He held out his hand.

"Go without me," she said. "I will meet you there."

She fell to her knees and reached under the log again, pulling out another cloth sack from beneath a layer of leaves. She opened it and drew out a short white cloak made of swan's feathers sewn to a linen lining.

Standing, she draped the soft, delicate garment over her shoulders, tied it at the neck, and pulled up the hood. The cloak's curved hem came to her hips. In the soft silvery light of dawn, the feathers were nearly luminous.

"My God," Gawain murmured, watching. "So the Swan Maiden does exist." He tilted his head and gave her a curious smile.

"For now, she does," Juliana admitted. "And she has been seen before, near the loch, and in the forest."

"No doubt. So this is your secret."

"Part of it. We have used the ruse of the Swan Maiden for years, to mislead the king's men and keep them away from certain places in the forest and along the loch."

"Ah. So other siege engines could be moved."

"And so the king's men would keep away from the rebels' forest homes. When De Soulis captured me, and you brought me back to Elladoune, I thought I need never do this again."

"And your silence? What is the reason for that?"

"To encourage the legend. To confuse the Sassenachs. To keep secrets. Gawain—"

He placed a finger on her lips. "No need to say it." He touched the same finger to his own lips. "I never saw this."

He turned at the sound of horses thudding along a forest path above the cove. In the distance, through the trees, torchlight moved in a column along a path, and split in two directions— toward the abbey, and toward the castle.

Juliana looked in the direction of the abbey. In the forest beyond, her friends would still be dragging the siege engine, bulky and slow, along its route.

"We must hurry," she said. "I will meet you at Elladoune when the machine is safely to the river." She stretched to kiss him quickly. "Put out the fire and save our friends, I beg you."

"I will do my best. Juliana." He grabbed her shoulders. "I cannot let you do this."

"I must," she said urgently, "though it doesna please you. Just as you choose what doesna suit me. We must accept that with each other, I think, for we are too stubborn to change easily. Go—I will come to you."

He pulled her to him roughly, and kissed her again. Closing her eyes for a moment, she wanted to melt, to linger. But he moved back, and she whirled and began to thread her way between the birches. She glanced back and saw that Gawain had already started back toward Elladoune.

Pausing, she assessed her direction. If she cut across the meadow toward the abbey, the shortest way to find the monks and their siege engine, the knights might see her in the open, and pursue her; she would be a clear target. Instead, she made her way along the fringe of the forest that skirted the meadow.

To her left, she could hear hoofbeats along the path. The route led through the forest behind the abbey grounds, and eventually trailed toward the path of monks with the siege engine. If they were not stopped or diverted, the knights would soon discover the rebels.

Carefully she wended her way through trees and thick undergrowth, through silvery light and deep shadows. Her white cape nearly glowed, and was easily visible. Soon they would see her. If they pursued her, she could lead them away from the rebels.

As she ran along a slope thick with trees, she could see the knights. Six, she counted; seven. De Soulis rode in the lead, his black armor and black horse like a heavy shadow.

The forest path forked nearby, one trail leading toward the rebels, the other swinging toward the town. Juliana ran toward the forking, and waited, watching.

She took a breath and skittered down the slope, balancing herself with arms out, until she reached the cleared path at an angle. Glancing left, she saw the horsemen on the track. She leaped down, far ahead of them, and stopped.

Breath heaving, she forced herself to wait. When one of the men shouted and spurred his horse forward, she whirled and took the fork toward the little town.

Without looking behind her, she ran as fast as she could. She heard the pounding and snorting of horses, heard shouts. They sounded well behind her. Pausing again, she turned.

Her pursuers were closer than she had thought. She dashed sideways through a stand of slender trees, where dense leaves shielded her progress. Glancing back, she stumbled on a hidden root, fell to her knees, and tried to catch her breath.

As she rose to her feet, a shadow emerged from the trees, and a man lunged toward her. She backed away, but he was fast and strong. His hand whipped out to grab hold of her cloak.

Pulled violently forward, she fell. Black gauntleted hands grabbed her arms, righted her, dragged her to her feet.

"Ah," De Soulis said, "the Swan Maiden is mine."

"Sergeant!" Gawain bellowed as he neared the swarm of guards clustered outside Elladoune's walls. One of the guards turned and walked toward him. "Who gave the order to fire this castle? 'Twas not to be done yet!"

"The sheriff, sir," the man answered. "We were told to send fire-tipped arrows into the bailey, and set the outbuildings aflame. He told us not to try to take it or to go inside. But there are people in there, sir." He gestured toward the wallwalk. "They have been shooting arrows down upon us. We do not know who they are."

"The place has not yet been cleared!" Gawain said angrily. "There are women in there, and old ones—and children, for love of God!" He glanced up at the battlements. He saw a few heads bobbing behind the merlons, and as one passed an opening, he recognized Laurie. He waved an arm and shouted. Someone looked down. Gawain pointed toward the massive wooden doors, now shut.

"Sir," the guard said. "We were told 'twas empty."

"I am going in there to vacate the castle," Gawain said

sharply. "In the meantime, do not attempt to attack further. You can take the men back to Dalbrae."

"Our orders are to stay here, sir," the man replied.

"Where is the sheriff?" Gawain demanded.

"Riding out after rebels, sir."

"You have done what he ordered. The castle is afire. Now be on your way." He strode past the guard toward the doors, hoping that those inside had seen him and would unbar the gate.

He heard a bolt slide free, and one of the huge, iron-studded wooden doors creaked open. Gawain slipped through the gap, stepping into shadows and smoke. Laurie slammed the door shut and he and Gawain turned to bar the doors shut again.

The portcullis was partially raised, and Gawain ducked beside Laurie as they passed beneath its iron teeth to enter the bailey. Gawain pushed back his chain-mail hood and stopped to stare at the bright blaze that filled one corner of the yard.

Flames consumed the thatched roof of the two kitchen buildings. Gawain saw a few of the MacDuffs—Teig, Uilleam, and some others—running across the yard with sloshing buckets of water, freshly drawn from the well on the other side of the garden plot. The gardens were aflame, too, bright ribbons of fire that ran up beanpoles and slicked across the greenery.

"Jesu," Gawain said, looking around. "Is everyone safe?"

"Aye, so far," Laurie said, wiping a hand across his brow. His face was streaked with soot. "We moved them all into the opposite tower, and wet the doors and walls thoroughly there. The horses and livestock were put into the ground-floor storage room in that tower, too, and we dampened the floors in there as well. And we have cleared a firebreak between the kitchen buildings and the rest of the outbuildings. The fire should be contained."

Gawain raised his brows. "Excellent," he said. "You must have had experience with castle fires."

"Och, in the Lowlands, a man gets used to this. The Southrons and the Scots are constantly burning each other out," Laurie answered. "We canna put out the fire in the kitchens, and those buildings will burn to cinders. But the rest may be safe."

"If the sheriff's men do not shoot more fire arrows in here," Gawain agreed. "Stone will not burn, but all else—"

"Aye. Should the stable roof, or any of the outbuildings closer to the keep catch fire, we will have a much bigger matter at hand. The castle would go down easily, then."

Gawain nodded, and ran toward the stone steps that led to the battlement. Laurie went with him, shouting out to the Highlanders to keep dousing the kitchen and gardens with water.

They strode along the wallwalk behind the crenellated battlement. Gawain kept a long-legged pace with Laurie as they encountered a few Highland men, each armed with bow and arrows, hiding behind the merlons and occasionally aiming a bow through the crenel space. Two or three men gave Gawain curious glances.

Gawain stopped to search anxiously beyond the meadow for any sign of Juliana.

"Man," Laurie said, "what is that you are wearing? What happened to the rest of your mail? And your surcoat?"

"I did not have time to put them back on," Gawain muttered.

"Huh," Laurie said. "And why was it off? Where were you the night, by the way?"

"I took Juliana away for safekeeping, if you must know."

"Well, she needed that, with the sheriff in a high fit after she put on that archery exhibition—though he only deserved it. And that armor he wears is but common blackened steel, they say now." Laurie laughed. "So why the Highlander's plaidie?"

"I had naught else at the time," Gawain replied.

Laurie grinned. "A wee bit of the pleasure making with the safekeeping, was it? No wonder these fellows look at you so odd. You're dressed like a MacDuff—a warrior MacDuff at that. Mayhap they resent it. Or wonder at it."

Gawain leaned his shoulder against a merlon and folded his arms across his chest. "Laurie," he said quietly, "did I ever tell you my name—my birth name?"

Laurie scratched his whiskered chin. "Mac . . . I dinna recall it—" He stopped and stared. "MacDuff?"

"I am Gabhan MacDuff by birth," Gawain murmured. "A few days ago, I found my grandfather's castle, Glenshie. 'Tis not far—alongside that tallest mountain across the loch."

"By heaven! Can you claim it as your own?"

"I have the right. But I must find the means to claim it."

Laurie's grin shifted into a frown. "Edward would never grant it. And who knows how long the English will hold these hills. I hear from my wife's cousin—the king's own general, Sir Aymer de Valence—that the king's military advisors nae longer find much advantage in keeping a tight hold on Highland areas."

"Too much effort, when they have to combat Bruce and his troops. That challenge grows daily."

"Look at the struggles here, and this but a small and sparse area, without the strong clan presence of other regions. Aye," Laurie said, nodding. "If you want Glenshie—and if Elladoune will go to your wife's kin—you will have to change fealties. You dinna have much choice that I can see."

Gawain stared, stunned by Laurie's rapid assessment of a matter with which he himself struggled. "Go over to the Scots?"

"Aye, what of it? You are born to it, after all."

Gawain turned to peer through the crenel at the sheriff's men, still standing idly below. He was relieved to see that an attack was not an imminent threat; the knights peered nervously up at the battlements, where the Highlanders kept bows trained down toward them. " 'Tis no simple matter. I do not want my family in England to pay the price again."

"Och," Laurie said. "Your family will fare well, as they always have. Big lads they are, and Henry in Edward's pocket so neatly. Dinna take so much upon yourself. Like me—I know I canna save the world. Sometimes we must do what the heart requires, and let the world fend for itself."

Gawain cocked a brow and looked at him steadily. "Uncommon wise. Have you been talking to Juliana?"

"Nah. Though it wouldna surprise me if we share like mind. From what I know of it, you did all you could to make up to your family for those transgressions. Now do what Gawain needs. I always expected you to jump the border sooner or later."

Gawain half laughed. "Between you and my wife, 'twill be a surprise to me if I am allowed to make up my own mind in this. You sound like you lean to the north side yourself."

"Me," Laurie said. "I am content enough. Come along. There are some MacDuffs here you havena met." Laurie stepped briskly along the wallwalk. "This is Angus MacDuff," Laurie said, indicating a brawny red-haired man, who turned and nodded. Beyond him were three lanky older boys with bows in their hands. "And these three fine lads are the sons of a man called Lucas MacDuff, who isna here—he's with the abbot, I hear."

"Ah, then I know what he is doing," Gawain said.

"Do you?" Laurie asked. "I just found out myself. I feel the fool. Rebels all, from the eldest to the youngest, and the abbot himself, and your own wife. All making a war machine in front of our faces, man, and we didna know it. Clever, that."

"Aye," Gawain said curtly. He nodded a greeting to each Highlander, and ran toward a section of wall that overlooked the gate. "Keep watch for Juliana," he said. "She should be coming toward the gate soon. We will have to find a way to get her inside the castle if the sheriff's men do not clear out."

"And if she doesna come soon?" Laurie asked.

"Now that I know all is secured here, I will go out to find her." He paced the walk, glancing over the crenellated wall toward the meadow, the forest beyond, even the loch itself, searching constantly. Something turned in his gut, a sense he did not like, and a prickling had started along his neck.

Laurie hurried away and came back with a longbow and quiver. "The garrison left us their spare weapons when they deserted this place," he said. "We are well armed with bows and bolts. We have been shooting down at the sheriff's men, and that convinced them to cease sending their fire arrows over the wall. But if we stop defending, they may attack again."

"I suggested they go back to Dalbrae." Gawain peered down.

"They dinna listen well," Laurie observed. "What can we expect from men under Sir Soul-less? Ill-trained, they are."

"Likely they are waiting for the sheriff to arrive."

"When he does, we will make good use of these arrows. Even better use, once we have your lady shooting beside us."

"She will not shoot to kill," Gawain said.

"Hah," Laurie retorted. "I have eyes in my head. I know what she can do."

Chapter 32

"Pity I do not have the golden chains with me," De Soulis murmured. "They suited you so well. But this will do for now." He finished the last of the knots and stood back. Juliana turned her head away and stood still and silent.

Her neck and wrists were bound with loops of rope, attached by a length of hemp. A long tether from the knot at her wrists was slung in the sheriff's hand. Caught fast, she had no hope of immediate escape.

"I know you can speak," he said. "I suppose 'tis contrary female temperament keeps you silent now."

She glared at him.

"The king wants an oath of fealty out of you," he said, "but 'tis pointless to do that. You will be tried for treason this time. And for threatening my life." He tied the tether to the back of his saddle.

Behind her, the sheriff's six guards sat their horses, watching. The soft snorting of the destriers was the only sound for a moment. There would be no help from that grim quarter.

"Well," De Soulis said. He tightened the knots. "The Master of Swans has caught a Swan Maiden again. Now let us see if he can catch a Swan Knight. There is some local legend to that effect, is there not?" He turned to her and smiled.

"There is one part of the legend you should know," she said. He raised a brow when she spoke, as if surprised and pleased. Her voice rang clear in the pale morning light. "One day a warrior will come who will defeat the evil man who tries to keep the swan maiden and her knight apart."

"And how will he do that?" De Soulis asked, swinging up

into his saddle. He pulled on the tether so that she had to walk toward him. "Tell me. I am interested in such things."

"He will fling a faery bolt into the loch. 'Twill release the spell that holds the maiden and her lover."

"Ah," he said. "Impossible. We are safe."

"You are not safe," she said, "because I will be set free." Her heart pounded at such a bold statement. If she had an arrow, she would have sent it true this time, without hesitation. Instead, she had only words to defend herself. And trust, which she found to be a steady shield—more powerful than silence.

Somehow, she felt sure that she would escape this. The first time De Soulis had caught her, she had been terrified and helpless. Now she felt apprehensive, but not truly afraid. Some inner certainty, newly gained, had diminished fear.

De Soulis glanced at her, narrowing his eyes. Then he yanked on the rope and stepped his horse ahead.

She stumbled after him. Her feathered cape hung over her shoulders, the hood fallen down. The horse walked ahead a few steps, and she strode after it, having no choice, but keeping up easily at that pace. She held her head high and mustered dignity like a cloak. Behind her, the other knights did not ride after them. De Soulis stopped and looked back.

"Come ahead," he snapped at them.

"Sir Sheriff," one said, " 'tis not right, sir, to treat a woman thus. None of us liked it overmuch the first time, but you said the king wanted the girl. But we will not do this again." The others nodded. "You had best find other guards to accompany you."

"This girl tried to kill me yesterday," De Soulis growled. "She is a rebel, a traitor—likely a witch. I have arrested her, and she will go on trial. Her treatment is just."

"Sir, she bested me at archery several times yesterday," another one said. She turned, and saw the man shove back his chain-mail hood, revealing thick blond hair. She recognized the best of the archers with whom she had competed.

"All the more reason," De Soulis snarled. "She won that damned Golden Arrow. You must be irate that a woman took it from you—Sir Rolfe de Lisle, the captain of the sheriff's archers!"

"The king's commanders will not look well upon this," another man said. "We could all be in trouble for it." The man beside him muttered agreement. "There are other ways—"

"I have every right to arrest her," De Soulis said. "Enough of this. We must hasten to Elladoune. No doubt her husband is there by now. I mean to arrest him as well."

The archer dismounted and walked his horse forward. "We do not dispute her arrest. But there is no cause to humiliate her. She is no witch—look, 'tis but a mummer's costume she wears. Naught to fear here. Instead, there is much to admire."

Listening, Juliana stared at him in utter gratitude.

"The lady is not a common criminal, to be dragged behind a horse," said another knight. "She is the wife of the constable of Elladoune, who is a son of Sir Henry Avenel himself. She deserves courtesy for that alone."

"What," De Soulis said disdainfully, "all of you, as one?"

"Sir," Rolfe de Lisle said, "let her ride my own destrier."

He reached out and untied the knot from De Soulis's saddle. Then he turned to lift Juliana to his own horse. The small wound in her side ached, bound with Gawain's bandaging, but she did not whimper. She put her roped hands on the man's shoulders as he boosted her up, and looked into a pair of steady blue eyes.

"There, my lady," he murmured. " 'Tis all we can do for you now. He does have the right to charge you with a crime."

" 'Tis enough, what you do," she said. "My thanks."

"Few have as keen a skill with the bow as you possess. In my mind, you are a comrade in arms." He gave her a crooked smile. "But you must face the rest on your own. Your own husband had the courage to ride away with you on that northern journey—my comrades were with you then—but he made a serious enemy in the sheriff. We will not do the same. We owe him our knight service." She nodded.

"Sir Rolfe," De Soulis said, "mount up."

"Aye, sir," Rolfe replied. "When the king's general inquires into this matter, he will learn of the lady's fair treatment, and 'twill look well for you."

De Soulis growled something and guided his horse ahead.

Sir Rolfe shifted Juliana sideways on the saddle and swung

up behind her, setting her legs over his thigh. They cantered along the path behind De Soulis. The others followed, riding to either side of her and Sir Rolfe.

Though she was a captive once again, she felt, oddly, as if she rode with her own honor guard toward Elladoune.

The sky had brightened with early morning, but the clouds were dull as pewter, made heavier by a pall of smoke in the air. A sense of dampness promised rain before long.

Rain would be welcome, Gawain thought, looking up. He wiped his forearm over his sweating, sooty brow. He had taken over from an exhausted Uilleam the task of carrying and dumping water buckets on the blazing garden. Moments ago, he had begun to wet down the thatch on another shed.

Flames still burned in the kitchen buildings, but the blaze now consumed itself, like the glowing embers of a hearth fire. Smoke trailed upward, stinging his eyes and clouding the air. Two buildings and the garden were ruined, but no sparks had spread.

He glanced toward the wallwalk, where Laurie watched for Juliana. Enough time had passed, Gawain thought; too much. He only hoped she was with the monks now, and all of them safe. But he felt dread spin in his gut.

He tossed the empty bucket to one of Lucas's sons, who ran to fill it again. Gawain charged toward the stone steps. "I am going out after Juliana!" he called to Laurie.

"Wait." Laurie pointed outward. "Your bride comes at last. But she has an escort. They just left the forest."

Gawain ran up the steps and strode toward the same section of the crenellation where Laurie hovered. Peering out, he swore under his breath.

Several knights headed across the meadow. De Soulis led them, and one man carried Juliana on his lap. Her white cloak seemed brilliant in the misty light.

He swore again. "I should have gone out there—I should never have let her do this." He grabbed the bow and quiver nearest him and loaded the bow.

"Likely she wouldna listen to you," Laurie remarked. "Well, let him inside. We will kill him and be done with it."

Gawain slid him a glance, and Laurie shrugged. But the thought had crossed his own mind. "Go down and open the gate," he said. "Take Angus with you. Do not let more than the sheriff and Juliana into the bailey if you can help it."

"Aye, I know what to do." Laurie slid his bow over his shoulder and jammed arrows into his belt, then headed down the steps into the bailey.

Ducking down, Gawain ran along the wallwalk to a better vantage point over the gate. The sheriff's men, some of whom had been lounging at the base of the castle walls, got up and came forward to meet their commander. While they conferred, Laurie and Angus ran inside the deep entrance arch and un-barred the great wooden doors beyond the portcullis.

Gawain watched from above as De Soulis motioned forward the rider who held Juliana in his custody. The tall knight, Gawain realized, was the same competitor Juliana had faced at archery. Narrowing his eyes as he studied the scene below, he drew some arrows from the pile at his feet, stuck a few in his belt for quick access, and loaded the longbow.

The sheriff and the knight riding with Juliana headed through the gate. Moments later, Gawain heard the horses in-side the entrance tunnel. He swore aloud when he saw some of the other knights follow inside.

Swiveling, he trained the bow on the entrance, coldly pre-pared to kill on an instant's impulse if it became necessary. He waited.

The groan and slam of the iron portcullis, followed by shouts, told him that Laurie and Angus had trapped some of the men inside the entrance arch. Then the sheriff, the knight, and Juliana rode into the bailey. Laurie and Angus followed.

While Laurie stood bow raised and arrow nocked, Angus fisted his hands on his hips. But Gawain noted that the big man had tensed to draw the great sword he wore sheathed at his back.

Keeping his own bow steady, Gawain looked at Juliana. Ropes were tied about her neck and wrists, which keyed his fury. But the pale courage on her face nearly broke his heart.

He sighted her captors—each a clear, easy bow shot away.

A damp wind touched the back of his neck, stirred his hair. He stood like stone.

"De Soulis!" he shouted. "Let her go!"

The sheriff looked upward. His black armor glinted like jet stone in the cloudy light. He motioned to the second knight, the archer, to release Juliana. The man dismounted and slid her carefully to the ground. De Soulis swung down himself and took Juliana's elbow in a tight grip. She winced.

The sheriff looked up again. "Avenel," he said smoothly, "this place was to be razed by king's order."

"It was to be cleared first," Gawain said. "You ignored that order."

"Burning clears sufficiently, where there are rodents."

"My wife's cousin Aymer will want to hear about your clearances," Laurie said, his voice carrying.

De Soulis turned. "Aymer?"

"De Valence." Laurie smiled flatly.

The sheriff snarled and turned back to Gawain. "You have transgressed yet again, Avenel. I am here to arrest you."

"What are your accusations?" Gawain asked mildly.

"Protecting Highland rebels. Aiding your wife in her assault against me. Aiding her escape—though I found her myself, as you can see. She is fond of that swan legend," he said, stroking her feathery shoulder. "But we upped her with no trouble." She flinched her shoulder away.

Suppressing fury, Gawain cautiously lowered the bow he held. He was sure that Laurie and Angus were prepared to rush the men if any move was made. Setting the bow upright, he stared down at De Soulis.

Elsewhere in the bailey, Uilleam, Beithag, and the others gathered slowly, coming closer. Behind them, the contained fire burned like a great hearth. A cool, damp wind whisked through Gawain's hair and stirred the plaid around his bare knees. The promise of rain grew stronger.

"You are dressed like a Highlander," De Soulis observed. "And how do you explain your other actions? What has become of you?" He said it with disgust. "An Avenel!"

"There was little I could do to assist my wife in her assault," Gawain said. "She had it nicely in her control that I could see.

And she freed her brothers from your unreasoning custody, which was her sole intention." His gaze was keen on Juliana as he spoke. She stood beside De Soulis, slim and straight, the breeze ruffling the white feathers against her throat, where the rope was noosed.

He narrowed his eyes, watching them. The blond knight standing with Juliana was an expert bowman, he knew, and his longbow was strapped to his saddle, but so far the man had made no move toward it.

"Secondly," he said, in a casual tone, "her escape. She fled all on her own, without anyone's aid—and with good reason," he added sharply, "with armed men in pursuit of a helpless girl."

"Helpless," De Soulis snorted. "Have you seen her shoot?"

"I have," Gawain said proudly. "Surely you noticed that I chased off after her with some of your men. I admit we crossed paths later, my wife and I."

"And you aided her then," De Soulis growled.

Gawain shrugged. "She needed no help from me. As for abetting Highland rebels . . ." He looked at the MacDuffs standing in the bailey. " 'Tis no crime to shelter one's own kin."

"Kin?" De Soulis shrieked. "You take your marriage too seriously. These are savages!"

"My marriage has naught to do with this. I was born among these savages," Gawain said, his gaze wholly on Uilleam now. "My birth name is Gabhan MacDuff."

In that instant, saying it aloud before witnesses, he made his decision. A burden, long carried, lifted from him and fled with the wind.

He looked at Juliana. Her eyes looked wide and dark in her pale face at this distance, but he knew they were as blue and deep as the loch beyond. The MacDuffs, beyond, whispered urgently. Uilleam stared up at him, unmoving.

"You have gone mad," De Soulis said slowly. "Mad."

"Not at all," Gawain said. "Now let my wife go."

"If you want her," the sheriff said, "you will have to join her." He pulled her nearly in front of him, and she gasped. "Sir Rolfe," he barked, "take him."

The blond knight took up his longbow and quiver and began

to stride across the yard. Juliana looked up at Gawain, her eyes large, pleading.

He tightened his gaze warily and took in the whole of the bailey. He could stand there demanding her release, but little would come of that. If he used one swift arrow to take De Soulis down in cold blood, he risked shooting Juliana; he had a fine aim, but it was not the match of hers. If he waited and let Laurie or Angus take the sheriff down, and Juliana was hurt, he would not be able to live with himself.

He strode slowly toward the steps. The sheriff's knight reached the middle of the yard. Gawain dropped his bow.

Juliana cried out then, and twisted violently in De Soulis's grip. She broke free and ran for the steps, launching past the knight, who reached for her and missed.

Gawain saw De Soulis spin and grab the longbow from his own horse. He snatched an arrow from the quiver and nocked it, aiming toward the battlement.

Knowing he was a ready target on the stone walk, Gawain turned to snatch his own bow. It lay too far away for him to reach it quickly. Juliana leaped onto the steps, bolting up.

De Soulis straightened his aim. And then Gawain knew.

Time slowed and vision sharpened even as he lengthened his stride toward Juliana, who came up the steps one by one. De Soulis drew back the string of the huge bow. Rage and hatred darkened his face as he sighted upon the girl.

In that instant, Gawain saw Laurie roar and raise his own bow, saw the knight swerve for De Soulis, knew Angus slid the great sword free. Unknowing, Juliana mounted the top step, her back to De Soulis. Gawain lunged, hand out, eyes keen.

He heard the deep twang of the bowstring, the only signal he needed, a key as paramount as tracking the arrow. That resonant sound sent him sailing toward her, body, arm, and hand extended.

The arrow soared in a pure arc. Focused wholly on its path, he felt, body and soul, as if he himself were a bolt leaving a bowstring. Somehow he knew where the arrow would curve; somehow he angled into that path.

His fingers closed around the shaft. He slammed into her, his shoulder knocking hers. They sank together to the walkway.

She gasped beneath him, and he lay over her, breath heaving, heart thundering. His grip nearly shattered the wooden shaft.

He heaved to his feet and dove for his bow. De Soulis shrieked out and lashed another arrow into the great bow.

Juliana began to get to her hands and knees. The sight of her, roped and crying, together with the slamming of his own heart, snapped the last of his control. Gawain snatched up his bow, nocked the arrow he gripped. He lifted, aimed at the sheriff, and drew the string so taut that his entire being quivered for the release. De Soulis, meanwhile, readied another arrow.

Before Gawain let go of the string, he saw De Soulis fall hard, dropping the bow he had been about to shoot. He slumped forward, an arrow protruding from his throat.

The knight in the middle of the yard lowered his bow and turned to look at Gawain. Then he nodded and walked toward his fallen commander, dropping to a knee as if to beg forgiveness.

Laurie stepped forward and stared down at the sheriff, then turned away. "That damned black armor," he said, his voice a growl that carried far, "didna protect all of him, did it."

Juliana was on her feet now, bound hands raised to her mouth, watching what had happened. Turning, she ran toward Gawain with a little cry.

He still held the drawn bowstring. The tension was enormous in his hands, the bow shaking for release. He turned to face over the wall, angled high, and let the shaft go.

The arrow sailed upward, its soaring arc perfect. The bolt came down in the center of the loch.

He spun then, just as Juliana came toward him, and swept her into his arms, holding her tightly. Stepping back, he began to loosen the ties of her white cape, fingers shaking. He tore it away from her shoulders and flung it over the wall. It sailed out like a bird and floated on the water.

"*Ach Dhia,*" Juliana whispered, looking through the crenel toward the loch's surface as the cloak sank. "The legend," she said. "Gawain, the legend! The arrow in the loch—my swan cloak—'tis as if the story itself has come into being!"

"'Tis just a tale, that," he murmured. He undid the ropes around her wrists and opened the knots at her neck. He sent the coil of rope over the wall, too, with an impatient whipping motion.

" 'Tis a tale, and not real," he went on as he pulled her into his embrace again, full and unencumbered. "What is real is that we are together, you and I. And we will stay here always, if 'tis what you want. At Elladoune."

"Home," she said, looking up at him. "Here, and at Glenshie."

"Aye, love," he whispered, and touched the silk of her hair. "Wherever you are is home to me."

"Gabhan," he heard then, and turned. Uilleam and Beithag stood on the wallwalk with Teig and Lucas's sons behind them. Mairead and her children came up the steps. All of them were soot-darkened from the fire, and all of them stared at him, eyes wide.

Gawain kept his arm around Juliana, and felt her hand at his waist. When Beithag and Uilleam walked closer, Juliana urged him forward with a little push. He took her with him as he went.

Beithag reached out and touched his face. "Gabhan," she said, smiling. Tears spilled from her eyes. She repeated his name again, lips trembling.

Uilleam grasped Gawain's hand in his own, leathery, warm, and strong. So much like his grandfather's hands. Gawain stared at them, then looked up into the old man's eyes.

"I am he," he said in Gaelic. "Gabhan."

"Welcome," Uilleam said. "We have missed you, Gabhan."

He smiled, and closed his eyes briefly in utter gratitude, and drew Juliana with him into the heart of the gathering.

Epilogue

Avenel Castle
Autumn, 1306

The room was shadowed and quiet. Gawain closed the book of psalms from which he had been reading, and looked at his mother. She rested her head back against the chair, eyes closed. He shut the volume and began to stand.

Juliana looked up from her seat on the floor, where she watched Eleanor and Catherine playing a game of backgammon. He smiled down at her.

"Do not go yet," Lady Clarice said. "I am not asleep."

He sat again. "I would not disturb you."

"You could not," she said, and looked up at him. "Gawain, I have been meaning to ask you—do you have aught else to tell me?"

"We have shared a great deal of news with you in the two days that we have been here, Mama," he said. "The resolution of our troubles at Elladoune, the decision of the king's general to leave Elladoune in my care for now, without a garrison, and under the jurisdiction of a new sheriff. And of course the welcome news about our child to come." He smiled.

"All that has been wonderful to hear," his mother said. "But I think there may be something that you withhold from me." She tilted her head and cast him a penetrating look.

He hesitated. "Aye," he said quietly.

"Then tell it," she said. "I am waiting."

He glanced at Juliana. Her eyes were bright and deep, their color even more brilliant since the child had been conceived within her. He would have thought he already loved her to the capacity of his being, but the feeling still grew and deepened within him.

Beside her, the twins paused in their game and kept silent,

hands quiet, faces demure and calm. They had matured and changed in just a few short months, he thought.

He turned to his mother. There was indeed something more to say, and time it was done.

"I have found Glenshie," he said.

Lady Clarice closed her eyes for a long moment. "Ah. 'Tis still standing, then. Good. Will you claim it for your own?"

"Through the King of Scots, aye," he answered carefully.

Her dark eyes, so like his, were intense. "You would have to reswear your allegiance for that."

"I already have," he answered. "I explained it to Henry and to the others, but I have not told you because—" He paused.

"You feared to tell me." She stretched out her hand, and he took it. "This family protects me too much."

"We do not mind," he answered. "Henry enjoys it, I think."

"He does. And I am sure he approved of what you told him."

"He did." Gawain smiled ruefully, remembering that quiet, late meeting with his stepfather. "He is a good man, a wise man. He knows how important this is to me—and to my Scottish kin."

"You did what you had to do. I am glad of it. 'Tis your heritage. There is much honor in claiming it."

He swallowed hard. "Tell me," he said, "of my father."

She sat still, her fingers, fragile and nearly translucent, wrapped in his. "He was one of the first of the rebels," she said finally, quietly. "And I loved him with all my heart."

More than enough, he thought, *for any man.* He stayed silent, holding her hand.

Lady Clarice nodded to herself, and he saw tears gather in her eyes. " 'Tis proper for you to want to find your home and your inheritance," she said. "And I must ask your forgiveness."

"Nay, Mama." He left his chair, knelt beside her, and kissed her hand.

"I should have told you about him long ago," she said. "I should have told you more about your Scots heritage. 'Twas wrong of me. I was . . . frightened for you. And still grieving."

"I understand," he murmured.

"We will talk, you and I, before you go back to Elladoune."

She smiled fondly. "Your father would be proud of you, Gab-han," she whispered.

He nodded, unable to speak. For some reason, he remembered trying to protect his mother with a wooden sword.

"Gawain," he said after a moment. "I am Gawain to you, Mama, if you wish it. I respect both of my names, and I will always be faithful to the tenets that Henry has taught me. Somehow I will bring this life, and my new life, together."

"Scotland can use such an honorable knight," Lady Clarice said. She patted his hand and smiled down at him as if he were a small child. He did not mind, for he knew that brought her joy. "But now we will not see you much at all," she added.

He glanced over at Juliana, who dashed tears away from her eyes. "Not for a while, true. But after our child is born next spring, we will visit here as soon as the child is old enough to travel. We will stay for a long while then, if you like."

"Come in the summer, when the swans are on the river!" Eleanor said. Beside her, Catherine nodded agreement.

Gawain looked at Juliana. "The summer would be a good time to visit. The swans are earthbound then, and cannot fly."

Lady Clarice nodded. "And I will be waiting here for you. I promise it," she added fervently, grasping his hand.

Elladoune

Juliana stood with Gawain on the shore of Loch nan Eala at sunset, beneath a pink and brilliant sky. The autumn leaves in the forest were masses of gold and wine and flame. Their colors spilled into the loch, where the swans glided, part of a perfect mirrored reflection.

The castle rose on its promontory, solid and sure. Beyond the loch, the face in the mountain appeared again, touched, as always, by setting or rising sunlight.

Juliana looked at Gawain. "Soon old Beira will be let loose from her prison, and winter will be upon us. And the swans will fly south again."

He smiled slightly as he studied the mountain. She loved those private, quiet expressions of contentment that she saw in him more often lately. He reached out to take her hand.

"Not all of the swans will fly away from here," he said, and lifted her hand to kiss it.

The sunset grew more fiery, a bright poem of a sky, and the shadows deepened. The wind had a crisp edge. Gawain turned and Juliana walked with him toward Elladoune, her hand still tucked inside his.

"Gabhan," she said. "I have something to tell you."

He slanted an affectionate glance at her. "I already know you are quick with child," he said. "Have you some other surprise for me?"

"I do. I have decided to take my oath."

He raised his brows. "Oh? You have been nicely avoiding that for months. I expected you to sidestep it indefinitely."

"I wanted to, but with a new sheriff appointed to Dalbrae, the matter will come up again. I have decided to say the words, and the sheriff will sign the affadavit, and 'twill be done."

"What caused this change of heart?"

"I havena decided to declare for the English, if that is what you are wondering—"

"Hardly," he drawled.

"I only thought to keep you out of prison. Charges of treason could come any day. I am surprised that the king hasna sent word to you already about that, but they say he is ill, and willna live long." She hoped it was not a great sin to wish Edward well away from Scotland, no matter what took him away.

"There are other measures that can be taken to keep me out of the king's dungeon, and free of another oath of obeisance."

"If my oath will help, I will do it." She stopped and looked up at him earnestly. "I would do anything for you."

"Offering me a rescue, Swan Maid?" he murmured, facing her.

"If you need it of me," she said.

He cupped her chin in his hand. "I thank you for your loyalty. But there is no need to take the pledge for my sake."

"I have made up my mind to do this. Send word to the sheriff that I will come to Dalbrae this week. What is his name?"

"You are a stubborn Highland lass, I know, and mean to see this through—but the signed writ for your oath has already been sent to the king."

She blinked, confused. "How could that be?"

"It was the first matter the new sheriff completed when he came to Dalbrae last week. He told me when I met with him this morning."

"You have seen him already? We just returned from Avenel late yesterday!"

"I rode out on patrol, but went to Dalbrae as well."

"Man of secrets, you are. Tell me," she said impatiently. "What sort of man is he? Why did he send that writ out?"

"I think," he said, his eyes twinkling deep, "that Sir Laurence will make an excellent sheriff for Glen Fillan."

"Laurie?" She laughed with delight. "You knew this, and didna tell me?"

"I wanted to surprise you," he answered, grinning. "He was appointed sheriff by his wife's cousin, Sir Aymer, and came to Dalbrae while we were gone. He found the writ for the oath among some other documents—De Soulis had it prepared before the fair. You never took the oath, but Laurie signed it, swearing that you had, and sent it by messenger to the king with some other documents. 'Tis done. His gift to us, he says."

Another laugh, this one of pure relief, bubbled up within her, and she stretched toward him. He gathered her into a warm hug, resting his chin on her head. She closed her eyes for a moment, savoring, while a cold autumn wind cut around them and his solid warmth shielded her.

"Laurie will make an excellent sheriff indeed," she said. "But what of the matter of Gabhan MacDuff, known to the English as Gawain Avenel? Will he pursue that man for treason?"

Gawain tucked her hand in his arm and began to stroll up the hill toward Elladoune. "Did you know that by Scots law—not English, but Scots—if a man is born in Scotland, he is obligated only to the King of Scots?"

"I thought that might be true," she said. "I hoped so."

"I have pledged to Edward and broken it three times now, and there is not much to be done about that," he explained. "But the king is so ill these days, and growing worse, that his advisors no longer care about trivial matters of justice any longer. They are leaving such things to the regional sheriffs and lords."

"Ah. And what will Sir Sheriff do about your case?"

"He says," Gawain went on, "that Glenshie is impossible to find, even if it is being rebuilt by this rogue MacDuff. Sir Laurie says it is hardly worth the trouble for a man in full mail on a warhorse to ride up there in search of one renegade, when there are so many other matters at hand—market fairs and farmers' disputes, and the like."

Juliana smiled as he spoke, then tugged on his arm so that he stopped and gazed down at her. She leaned forward and kissed him on the mouth.

His hand steadied her at the small of the back, and his other hand brushed along her jaw. Warm and hungry, his lips slanted over hers.

"Ah," he said, drawing back a little, "I think you approve of the sheriff's decision."

"Very much," she answered.

"Then perhaps you will approve of this—he has offered to foster Alec and Iain at Dalbrae. What do you think, my love? Are you ready to let the young ones out of the nest, after keeping them so close these last few months? Laurie and I thought you might be ready to part with them soon."

"Not immediately," she said, wrinkling her brow, thinking ahead to the spring, when their child would be with them at Elladoune. She very much wanted her younger brothers to enjoy a sense of family—and she wanted to cherish it herself. "But when they are ready, that would be a good place for them. They adore Sir Laurie."

"And they know Dalbrae quite well and will have the run of the place, no doubt," Gawain drawled. "Laurie says his wife will be coming north soon. She is too impatient to wait for her child to be born first, and will risk the journey—she assures Laurie in her letters that she is robustly healthy, and told him to stop fretting about her condition." He grinned. "Lady Maude will be a good friend to you, I think."

She held his hand tightly and tilted her head back to laugh. "Gabhan, my love, sometimes I wonder if I can hold any more happiness inside. Truly. Our life is more wonderful than I ever could have dreamed."

"Just one more part of the dream," he said softly. "The ransom for Niall and Will has been paid. They will come back to Elladoune before winter."

She gasped. Tears started in her eyes. "Paid? I never saw the request!"

"I asked Henry to send the coin from my revenues," Gawain said quietly. "I have some land in Northumberland that is farmed by tenants and produces well. The coin was readily available."

She took both of his hands, his fingers warm and sure over her own, and gazed up into his eyes. "I can never thank you enough for that," she whispered.

"No need to try," he murmured. "They are my brothers by law. I wanted to help them."

"You just released two rebels, you know," she said, tears floating in her eyes.

"I know. Now you will be surrounded by them." A little smile played at his lips. "There is something more to tell you, and I ask your blessing for it. I am going to send word to James Lindsay soon, and request that he come here to meet with me."

"Jamie? Of course you have my blessing for it. Why?"

"I have decided to offer my services as a spy for the Bruce," he answered. "I have contacts and influence as constable of an English-held castle."

"Gabhan," she breathed out, "'tis a great risk."

"I know." He paused, and his gaze swept the castle, the loch, the mountains. "'Tis something I must do."

"What of Laurie? The sheriff wouldna want you to place him in the poor position of being your enemy."

"Laurie," he said, "suggested it to me himself."

She stared up at him. "Laurie?"

"I told you that he leaned that way."

"He has fallen, then. In a manner of speaking."

"Well," he said as he took her arm again, "he says he likes Scots ale too well to be unkind to those who make it. And the sheriff of Dalbrae gets the best ale in the region, after all." He laughed then, deep and mellow, and hugged her to him as they climbed the hill toward the castle.

Hearing a sound, fast and rhythmic and growing louder, Juliana turned and looked overhead. Gawain turned with her.

A huge white swan flew toward the loch, its great wings beating in a steady cadence. Dipping, sinking, the bird landed on the loch with a flurry and a splash. Then it settled on the water, curving head and neck in a graceful arc.

"*Ach Dhia,*" Juliana breathed. "Look!"

"What is it?" Gawain asked, glancing where she pointed.

Guinevere glided across the loch with her four cygnets, now grown larger, their grayish feathers mingled with white. They streamed in a line toward the newcomer.

"'Tis Artan," she said. Tears pooled in her eyes. "He is back." She looked at Gawain. "He found his way home after all."

"I knew he would," he said, drawing her into the circle of his arm. "Somehow I knew he would do that, though it took him all his life to find his way here."

Juliana tilted her head, and he kissed her, familiar and welcome and comforting. The child within her tumbled, and she looped her arms around her husband's neck and smiled. "And whatever comes in the future," she said, "we will be together here."

Gawain nodded. "Aye, love," he murmured.

Author's Note

Swans and swan lore are shining threads in the Celtic as well as the medieval fabric. The history, the legends, and the natural care of these beautiful birds, who lend themselves so well to imagery and metaphor, were a pleasure to research. As early as the twelfth century, swans in Britain were regarded as the exclusive property of the English monarchs. Masters of Swans were appointed by the crown to care for the birds, and to raise them for table and captivity on rivers and lakes. Today, swans in Britain are carefully tended and protected, and thrive there.

Symbolism was never far from the medieval mind, and swans have always lent themselves to that. Medieval chronicles record that in May, 1306, Edward I of England held a grandiose feast at Westminster, in which he knighted, en masse, three hundred knights. Later in the festivities, two captive swans were brought into the great hall:

"Two swans were brought before the king in pomp and splendour, adorned with golden nets and gilded reeds . . . an astounding sight to the onlookers. The king swore by the God of Heaven and by the swans that he wished to set out for Scotland . . . to avenge the breach of faith by the Scots" (transcribed in Elizabeth Hallam, *Four Gothic Kings,* Wiedenfeld and Nicolson, New York, 1987).

The link between swans and Scotland led me to the rich Celtic tradition of swan legends and tales; the Lindsay crest itself features a swan with wings raised. For purposes of the story, the legend of the swans of Elladoune was invented, and a second Feast of the Swans was created in Newcastle, where the English king stayed in 1306 while gathering his armies.

Readers who are familiar with my previous novel, *Laird of*

the Wind, will recognize Sir Gawain Avenel from his introduction there, and will know James Lindsay and Isobel Seton and their involvement in the cause of Scotland. I hope *The Swan Maiden* proved enjoyable, independent of its connection to another novel.

Finally, while arrow catching is quite possible to do, it is a technique best left to experts. I was fortunate enough to be instructed carefully in how to catch arrows by Sensei Tim Gilbert, a sixth degree black belt, who has been snatching bolts out of midair with ease, style, and courage for twenty years.

I hope you enjoyed *The Swan Maiden,* the second in my trilogy of stories involving legends of maidens in the Highlands of Scotland. Please look for *The Sword Maiden,* my next release from Signet books. I love to hear from readers—you can reach me by e-mail through my Web site at *www.susanking.net;* or send a note with a self-addressed, stamped envelope to: P.O. Box 356, Damascus, MD, 20872.

If you enjoyed the first two books in Susan King's
wonderful "Maiden" trilogy, you won't want to miss
the next novel in the series, *The Sword Maiden*.
Set in the magnificent Scottish Highlands, it tells of
ancient legends, searing passions, and an enduring
love. Experience the thrilling romance and wild
adventure that readers have come to love and expect
from this extraordinary author. Turn the page
for a special preview.

The Sword Maiden

A Signet paperback coming in Fall 2001

Chapter 1

Scotland, Argyll
1428

Wild as blackberries she was, sweet and dark and unruly, and she would never be his. Lachlann MacKerron knew it, had always known it. Yet he paused in his work and leaned in the doorway of the smithy to watch her. He allowed himself that much.

Eva MacArthur, daughter of the clan chief, stood in the yard talking quietly with Lachlann's foster mother, holding a basket of cheese and oatcakes as an offering of comfort for the new widow. Ever since his foster father's death, many neighbors had made kind gestures, but only Eva had come to visit every week.

Inside the smithy, a piece of steel heated in the forge, but it could be left for a few moments. Lachlann lingered in the doorway. Sunshine gave Eva's dark hair a warm sheen, and he knew without having to look that her eyes were the gray green of a stormy sky. He tipped his head to admire the lean line of her body; she was not tall, but she was made with grace and strength.

She had outrun him often enough in childhood when they had played together in the hills with her MacArthur cousins. He did not doubt she could outrun him still, had she wanted. In the past few years, womanhood had tempered her natural penchant for boldness. He liked that softening well upon her. She would make a fine wife for a man—but she was not for him.

The chief's only daughter would never be matched to the smith's foster son, even though the young smith's true birth name and birthright was grander by far than anyone suspected.

Lachlann frowned, sensing the burden of secrets keen upon his shoulders. What he had learned as his foster father lay dying had changed him forever. His past, his identity, his future were suddenly different. In the past weeks, he had tried to accept it, though it would take him along a new path in life.

Shaking his head, he stirred himself away from his thoughts and watched Eva as she continued to talk to his foster mother. Changes had come into Eva's life, too, he knew. Recently he had heard that the MacArthur, Eva's father, had betrothed his daughter to a Campbell. News and gossip spread quickly at the smithy, and Lachlann listened to little of it—but he had given discreet attention to the discussion of the coming marriage. Eva MacArthur, his customers said, seemed willing to wed the handsome Campbell, who was far older than his bride.

Eva turned just then and smiled at him, and it seemed as if a sunbeam came through a cloud. Grief and hard resolve had tormented him for weeks, but he felt himself brighten a little in the bask of that smile.

He nodded at her, brisk and somber, and wiped his hands on his leather apron. He was aware that he filled the space of the doorway awkwardly, too tall, too broad in the shoulders, his head bowed beneath the lintel. He felt large and clumsy and crudely made, suddenly, with her clear-eyed gaze upon him. His dark hair sifted over his eyes, and he shoved it back, his long fingers grimed with ash and the handling of iron.

Eva embraced his foster mother and took her leave, and Lachlann turned away. He entered the dark, warm haven of the smithy, where the fire glowed red and his work awaited him.

Soon enough, Eva MacArthur would marry. Before the wedding took place, Lachlann would leave the region of Argyll. When their paths crossed again—years from now, he thought—she would surely despise him for what he would do.

His decision was made, his resolve private and intense. He could not turn away from his new responsibility of vengeance—even though the man he was obliged to hate was about to wed Eva.

Lachlann turned toward the forge, still hearing Eva's voice in the yard. Though the girl had captured his heart long ago, she did not know it. He would keep that to himself with the rest of his secrets. But some part of him, deep within, hurt savagely to know that she would be wife to his enemy.

Eva walked past the door of the smithy and stopped to peer inside. Lachlann stood just beyond the rectangle of sunlight that spilled into the doorway. Her shadow touched his feet.

"God's greeting to you, Lachlann MacKerron." Her voice was soothing, low-pitched, and mellow as honey.

"And to you, Eva MacArthur." His words created a deep thrum inside the dim, stone-walled smithy. "I thank you for visiting my foster mother so often. She values your kindness."

Eva smiled ruefully. "We all care about her and miss your foster father. Finlay MacKerron was a good man. My father laments that he will never find an armorer of his merit again. He says you will be as good, if not better. He very much likes the blades you have made for him."

"My thanks."

"But we have heard that you will be leaving Scotland soon. My cousins say that you plan to go with them to join the king's army and perhaps even sail to France to fight the English there."

He nodded. "Scotsmen can earn land grants and knighthoods by doing so."

"But men must endure a brutal war, one that is not our own, to earn such honors," she murmured.

"True." He watched her steadily.

"Will you leave your foster mother then? It surprised me to hear it of you."

"Her sister—your own cook at the castle—is coming here to live with her, along with her daughter and son-by-marriage and their children. I would be underfoot among so many."

"Will you be gone long?"

He shrugged. "Who can say? Tell your father that there is a fine smith across the glen who can do whatever is needed."

"Until you return." She placed a hand on the doorframe.

He paused. "I might come back," he said cautiously.

"You will." She smiled again. "You know that I am blessed with the Sight—or cursed, depending on who you hear it from." She laughed softly. "But I feel certain you will return to us."

He frowned, knowing that when he returned his mission would destroy her life. Hoping she would not foresee the dark intent in him, he glanced away.

"*Ach*, Lachlann MacKerron," she said quietly, "how could you stay away from this lovely glen, with its loch and its legend of a magical sword, and you a bladesmith?" She tilted her head and watched him, still smiling, teasing him gently.

"How indeed?" he murmured. He turned and picked up a leather gauntlet, drawing it slowly over his left hand.

"You have work to do, I see."

"I do," he answered. "Tell your father that I intend to finish the work that Finlay left undone at his death. The weapons and armor that your father commissioned from our smithy will be completed before I leave."

"You would have to labor as hard as two men, or three, to finish all of those pieces alone."

"I do not mind." He found deep satisfaction in the solitary nature of his craft, and could work for endless hours unaided but for specific tasks. "Tell him it will be done."

"Well, then." She hesitated. "I must go." But she lingered in the doorway.

"Congratulations to you," he said stiffly after a moment. "I hear the banns of your marriage were posted last week."

"They were." She glanced down at her feet, bare and slim, as she stood outside the doorway. "In another month I suppose I shall be wed."

"Ah," he said noncommittally and picked up a pair of tongs. He was grateful, suddenly, that shadows and smoke surrounded him as he stepped toward the forge.

"Farewell, Lachlann," Eva said. "A thousand blessings to you on your journey, when you go."

"Blessings to you, Eva MacArthur . . . in your future."
Using the tongs, he lifted up the length of steel resting in the
fiery coal bed. The metal glowed pale yellow.

Eva stayed in the doorway for several moments, then left.
Lachlann did not glance up, but knew she was gone. Felt it
somehow. He turned his attention to the work.

Hot new steel gleamed as he tipped the raw blade into the
fire and watched yellow flow into orange red. The dirk would
be strong and true when it was done, as fine as any weapon
made in this smithy when his foster father was alive.

He would work late again that night, he thought. The colors that told the state of the metal were brightest in the darkness, and he still had much to do. He had worked entirely
alone since Finlay MacKerron's death.

Lachlann had become a master smith himself several
years ago, while still a lanky youth; he could handle the tasks
at hand easily. But there were moments when he keenly
missed Finlay's wry wit, guidance, and companionship, in
the smithy and at home.

He glanced toward the pile of weapons and armor pieces
in the corner, much of it hammered out by Finlay in the last
few months. The work already promised to Eva's father and
kinsmen, partly paid in good coin, was nearly done. In addition, Lachlann also had the usual tasks of making horseshoes
and nails and repairing farm tools. He had begun to refer that
work to the smith across the glen.

Weapon smithing had proven strong medicine for grief—
and for rage. Heating iron into steel, hammering it, shaping
and cooling it, Lachlann was able to forget, for brief periods
of time, all but the work itself.

When this lot was finished, Clan MacArthur would be
well armed. Some of them would sail for France to help the
French fight the English. Lachlann would go with them, for
that seemed the swiftest way to his new goal. He must set
aside his smithing to become a warrior and a knight. Only
then could he satisfy the obligation for revenge that had been
placed upon him.

Once, when life had been more peaceful and the future
had seemed a reliable thing, he had hoped to become a fine

bladesmith and establish his own forge one day. But Finlay had died unexpectedly, uttering in his last breaths the truth of Lachlann's past and the name of his enemy. Those revelations had heated and reshaped him, as if he were a bloom of iron newly fetched from the fire.

He held the length of steel in the coal fire, watching the hues: pale straw, glowing red, then brown and a burst of purple. Seeing that, Lachlann knew the heat had peaked enough.

He pulled out the blade and plunged it into a trough of warm brine. The metal sizzled and the quench bubbled as the brittle steel was tempered in the salty water.

Lately he felt like a blade himself, one much in need of tempering—but the time was not right for that. His anger had hardly peaked, had scarcely begun to harden him. Waiting years to learn the full truth of his childhood, he was now trapped by his knowledge. His pursuit of vengeance would hurt the girl he loved irrevocably.

He turned the steaming blade in the brine, frowning. Surely Eva MacArthur regarded him as little more than a childhood friend. To her he was only the smith's lad who had run with her in the hills years ago, and who now made blades for her kinsmen and repaired her pony's shoes.

And if the blacksmith's lad killed Eva's husband, as he ought to do, then she would regard him as a murderer and as the one who destroyed her happiness.

A poor choice indeed for a man's future.

He pulled the hot blade from the water, its length still steaming. Etched by the brine, the blade showed the markings of iron and steel, finely layered to make a strong and flexible weapon. The old methods that Finlay had taught him were guarded closely, understood only by a few.

He sat down at a workbench and scooped a handful of sand from a sack, pouring it slowly over the new blade to begin the careful task of polishing. He would need to collect more sand to make himself a sword blade for his journey. White sand gathered under a new moon would make the steel brilliant.

Another secret of his craft, the gathering of the materials. Like most blacksmiths, Lachlann was accustomed to keeping his knowledge private. But the newest secret in his cache had to do with the smith, not the smithing.

He rubbed a bit of leather along the slender length of the blade. No one, he was certain, not even his foster mother, suspected that he yearned for a wild-spirited, dark-haired girl who could never belong to him.

He would not stay to watch her wed the man he ought to kill. Eventually, though, he would return and see her again—and see his obligation through to its end.

Before that day arrived, he must harden his heart.